Critical acclaim for *Removal*

'A brilliant thriller by a striking new
Constitution like a walnut. This is *Se*
— **Clem Chambers, author**

'Peter Murphy's debut *Removal* intr
thriller genre. Murphy skilfully build   ...p prose. When
murder threatens the security of the most powerful nation in the
world, the stakes are high!'
— **Leigh Russell, author of the Geraldine Steel mysteries**

Critical acclaim for *A Higher Duty*

'A gripping page-turner. A compelling and disturbing tale of English
law courts, lawyers, and their clients, told with the authenticity that
only an insider like Murphy can deliver. The best read I've come
across in a long time'
— **David Ambrose**

'Weighty and impressive' — **Barry Forshaw *Crime Time***

'An absorbing read' — *Mystery People*

'A very satisfying read' — ***Fiction is Stranger than Fact***

His 'racy legal thrillers lift the lid on sex and racial prejudice at the bar'
— **Hugh Muir, *Guardian***

'If anyone's looking for the next big courtroom drama…
look no further. Murphy is your man'
— Paul Magrath, ***The Incorporated Council
of Law Reporting Blog***

'Peter Murphy's novel is an excellent read from start to finish and highly
recommended' — *Historical Novel Review*

'This beautifully written book had me captivated
from start to finish' — *Old Dogs — New Tricks*

Also by Peter Murphy

Removal (2012)
Test of Resolve (2014)

The Ben Schroeder series
A Higher Duty (2013)

A MATTER FOR THE JURY

Peter Murphy

NO EXIT PRESS

First published in 2014 by No Exit Press,
an imprint of Oldcastle Books Ltd,
PO Box 394,
Harpenden, Herts,
AL5 1XJ

noexit.co.uk

ISBN
978-1-84344-285-1 (print)
978-1-84344-286-8 (epub)
978-1-84344-287-5 (kindle)
978-1-84344-288-2 (pdf)

2 4 6 8 10 9 7 5 3 1

Typeset in 11pt Monotype Garamond
by Avocet Typeset, Somerton, Somerset
Printed in Great Britain by Clays Ltd, St Ives plc

For more about Crime Fiction go to www.crimetime.co.uk / @crimetimeuk

Dedication

This book is dedicated to the memory of the judges, barristers and solicitors who, at such cost to their own lives and well-being, undertook the extraordinary burden of dealing with capital murder cases in this country before the Murder (Abolition of Death Penalty) Act 1965.

1

January 1964

THE FENSTANTON LOCK keeper's house was the only home Billy Cottage had ever known. The house stood by itself on a small plot of muddy, barren ground, less than a hundred yards from the lock. The lock lay about half a mile from Fenstanton and about a mile from St Ives, as the crow flies – though neither the river nor the walkways along its banks followed a path anything like the crow. Billy's father, Tommy, had been the Fenstanton lock keeper for more than thirty years. Billy and his sister Eve, two years his junior, had been born in the house to Tommy and his wife, Marjorie, and had never lived even a minute of their lives anywhere else. Tommy had died suddenly, some seven years earlier, followed in a matter of months by Marjorie. No one inquired into the two relatively early deaths, both almost certainly the result of years of heavy drinking, and as no one seemed to object or suggest any alternative, Billy simply took over his father's role as lock keeper. He was now 28 years of age.

The house was a small two-storey stone structure with a grey tiled roof, the exterior walls painted in a rough off-white cement paint. At the rear was a garden, marked off by a low brick wall, in which someone more enterprising than Billy might have grown vegetables, or at least flowers. The ground floor consisted of a living room and kitchen, with a storage area under the stairs. Upstairs were two bedrooms, separated by an airing cupboard. The airing cupboard also housed the geyser, which supplied the house with modest quantities of hot water. The walls of the living room and bedrooms were papered, in green or blue floral patterns; the doors varnished in a dark brown. The wallpaper was faded and torn, the plaster crumbling, and the window panes cracked in places. Billy had no idea how long the house had looked like this, though it was certainly for as long as he could remember. The only improvement made during his lifetime had been made by Tommy, who had converted the outside earth closet at the rear of the house into a water closet, a venture which seemed to exhaust all the energy and money he had to spend on the house. Its exposed position made it vulnerable to the bone-chilling east winds which blew in from the fens in winter. Even in summer it was rarely warm.

The lock keeper's work was hard. His main duty was to open and close the gates of the lock, and control the sluices. When a craft arrived, the pilot would summon him by ringing a large school bell affixed to a post by the gate. The pilot would pay the fee, manoeuvre his craft in and out of the lock, and be on his way. That was the easy part. There was no money to pay other workers to cut back the reeds or shovel away the silt, tasks which must be performed diligently for the river to remain navigable. Already, parts of the Great Ouse upstream towards Northamptonshire, where the river rose, were almost impassable; and long stretches towards the Wash, where it ran to sea, were difficult for larger craft. Tommy had taken it upon himself to work the banks for almost a quarter of a mile, upstream and downstream of his lock. The St Ives keeper did the same on the opposite bank and, between them, they kept their section of the river flowing between the infrequent visits of the dredging barges sent by the Great Ouse Catchment Board.

Neither Billy nor Eve had received much in the way of education. Billy was too useful to Tommy to be wasted on something with as little practical value as reading and writing, and he was always in trouble for playing truant. He was cutting back reeds by the age of seven. At ten he could help with the removal of silt. At twelve he could operate the lock just as well as Tommy and, in the case of an unpowered barge, he would assist the pilot in guiding his horse along the tow path in and out of the lock. Trade had slowed during the years when Tommy was keeper, and even before. Ever since the coming of the railways, river traffic had been in decline. The Great Ouse had fared better than some waterways, and some commercial traffic still continued. There was a slowly increasing volume of leisure traffic. But few locks had full-time keepers now. It was difficult to eke out a decent living and, within a year or two of taking over, Billy found himself working evenings behind the bar at pubs in St Ives to make some extra cash.

Eve kept house and looked after Billy. It had never occurred to her to move away from home. At primary school she had been labelled 'slow', based on no particular evidence, by a teacher who found her natural quietness disturbing. It was a label Eve and her family had accepted without critical inquiry as an accident of life. Every day she did the housework, put on a clean dress, and went shopping for the essentials in Fenstanton or St Ives, walking both ways, and carrying her purchases in large cotton shopping bags. She prepared Billy's supper before he went to St Ives and was in bed by eight.

2

WHAT BILLY LIKED most about working in pubs was that it got him out of the house during the quiet evenings, when the memories returned with a particular vengeance. There was not much to do at home in the evenings. There was an old, temperamental wireless set which picked up signals spasmodically, but the programmes rarely interested him. His reading skills were limited. He could thread his way painstakingly through a simply written book, but he did not often find the patience for it in the dim gas lighting – Tommy had never seen the point in installing electric lights. It was easier for Billy to follow the example he had been set. Whisky was not a cheap commodity. He assumed that the nameless hooch Tommy and Marjorie had drunk every night must have been cheaper. No doubt it was produced locally, but Tommy had never divulged the source. So Billy had to hoard some money away for whisky or, occasionally, persuade a colleague at the pub to turn a blind eye while a bottle vanished from the cellar. But it was during those long evenings at home, with only the silent Eve and his bottle for company, that the memories were at their most potent.

It was not that sex had ever been much of a mystery to either Billy or Eve. Tommy and Marjorie had sex several times a week after two or three hours of drinking hooch, and never made any secret of it. Often they left the door of their bedroom open. Billy and Eve shared the other bedroom, occupying single beds. There was nowhere else for them to sleep. When the noise woke them up, they would often creep along the short stretch of corridor and peer in through the open door, to see Tommy and Marjorie naked on the bed, the covers thrown back, in the throes, or immediate aftermath, of sexual intercourse. Marjorie's usual reaction, on seeing the children at the door, was to laugh. Sometimes she would seize Tommy's penis and wave it in their direction.

'Look at that,' she would say. 'Daddy's giving Mummy a right bloody seeing to, isn't he? Isn't Mummy a lucky girl?'

'Shut up, you silly bitch,' Tommy would say. But this only made Marjorie laugh even more.

But the memories that truly disturbed Billy were of what came later. Later, when Marjorie was asleep, Tommy would start the singing. Tommy was a Lincolnshire man and made a show of being proud of it, though he had not returned to his native county once during the thirty-five years before his death. As a Lincolnshire man, more than any other song, he liked the *Lincolnshire Poacher*. Tommy knew every verse, of course, and as a child Billy could sing each one with him. But now he remembered only the first and the last.

When I was bound apprentice in famous Lincolnshire,
Full well I served my master for nigh on seven years,
Till I took up to poaching, as you shall quickly hear,
Oh, 'tis my delight on a shiny night in the season of the year.

Success to every gentleman that lives in Lincolnshire,
Success to every poacher that wants to sell a hare,
Bad luck to every gamekeeper that will not sell his deer,
Oh, 'tis my delight on a shiny night in the season of the year.

Often Tommy would sing during the day, while operating the lock or shovelling silt. But what Billy and Eve remembered most clearly was when he sang late at night. They would hear him singing softly as he lifted himself quietly out of bed, and during the short walk from his bedroom to theirs. When it started, Billy could never recall. It was a long time ago, that was certain. Eve could not have been more than ten or eleven. But once it started, it happened so often that no one occasion stood out particularly. Tommy would wear a cotton dressing gown, under which he was naked. He would point towards Billy's bed.

'You – turn the other way and go to sleep,' he would command Billy. 'Or else.'

Billy would turn the other way as commanded, but of course, as soon as Tommy's attention was fully fixed on Eve, his curiosity made him turn back quietly to watch. The pattern never varied very much. First, Tommy would take off his dressing gown. By that time, if Eve had been asleep before, she would be wide awake. And the whole time, the singing, now almost a whisper.

When I was bound apprentice in famous Lincolnshire,
Full well I served my master for nigh on seven years,…

He would take off Eve's nightdress and underwear and pull back the covers on her bed.

'You are such a special girl. You are Daddy's little princess.'

Then he would kiss her, up and down her body, as she lay in place on her back, frozen and motionless.

'Daddy's little princess. Be a good girl for Daddy. You know what Daddy likes, don't you?'

Till I took up to poaching as you shall quickly hear,
Oh, 'tis my delight on a shiny night in the season of the year.

Then he would take her frozen hand, unclench her fingers, which she held stiff without actively resisting, and place them where he wanted them. She never tried to remove them, but neither did she actively cooperate, so Tommy had to put his hand over hers and move it up and down until he was satisfied. When she was about twelve, he began to vary it sometimes by pulling Eve up off the bed and bringing her head down to his groin. Billy would see him holding her hair and moving her head up and down until his body suddenly went limp, he released her hair, and her body sank back down on to her bed.

'You are such a perfect little girl. Daddy's little princess.'

Once she was about thirteen, and her breasts had grown nicely, he began to lie down on top of her, just as he did with Marjorie.

Success to every gentleman that lives in Lincolnshire,
Success to every poacher that wants to sell a hare…

When it came time to return to the marital bed, he would place a finger over her lips.

'Remember, princess, this is our secret. No one must ever know. My beautiful little princess.'

They would hear his footsteps retreat along the corridor outside.

Bad luck to every gamekeeper that will not sell his deer,
Oh, 'tis my delight on a shiny night in the season of the year.

Billy could never remember whether he had ever heard Eve protest or complain. If she ever had, she gave up at an early stage. She never cried, and she appeared to go to sleep soon after Tommy left. Whether his mother ever knew about Daddy giving Eve a right bloody seeing to, Billy never knew. If she did, he never heard her mention it, nor did he detect any change in her behaviour towards his father. Having no other frame of reference, Billy concluded that what he had witnessed must be normal behaviour for men and women. After all, his parents made no secret of it. Marjorie obviously enjoyed what Tommy did, so perhaps Eve did too. When this view took shape in his mind, Billy was seventeen and struggling to deal with his own emerging sexual desires. One night it seemed to him natural enough to approach Eve himself. She did not seem surprised, and cooperated by undressing herself and guiding him inside her.

'I like it better with you,' she told him, as he left her bed to return to his own. 'You don't smell of drink.' It was the only comment she ever made to him about it.

Billy's insight into human sexuality was now fully developed.

* * *

For some years, Billy had no real opportunity to meet women other than Eve and his mother. By the time his parents died, he and Eve had settled into a comfortable routine. But when he began to see young women in the pubs in St Ives, it seemed obvious that, just like Eve, they would be freely available to him if only he could arrange the right circumstances. Often the young women would be with young men. But Billy had no reason to see that as a drawback. The young woman would surely be available if he wanted her. He watched many of these couples closely, and sometimes followed them along the street when they left the pub.

One evening he followed a young couple for about half a mile to the girl's home. They kissed and cuddled for a few minutes on the doorstep while Billy watched from behind a tree. When the young man left, Billy approached the house and hid in some bushes in the garden to the left of the front door. It was not the first time he had kept watch on a house, but it was the first time he had any real luck. A few minutes later the girl appeared at the window of an upstairs room, no doubt her bedroom. Billy watched, fascinated, as she undressed in the most natural way imaginable, utterly oblivious to his presence. She seated herself, naked, at a dressing table, still clearly visible. By now, Billy had unbuttoned his flies and was touching himself as she began to remove her make-up. He was summoning up his nerve to knock on the door and ask if he could come in. He was so absorbed that he failed to notice the approach of PC Willis. The officer happened on the scene purely by chance in the course of a routine patrol and, in the stillness of the evening, easily spotted the movement in the bushes as he cycled past. As he got closer, he distinctly heard the whispered tones of a verse of the *Lincolnshire Poacher*, which struck him as odd.

Having put his hand on Billy's shoulder, PC Willis thought briefly about what to do. Willis was an old-fashioned copper who believed in dealing with situations as quietly as possible and not getting people into too much trouble if it could be avoided. If Billy had been a teenager, he would have given him a clip around the ear and warned him not to do it again. But at his age, Willis thought with regret, that wouldn't do. He might move on to something more serious; he needed a bit more of a lesson. So he arrested Billy, charged him with indecent exposure, and kept him in a cell overnight. The next morning he took Billy to the magistrates' court, where Billy pleaded guilty to the charge and was conditionally discharged for twelve months. Eve did not ask where he had been. Billy told her that he had had a couple of drinks too many at the pub and had spent the night there rather than trying to walk home.

After that, Billy became more cautious. He had to make sure to keep out of trouble for the next twelve months. So he abandoned his pursuit if the couple lived close to town, where he might encounter PC Willis again, and he did not lurk outside any more houses. He confined himself to following couples who walked a little way out of town. That was how he first found out about the *Rosemary D*.

3

THE *ROSEMARY D* WAS moored at Holywell Fen, about a mile along the river from the bridge at St Ives. The fen behind the river was remote and treacherous, an expanse of marsh covered by reeds and clumps of rough grass, often cut off by the river mists; and a bend in the river to the north took the mooring behind some trees and away from the distant lights of the town. The *Rosemary D* had belonged to Ken and Rosemary Douglas, who were still something of a legend in St Ives. They had arrived in the town from London in 1959 with a great deal of money and a great deal of fanfare. They bought and renovated a large town house in the High Street. They also bought the *Rosemary D*. Rosemary became an active member of the Civic Society. Ken joined the Rotary Club and submitted an application for appointment as a magistrate.

The *Rosemary D* was a Dutch houseboat. Her original name was *De Grachtprinses*. They found her berthed, apparently abandoned, on the Herengracht in Amsterdam. They fell in love with her, renamed her, and had her towed with enormous care to the Wash and up the river to St Ives. She was all of forty feet long, and had two sections – living quarters with a makeshift kitchen and a minute toilet forward, and sleeping quarters aft. Her exterior was painted in bright shades of red and green, with wispy harlequin figures in brown, silver and gold executing macabre dance moves, their arms and legs grotesquely hyper-extended along her sides. A number of hardy plants in large earthenware pots were strategically placed around the deck. Both the town house and the *Rosemary D* provided settings for extravagant parties, noted for the quantity and quality of food and drink. It was rumoured that more exotic substances were also available. There were whispered stories about scandalous goings on late into the night.

Then, in 1962, the bubble burst. One morning in May, the town house was suddenly cleared out, and Ken and Rosemary Douglas left St Ives abruptly, never to be seen again. The police had uncovered the source of their money, and were seeking Ken and Rosemary's help with their inquiries into a number of serious frauds. With the police and the bailiffs hot on their trail, they made good their escape to a warmer clime, a South American country which had not found it necessary to enter into an extradition treaty with the United Kingdom. Soon afterwards, the bailiffs put padlocks on both the house and the *Rosemary D* and it was generally assumed that both would be sold to satisfy the creditors. The house was indeed sold but, for whatever reason, whether through an oversight, a lack of energy, or a slow market in houseboats, the *Rosemary D* remained at her berth at Holywell Fen – deserted, locked, and apparently fated to begin a gradual decline.

Enter the young courting couples of the surrounding countryside, from St Ives, Fenstanton, Hemingford Grey, Needingworth, Over, and Swavesey, who found the padlocks easy enough to pick, and began to make regular use of the *Rosemary D* for assignations forbidden to them in their parents' houses. The Douglases had not had time to clear out the *Rosemary D* before fleeing the country, so the bed, bedding, chairs, kitchen table, glassware and cutlery remained in place. Word soon spread that an ideal spot for courting had been found and, in a remarkable show of social cooperation, a number of house rules developed and were generally obeyed. A length of rope daubed with red paint was to be left hanging from the door leading to the living quarters to show that they were occupied. No one was to occupy the boat for more than an hour, and at busy periods, forty-five minutes. The boat was to be kept reasonably clean and tidy (one couple regularly took the bedding away and returned it washed and dried) and all items brought on board were to be removed on leaving. The windows were to be closed. The padlocks were to be positioned so as to appear to be locked, but not actually locked. Above all, conversation about the venue was to be kept to a minimum, to reduce the chances of the bailiffs taking a renewed interest.

Frank Gilliam found out about the *Rosemary D* from a friend at work. Frank was twenty-three, a management trainee at Lloyds Bank in St Ives, and over lunch one day he heard about her from Molly Smith, one of the tellers. Molly's boyfriend, Sam, had taken her there several times, she confided. She did not go into great detail, but in hushed tones she confided to Frank that, the last time, something had gone a bit wrong, and she had spent almost two weeks worrying herself to death, and worrying Sam to death until, mercifully, her period arrived exactly on time. Frank was all ears.

Frank was a handsome young man – almost six feet tall and fairly slim, with light brown hair and eyes. He had been going out with Jennifer Doyce for about two months. Jennifer was a couple of years younger than Frank, a slight girl of medium height, with black hair and blue-grey eyes. She also lived in St Ives, but was training as a librarian in Huntingdon. Their outings were confined to the weekends, and consisted of visits to cafés, pubs, or the cinema. Jennifer was by no means unwilling, but opportunities for physical intimacy were few and far between. Both Frank and Jennifer still lived at home with their parents and, when he walked her home, it was usually too cold for anything more than a brief kiss and a suggestive fondle. At the cinema, with their coats over their laps, she would use her hand to good effect. But then there was the problem of concealing the inevitable stains from his mother. And Jennifer did not feel comfortable enough in the cinema to let him do anything similar for her.

Frank was ready for more; and he was prepared. On his last visit to the barber, he had summoned up his courage sufficiently to buy a packet of three condoms.

'Will there be anything else, sir?' Geoffrey, the barber, inquired as usual, taking his half crown and depositing it in the till.

Geoffrey had been asking the same question of Frank for at least two years. In theory, he might have been referring to shaving cream or razor blades. But the context always suggested otherwise. The question was asked with a knowing grin, and an upward glance towards the condoms, which were kept on a high shelf, almost invisible unless you knew exactly where to look, to avoid any shock or offence to older customers or mothers bringing in their young sons for their short back and sides. It always made Frank feel horribly awkward. When he replied, 'No, I'm fine, thank you,' he would try to give the impression of a man who was already provided for, though he felt sure that Geoffrey saw straight through him. But on this occasion Frank was determined to overcome his self-consciousness.

'Yes, actually, a packet of the…' He allowed the sentence to die, unfinished, in the air.

'Of course, sir.' Geoffrey looked around quickly. There was only one customer waiting, a youngish man immersed in the sports pages of the *Daily Mirror*. No danger of scandal. He quickly mounted a small stool kept behind the till for the purpose, and swiftly removed one packet, which almost immediately disappeared into an anonymous brown paper bag.

'There you go, sir,' he said quietly. 'That will be another half crown.'

'Good luck, sir,' he added in a confidential whisper as Frank left. 'Pop in any time if you need some more.'

So Frank was all set. All he needed to do now was to tell Jennifer about the *Rosemary D.*

4

THEY DECIDED TO go to the Oliver Cromwell for a drink to settle their nerves, and to warm themselves up a bit, before setting out for their big adventure. They arrived at 9.45. The Oliver Cromwell was a basic locals' pub in Wellington Street, a stone's throw from the historic Quay and the ancient bridge which spans the Great Ouse at St Ives. It was an overwhelmingly male establishment. Few women drank there – perhaps the occasional widow sitting on her own in a corner of the snug – it was very different from the new, more glitzy town-centre pubs where women, even women on their own, were no longer so unusual. Jennifer turned one or two heads when they entered. But they did not much care about that. They needed a drink, and the Oliver Cromwell was convenient. It would be a short walk to the end of Wellington Street, then a right turn on to Priory Road, leading, through a metal turnstile gate, to the seemingly endless expanse of meadow which formed the bank of the river until you reached the fen.

The decision to pay a visit to the *Rosemary D* that Saturday night had been taken. Both knew what it meant, and both knew there would be no turning back. Separately, they had taken advice in advance of the occasion. Frank's elder brother Jim, who was independent and living in a flat of his own, showed him how to prepare and put on a condom. Jennifer's elder sister, Marion, who was married, warned her not to expect too much of the first time, and gave her tips on reviving him for the second session which, she assured Jennifer, would be far better. Jennifer did not tell Marion about the *Rosemary D*. It was not exactly the setting she had imagined for her first time. But things were as they were; she genuinely liked Frank; and a comfortable boat on the river seemed romantic enough. She put on her smartest blouse and skirt, and a new warm cardigan against the cold and, as always, she wore around her neck the large gold cross and chain her grandmother had given her when she was confirmed.

Frank went to the bar and ordered a pint and a half of bitter. Billy Cottage served him and then watched as they sat together at a table by the fireplace, holding hands, but talking very little.

The landlord called for last orders at 10.30. They took a few minutes to finish their drinks. Frank checked his pocket for the condoms for the fiftieth time that evening. They put on their coats and hats and left the pub. The night was bitterly cold, but they had anticipated this, and had warm coats, scarves and gloves. There was no question of undressing very much on the boat – it would be far too cold. That was a drawback. But on the other hand, the coldness of the night was likely to discourage potential rivals for the boat from venturing out. Indeed, they had every expectation of being the only visitors. They might be able to stay for longer than an hour, if the cold was not too much for them. They walked briskly towards the meadow. Billy Cottage left the Oliver Cromwell almost immediately and followed, keeping a safe distance behind.

At the end of Priory Road Mavis Brown was preparing to lock up the corner shop for the night. The shop faced into town down Wellington Street. Mavis was just nineteen, and the shop belonged to her widowed father. She lived with him in the flat upstairs and worked alongside him in the shop. They sold newspapers, magazines, sweets, cigarettes and tobacco and a small selection of groceries and household items. The shop was not officially open at that late hour on a Saturday. Mavis had been doing some stock-taking over the weekend and had worked later than she had intended. But she saw Frank and Jennifer peering in through the lighted window and, being a kind and helpful girl, she took the trouble to open up long enough to sell them two packets of Woodbines. Billy Cottage paused until they emerged from the shop and continued walking. Mavis was just about to switch the lights off and go upstairs when Billy passed the shop. She did not know him, but she was at the large shop window and could not help seeing him. There was a street light on the corner. She had a clear view. She noticed that, despite the cold, he had his raincoat open. He was wearing a dark jacket and a red and white checked shirt. He had a dark woollen hat on his head. His heavy brown shoes looked as though they had not been cleaned for a long time. She even heard him singing in a cheerful tone.

When I was bound apprentice in famous Lincolnshire,
Full well I served my master for nigh on seven years...

Mavis probably wouldn't have paid much attention to that, except that she was sure she had heard the same song just the other day. There had been a folk music concert on the radio just before bedtime. She had listened to it with her father over their cups of cocoa. A singer called Steve Benbow had performed that same song. Billy walked on. As she switched off the lights Mavis glanced at the clock on the wall at the back of the shop. The time was 10.45.

5

27 January

At 8.30 on Monday morning it was still barely light. The morning was grey and cheerless and the day seemed destined to be every bit as cold as the five that had preceded it. But it would have taken more than a little cold weather to keep Archie Knights and Bouncer at home. Archie had retired from the former Suffolk Regiment with the rank of major three years before, and getting up early was a habit he had been unable to shake off. He had been awake since 5.30, although on this morning he had allowed himself the indulgence of a cup of tea and an attempt, only partially successful, on the *Times* crossword before calling his golden retriever for their daily walk. Archie pulled on his wellingtons, and man and dog set out for the river bank at a brisk pace.

Archie passed the *Rosemary D* during his walk two or three times a week. He had met Ken and Rosemary Douglas socially once or twice, and he had heard the rumours about the parties on the boat. But that was history now, and when the police started to take an interest in them his wife had instructed him to disapprove of the Douglases and their parties. Usually, he gave the *Rosemary D* no more than a passing glance, wondering vaguely when someone would either come and occupy her or tow her away before she started to deteriorate. But on this morning he stopped abruptly alongside. This was partly because he noticed that the door leading down to the quarters was not firmly closed as usual, but was ajar; and partly because Bouncer had stopped and was making an unfamiliar soft whining noise. After hesitating for some time, Archie made his way carefully on to the small, muddy wooden dock. He approached the boat, put one foot up on the deck and called out.

'Hello. Anyone aboard?'

There was no reply. Bouncer was still whining and was straining at the leash, trying to turn Archie around, as if he wanted to leave.

'It's all right, boy,' Archie reassured him. 'Someone probably left it unlocked by mistake.'

He tried to peer through the opening, but it was too narrow, and he could see no light inside. The window curtains were closed.

'Come on, Bouncer, we'll just take a quick look.'

He stepped fully on to the deck, pulling the unwilling Bouncer behind him, and gingerly approached the door. He knocked.

'Anyone home?' he called again. 'Can I come in?'

No reply. He pushed the door open. There was just enough light for him to see. There was no one in the living quarters, and everything seemed in order, except for a single chair overturned on his left. But there was a smell hanging in the air. He closed his eyes. It was a smell which brought to mind his days in combat as a captain in North Africa and Italy. There was no mistaking it. Dreading what he now knew he was going to find, he trod quietly towards the sleeping quarters. The door was open. One look, even in the dim light, was enough. He turned and ran hell for leather for the door, for fresh air and daylight. The horror of what he had seen did not hit him fully until he had jumped back from the dock on to the river bank. He turned slowly back to look at the boat, one hand over his mouth, breathing heavily. He felt sick.

'Oh, my dear God,' he muttered. Bouncer had sat down on the grass, his head against Archie's leg, quiet now. Archie breathed deeply several times to ward off the nausea. There was no time for that. He forced himself to concentrate and pulled sharply on the leash.

'Come on, boy,' he said. 'We have to go and find Constable Willis.'

* * *

In Sergeant Livermore's absence on leave, PC Willis was the ranking officer at St Ives police station. Only PC Hawthorne, who had been with the force less than three months, was available to assist him. As he ordered Hawthorne to summon up the one river boat the force had at its disposal, Willis had the uncomfortable sensation of leaving the citizens of St Ives at the mercy of whatever burglars and other assorted malefactors might be disposed to ply their trade early on a Monday morning, with the police station temporarily unattended except for Sylvia, the civilian receptionist.

But there was nothing to be done about it. What Archie Knights had told him needed immediate attention, and once he was sure of what he was dealing with, Sylvia was going to have to call Huntingdon and Cambridge and get CID officers involved. Meanwhile, he and Hawthorne would have to cordon off and secure the scene and make preliminary notes. There would be hell to pay if everything was not in order when CID arrived, and Willis had no intention of allowing that to happen. The river boat was kept at Bert's boatyard, just out of town to the east. The force had no specialist marine officer and, if Bert was out, any investigation had to wait until he returned. Fortunately, on this occasion Bert was in the office and answered the phone as soon as it rang. Within a few minutes he had collected the officers and conveyed them to Holywell Fen at full throttle. On approach, he throttled back and expertly pulled up alongside the *Rosemary D.* As soon as Bert had tied off the lines to secure the boat in place, Willis and Hawthorne clambered aboard.

The scene was too much for young PC Hawthorne. He turned and ran back through the living quarters to the side of the boat, where he vomited violently over the side. Willis felt queasy himself, but he put a handkerchief over his mouth, and slowly, with infinite care, made his way around to his right until he was able to pull open the nearest window curtain. He would gladly have opened a window to let in some fresh air, but his training prevailed. CID would call that contaminating the scene. With the benefit of daylight he saw the details of the scene clearly for the first time. There were two victims, one male, one female. The male was straight ahead of him on the floor, to the right of the bed. He appeared to have several serious head wounds, which must have been inflicted, Willis thought, with great force and using a heavy object. There was a lot of blood all over his clothes and on the floor. The female was lying on the bed. She also appeared to have head wounds. Her skirt had been pushed up; her knickers were around her ankles. Her genitals were fully exposed. Willis shook his head. He was about to look around for a murder weapon, when he looked again at the girl's face. He bent down and seized her wrist, feeling for a pulse, watching her face carefully. Then he dropped her wrist, turned and ran the full length of the *Rosemary D*, shouting Hawthorne's name loudly as he ran. Once on deck, he tore Hawthorne away from the side, as he was still wiping his mouth.

'Do that later,' he shouted. 'The girl's alive. Barely, but she's breathing. Bert, get the river ambulance here. Now, for God's sake!'

6

BEN SCHROEDER WAS one of the two newest members of the Chambers of Bernard Wesley QC The set occupied two floors of 2 Wessex Buildings, under the shadow of the magnificent arch at the bottom of Middle Temple Lane which leads the visitor out of the extraordinary quiet of the Temple into the incessant growl of the traffic on Victoria Embankment. The barrister's rooms in Chambers looked out over Middle Temple Gardens and provided a peaceful haven in which to work, one which the noise of the traffic failed to disturb. The names of the members of Chambers, in order of seniority, were hand-painted in black by the Temple signwriter on the white panels at the side of the doorway at street level and on the main door of Chambers itself, two floors above. One last name appeared at the end of the list in italics and it was in some ways the most important of all. It was the name of the clerk, Merlin Walters. The barristers' clerk was the Bar's version of the theatrical agent, and his work was absolutely vital to the success of each member of Chambers, however able that member might be. By a long-standing rule of the profession, barristers did not form firms or partnerships. Each barrister was a sole practitioner. In return for a fee of one tenth of each barrister's earnings, the clerk managed that barrister's career; assessing his strengths and weaknesses, recommending the kind of legal work most suited to his talents; negotiating fees with the solicitors who instructed the barrister; and receiving the fees on his behalf; all the while doing all he could to attract new solicitors. And now, also, on *her* behalf; the second new member of Chambers was Harriet Fisk, whose very presence was the harbinger of a coming revolution in the most traditional of professions.

As the two newest members, Ben and Harriet shared a room. When one had a conference with a solicitor, the other would retire to another room or walk the few yards up Middle Temple Lane to the library. The room was tastefully decorated. Without in any way insisting, Harriet had gradually taken responsibility for the decoration. They had already shared a room together for a year as pupils, and he had long been aware of her flair for bringing a room to life. Now that they were going to share on a longer-term basis, Ben had gladly stood back and allowed her good taste to transform the drab interior they had inherited from Peter Elliot and Roger Horan. The result was not the usual barrister's room, full of hunting scenes, Punch or Dornier prints, and antique but seriously battered desks. Instead, the walls, painted in a light shade of green, boasted three original landscapes and an elegant gold-framed mirror. The chairs and the single sofa were upholstered in a soft fabric, a soft green one or two shades darker than the walls. The several small tables were mahogany and contemporary, and the room was richly carpeted in a light brown. The desks, which stood in the two corners of the room, diagonally opposite each other, were a rich deep walnut with brass fittings and dark green leather inlaid tops. Today it was Ben who had the conference and Harriet who had taken her papers to the library. Conferences were still a new experience for him. The Bar was the senior branch of the profession, and etiquette demanded that the solicitor, however senior, bring his client to the Chambers of the barrister, however junior, for conferences. As a very junior member of the Bar, Ben had not yet ceased to be self-conscious about this presumption.

Bernard Wesley's set was a small one, and thought of itself as an élite group of skilled advocates. Wesley himself, the only QC in Chambers and an intense and introverted man out of court, specialised in complicated commercial work, but also appeared frequently in high-profile divorce cases. Gareth Morgan-Davies, with whom Ben had served his pupillage, a Welshman with a passion for rugby and opera, had a variety of heavy work, both civil and criminal, and was generally believed to be on the verge of taking Silk. Harriet's pupil-master, Aubrey Smith-Gurney, whose amiable demeanour masked an exceptionally keen legal mind, preferred life out of London at his home in Sussex whenever a busy civil practice permitted, which was increasingly infrequently. Kenneth Gaskell and Anthony Norris were somewhat less senior but were building considerable reputations in divorce and criminal law respectively; though Norris's abrasive brilliance in court was matched by a marked tendency to alienate people, including members of his own Chambers, because of an almost contemptuous brusqueness, and often downright rudeness. Peter Elliot and Roger Horan had joined Chambers within the last three years and were still beginning to build their practices. Ben had no reservations about his own ability, and no fears about competing within this talented set. No inner demon questioned his skill as an advocate. He had every confidence in his future success.

But a different demon whispered to him about his background. He was the son of a family of Jewish traders. The family had emigrated from Austria, settling in Whitechapel three generations previously, and had built a successful business selling furs and expensive clothing in the Commercial Road. Ben was the product of a grammar school and then London University, which in almost any walk of life was an enviable start. But the Bar was the last refuge of a vanished professional age. No one had ever said to his face that his background was an obstacle to success at the Bar. Indeed, there were many, especially his pupil-master, Gareth Morgan-Davies, who had assured him that in a rapidly changing profession it was irrelevant. Indeed, both his and Harriet's presence in Chambers seemed to confirm that the legal landscape was rapidly changing. But Ben's mind was not yet at ease. All the men senior to him in Chambers had come to the Bar by way of public school and Oxford or Cambridge. Outside Chambers they were all members of the same select London Gentleman's club, which would never accept Harriet as a member and would not accept Ben without a demeaning campaign of lobbying on his behalf by Bernard Wesley – something Ben had not sought and would never seek. There was no overt obstacle to his advancement in his profession; but he felt that there was an unseen barrier, that in its innermost essence, the Bar remained a close professional caste immune to change, a caste which would allow him to advance so far, but no farther; a caste which jealously guarded an inner sanctum to which he would never be admitted, however great his ability and however distinguished his achievements. The demon came to whisper to him, not only at night, but also in Chambers and in court, even after a victory, and was not easily deflected.

He was a handsome young man, now twenty-six years of age, and he did not wear his concerns on his sleeve. He had a ready smile, a cheerful disposition, and an assured, decisive manner when delivering his legal advice. A solicitor coming to Chambers would never have guessed that he harboured any self-doubt at all. He was just short of six feet in height with a thin build, not exactly athletic, but quick and graceful in movement. His hair was solidly black. His eyes were a deep brown, seemingly set rather deep in his face because of strikingly prominent cheek bones, and when he fixed a witness with those eyes during cross-examination it added another layer of disconcerting intensity. His jaw was narrow, and made his chin look almost pointed when viewed from certain angles. If his face had a weakness at all, it was that it cried out for a very thin, neatly groomed moustache and beard, but it would be many years before he had the confidence to add that adornment – it would have been a step too far in the conservative legal world he had so recently entered. His clothes reflected his need to conform. With his family connections, he had his choice of the finest Jewish tailors in the East End, an asset of which he had taken full advantage. His three-piece suits were immaculately made to measure in dark grey with the lightest of white pinstripes. He wore a thin gold pocket watch, attached to a thin gold chain threaded through the middle buttonhole of his waistcoat. His shirts, also made to measure, were of the highest quality cotton. His ties were silk, restrained darker reds and blues in colour, but at the same time they engaged the eye. He had learned from Gareth Morgan-Davies always to wear a fluted white handkerchief in the top pocket of his jacket.

Ben stood by a window, looking out over the Middle Temple gardens. He glanced at his pocket watch. Almost time.

7

MERLIN KNOCKED ON the door, and stepped quietly into the room.

'Your conference is here, Mr Schroeder, if you're ready, sir.'

'Quite ready, Merlin,' Ben Schroeder replied. 'Please show them in.'

Merlin had kept him busy with small criminal cases in the magistrates' courts and small civil disputes in the county courts. Ben's personal preference was for criminal cases, and Merlin believed that was where his strength lay, but as the most junior tenant he gratefully accepted whatever work came his way and did his best to cultivate the solicitors who entrusted him with it, almost all regular clients of Chambers whom Merlin had courted painstakingly over many years.

Barratt Davis was one of the regulars. He was one of two partners in the firm of Bourne & Davis, whose offices were in Essex Street, just outside the Middle Temple. It was a short walk for him to Chambers through the little gate into the Inn of Court, past the famous fountain and the Inn's historic dining hall, and down Middle Temple Lane. Davis was a tall, vigorous man in his late forties, with a large shock of thick brown hair, which his comb could never quite control, running fiercely from his neck to his brow, where it rose abruptly in a wave. As a solicitor with offices just outside the Temple he made himself wear dark grey suits in deference to the conventional professional taste, but as a gesture of defiance he also wore brightly coloured shirts and ties, today yellow, with a matching handkerchief in the top pocket of his jacket. Following close on his heels into Ben's room was a young woman in her mid-twenties, dressed in a black jacket and knee-length skirt, a white blouse and low-heeled black shoes. Her dark brown hair was swept back and held in place by a silver pin, and she wore a thin silver chain around her neck.

'Good afternoon, Mr Schroeder,' Barratt Davis said, seizing Ben's hand in a vice-like grip. 'I'm not sure you've met my new assistant, Jess Farrar? She's only just come on board. She will be working with you on this case.'

Ben smiled at Jess.

'No, we haven't met before.'

He gratefully extricated his hand from Davis's grip and offered it to Jess. She took it warmly but, to his relief, far more gently.

'I'm glad to meet you,' she said.

Two other men had entered Ben's room and were standing uncertainly by the door. Barratt Davis walked back to the door and ushered the older of the two forward. He was wearing a brown tweed suit over a light blue shirt, and a brown bow tie with white dots, and looked rather out of place in the formal atmosphere of counsel's Chambers.

'Mr Schroeder, may I introduce a professional colleague, Mr John Singer, a solicitor from St Ives in Huntingdonshire? We have collaborated on a number of matters in the past, and I think I am right in saying that members of his family have been solicitors in the town for almost a hundred years.'

'Indeed so,' John Singer smiled. Ben shook his hand.

'And this is Mr Singer's client,' Davis continued, beckoning to the second man to leave the safety of the door and venture into the room. He was dressed in a dark grey jacket, with a black shirt and a white clerical collar. 'The Reverend Ignatius Little, Vicar of St Martin's Church in St Ives.'

'My firm represents the Diocese of Ely in various church matters, Mr Schroeder,' Singer added. 'The diocesan office consulted us about Mr Little. We advise the Diocese in a wide range of legal matters. But we have no experience of... ,' he hesitated, 'of... representing a defendant in this kind of case. So we sought the advice of Mr Davis, as we have in the past.'

'Please sit down,' Ben said. He ushered them all into the chairs that formed a semi-circle in front of his desk. 'Did the clerks offer you some tea?'

'Yes, but we are all right, thank you,' Davis said. He turned to the Reverend Ignatius Little. 'Mr Little, you can have every confidence in Mr Schroeder. Bourne & Davis instructs him regularly.' He smiled at Ben. 'In fact, we instructed him in his very first case, which was something of a triumph.'

Ben returned the smile across the desk, but hesitantly, remembering that his first case had been a relatively recent experience.

'Mr Schroeder represented a client of ours, a police sergeant from Essex. He was charged with an offence which could have ended his career.'

Going through a red light on his motor cycle, Ben recalled silently. Not a particularly grave matter in itself, but Sergeant James Mulcahy was the officer responsible for training police motor cyclists in Essex, and in his case a conviction would have been catastrophic.

'Mr Schroeder had the charge thrown out after cross-examining the officer who stopped our client.'

In Hackney, at the junction of Dalston Lane and Kingsland Road, Ben reminded himself. And it was the magistrate, Horatio Templeton, who had the charge thrown out. All I did was exploit the officer's ill-advised insistence that he had seen no less than four vehicles cross a red light at exactly the same time, even though there were only two lanes of traffic at the junction. Sergeant Mulcahy did not believe that was possible. Neither did I. Neither, mercifully, did Horatio Templeton. Result: reasonable doubt. One career saved, one getting off to a decent start.

If the Reverend Ignatius Little was impressed by Davis's complimentary introduction of his defence barrister, he did not show it. Davis had opened a brown file folder which he had removed from his briefcase. He stared at the papers inside the file for some time before continuing.

'Mr Schroeder, the Reverend Little was arrested last Thursday morning in St Ives and charged with indecent assault on a male under the age of sixteen, to wit, ten years of age. He was granted bail by the magistrates yesterday. He will elect to go before a judge and jury at quarter sessions, of course. No question of letting the magistrates loose on this. Far too much at stake, goes without saying. We have a date for committal proceedings on the 13th February. It seems a long time to wait for a committal out in the country, but the police told the magistrates that they want to make further inquiries.'

Ben raised his eyebrows.

'They want to find out whether there have been other complaints against Mr Little,' John Singer explained. 'Mr Little has been suspended from his living pending the outcome of the case. That's standard practice in any such circumstances. That's how I became involved. The Diocese always consults us before taking a step such as suspending a priest. But of course, that came to the notice of the police. They have been asking questions of the Diocese. Where has he served in the Diocese before? Why did he move? Has he served in any other diocese? Have there been any complaints against him? Has he ever been suspended before? The Diocese tells me there is nothing known against Mr Little at all. He has been a popular vicar. His parishioners like him, and there has been no hint of scandal or trouble of any kind.'

Davis nodded. 'We will make sure witnesses are available from the Diocese to give evidence about all that,' he said. 'But that won't stop the police digging as deep as they can. I have advised Mr Little that he must be as frank as possible with us. If there is anything, anything at all, which reflects badly on him in any way, he must tell us about it.'

Ben looked across at the Reverend Ignatius Little. He was sitting dejectedly, his head bowed, his hands in his lap. He had not said a word. Ben had read a short written proof of the evidence Little would give about the allegation, prepared, he imagined, by Jess Farrar. He understood the allegation and Little's response to it. But it was important to get Little to talk about it himself, out loud. He had not yet recovered from the trauma of being arrested. He was still in shock. He had the air of a man who preferred to believe that this was not happening, that he would soon wake up to find that it was all a terrible dream, that it was time for him to stroll from the vicarage to his church for matins, as usual. But usual was a thing of the past now. The sooner that illusion went away, the better. It was time to wake up and deal with reality.

'Tell me something about yourself, Mr Little. I see you are thirty-four years of age. How long have you been Vicar of St Martin's?' he asked quietly.

Little raised his head to look at Ben for the first time. 'For just over a year,' he replied. 'It's my first living.'

'And before that?'

'I was curate at St Anthony's, Great Shelford, for almost three years. I was ordained priest in 1959. Before that, I was at Cambridge. I read Classics at Selwyn, and then went on to Ridley Hall to train for the ministry.'

'You will have to forgive me,' Ben smiled. 'I'm from a rather different religious tradition.' For the first time, Little ventured a weak smile in return. 'So I'm not familiar with what goes on in the Church of England. But I am quite sure that at some point, when you are selected as a candidate for the ministry, they make some kind of inquiry into your character.'

'I can answer that,' John Singer said. 'The Diocese makes a thorough inquiry in all cases. Not just police records, though they do look at those, of course. But inquiries are made of family, friends, neighbours, school, college. We consult with the Diocese in that process if anything comes up that may need to be investigated further. Nothing came up in Mr Little's case to raise any concern at all.'

'They give you a thorough grilling, I can assure you,' Little added. 'In my case I was grilled by the Archdeacon personally. Did I drink? Did I gamble? Would I be on the lookout for rich old ladies to fleece? It was like the Inquisition, I don't mind telling you.'

Ben smiled.

'Well, let's not worry about rich old ladies. What about younger ladies, whether rich or otherwise? Did the Archdeacon ask you about that?'

'Mr Little is engaged to be married,' John Singer said, in a tone which suggested that that fact was enough to make any further inquiry unnecessary.

Ben nodded. 'So I understand. My question to Mr Little was whether the Archdeacon had asked him about his interest in women. Given the circumstances in which we are all here, it is a subject we can hardly avoid.'

'He did,' Little replied. 'He asked me whether I had a normal sexual interest in women. I answered in the affirmative, of course.'

'Of course,' Ben repeated. 'You must forgive me, Mr Little, but you are going to be asked questions about this in court, and we have to be prepared for them. So let me ask you this as plainly as I can. Do you have any sexual interest in men or, more importantly, in ten-year-old boys?'

Singer sat upright in his chair, and appeared to be on the verge of renewing his protest. But Barratt Davis placed a hand on his arm and shook his head.

Little went red and bit his lip.

'No,' he replied firmly, though not immediately.

'The jury will want to see a more confident reaction to that question, when I ask you in court,' Ben said.

Little shifted uneasily in his chair.

'If there is anything you want to add,' Ben said, 'this is the time to do it.'

'Well...'

There was a silence.

'Perhaps if I stepped outside for a moment?' Jess Farrar asked quietly.

'No. Thank you,' Ben replied. 'There will be both men and women in court when I ask Mr Little these questions. We may have a woman on the jury. Please understand, Mr Little, that whatever you say today is protected by legal privilege. No one can ever repeat it. But once we are in court, everything you say will be a matter of public record. So I have to know what you will say, if asked, before we go to court.'

Little nodded. He considered for some moments.

'I went to a minor public school', he replied. 'Boys only, of course. Like all boys, I went through a phase of having a crush on other boys when I was twelve or thirteen. We would see each other undressed after gym or football, of course, and everyone went through a phase of being attracted to another boy. But nothing came of it. At my school, it wasn't like other public schools where they turn a blind eye to that kind of thing. So I'm told. It isn't a religious institution, but the school has a history of boys going on to the Anglican priesthood. They would never have tolerated any... misconduct. The phase ended, and that was that.'

'Thank you,' Ben said. 'I know that couldn't have been easy for you. But it is important that I know.'

He looked down at Little's proof of evidence.

'Tell me about your fiancée, Joan Heppenstall.'

Little slumped back down in his chair. 'Ex-fiancée now, no doubt,' he said sadly. 'I haven't seen her since I was arrested. I understand she has gone back to Yorkshire to stay with her parents.'

'Her family live in York,' Davis said. 'She's a primary school teacher, and has been teaching at the school in St Ives, but they haven't seen her since the weekend. She didn't report for work on Monday morning. We will speak to her, of course, and take a proof of evidence. I'm sure she is in a state of shock at the moment, but she is bound to calm down and think about what she's doing eventually. I can't think of any reason why she wouldn't give evidence for Mr Little. Can you, Mr Singer?'

'No,' Singer agreed. 'She seems a very pleasant young lady. She's very well thought of at the primary school.'

'It might be a good idea to let Miss Farrar talk to her,' Ben suggested. 'She might open up more to a woman.'

Davis glanced over at Jess, who nodded brightly.

'Point taken. We will try to get that done next week,' he replied.

'What about the boy who is making this allegation against you?' Ben asked. 'Raymond Stone. What can you tell me about him?'

'I don't know why he would say these things about me, Mr Schroeder,' Little replied. 'His family are loyal members of the St Martin's congregation. His parents and grandparents are very active.'

'I understand from your proof of evidence that he is a choir boy, and that he also helps you prepare for services?'

'Yes.'

'He says that this incident occurred when the two of you were alone in the vestry after choir practice.'

'Choir practice always takes place on Wednesday evenings in the church,' Little replied. 'It ends a little after 8, no later than 8.30, even if we are preparing for a special occasion, such as Easter. There is no reason for the members of the choir to remain behind once practice is over. But one of the boys may volunteer to give me a hand in the vestry for a few minutes afterwards, laying out my vestments for Sunday, fetching the communion wine, putting the numbers of the hymns and psalms into the wooden holders, that kind of thing. But that would never take more than about ten to fifteen minutes at most.'

'Would anyone else still have been at the church by that time?'

'Possibly John Sharples. He is the organist and choir master. John sometimes stays for a while, getting his music organised for the

Sunday services. But he would be in the church. He would have no reason to come into the vestry.'

Ben looked up briefly, across his room, and out into the distance, out across the Victoria Embankment, and down to the southwest corner of the Middle Temple Gardens, which lay below his windows.

'Well, we won't know in detail what Raymond is going to say before the committal proceedings,' Ben said. 'But the police have given Mr Davis what they say is an outline of the allegation. According to the police, Raymond will say that you unzipped your trousers, took out your penis, and invited him to touch it. He also says that you grabbed his penis through his clothes and fondled it. What do you say about that?'

'It's a pack of lies,' John Singer insisted. 'Mr Little would not do such a thing. In any case, why would he do it in the vestry when anyone could walk in, and why would he do it with a boy whose parents are parishioners?'

'Again, Mr Singer, my question was directed to Mr Little. I must ask you to let him answer for himself.'

'It is not true,' Little said, again firmly, but not immediately.

Ben nodded.

'I am sure Mr Davis has already explained this to you, Mr Little. This is a criminal case. The prosecution has the burden of proof. You don't have to prove your innocence. You don't have to prove anything at all. You don't even have to give evidence at trial unless you want to. Unless the prosecution proves your guilt beyond reasonable doubt, the jury must return a verdict of not guilty.' He paused. 'But as a matter of practical reality, a jury is bound to wonder why a ten-year-old boy would make up a story like this if it isn't true? I would like to be in a position to answer that question for them if possible. Can you shed any light on it?'

'I've been asking myself that question ever since I was arrested,' Little replied. 'The only thing I can think of is that I wouldn't give him a reference for the King's School. To be honest, and I know this is going to sound strange, I don't even know much about that situation. I know you want me to answer for myself, Mr Schroeder, but Mr Singer actually knows more about it than I do.'

Ben looked inquiringly at Singer.

'You may know, Mr Schroeder,' he said, 'that cathedral choir schools can offer great opportunities for any boy with a gift for singing. The King's School at Ely is as good as any in the country. A boy who has been a chorister can go on from King's to a choral scholarship at one of the Cambridge colleges. If the boy also studies music and learns the organ, he may go up as an organ scholar. In addition to music, the boys receive a first-rate general education, so in any case their chances of going to the university are quite good. But there are very few places available for choristers, only eighteen to twenty-two at any given time, and they are greatly sought after. Naturally, to some extent, the school relies on local schools and choir masters to identify boys who may have the necessary talent.'

'And Raymond had ambitions to go to the King's School?'

'He had ambitions and, more importantly, his parents had ambitions,' Singer replied. 'Ironically, this was all going on long before Mr Little was appointed vicar. Boys are choristers between the ages of eight and thirteen, and by ten it would usually be a bit late to join, though in the case of a boy with exceptional talent, it is not unknown for the school to accept him at that age.'

'Had Raymond applied?' Ben asked.

'Yes, I understand so,' Singer replied. 'That's something we would have to check with the school.'

Ben glanced at Barratt Davis, who nodded and made a note.

'But it was no secret in St Ives that the Stone family thought Raymond had the talent, or that they wanted him to be a chorister at King's.'

'But...?' Ben asked.

'John Sharples didn't think he was good enough,' Little replied. 'He had said so before, when Raymond was about eight. That was when my predecessor, Alec Whittle, was the incumbent. Mr and Mrs Stone had pestered him about it, and they came to see me just after I arrived. They said that, even if John didn't think Raymond was good enough, the school would at least audition him if they had a recommendation from his vicar. Alec Whittle didn't want to do it in the face of John's advice. Neither did I, and that's what I told them. I'm not a musician, and I am no judge of such matters. To be honest, I didn't think anything of it, really. I had enough to do – settling into my first living, getting used to dealing with the Parish Council, taking on my legal responsibilities, worrying about how to pay for repairs to the church building, being responsible for planning all the services, running counselling sessions for couples intending to be married, running the youth club. I have no curate to help me. Whether Raymond Stone could sing or not was the least of my worries. I didn't pay much attention to him. Now, I wish I had. But at the time, it didn't seem very important. Obviously, it must have caused resentment. It may be that I took away Raymond's last chance of going to King's.'

'If so,' Ben replied, 'I would have thought Raymond had more cause to be angry with John Sharples than with you.'

No one responded to this observation. Ben nodded.

'Well, there it is. Mr Davis will make further inquiries at King's and with your fiancée. That's all we can do until the committal proceedings.'

He looked at Singer.

'I think we should try to ask the magistrates to commit to Quarter Sessions well away from St Ives. There is bound to be a lot of local feeling. I'm not sure we could find an impartial jury. Where would it usually go?'

'Huntingdon, where, I'm afraid, Mr Little will be the talk of the town until the case is over,' Singer agreed ruefully. 'Small country town – they love to gossip, and there's nothing you can do about it.'

'I quite agree, Mr Schroeder,' Davis replied. 'Cambridge would probably be best. It's not too far away, but we would have a large urban jury pool to select from.'

As the party rose to leave Barratt Davis contrived to usher everyone else out of Ben Schroeder's room before positioning himself in the doorway.

'Preliminary thoughts?' he asked.

Ben shook his head.

'It's not the most compelling explanation for a ten-year-old inventing a story like this, is it? But, in the end, it will probably depend on how well Raymond does in the witness box, and how well Mr Little does.'

'I was afraid you might say that,' Davis said.

* * *

When Davis had gone, Ben sat back down at his desk and gazed
out of his window for some time. He glanced at his watch: 5.45.
He might be able to catch Gareth before he left Chambers for the
day. As his pupil-master, Gareth Morgan-Davies had been Ben's
teacher and mentor from the moment he entered the profession.
Ben had learned much of what he knew about the Bar and about
advocacy from watching and listening to Gareth, in and out
of court. Almost unconsciously, he had adopted much of his
phraseology and many of his courtroom mannerisms, although,
as a young Jewish man from the East End, he had not attempted
to mimic his pupil-master's rich Welsh accent. The relationship of
pupil and pupil-master did not necessarily end with six or twelve
months of pupillage. If successful, it would be a mentorship that
would continue throughout their working lives, and in his first days
of practice Ben had used Gareth as his first port of call for advice
with cases and professional dilemmas. There had been another
mentor in his life during his pupillage, but Arthur Creighton, a
kind, elderly, but declining member of Chambers, had died just over
a year ago. Creighton had taken a kindly interest in all the pupils
in Chambers and had provided a safe source of advice at almost
any hour of the day or night, when pupil-masters were not to be
disturbed, or were not to hear of a particular uncertainty or fear in a
pupil's mind; a second and more intimate oracle. The loss had been
a huge one for Ben, because it deprived him in a single moment of a
trusted friend and of the wisdom of a long professional lifetime. But
at least he still had Gareth and, to his relief, Gareth was in his room,
immersed in a set of papers, showing no sign of being in a hurry to
leave. He looked up in response to Ben's knock.

'Come in, Ben.'

'I don't want to keep you, Gareth. It can wait if you're busy. I've
just had a conference and I wanted to run it by you and get a quick
reaction to the facts.'

Gareth laid his reading glasses on his desk and waved Ben into a
chair.

'By all means. I'm sure it's more interesting than this nonsense
I've got to deal with – two people with more than enough money
getting divorced and trying to bring each other to ruin just for the
sheer spite of it. The only good thing to be said for either of them is

that they don't mind paying counsel decent fees to help them do it. So, what have you got?'

'I've got a vicar who, according to the prosecution, is rather too fond of his choir boys – well, one choir boy, anyway.'

Gareth laughed. 'That's a bit of a cliché, isn't it? Not very imaginative of him.'

'No, I suppose not,' Ben replied, laughing in return. 'I'm not sure I will ever understand the Church of England. I don't have quite the cultural background for it.'

'I hope you're not coming to me for that,' Gareth said. 'For the record, I belong to the Church *in* Wales, which is *not* an established church. Quite a different kettle of fish.'

'I'll take your word for it, Gareth,' Ben said. 'What I wanted to ask you about was...'

But Gareth was holding up a hand, clearly telling him to stop.

'Just a minute, Ben. Just a minute. Don't say any more. This wouldn't by any chance be the St Ives case, would it?'

Ben was taken aback. 'Yes. But how do you know...?'

Gareth stared at him for some seconds before laughing again, this time more heartily. It took him a full half-minute and a relieving blow of his nose into a handkerchief before he could reply.

'Ben, I'm delighted that you have the case. But we can't talk about it, I'm afraid.'

'Why on earth not?' Ben asked, genuinely puzzled.

Gareth leaned forward across his desk.

'Because, my dear boy, I'm going to be prosecuting you.'

Ben sat back in his chair and took a series of deep breaths. For some seconds he was unable to speak. Gareth continued to chuckle.

'You're...? You are not serious.'

'I'm perfectly serious,' Gareth replied. 'I haven't got any papers yet, but Merlin told me about the case this morning. He has been trying to get me to do more prosecuting for some time. I prefer the other side, as you know, but Merlin thinks it will be useful for me when I apply for Silk in a year or two. He has a contact with the prosecuting solicitor for Huntingdonshire. If it works out well, they may start sending work to Chambers regularly. So not only can I not talk about the case with you, but I have to make sure I give you a bloody good hiding in court.'

'Sorry, Ben,' he added, as Ben walked slowly to the door. 'You'll have to find someone else to talk to about this one. Unless your chap wants to plead, of course.'

8

BEN RETURNED TO his room and opened the door slowly to see Harriet at her desk. She smiled brightly.

'You look as though you've seen a ghost!' she said. 'I take it your conference has finished?'

'Yes, all finished,' he replied, crossing the room to stand beside her desk. 'Actually, I have just been visited by the Spirit of Trials Yet to Come.'

She laughed. Harriet was almost as tall as Ben, with black hair and green eyes and was, as always, fastidiously dressed in a black suit and starched white shirt, her hair held up at the back by a small silver pin. She was some two years older than Ben, and her upbringing had been very different. Her father, Sir John Fisk, had worked in a number of countries as a senior diplomat. Neither of her parents wanted to be separated from her, and boarding schools had been ruled out, so Harriet had received a broad education from British schools abroad and from several local populations with widely different cultures. It was only when her father retired from the Diplomatic Service to become Master of a Cambridge college that her life became more settled and she made her way through University at Girton. But she came to the Bar with an exceptional knowledge and understanding of people and a rare self-confidence. She had a good legal mind, and had inherited her father's abilities as a diplomat. These qualities had played a large part in her becoming the first woman in Chambers, despite considerable initial resistance.

'I see,' she replied. 'And how am I to picture the Spirit of Trials Yet to Come? With a long black gown covering his entire body and long, thin fingers to point at you?'

'No. In fact, he has a perfectly normal suit and tie, quite normal fingers, and a Welsh accent,' Ben replied.

She laughed again. 'Ah, now I understand. What has Gareth done to earn the title?'

'He's prosecuting me in my child molestation case,' he replied. 'I can't believe it. I've just had a conference, I go to his room expecting the usual sage advice and he drops that bombshell.'

'Good experience for you,' she said. 'And a chance to show off everything you learned during pupillage.'

'Oh, yes? Just you wait till you have a case against Aubrey in the High Court.'

'He will be a sitting duck,' she smiled. 'I know all his tricks. He will be defenceless.'

He returned the smile.

'Somehow I can't quite picture Aubrey as a sitting duck,' he replied, 'any more than I can Gareth.'

'How does the case look?' she asked.

'Difficult, to say the least. I'm not sure he will be a very good witness, and his explanation for the lies of this young choir boy is not the most compelling.'

'Perhaps he's guilty?' she suggested. 'God forbid a client of Ben Schroeder should be guilty, but you never know.'

'No, you don't', he agreed. 'Well, there's nothing I can do about it. At least with Gareth I know I will have a fair prosecutor.'

'True.' She began to push her chair back from her desk. 'Do you still want a natter?'

Ben looked blank.

'Before your conference, you said there was something you wanted to talk to me about.'

He closed his eyes. 'Oh, yes. This business with Gareth distracted me. Yes, I would like a word, but it would be better somewhere other than Chambers, and I can see you are busy...'

He had been looking at the large stack of papers on Harriet's desk.

'Oh, this? No, that's a long-term project, an advice I must get around to one of these days. I just have an application in the West London County Court tomorrow morning and I got that under control in the library. So I am as free as a bird. Do you want to take me for a drink?'

'A very good idea,' Ben replied. 'Where shall we go?'

'Why don't you take me to the Club?' she suggested mischievously, rising to her feet.

'Ha-ha, very funny,' he replied. 'What about the Dev?'

'The Dev it is.'

It was after six. They walked unhurriedly down the stairs and into the chilly air of Middle Temple Lane. The Temple had fallen almost silent for the evening, and they made their way up the Lane, crossing diagonally in front of Middle Temple Hall, past the fountain, to the little gate which led out of the Temple and almost directly into the Devereux. The Devereux was a favourite resort of the Bar, mainly because of its convenient location, but it was also an old house, named after the turbulent Devereux family, and a convivial one. It was often very busy when the barristers were ready to abandon Chambers for the night, but on this evening it was quiet. They found a table in a corner to the right of the door, and Ben bought a pint of bitter for himself and a gin and tonic for Harriet. He allowed a couple of minutes to pass in silence and she did not try to rush him.

'I want to know why I was taken on in Chambers,' he said eventually.

She took a long sip of her gin and tonic.

'You mean, apart from the fact that you are a first-rate advocate who had a spectacular result in his first jury trial?' she replied.

'Yes, apart from that.'

'Ben…'

'Look, Harriet, you know that Chambers works on a blackball system. All it takes is one vote against you in the Chambers meeting. We both know that Anthony Norris opposed me because I'm Jewish. He didn't even try to hide it.'

'That was before you won a rape case at the Old Bailey for his favourite solicitor while he was away skiing in Switzerland,' she replied.

'Even so…'

'No, Ben. Look, I agree with you that it's tempting to blame all the ills of the world on Anthony Norris. I'm pretty sure he was against me at one stage, just because I'm a woman. But in all fairness, he did seem to change towards you after the Bailey case. I heard him singing your praises to Aubrey one day, telling him the story of how you stood up to Judge Weston when he wouldn't let you cross-examine, and how the jury took it upon themselves to stop the case at half time. If he wanted to blackball you, he could have done it, but it would have been difficult for anyone to oppose you after that. I thought I was the one who would be moving on.'

'But you're a great lawyer,' Ben replied, 'and…'

'And my father is the Master of the Cambridge college where Bernard Wesley and Aubrey both went, and because of his connections I have my own supply of work, and…'

'That's not what I meant,' Ben insisted. 'I'm sure you remember, there was a lot of talk about Chambers not expanding too quickly. Peter and Roger were just getting started, and they were not sure there was room for two.'

'That was always a silly excuse,' Harriet interrupted. 'With the explosion of legal aid cases, Chambers was too small to benefit from all the work that was becoming available. Even with the two of us, we still need to expand to take full advantage of it.'

'I know that's what Gareth thought,' Ben said. 'For a long time he was telling me that everyone would see sense and realise that they needed both of us.'

'And apparently, they did,' she pointed out. She laughed. 'Ben, we shared a room for a year as pupils, and I think I have come to know you pretty well. I know you worry a lot because you are not sure your background is right for the Bar, and I don't blame you at all. With people like Anthony Norris around, I couldn't blame you – or me, for that matter – for being paranoid. But it's not paranoia. It is real. There is prejudice against both of us at the Bar. We have to recognise that. But, Ben, the point is, it's up to us to break it down, to change it, and we have made a good start. And now, we have to keep going, not look back. You know, that's what Arthur Creighton would have said, and he would be proud of us.'

Ben sat back in his chair.

'God, I miss that man,' he said quietly.

'So do I,' she replied.

'Life dealt him so many blows, didn't it?' Ben continued. 'He lost several years of practice because of the War. He got wounded twice, which meant he was always in pain. His practice never picked up again. It must have been galling for him to watch Bernard climbing to dizzying heights while he was running around the county courts and the magistrates' courts, often doing stuff a pupil could have done; then his wife getting run over, getting killed. Then, finally, not being able to pay his clerk's fees and his Chambers rent. And even with all that, I never once heard him complain about how unfairly life had treated him.'

'Neither did I.'

'Not once. And since he wasn't busy, he chose to spend his time with the pupils. Giving us hours of his time, making himself available at all times of the day or night. And he was such a source of wisdom, you know. He had been around so long, he knew all the judges, and he could sum up a case perfectly in a minute. But he never boasted about it. He always made you feel that you would have come to exactly the same conclusion yourself if you had just had another minute or two to think about it. You could ask him anything without feeling stupid – which is not always the case with pupil-masters.'

'Very true,' she said. She finished her drink, and they both fell silent for some time.

'Same again?' he asked.

'Please.'

As he returned from the bar, she pulled herself up in her chair. They touched their glasses without speaking. She smiled.

'You earned your place, Ben. Why can't it be as simple as that? You proved your worth, and they recognised it, if only belatedly. Can't you accept that and move on?'

He was silent for some time.

'I hope I can,' he replied.

'It is also possible that the ghost of Arthur Creighton was looking down benevolently and putting in a good word for you,' she added, smiling. 'For us both.'

He returned the smile.

'If there are such things as ghosts, that's exactly what he was doing,' he said.

9

DETECTIVE SUPERINTENDENT STANLEY Arnold gingerly lowered his large frame into the hard wooden chair. It was not the most comfortable of circumstances. It wasn't like his home station at Cambridge, where he had room to move and people to help him. These country police stations were all the same, he reflected. Far too small, no real space to work, lucky if you had a phone and a serviceable typewriter most of the time. A decent cup of tea, if you were really lucky, and that was it. There were usually only one or two officers attached. Hopefully one would be a sergeant, or at least a constable with a good few years of experience – like Willis, a good copper if ever Arnold had seen one, a copper who kept his eyes open and knew how to look after a crime scene until help arrived. You couldn't always rely on local officers for that. Arnold had lost a good few cases over the years because of some inexperienced young officer trampling all over the evidence without even realising it. Why didn't Willis have his sergeant's stripes by now? He must remember to mention it to the Assistant Chief Constable. Still, what on earth did they find to keep themselves busy at St Ives? Look for stolen bicycles, arrest the odd shoplifter, deal with a few vagrants and drunks, get the ladder out and bring the odd cat down from a tree? The occasional serious burglary would offer some real excitement, but chances were they would call for help from Huntingdon or Cambridge even for that. And this case was going to be a headache – a big headache.

After so many years in the job, Arnold was no longer easily surprised, but he had been surprised by the violence of the assault on Frank Gilliam. It suggested an onset of blind rage, of an uncontrolled frenzy. The pathologist's report would take some time. Whatever the murder weapon was, it was large and heavy, and it had not been left at the scene. Probably metal, the pathologist said, but he would need to check the wounds before he could be sure. Gilliam had died during the early hours of Sunday morning, probably not long after midnight. A more accurate time would also be available in due course. Frank's parents said he was a popular boy who made friends easily; they could not even understand the idea that someone could hate him enough to do him such violence. But whether because of hate or some other cause, someone had.

Jennifer Doyce was unconscious and still in a critical condition at Addenbrookes Hospital in Cambridge. She had almost certainly had sexual intercourse. The bruising and lacerations around her vaginal area suggested a violent act of rape by the assailant, though it was not clear whether she had also had sex with Frank. Jennifer's mother said that there had been no boyfriend before Frank; there was no one who wished her harm, no one she knew of. But that was not all she said. Even in the midst of her overpowering grief and lack of comprehension, she wanted to know what had happened to Jennifer's gold cross and chain. It was valuable and it had belonged to Jennifer's grandmother. Arnold wanted to know, too. Willis did not remember seeing it on her when she was taken to hospital. At Arnold's request, he had searched the *Rosemary D* again, without result.

That was another headache. He had talked to the prosecuting solicitor. It was a fair inference that the assailant had taken it. If so, the killing of Frank Gilliam might have been in the course or furtherance of theft. That made his murder a capital crime. If Jennifer Doyce died, that would make two capital murders. When the killer was caught, he would hang. The Director of Public Prosecutions would be taking an interest in the case. That fact would not escape the attention of his Chief Constable, whose first instinct would be to call in Scotland Yard. Arnold would try to talk him out of it unless they ran into a serious forensic problem that could not be solved locally. Too many cooks often spoiled the broth, in his experience. The only real reason for the Chief Constable to call in the Yard was to cover his own back if something went wrong. Arnold had no intention of allowing that to happen. And, after all, he was a detective superintendent. Who would the Yard send to tell *him* what to do?

Promotion to detective superintendent had come as a surprise to Stanley Arnold. He had fully expected to retire as a detective inspector, the rank he had held until about three years earlier. Not bad, for an officer who had worked his way painstakingly up through the ranks. There had been none of this nonsense about graduate entrant schemes back then. In his day, you pounded the beat and learned your craft the hard way before they trusted you to put on a suit and tie and investigate serious crimes. Even then, promotion was usually slow. But in the early hours of a frigid December morning in 1960, Arnold had been called out to look into the death of a Cambridge undergraduate called William Bosworth, who had been thrown into the river Cam by a group of his fellow students who had got drunk at their annual rugby club dinner. Arnold had quickly arrested the young men concerned. It had not been difficult. Several had been arrested near the scene for being drunk and disorderly, which had led to the discovery of Bosworth's body. The rest, including the apparent ringleader, Clive Overton, had returned to college to sleep it off. Arnold remembered Clive Overton in particular. His father, Miles Overton QC, was a leading figure at the Bar. Arnold had been the victim of his powers of cross-examination earlier in his career. Arnold had these young men all ready to appear before the magistrates at 10 o'clock that same morning. As far as he was concerned, they were all bang to rights for manslaughter, if not murder.

But at that point, something very odd had happened. The Master of the college had appeared at court; Arnold had been instructed to limit the charge to assault, occasioning actual bodily harm; the accused had been granted bail; and within a day or two he had been told, politely but firmly, by someone very high up, that the matter would go no further. Not long after that, Arnold was promoted to the rank of detective superintendent, a rank for which there was no obvious vacancy at the time. His regular detective sergeant, Ted Phillips, who had been at his side on that fateful evening, was promoted to detective inspector. Since then, they had continued to work together, much as before. Arnold had heard that, after spending some time in America, Clive Overton was on his way to becoming a barrister. Perhaps he would cross-examine Arnold one day. All very strange, but there it was. Nothing to be done but to keep working the cases. And this one was going to take some work.

Arnold's reflections were interrupted by Phillips and Willis, who had just returned to the station together. Arnold looked up inquiringly.

'Nothing so far, sir,' Phillips said. 'Forensic are working on the boat. It's going to take them some time. We've got two frogmen in the water looking for a murder weapon, just in case the murderer chucked it overboard. It's not going to be easy to find, even assuming it's there. It might have drifted downstream a bit, and the water is very murky. We have some of our lads searching the immediate area around the boat. If that doesn't turn something up we may have to start working the whole fen. We will need some serious local help with that.'

'Anything on Jennifer Doyce?'

'No. She's still unconscious, and nobody's putting money on her waking up again.'

'You haven't seen Hawthorne, have you, sir?' Willis asked.

'No.'

Willis shook his head. 'That's young coppers for you these days. Never here when you need them.'

Arnold smiled.

'I've been thinking about where we go from here' he said. 'I want leaflets asking for information distributed in every town and village within a radius of 20 miles. The local stations can help us with that while we continue inquiries here'.

'You want to limit it to 20 miles? You reckon he's definitely local, do you, sir?' Phillips asked. He sounded surprised.

Arnold's mind took him back to the *Rosemary D*. The extraordinary frenzied level of violence, the horrific injuries, the quantity of blood at the scene, the sheer brutality of it all. This had been about the boat and about those who visited her. He nodded.

'I'm certain of it.' He turned to Willis. 'We need to speak to as many of the young couples who were using the boat as possible. Do you have any information at all about them?'

'No names. We know it's been going on for a while. We've been up there and banged on the door once or twice, to discourage it. But we don't have the manpower to do more than that. Besides, trespass is a civil matter, sir, as you know. We wouldn't go in unless we had information that an offence was being committed, and even then I would have to get a warrant. I could make a few inquiries, put the word around.' He paused. 'Of course, sir, they may be a bit nervous about coming forward... in the circumstances, you understand.'

'Put the word out that no one is going to get into trouble, and that any statements given can be kept private,' Arnold suggested. 'All we are interested in is the information. I want to know whether they may have noticed anything suspicious – anyone lurking on or around the tow path while they were walking to or from the boat – even if it didn't seem significant at the time. Any description might help.'

'Right you are, sir,' Willis replied.

'We can't rule out the possibility that the assailant used the boat himself,' Phillips pointed out. 'He might have got to know about the boat through going there. Perhaps that's what gave him the idea.'

Arnold stood and walked over to the window slowly, hands on hips.

'Possibly,' he replied. 'But my money is on someone who wanted to be part of the *Rosemary D* scene and was feeling left out, rather than someone who was a regular visitor.'

'Someone who wanted to join in the fun and was watching, biding his time?' Willis suggested.

'Exactly. Besides, we have to start somewhere. We don't want to frighten them off. We need any help they can give us. Obviously, if one of them gives you any reason to suspect him, see if you can find out more. Ask about his movements on Saturday. See if he will give you his fingerprints, so that we can eliminate him. See how he reacts to that.'

'Leave it to me, sir,' Willis said. 'They're all local lads. I know how to approach them. I'm likely to know most of them, anyway. But if something doesn't feel right I'll pick up on it and let you know.'

'I don't doubt it for a moment,' Arnold replied. 'I also want a list of everyone within the same 20-mile radius who's been convicted of a sexual offence during the past ten years.'

'Some of them will still be inside,' Phillips said. 'The perfect alibi.'

'The more serious offenders, yes' Arnold agreed. 'But I'm not thinking about them. Something happened here to make our man react to this couple with massive violence. There was probably a sexual motive, but these offences resulted mainly from extreme rage.

Remember: our theory is that he wanted to be part of the *Rosemary D* scene, but couldn't for some reason. He may be inadequate – unsure of his ability to perform sexually. He may never have gone as far as rape before. He may not have a record at all. But if he does, what kind of offences would this man have committed?'

There was a silence for some time.

'I see what you're saying,' Willis replied eventually. 'Something like indecent assault – nothing too serious, groping, feeling a girl up, that kind of thing; or even indecent exposure.'

'Soliciting prostitution,' Phillips added.

'Yes,' Arnold replied. 'And check anything to do with pornography – books, magazines, films, whatever.'

'I'll need some more help,' Willis said.

'I'll put the call out,' Arnold said. 'I'm not sure how many more men we can divert from Cambridge. But we've got Huntingdon – after all, it's on their patch. And the Chief Constable can put the word out to other forces that we need help with this one. That's what chief constables are for. It will give him something to do, make him feel useful.'

'Speaking of making yourself useful,' Willis said, in the direction of the door, 'where do you think you've been? You were supposed to be back long before this. I have a couple of inquiries for you to make.'

The uniformed figure of PC Hawthorne had appeared in the doorway. Far from appearing uncomfortable at being derelict in his duty, he seemed rather pleased with himself.

'Sorry. I was interviewing a witness,' he replied proudly.

'Oh, yes?' Willis replied. 'And where would you have run into a witness, Hawthorne?'

'At Mr Brown's corner shop. It's on Priory Road,' Hawthorne replied. 'He sells cigarettes and newspapers and...'

'Yes, Hawthorne, I know. I've known Joey Brown since before you were born. What does he know about this?'

'He doesn't,' Hawthorne replied defiantly, taking his notebook from the top left pocket of his uniform jacket. 'But his daughter Mavis does.'

He opened the notebook at the page he wanted, but seemed unsure of whether to continue.

'Go on, officer,' Arnold said encouragingly.

'Mavis was in the shop on Saturday night,' Hawthorne began, studying the notebook intently. 'It was just before 11 o'clock. She had been doing some stock-taking and she was about to lock up for the night and go upstairs. They live above the shop, you see...'

'Go on,' Arnold said again.

'Yes, sir. Just as she was about to turn the lights out she saw a young couple at the shop window. They wanted to buy some cigarettes. She opened up for them and sold them two packets of Woodbines. When they left, they were walking towards the meadow. She didn't see them again. But she did give me a description.'

'Jennifer and Frank both had Woodbines with them,' Phillips said.

'Well, I'm damned,' Arnold breathed. 'Well done, lad. You've probably found the last person to see them before it happened. I want you to bring her in tomorrow morning. I would like to test her memory a bit more.'

Hawthorne positively beamed. 'Yes, sir.' He paused. 'Actually, there is more...'

Arnold nodded encouragingly.

'Well, sir, Mavis also saw a man pass the shop just a minute or two after the couple. She had put the lights out by then, and she could see him clearly under a street light. He was walking in the same direction as the couple, towards the meadow. She also gave me a description of this man. He was about the same height as her dad...'

'Five seven, five eight,' Willis interjected.

'He was wearing a raincoat, open, a dark jacket and a red and white checked shirt. He had a dark woollen hat on, so she couldn't see his hair or eyes. He had heavy brown shoes. She noticed that the shoes looked dirty.'

Hawthorne turned over to the next page of his notebook.

'And he was whistling a tune.'

'Oh, yes?' Arnold asked.

'Yes, sir,' Hawthorne replied. 'She recognised it from a programme on the radio, and she whistled it for her dad when she got upstairs, and asked him what it was. It was the *Lincolnshire Poacher*.'

Willis had been leaning on the table in front of the desk at which Arnold was sitting. But now he suddenly pushed himself up, quickly, firmly, holding up one arm as if to request silence, and walked over to the window. For some time he stared outside. Eventually, he turned back to Hawthorne.

'Is she sure about that, Hawthorne?' he asked. 'Is she quite sure about that?'

Hawthorne nodded. 'Positive,' he replied.

'Bloody hell,' Willis said.

10

PC WILLIS TURNED the black Humber Hawk police car off the tow path and drove slowly across the muddy ground to park in front of the lock keeper's house, at right angles to the house, just to the left of the front door. He switched off the engine and turned towards Detective Superintendent Arnold, who occupied the front passenger seat.

'This is the house, sir' he said. 'If he's not here, he will be down at the lock, I daresay. We can walk down to the lock in a minute or two if we need to.' He glanced at his watch. 'It's almost lunch time. He will probably be making his way back to the house about now.'

They climbed out of the car and surveyed the house. DI Phillips, getting out of the back of the car, joined them.

'He wouldn't spend all day at the lock then, in case there are boats wanting to use it?' he asked.

Willis shook his head. 'There's not the volume of traffic for that. He will have his regulars, and he will know roughly what time to expect them. A lot of the traffic depends on the tides, anyway, and he knows all about the tides. But if anyone else comes unannounced, a leisure boat, say, on no particular schedule, they just have to ring the bell and wait for him. They have no choice, really. He would get there quickly enough unless he's upstream, doing maintenance.'

'Let's see if there's anyone at home,' Arnold said. He approached the front door and knocked loudly three times. There was no response. Arnold knocked again. This time, he shouted out. 'It's the police. Is there anyone home?'

Again, there was no response from the door. But a small, thin woman made her way cautiously around the side of the house from the rear. She wore a clean blue dress with a design of white leaves, and flat blue shoes. Over the dress she wore a white apron, tied at the back; and over the apron, hanging down between her small breasts, she wore a striking gold cross on a chain. She paused at the corner of the house, as if uncertain whether to approach any further.

'Can I help you?' she asked timidly.

Willis, the only one in uniform, walked over to her quietly. He had noticed her hesitancy, and had no wish to alarm her.

'I'm PC Willis, from St Ives, Miss Cottage,' he said. 'It's Eve, isn't it?'

She nodded silently.

'These gentlemen with me are plain clothes officers from Cambridge, Detective Superintendent Arnold and Detective Inspector Phillips. We would like a word with your brother, Billy. Is he at home?'

She shook her head, again silently.

'Are you expecting him back? Do you know where we might find him?'

She seemed lost in thought for some seconds.

'He's at the lock,' she replied. 'There was a long unpowered barge due in, mid-morning. He has to open the lock and walk the horse. They take some time to deal with, those long ones. Then he was due home for lunch. But those unpowered barges are often late. It can be the weather, the currents, you know, or some problem with the horse. You never know. He's probably been held up. Would you like to come in and wait?'

'Thank you,' Willis replied.

She left her refuge by the wall and led the way slowly to the front door, which was unlocked. She pushed it open and walked into the living room. The officers followed. She stood still in front of the battered oak sideboard on the far side of the room, arms folded, looking down at the floor.

'Would you like some tea?' she asked, mechanically, without looking up.

'No, thank you, Miss Cottage. Don't let us stop you if you have things to do. We will be perfectly all right here until Billy gets back.' Willis replied.

He turned towards Arnold and Phillips, who were looking

around the room. It was cluttered and untidy. A bottle of Dewars, half empty, stood on a small table at the side of the armchair, next to a single dirty glass. On the dining table were two white candles in cheap wooden candlesticks, the candles burned most of the way down, and around the bases of the candlesticks, pools of solid candle wax, attached like rough white limpets to the yellowing lace table cloth. Looking at Arnold, Willis diverted his gaze to the gold cross and back again, no more than a second or two. An almost imperceptible nod from Arnold told him he had not missed it.

Eve raised her head slightly and smiled nervously. 'I'm sorry the house is such a mess,' she said quietly. 'I've been into town, shopping, this morning. I haven't had time to clear up.'

'Not to worry, Miss Cottage,' Arnold said. 'You weren't expecting us.'

Her head sank back down. 'No,' she replied.

Arnold took two steps towards her, as if to get a better look.

'I hope you don't think I'm staring,' he said. 'That's a beautiful cross and chain you have. It reminds me of one I've seen before, in a photograph. Have you had it long? Family heirloom, perhaps?'

She unfolded her arms to take the cross in her left hand. She looked at it intently before looking back up at Arnold and smiling, less nervously now.

'Billy gave it to me,' she said proudly. 'He takes good care of me, he is very nice to me.'

'I'm sure he is,' Arnold replied. 'When did he give it to you? For Christmas, your birthday?'

'No. My birthday is not until May. He gives me things all the time. He gave me this on Tuesday.'

'What, this Tuesday, just gone?'

'Yes.'

Phillips had also approached.

'I bet that cost a few bob,' he said, introducing a hint of jealousy into his tone. 'I wish I could afford something like that for my wife. On my salary I'd have to save up for it for years.'

She laughed out loud at their ignorance.

'He didn't *buy* it,' she explained. 'He *found* it. He finds all kinds of things when he's working, doesn't he?'

'Oh, does he?' Phillips asked. 'That must come in handy. Where does he find things, what kinds of places?'

'Everywhere,' she said. 'At the lock after a boat has passed through; on the banks of the river after they've had a picnic; in town; on the banks of the river, mostly. Billy says people leave all kinds of things there. He says you'd be amazed how careless people can be.' Her head sank again. 'I suppose I should have taken it to the police station really, shouldn't I? But... am I in trouble?' Her voice was quiet again now, sad.

Arnold smiled. 'Not from us,' he said. 'And I'm sure Constable Willis understands.'

'No need to worry about it,' Willis agreed soothingly.

'But, Eve,' Arnold said, 'I think I may know who lost this cross and chain. As I say, I'm sure I've seen a photograph of it. It's quite valuable, and it's of sentimental value to the owner – it belonged to her grandmother. I'm going to have to take it to see if it's the one she lost. If not, I'll bring it back, I promise.'

For some moments, Eve clutched the cross desperately, looking stricken. But then, with a look of resignation, she lifted the chain up over her head and held it out in front of her, offering it to him, giving it one last squeeze. Arnold took it gently from her, wrapping it in a clean white handkerchief.

'Did she lose it on the bank of the river?' she asked.

'Yes,' Arnold replied. 'Well, close to the river.'

'She must be very sad. I hope she will be happy to get it back.'

'I'm sure she will,' Arnold said.

The front door opened behind him. A male voice, calling out loudly.

'Eve, I'm back. Where's my lunch?'

Arnold turned towards the door.

'You will be having lunch with us today, Billy,' he said.

Billy Cottage stared blankly at the intruders in his house. Eve tried to make herself as small as possible in front of the sideboard.

'Who are these people?' he demanded of her. 'If they need the lock they can ring the bell and wait, can't they? They are not supposed to come to the house.'

'I'm sorry, Billy,' she said. 'I...'

'You shouldn't have let them in.'

'I'm sorry.'

Then Billy saw PC Willis in his uniform and froze.

Phillips took one arm. Willis approached and took the other.

'Billy Cottage,' Phillips said. 'I am arresting you on suspicion of…'

He looked at Arnold.

'Larceny by finding,' Arnold said. 'For now.'

'…on suspicion of larceny by finding. Do you wish to say anything? You are not obliged to say anything unless you wish to do so, but what you say may be put in writing and given in evidence.'

'I don't know what you are talking about,' Billy replied.

Phillips jotted his response in his notebook.

* * *

Billy sat between Arnold and Phillips in the back of the Hawk as Willis drove them back to St Ives police station. Billy made no further statement, but the officers distinctly heard him singing to himself, softly, under his breath.

When I was bound apprentice in famous Lincolnshire,
Full well I served my master for nigh on seven years,
Till I took up to poaching as you shall quickly hear,
Oh, 'tis my delight on a shiny night in the season of the year.

Success to every gentleman that lives in Lincolnshire,
Success to every poacher that wants to sell a hare,
Bad luck to every gamekeeper that will not sell his deer,
Oh, 'tis my delight on a shiny night in the season of the year.

11

ST IVES POLICE station had only one room that could be used for interviews, and it was far too small for the purpose. As he lowered himself carefully on to the hard wooden chair, square and solid, with its straight back and hard padded seat, and placed his file of papers on the small wooden table that separated him from Billy Cottage, Detective Superintendent Arnold reflected that this was hardly surprising. They probably didn't have too many long interviews to conduct in St Ives during a normal year. But this was not turning out to be a normal year at St Ives police station. Instead of its normal complement of two or three officers, the place was swarming with uniformed officers from Huntingdon and Cambridge. They went out periodically to comb the river bank by the *Rosemary D*, and to make inquiries in town, then returned to hand in their reports to PS Livermore. The sergeant had been recalled urgently from leave, and was none too pleased about it. But he was now working with DI Phillips to coordinate and analyse the information obtained. Mercifully, Arnold's chief constable had so far kept Scotland Yard at bay, but Arnold had to phone in reports on a regular basis to allay the concerns that went up to a very high level in any case such as this. The hours of work put in by so many officers were beginning to pay off. Arnold now had some solid information, and the time had come to ask Billy Cottage some questions.

'As you already know, Mr Cottage, I am Detective Superintendent Arnold, from Cambridgeshire Police. We are working with Huntingdonshire Police on this case. My colleague here, Detective Inspector Phillips, will be making notes of this interview. First, I must remind you of the caution you were given earlier. You are not obliged to say anything unless you wish to do so, but what you say may be put in writing and given in evidence. But whether or not you wish to speak to me, I will now put certain questions to you. First, can you confirm that you are William Cottage, and that you live at the lock keeper's house at Fenstanton, near St Ives?'

'Yes.'

'Mr Cottage... It's Billy, isn't it? Do you mind if I call you Billy? It will make it easier, won't it?'

'If you like.'

'Good. So, Billy, you are the lock keeper at Fenstanton, are you?'

'That's right.'

'And you live at the lock keeper's house with your sister. Her name is Eve, is that right?'

'Yes.'

'Just the two of you?'

'My parents are both dead.'

'Your date of birth is 10th October 1935, which makes you, what? Twenty-eight. Is that right?'

'Yes.'

Arnold leaned back, reached down into his briefcase, which he had placed on the floor beside his chair, and took out the gold chain and cross, reluctantly yielded to him earlier by the sister of the man he now had to question.

'All right. Now, Billy, I wish to ask you some questions about this gold cross and chain. I got it from Eve when DI Phillips and I were at your house today with PC Willis. Eve told me that you had given it to her on Tuesday. Is that correct?'

'I found it.'

Arnold nodded encouragingly.

'That's what Eve told us.'

'I thought it would look nice on Eve. It's pretty.'

'It *is* pretty,' Arnold agreed. 'Where did you find it, Billy?'

Billy frowned, as if concentrating hard on the question.

'Where did I find it?'

'Yes. Where?'

Billy gave an apparently careless shrug.

'Down by the lock, I expect. That's where I generally find things.'

Arnold held the cross a little closer to him.

'Let's see if we can do a little better. I would expect you to remember exactly where you found this. It was just a few days ago, and I daresay it's not every day you come across something as pretty as this, is it? Try a bit harder, Billy. Where did you find it?'

Billy looked at the cross, then suddenly away across the room.

'It was at the lock,' he replied. 'On the bank, just up from the lock gate.'

'How did you notice it? It was just lying there, was it?'

'I expect so. I remember seeing something shiny...' Billy's concentration seemed to desert him for a moment.

Oh, 'tis my delight on a shiny night...

'Go on, Billy,' Arnold was saying. 'You saw something shiny. Then what?'

Billy seemed to come back.

'I saw it shining in the grass and I picked it up. That was it. I took it home and asked Eve if she liked it. She said she did, so I gave it to her.'

'So, it was definitely down by the lock, which means you found it on this side of the river?'

'Yes.'

Arnold nodded. He paused for some time to allow Phillips to catch up with his notes.

'Did you think of handing it in at the police station at all? I mean, it says it's 22 carat gold. It's really heavy, isn't it? Didn't you think it might be valuable?'

A shrug again.

'I didn't really think about it.'

Arnold waited, silent.

'Look, I find stuff by the river all the time. If I took everything I find to the police station, I wouldn't have any time left to work the lock, would I?'

Billy smiled, as if he had scored a point. Arnold returned the smile.

'Of course, you couldn't hand everything in, Billy. We all understand that.' He held the cross up to the light. 'Still, even leaving aside the value, whoever it belonged to would be upset to lose something like this, wouldn't she? Did you think about that at all?'

'Not really.'

Arnold pulled the cross and chain towards him and it disappeared into his briefcase as quickly as it had appeared. He rummaged among the papers he had placed on the table until he found a photograph. He pushed it across the table to Billy.

'All right. Well. Let me ask you about something else. Do you recognise the boat in this photograph?'

Billy snorted contemptuously.

'She's moored up by Holywell Fen, she is,' he said authoritatively. 'But she wouldn't be, not if I had my way.'

'Oh?' Arnold asked. 'And why would that be?'

With another snort, Billy pulled the photograph towards him and looked at it closely.

'She's a hazard,' he replied. 'Look at her. She's a big craft to be moored there. She never runs any lights. You can't see her in the dark, or in the fog. Someone is going to ram her one of these days, you mark my words. She should be removed. I've told the River Board, but they never listen to me. Might as well be talking to myself.'

'Do you know her name?' Arnold asked.

Billy nodded.

'*Rosemary D*', he replied. 'That's what they call her. Bloody nuisance, that's what I call her.'

'Have you ever been on board?'

Billy's focus seemed to slip again.

Success to every gentleman that lives in Lincolnshire...

'Why would I want to board her?'

Arnold spread his arms out wide.

'Oh, I don't know. Perhaps to check on her lights, or to see if you could find out who owns her, who you could approach about moving her?'

'No. Never.'

Success to every poacher that wants to sell a hare...

'Well, there we are, then,' Arnold said. He paused again, waiting for Phillips to signal that he was ready. 'You see, Billy, the reason I ask is this. We have reason to believe that the lady who owns the cross and chain I showed you lost it on Saturday night while she was on board the *Rosemary D*. So I'm wondering, if she lost it on the *Rosemary D*, what was it doing on the opposite bank, down by your lock on Tuesday? Can you help me about that at all?'

Bad luck to every gamekeeper that will not sell his deer...

'I don't know, do I? Perhaps she made a mistake. Perhaps she lost it later, down by the lock.'

Arnold produced another photograph from the stack of papers.

'Well, the problem with that, Billy, is that she wasn't in any condition to move from the *Rosemary D* down to the lock. This is what she looked like on Monday morning.'

Arnold pushed the photograph towards Billy, who pushed it back violently, barely glancing at it.

'I don't want to look at that.'

'I can't say I blame you. It's not very nice, is it, Billy?'

'Take it away.'

'All right. I'm just trying to show you how important it is that you tell me where you found the cross and chain you gave to Eve.'

'I already told you.'

'But you haven't told me the truth, have you, Billy?'

'Yes, I have.'

'If necessary,' Arnold said, 'I can show you on the photo the mark that was made on her neck when the thief took the chain off her. Would you like to see it again?'

Billy turned almost all the way around in his chair.

'No. Take it away.'

Oh, 'tis my delight on a shiny night in the season of the year.

Silence. Then suddenly, unprompted...

'All right, I found it near that craft, the *Rosemary D.*'

Phillips looked up sharply. A raised finger asked for time. Arnold waited.

'Well, that wasn't too difficult, was it? Why didn't you say so before?'

The focus seemed to return.

'It wasn't nothing to do with that,' Billy protested.

'To do with what?'

'That – in that photograph.'

'I don't remember suggesting it was,' Arnold said. 'So, where exactly did you find it?'

'It was like I said,' Billy replied defiantly. 'It was on the bank, in the grass. I saw it shining. I picked it up and went home.'

'Not on Tuesday, you didn't,' Arnold said. 'Since Monday, the whole area has been cordoned off. It's a crime scene – police officers swarming all over it.'

'I never said it was Tuesday.'

Arnold looked at Phillips, who nodded.

'You did, actually, Billy,' he said.

'Well, that was wrong, then.'

'Well, when was it, then?'

Oh, 'tis my delight…

There was a knock on the door. Without waiting for a response, PC Willis opened the door and stepped smartly into the room. Arnold was momentarily vexed, but he knew that an officer as experienced as Willis would not interrupt a detective superintendent in the middle of an interview in a murder case without good reason. Besides, there was no harm in giving Billy Cottage a few minutes in which to reflect on his position.

'Sorry to disturb you, sir, but there's something come up that Sergeant Livermore and I thought you should know about without delay. Would it be possible to take a short break?'

'Certainly, Constable,' Arnold replied. 'I'm sure DI Phillips wouldn't mind a bit of a rest. While we're at it, why don't we all have a nice cup of tea? Sit tight, Billy, we will bring you some tea and then we will continue.'

'Can I use the toilet?'

'Of course you can. PC Willis will take you in a couple of minutes. Just sit tight for a short while.'

Phillips stood gratefully, massaging his right hand vigorously. Arnold closed the door of the interview room and the three officers stood in a huddle just outside the door. Sergeant Livermore joined them.

'Good news, sir,' he announced. 'Jennifer Doyce has just woken up in Addenbrooke's, and she is able to talk.'

Arnold's jaw dropped.

'You're joking. When they took her in, they didn't give her a snowball's chance in hell. What happened?'

'The doctors are just as surprised as you are, sir. They can't really explain it. Under any normal circumstances, her injuries should have been fatal, or at the very least she should have irreversible brain damage. But somehow, she's survived. Mind you, she's not out of the woods yet – not by a long way. She's still listed as critical. She's got a fractured skull, a couple of broken ribs, and she suffered some injuries around the genital area. There may be internal injuries. But she has regained consciousness, and her vision and hearing are fine. She's talked to the nurses a bit. They are keeping her sedated and on a morphine drip for the foreseeable future. There's no way to tell yet how much she remembers, but apparently she did ask something about Frank, and they don't want to upset her. No promises, but they might let you talk to her for no more than five minutes tomorrow if her condition doesn't worsen. It will be some time before we know whether she can make a full statement. Her mother is with her, and I've asked her just to make a note of anything Jennifer says, not to ask any questions, just to make a note.'

'Well, I'm damned,' Arnold said. He stood, lost in thought, for some time, hands on hips. 'All right, let's detain Sonny Jim overnight. I want to have a word with Jennifer before we resume the interview, if they will let us. We will drive back to Cambridge later this afternoon, so that we can be there at whatever time the hospital will let us in.'

He turned to face Phillips, who was still rubbing his writing hand, though now more gently.

'Good news, sir,' Phillips said, smiling.

'Yes. Makes a nice change, doesn't it?' Arnold replied. 'Let's hope her luck holds – and ours.'

12

JESS FARRAR STEPPED down from the train on to the platform and pulled her overcoat tightly around her body to fend off the chilly wind sweeping through the station. Underneath her coat, her suit and blouse felt rumpled and uncomfortable. The journey had taken more than three hours in an uncomfortable seat; the train's relentless heating had been oppressive rather than comforting; and the sandwich and coffee she had bought in the dining car had been stale and tasteless. She took a deep breath. Perhaps Bettys Tea Rooms would offer something more appetising. Looking around her, Jess found an exit sign and made her way up the stairs and along the bridge that led to the station's main entrance hall. Once outside, she paused briefly, recalling the street plan of York city centre she had memorised earlier. She left the shelter of the station awning, turned left on to Station Road and, with her head down against the wind, made her way as quickly as she could along Museum Street into town. Once over the river, she turned right on Lendal Street, passed the lodgings used by the High Court judges at assize time, and from there left into St Helen's Square, where Bettys occupied a corner of its own.

Jess was not sure that Joan Heppenstall would turn up. She had made the arrangement to meet by phone, after two days of delicate negotiation. At first, she could not get past Joan's father, who advised Jess in no uncertain terms that his daughter was too upset to talk to her and, in any case, did not see why she should; she had been insulted and humiliated enough and wanted nothing more to do with her former fiancé. But Jess had persisted, and eventually he put Joan on the line to speak for herself. Even then, it had been an uphill task. It had taken two further calls to persuade her that Ignatius

Little was in a serious situation, and that she ought at least to give him the benefit of some doubt in the matter. Finally, Jess made it clear that Joan had no obligation to give evidence on his behalf; she just wanted to get some background information that might assist in preparing his defence. After much cajoling, Joan had agreed to meet for afternoon tea at Bettys. Jess would not have been surprised if she had changed her mind but, to her relief, Joan was already in the tea room when she arrived. The waitress escorted her through the elegant room to the far corner table at which Joan was seated. They shook hands formally.

'Did you have any trouble finding your way?'

Joan was very nervous, Jess saw at once. Tearful, too. There was a small embroidered white handkerchief on the table, which looked damp and creased.

'No, not at all. It is quite an easy walk from the station – if you don't get blown away. Is it always this windy in York?'

'The wind can be quite strong at this time of year.'

A silence. Joan felt the need to fill the vacuum.

'Is this your first visit to York, Miss Farrar? I'm sure you told me, but I can't remember. I'm sorry.'

Jess smiled.

'It's Jess, please, and there is no reason why you should remember. Yes, it is my first visit. It's obviously a beautiful city. I thought I might take a walk around when we've finished, before I go back to the station. I read a little about it in a guide book on the journey. I know there are all sorts of interesting things to see.'

Joan nodded.

'Most people make straight for the Minster, of course. It's just a couple of minutes' walk along Stonegate.' She waved a hand vaguely towards the wall to her left. 'But the whole city is beautiful, so many lovely buildings. The Railway Museum is well known, too, of course – if you like that kind of thing.'

A waitress wearing a pristine white apron over a black dress, and a delicate white cap balanced on the front of her head, approached with menus.

'What do you recommend, Joan?' Jess asked. 'Is it all right if I call you Joan?'

Joan nodded.

'They do very good sandwiches and scones, and different kinds of cake. They will bring the cakes around on a trolley so that you can choose.'

Trying to put the railway sandwich out of her mind, Jess closed her menu.

'I'm going to have a ham sandwich and some tea,' she said decisively. 'And I will think about the cake later.'

She raised her eyebrows in the direction of the waitress, who was hovering expectantly nearby, and placed her order. The waitress turned to Joan.

'I'll just have tea, thank you,' she said.

The waitress retreated.

'My mother makes tea for me every day at five,' Joan said, 'and she's very proud of her fruit cake. If I spoil my appetite too much I won't hear the last of it for the rest of the day.'

Jess laughed.

'Ah, so you have a mother like that too, do you? I know exactly what you mean. My mother's speciality is Victoria sponge cake.'

Another silence, but more comfortable this time. Joan was warming to her a little, but she was not yet ready to have the conversation Jess needed to have with her.

'So, you work in London?' Joan asked. 'Is that where you're from?'

'No, I'm a Sussex girl,' Jess replied. 'My family lives near Hastings. But I've always spent a lot of time in London. My father is a stockbroker; he works in the City. So I'm quite used to London, but I don't think of myself as a Londoner. Perhaps I will after I've lived in town longer.'

'I don't know any women who are in the law. Isn't it a bit unusual?'

'Yes, I suppose it is, a bit' Jess agreed. 'But not as much as it used to be. Things are changing. It's much more open than it used to be.'

'Did you study law then? Did you go to university?'

The waitress arrived with their tea and Jess's sandwiches. She artfully contrived to arrange tea pot, hot water jug, milk jug, sugar bowl, sandwiches and plates on the small table with barely a fraction of an inch separating them, but without the table seeming cluttered.

Jess took responsibility for pouring the tea.

'I did go to university, at Bristol,' she said. 'But I studied history, not law. After I came down I had no idea what I wanted to do. For some reason, the idea of the law came into my head. I'm not quite sure why. It may have been through reading about some sensational trial in the papers, or seeing a film. Anyway, my uncle is a solicitor and, to cut a long story short, I made his life a misery until he agreed to ask a few people he knew whether they were interested in taking on a female historian. Barratt Davis is an old friend of my uncle's and he offered me a job. I've only been with him for a month or two. In fact, to be honest, this is my first solo assignment.'

Joan looked at her thoughtfully.

'It makes sense that they would send a woman,' she said. 'Actually, I'm quite relieved that they did.'

Jess nodded.

'Tell me a bit about your family.'

Joan poured more tea as Jess started on her sandwich.

'My father is a canon at the Minster,' she said. 'Before that he was a priest at different churches in and around York, so the church has always been part of my life. My mother was a teacher, but she hasn't worked for a number of years. I have a younger sister, Ellen, who is, well, she can't walk very well. One of her legs doesn't work properly. She was born that way. The doctors don't seem to understand why. She's had several operations, but nothing seems to make it right, so my mother has to take care of her. I help out, of course, whenever I'm at home, but it's still quite a strain for her.'

'Yes, I'm sure,' Jess said. 'Tell me, how did you meet Ignatius?'

Joan drained her tea cup and poured more tea for them both before replying.

'It was through the church, of course. Story of my life. He came up to York for a meeting of ordinands while he was in training at Ridley Hall. My father had them all over to the house one evening for sherry and cakes – very Church of England. I talked to Ignatius…'

Jess suddenly giggled.

'I'm sorry,' she said. 'I'm sorry. I don't mean to be rude. But do you really call him Ignatius? It's a bit of a mouthful, isn't it? You must have a…'

To Jess's relief, Joan giggled in return.

'I call him Iggy,' she said.

'Iggy?'

'Yes, but only when he's not around. He's a bit sensitive. He really is an Ignatius by temperament.'

'Well, I prefer Iggy,' Jess replied.

'So do I. Well, I talked to Iggy over sherry, but I also talked to all the other ordinands and, I have to say, he didn't make any particular impression on me. But he phoned a day or two later, completely out of the blue, and asked whether he could see me again if he came up to York. I didn't really know what to say. I asked my father about him, but of course, as Iggy was an ordinand, he thought it was a great idea. He would love to see me married to a minister. So I said I would see him if he came to York, which he did. Then I went down to Cambridge to see him there, and that became the pattern, Iggy would come up here, then I would go down there, until he was ordained. It was then that he asked me to marry him. I'd finished my teacher training by then and I was able to get a job at the school at St Ives. So it all worked out well.'

She paused and picked up the handkerchief.

'Or so I thought.'

The tears came again. She picked up the handkerchief and dried her eyes. Jess finished her sandwich, giving her companion time to compose herself. At length, Joan replaced the handkerchief in her handbag.

'Look, I know it's not really walking weather,' she said abruptly. 'But would you mind if we walked around for a while and got some fresh air? Do you need to be inside to make notes?'

'No, that's fine,' Jess replied. 'I managed to keep my feet on my way from the station, so I am sure I can do it again. Show me the Minster – from the outside, anyway.'

They paid the bill and walked slowly along Stonegate in the face of wind and light drizzle until the majestic outline of York Minster came into view and, as they got closer, grew ever more imposing until it seemed almost to engulf them. They entered the grounds surrounding the ancient cathedral and stood together under the walls, shielded for the moment from the wind.

'I know what you want to ask me, Jess,' Joan said.

Jess nodded.

'I have no reason to believe that Iggy has any... any interest in boys. Of course, I haven't really seen him with boys, except at church when I'm there as well; so I don't really know.'

Jess touched her hand briefly.

'Joan, I know how difficult this must be for you. I don't want to cause you any more pain than you've suffered already. But I know you understand how serious this is, what it means to Iggy, not just in terms of his future in the ministry, but possibly going to prison and then having to live with a criminal record. So his solicitors and his barrister need to know what they are dealing with. Has he... has he ever said anything, anything at all to make you suspicious?'

Joan turned her head away slightly.

'No, he's never *said* anything.'

Jess nodded. 'All right.' She watched Joan carefully. She knew there was more to come, and it was costing her a lot to say it.

'But...'

She touched Joan's hand again.

'It's all right.'

Joan turned her head fully away for some moments, before turning back to look Jess full in the face.

'I can't believe that I'm here, talking about things like this with a complete stranger. But... I don't think he is very interested in me. Sexually, I mean.'

'You were engaged to be married,' Jess pointed out. 'Are you saying...?'

Joan folded her arms tightly around her. Suddenly, her resistance melted away.

'I was assuming that things would be different once we were married,' she said. 'I'm sure that was very naive of me. But you must understand, in my family there was never any discussion about sex. It's not the kind of thing you talk about in a church family.'

Jess smiled.

'It's not the kind of thing you talk about in most families,' she said. 'It was the same with my parents.'

'I got the usual platitudes about marriage and how wonderful it all is,' Joan said, 'but not much information about what to actually expect. But I can't blame my parents. I'm an adult. All the signs were there, and I didn't pay attention.'

'What signs?' Jess asked quietly.

Joan took a deep breath.

'Obviously, in our situation, there was no question of sex before marriage. Not the done thing, of course. But we had time alone together and I thought: he must have desires and... well, I didn't see any harm in relieving the pressure occasionally, so to speak. I'm not totally ignorant about the mechanics of sex, you know. I'd been out with another boy a few times. So I... I tried rubbing his... his... you know, his penis; through his trousers at first. He seemed to like it. I mean, he would kiss me and swear his undying love and so on, and he would give my breasts a squeeze. But that was it. He never became really hard at all. The only time he seemed excited was once when I actually unbuttoned his flies and took it out. I think that gave him a thrill, because he did get hard that time, and after I had played with him he even managed to... you know... ejaculate all over my fingers. I felt good about that, but it took a very long time, and he never asked me to do it again. So, in all honesty, I don't know what to think.'

She put a hand on Jess's arm.

'Jess, I've never told anyone what I've just told you – not even my closest friend. And I'm not sure what it means, if it means anything at all. It's just that, when you asked me to meet you and talk about being a witness for Igg... well, it's not that I don't want to help – I know I owe him that. It's just that... well, I'm not sure I would make a particularly good witness.'

13

DETECTIVE SUPERINTENDENT ARNOLD and Detective Inspector Phillips made a deliberately vigorous entry into the small interview room, throwing back the door so that the knob crashed into the wall, pulling out their chairs from under the table with a clatter, and seating themselves purposefully. Arnold had arranged for Billy Cottage to be brought up from the cells half an hour before commencing the interview. He wanted to give him time to reflect after a night, and a good part of the following day, in the cells. Phillips was poised to resume writing in his notebook. Arnold folded his hands in front of him on the table.

'I tell you what, Billy,' he said. 'Let's not waste any more time. I'm going to explain to you what happened on the *Rosemary D* late Saturday night, early Sunday morning. The young lady who owns the cross you found – her name is Jennifer Doyce. She went on board the *Rosemary D* with her boyfriend, Frank Gilliam. This was on Saturday night, some time just before midnight. Someone attacked them. With this...'

Arnold reached down to his left and picked up a thick plastic sack, which had several yellow exhibit labels carefully attached to the tape around its neck. It contained a heavy-looking winch handle with a number of rust-coloured stains.

'This would have been used for lowering and raising the anchor. But of course, you'd know all about that, wouldn't you? It's been in the water for a while. Whoever attacked Frank and Jennifer would have thrown it overboard, hoping it might drift downstream with the silt. But, as luck would have it, it caught on the anchor line, and didn't go anywhere. The frogmen we sent down to look for a weapon swam right into it. The blood stains are a bit degraded, but there is still enough to be identified as the same blood groups as the victims'.

Arnold banged the winch handle on the table for emphasis.

'Jennifer is still alive – just,' he said. 'She has serious head injuries, and she was raped. She's in a bad way but, unfortunately for whoever did this, she survived, and she may well make a good recovery over time. In fact, DI Phillips and I spoke to her for a few minutes this morning.'

He paused to allow this to sink in. Billy appeared cowed, but Arnold was not sure whether his expression changed much in response to hearing the news.

'Frank, on the other hand, is dead. The cause of death was a series of blows to the head with a heavy blunt instrument, resulting in a fractured skull. So we have one charge of murder, one charge of attempted murder, and one charge of rape. And here you are, with her gold cross and chain in your possession, lying to us about where you found it, telling us you found it in the grass, even after we've explained to you that it was taken from her neck by her attacker.'

Billy was staring into the distance at no one and nothing in particular.

'I think I should caution you again, Billy,' Arnold said, 'because I must tell you honestly, I suspect that you may be responsible for the attack on Jennifer and Frank.'

'No…' Billy began to protest, his voice almost plaintive.

'Just listen to me, Billy. Again, I must remind you that you are not obliged to say anything unless you wish to do so, but anything you do say will be taken down and may be given in evidence. Now, do you wish to say anything? Do you wish to explain where you got the cross and chain?'

When I was bound apprentice in famous Lincolnshire…

Billy seemed lost in thought.

'It might not have been by the boat. It might have been in the reeds, further along the tow path, closer to town.'

'*Might* have been?'

'I don't remember exactly. But it must have been, otherwise the police would have found it before I did, wouldn't they?'

'So now,' Arnold said, 'you're saying it wasn't by the lock, on your side of the river, as you originally told us, or by the boat itself, on the other side, as you also suggested. Now, you're saying it was on the bank but closer to town? That's what you're saying now, is it?'

Full well I served my master for nigh on seven years...

'I think so.'

Arnold sat back in his chair, pausing, allowing Phillips to catch up.

'Let's consider that for a moment,' he said. 'First question: when was this?'

'I already told you,' Billy replied, with a show of defiance, 'on Tuesday morning.'

'Let's accept that for the moment, even though there would have been police officers walking up and down the river bank all day. What were you doing on the other side of the river, anyway?'

'I often go over to that side. I have to be aware of possible hazards to river craft, reeds, flotsam and jetsam. You can't see everything from the lock. You have to go and look for yourself. People coming through the lock expect me to tell them about things like that. If I didn't, and a craft met with an accident, the River Board would be down on me like a ton of bricks.'

'Are you sure you didn't cross the river to get a look inside the *Rosemary D*?'

Till I took up to poaching as you shall quickly hear...

'Why would I do that? I know where she is. She's a hazard, like I said. But there's nothing I can do about it. If the River Board...'

'I don't think it's got anything to do with the River Board, Billy,' Arnold said. 'I think it's got more to do with what goes on inside the boat, rather than around her.'

Oh, 'tis my delight on a shiny night in the season of the year.

'I don't know what you mean.'

'Yes, you do. All those young courting couples going there and getting up to all kinds of mischief. You know all about that, Billy. You know what goes on. You like to watch, don't you?'

'No.'

'Of course you do. PC Willis nicked you for it before, didn't he? You were standing outside a girl's house watching her undress and playing with yourself. You got a conditional discharge from the magistrates.'

'That's not how it was. I can explain that.'

'No conditional discharge this time, Billy. Not for murder. Not for rape. You went to watch, didn't you? What happened? Did you decide it wasn't enough to watch? Did you want to join in? Wouldn't they let you, is that it? Did they try to send you on your way?'

'No.'

'And you got angry. I understand that. Why wouldn't you? Why wouldn't they let you have a bit of fun with them?'

'No.'

'So you get angry. You start to leave, but then you think, sod it, they're not going to treat me like this. So you pick up the winch handle, and you go after them. Who do you attack first? Frank, I would think. Get him out of the way, so he can't interfere. Then you take Jennifer, once you've clobbered her over the head as well, and she can't resist any more. Was she your first, Billy? Do you want to tell me all about it?'

Billy was rocking back and forth in his chair. He appeared to be having trouble breathing. Phillips looked across at Arnold questioningly, but Arnold raised a hand slightly. There was a long silence. Arnold waited.

'I've never even been on that boat,' Billy said eventually.

Arnold sat up in his chair.

'I want you to think very carefully about that answer, Billy,' he replied quietly. 'I'm going to give you the chance to change your mind, to tell us the truth. Perhaps you were on board, but nothing happened, at least nothing to do with you? Perhaps you discovered the scene and panicked, didn't know what to do, just ran away?'

Billy shook his head.

'I never went on board,' he said. 'I never had the need to.'

'In that case,' Arnold asked, 'why did my forensic officer find your fingerprint on a window ledge in the aft cabin – an inside window ledge? The police have your fingerprints from your last arrest, or had you forgotten? The print has some blood around it, by the way – same group as Jennifer's, as it turns out.'

Billy was staring helplessly up at the ceiling.

Arnold stood up.

'The other strange thing,' he added, almost as an afterthought, 'is that when we spoke to Jennifer today, she told us that she remembered the man who attacked her was humming a tune to himself, almost under his breath, but she could hear it. This was while he was raping her, before she lost consciousness. Care to guess what tune he was humming, Billy?'

Phillips also stood.

'I'm going to arrange for you to see a solicitor,' Arnold said. 'I think you need some legal advice. In the meanwhile, I am going to speak to my superiors in Cambridge, and I am going to recommend that you be charged with the murder of Frank Gilliam and with the attempted murder and rape of Jennifer Doyce.'

He turned towards the door.

'Oh – and also, larceny of the gold cross and chain. Jennifer recognised it as hers. Mustn't forget that, must we?'

Sergeant Livermore was approaching as Arnold and Phillips left the interview room.

'You were asking about solicitors earlier, sir. There is actually a solicitor at the station at the moment,' he said. 'John Singer, local chap, well regarded. He was here on another matter.' He leaned towards the two detectives knowingly, confidentially. 'Vicar with an unhealthy interest in choir boys. He said he would be happy to have a word with Billy.'

'Sounds like the perfect man for the job,' Arnold said.

14

IT WAS A FEW minutes after seven in the evening. Barratt and Suzie Davis had just settled down in the living room of their home in Kensington with a bottle of White Burgundy, some olives, and a prized recording of Elgar's *Enigma Variations* – the London Philharmonic, conducted by Sir Adrian Boult. When the phone rang, they exchanged frustrated glances. They had both had an extremely busy day. Barratt's clients had been especially challenging. Suzie ran a small fashion boutique with a growing reputation in the Kings Road, Chelsea, and had been run off her feet. This was their time to unwind. For a moment Barratt considered letting the phone ring unanswered, but the habit of a lifetime was not to be broken now. Turning Elgar down a little, he walked slowly across the room, giving whoever was calling ample time to change their mind and hang up. No such luck. He picked up the phone.

'Barratt Davis.'

The voice on the other end of the line sounded breathless, as if its owner had run some distance to the phone.

'Barratt, this is John Singer. I'm awfully sorry to disturb your evening. I've been at the police station all afternoon, and I've only just got back to the office.'

'Hello, John,' Barratt replied. 'This is a surprise. What's the matter? Has the Reverend Mr Little been on the rampage again?'

Suzie made a face at him. She stood, walked to the record player, gently lifted the needle and replaced it carefully in its cradle. Returning to the coffee table, she picked up Barratt's glass, crossed the room again and handed it to him with a sympathetic kiss on the cheek. He smiled and blew her a kiss in return.

'No, something far worse, I'm afraid,' Singer was saying. 'It's right out of my league. I'm hoping you will take it, Barratt, but in any case it will need a London solicitor and counsel. It's a dreadful business.'

There was a silence on the line.

'Barratt, have you ever defended a capital murder?'

The question hit Barratt like a jug of iced water in the face. For some moments, he stared vacantly ahead of him, as a torrent of memories cascaded unchecked through his mind. Three cases: all convictions; the evidence overwhelming; the defence impossible; the result a certainty from the beginning; the dreadful consequences of conviction seemingly quite inevitable. The former Army lieutenant who caught his wife in bed with a close friend. He had brought his service revolver back home with him after the War. He had probably never fully recovered from the stress of combat, and by the time he managed to bring himself under control, he had shot both of them in the head, twice, at close range. Tried, convicted, sentenced, and executed. The twenty-year-old lad who surprised the owner during a burglary of an electrical store. The store should have been locked and unoccupied at that time of night, but the elderly owner was preparing for his annual audit, and had some late-night paperwork to do in the back office. The lad panicked and hit him once over the head with the solid brass lamp he kept on his desk. It was a blow that would not have killed everyone, but it killed this man. Tried, convicted, sentenced, and executed. The thirty-year-old mother, abandoned by her husband, who smothered her disabled seven-year-old son with a pillow out of sheer desperation, after she had gone for weeks without sleep and did not know where to turn. Tried, convicted, sentenced but, at the very last moment, reprieved by the Home Secretary, sentence commuted to life imprisonment – a victory of a kind. He remembered, indeed he could still feel, and even smell, the atmosphere of those trials: sweaty, tense, nervous, gut-wrenching; the constant and mostly vain efforts to reassure a client who was probably going to be dead at the hands of the public executioner within three months; the sleepless nights; the obsessive going over the facts, time and time again, searching for something – anything – that might offer a way out; the endless analysis of simple points of law, searching for any loophole that might have been overlooked. After conviction, the moment of sentence, the judge's clerk carefully placing the black cap on top of his wig, the 'Red Judge' in his terrifying red robes, the colour of retribution. After sentence, the hopeless trip to the Court of Criminal Appeal, in which any remaining glimmer of hope was summarily snuffed out by three dismissive appellate judges. Finally, the night before the execution, the Home Secretary's final rejection of the plea for clemency – 'the law must take its course'; the hours of drinking in a futile bid to release the tension; the sleepless night; the announcement of the execution on the radio the next morning. Then, somehow, back to the office as if it were just another day at work, completely hung over, barely capable of carrying on a normal conversation, trying to summon up the will to deal with a shoplifting prosecution or a routine contractual dispute. Yes, he had defended capital murders, and he never wanted to do it again.

'The client is a man called Billy Cottage,' Singer was saying. 'He was charged late this afternoon, he appeared before the magistrates, and he was remanded in custody. He is at Bedford Gaol. It was a brutal attack on a courting couple making love on a houseboat on the river, just outside St Ives. They were both savagely beaten with a winch handle, and the girl was raped. The young man died. The young woman is still on the critical list in Addenbrooke's. They are not sure whether she will pull through.This was not this weekend but the previous one – 25 and 26 of January – late Saturday night or early Sunday morning'

It came back to Barratt immediately.

'Yes, I read about it in the papers,' he said. He hesitated, conscious that he was about to mortgage yet another chapter of his life. 'Do we know what evidence they have against him?'

'I haven't seen any forensic reports yet, but the detective superintendent in charge of the case told me that they found a fingerprint inside the boat, on an inside window ledge, with a blood stain of the same group as the girl. Then there's something I don't understand about witnesses who heard him humming some tune. I'm not sure whether there is anything in that. It won't become clear till the committal proceedings.'

There was a lengthy silence, while Barratt Davis weighed his personal feelings against his sense of responsibility.

'What counsel would you use for this?' Singer asked eventually.

'Martin Hardcastle QC,' Barratt replied, without hesitation. 'I used him in the last two of the three capital cases I've been involved in, and in many other cases also, over the years. Martin is brilliant in court, but he will need a hard-working junior to organise the evidence for him and help with the law. I think I would be inclined to go with Ben Schroeder again.'

'He's a bit young for a murder, isn't he?' Singer commented. 'I must say I was very impressed with him in the conference, and he seems to be taking charge of the Reverend Little's case very well. But, still, he...'

'Young men have to grow up quickly at the Bar these days, John,' Barratt replied. 'Martin did four capital murders on his own in his first two years of practice as a junior. Ben will never have to do that, thank God. In any case, Martin will do all the work in court. Ben will be there at his beck and call, to make sure he has whatever he needs.'

'Whatever you think best,' Singer said. 'I'm just glad you're on board. It's a weight off my mind, I don't mind telling you. I'll make arrangements for an initial conference if you will ask your secretary to phone the office tomorrow. I just want rid of it. I want to get back to being a country solicitor.'

'That suddenly sounds very appealing,' Barratt said, wishing Singer a good evening. 'Perhaps I will give it a try myself. You don't happen to need a partner, do you?'

Singer laughed out loud. 'Come off it, Barratt,' he replied. 'You would be bored to death. You wouldn't last a month.'

* * *

Martin Hardcastle said very little during the phone call from Barratt Davis. It was better that way, at that time of night. It was, in any case, no more than a courtesy call from a man who was his friend, as well as a professional client. As professional etiquette demanded, Davis would call Vernon, Hardcastle's clerk, in the morning to retain him formally, and Vernon would make all the necessary arrangements. That was when the real business began. All that was needed tonight was an exchange of greetings and familiar expressions of confidence. These days, in the blur his life had become, cases came and went –

even capital murders – and Hardcastle had done enough of those by now to have abandoned any pretence that he could wave a magic wand, swoop down from on high to save a life by his forensic brilliance. He also knew that a solicitor of Barratt Davis's experience and competence would not believe for a moment that he could. On the other hand, he had won a few – cases where the evidence was not strong; or where the jury, conscious of the looming penalty and having some sympathy for the defendant, found a reason to convict of manslaughter rather than murder; or occasionally even to acquit altogether because of self-defence. And there was still the reassurance of being instructed in a case, the elusive security of being in work, the feeling of being wanted, that never seemed to go away – forever an integral part of the psyche of the barrister. Just before Davis's call, Hardcastle had, with determination, put the cap back on his bottle of Bell's whisky. He had to be in court the next morning, to make his closing speech to the jury in a fraud case. But a new case called for a reward.

Rewards. Martin Hardcastle had come to the Bar with impressive credentials. He had taken a first in Law at Cambridge, followed by the degree of Bachelor of Civil Law at Oxford. He passed his bar examinations, also with first-class honours, and was invited back to Trinity Hall to give supervisions in criminal law while he did his pupillage. A fellowship was within his grasp if he wanted it. So was a tenancy in excellent Chambers, the Chambers of Miles Overton QC, which offered a range of first-rate work, especially in crime and divorce. Unusually, he had to make the choice between academia and practice, and chose the cut and thrust of practice as more suited to his temperament. Once he gained a place in Chambers his career flourished. His command of the law was obvious, his style in court patient and courteous, yet forceful and precise. Judges liked him; juries ate out of his hand. After fifteen years, he took Silk, and he seemed poised to collect every reward the Bar offered. In addition to those he gave himself.

The rewards Martin Hardcastle gave himself started harmlessly enough, not long after his call to the Bar. They were not his idea. Occasionally, a member of Chambers would celebrate a really good result in court with a bottle or two of champagne in Chambers, to be shared with everyone, or a pint or two in the Devereux with one or two colleagues. Drinking more than that during the week was discouraged in Chambers. At weekends it was a different story. Dinner parties and weekends in the country were part of Chambers life, and the wine flowed freely. But during the week, the expectation was that the drinking would stop – unless there was a good result to celebrate. So Martin was scrupulous in limiting the rewards he shared with colleagues – there was no point in giving the wrong impression in Chambers. He started smoking cigarettes to take his mind off the rewards while he was working but, on the other hand, he saw no reason to deprive himself of the rewards completely. He had earned them, and he deserved them more than most. He had many good results in court. It was just a question of practicality to reward himself at home, rather than in Chambers or in the Devereux.

Home was a flat on the top floor of a building in Gray's Inn, a respectable distance from his Chambers in Brick Court, in the Middle Temple. At home, he could keep an ample supply of wine for dinner – he was a respectable home cook in those days – and an ample supply of Bell's for after dinner. At home, there was no one to judge him. In any case, if people knew how hard he worked, if they knew how good he was in court, they would understand. Of course, you couldn't guarantee a really good result in court. Sometimes, the other side held all the aces, and it was a matter of damage control rather than victory. Then, any result was a cause for celebration. They all mattered to the client, and damage control took just as much skill as winning. That deserved a reward, too. Sometimes, there was no result at all, nothing particular happening, just a trial dragging interminably on. So then, he celebrated the fact that the next day was Friday; or Thursday. Sometimes, he celebrated something as simple as getting through the day and, sometimes, he celebrated getting through the day without anyone noticing that he was not his usual self; because there were days when he woke up not feeling his usual self, and the symptoms tended to persist throughout the day. Probably just stress, and not getting enough sleep he told himself. But he managed; he was in control.

Fair enough, there had been the odd day here and there when he was not up to going to court in the morning. He always phoned Vernon early to explain: it was the Indian food consumed at a dodgy restaurant the night before; it was the stomach bug that was doing the rounds: 'you must have heard about it, Vernon, everybody's going down with it, no need to worry, just a 24-hour job, be as right as rain tomorrow'. Vernon would duly phone the court and pass on Mr Hardcastle's regrets and, after all, he had a junior at court to hold the fort. He would appear at court the next day, apologise profusely to the judge, the jury and his client, he would forego the rewards for a day or two, and he would begin to feel better again.

On days like that, as he lay in bed at home, it would occur to him that perhaps the rewards should stop; or perhaps he should save them up for the weekend, or make sure they ended by, say, 9 o'clock at night. But eventually, to his relief, he would realise that the day off work was nothing more than the result of too much stress. He was working too hard. There was no need to deprive himself of his rewards. He just needed to be more careful. On one really bad day, it was true, he had panicked and had systematically poured every drop of alcoholic drink he possessed down the kitchen sink. The process had lasted for almost an hour, and the liquid represented a lot of money. For a day, he felt better. But the following evening, he again panicked. He rushed to an off-licence on Gray's Inn Road just before it closed and replenished his stock. He had been over-reacting when he poured his drink away, he realised. He was taking it all too seriously. Everybody needed a drink. In a profession as stressful as the Bar, that was just the way it was. You just needed to control it, that was all. Perhaps it was time to take some holiday. That was it. He had not had a real break since… well, it must be almost two years. He must speak to Vernon about it. After the next case.

One morning, about a year earlier, Martin Hardcastle had woken up with a start and realised that he was forty-eight years of age. He had spent eighteen years in practice at the Bar; and had been in Silk for three years; but suddenly he could not account for those years in any detail. It was all a blur. Where had the time gone, for God's sake? He was still living in his flat in Gray's Inn. He had no home in the country, as most of his colleagues did. He had never married and had children, as they had. There had been a few women along the way, but they survived in his mind mainly as images. He had no clear recollection of who they were, how long they had stayed, or what they had meant to him. A large part of his life had passed him by without his noticing it. What lay ahead seemed like an abyss. He was still successful in court, but those who knew him noted the loss of the youthful enthusiasm they expected in his advocacy, and the development of a world-weary, cynical, even bored tone.

By now, it was more a matter of survival. He had developed strategies. There would be no drinking before 8 o'clock in the evening. That had the merit that he could decline drinks in Chambers, and so reassure his colleagues that he was going home to work. He would avoid social engagements as far as possible, unless he could be sure of being home no later than 9 o'clock. That had the merit that he could manage with just one or two drinks away from home. He would drink a pint or two of milk before going out, and copious amounts of water before going to bed, which greatly improved his powers of recovery in the morning. There were still days when he left his junior to run things in court. But he would have done that anyway. He was a Silk. The case was his responsibility. He was preparing a cross-examination or closing speech. He could think better at home. No point wasting a day in court when he wasn't needed, and he had important work to do. Occasionally, a judge would mutter something about QCs having a duty to be present throughout the case. But a suitable display of contrition always seemed to do the trick. That was one good thing about being in Silk – no judge was going to be too hard on you.

Now, he had a new capital murder. There was no case more important, and it came from Barratt Davis, his most loyal instructing solicitor. This might be just the tonic he needed.

15

'YOU MEAN YOU'RE not going to ask any questions at all? Aren't we wasting a good opportunity? May I remind you that I would like to bring this to an end as soon as possible, Mr Schroeder?'

The Rev Ignatius Little was using his best pulpit voice to sound assertive, but his darting eyes and restless manner did not match, and gave the game away. The man was frightened, and searching for reassurance.

'So would I,' Ben replied. 'But it's rarely a good idea to ask questions at the committal stage. There are sometimes cases which are so weak that there is a reasonable chance the magistrates might refuse to commit for trial. But cases like that are very unusual, and I'm afraid your case isn't one of them. So if we ask questions at this stage, it serves no useful purpose. All we do is give away our defence and allow the prosecution witnesses the advantage of a dress rehearsal.'

'Best to keep our powder dry,' Barratt Davis nodded in agreement. 'Keep them guessing.'

It was 8.30 on a bright and bitterly cold morning. They were sitting, with Jess Farrar and John Singer, in the lounge of the George Hotel in Huntingdon, a short walk from the station, and an even shorter walk across Market Square to the Town Hall where, in two hours time, the Huntingdonshire magistrates would convene to hear the committal proceedings against Ignatius Little. Ben, Barratt, and Jess had caught an early train from King's Cross. John Singer had arranged to meet them at the George with Little, and had taken possession of a quiet corner table, where the few breakfasting commercial travellers and local businessmen were less likely to overhear them. A large tea pot and an equally large coffee pot occupied the centre of the table, surrounded by their accompanying milk jugs, a sugar bowl and a hot water jug. Untouched slices of brown and white toast were growing cold and brittle in their silver toast racks.

'I don't understand why you say the case isn't weak,' Little protested. 'As you say, Mr Schroeder, there is no supporting evidence. It's just that wretched boy's word against mine. What sort of case is that to ruin a man's name with? Why couldn't we stop it now? We could at least try.'

Ben took a deep breath. It was not the first time they had been over this question. But Ben knew he must be patient. This was Little's case, and the consequences of conviction were unimaginable for him. Overall Ben was pleased that Little had abandoned the meek, resigned demeanour he had displayed at the first conference. If he was going to be a good witness eventually, he needed to show some outrage, some sense of injustice, about the charge. But he also needed to remain calm.

'On a charge of indecent assault, you have the right to be tried either by the magistrates or by a judge and jury at Quarter Sessions,' he explained. 'But, in our case, it's not really a choice. Letting a bench of local magistrates try their local vicar is not a good idea, for obvious reasons. So we are electing trial by jury. Once we make that election, the magistrates' only function is to commit the case for trial. All they need in order to do that is enough evidence to support the charge; in other words, evidence that would allow a jury to convict. It doesn't take much. If Raymond Stone tells them that you touched him in an indecent manner, that's all it will take.'

Ben paused to allow what he had said to sink in.

'When we get to trial in front of a jury, it will be quite different. For a jury to convict, the case has to be proved beyond reasonable doubt, and the jury has to be warned that it would be dangerous to convict without corroborating evidence. That's why I think it is not going to be easy for the prosecution, once we get to Quarter Sessions. But that's not today. We have to choose our battles carefully.'

Little nodded in compliance. Ben hoped he had made his point, but he fully expected the question to be raised again later in the morning. Reassurance was a long process with clients, sometimes. There were no short-cuts.

'What if the magistrates want to ask me questions?'

'The only question they are allowed to ask you is where you want to be tried.' Ben smiled. 'You are not going to give evidence today. I will tell the court that we reserve our defence for trial. Once we have got today over and done with, and we have Raymond's deposition, we can begin to prepare our defence in more detail.'

Ignatius Little looked down at the table for some time. Ben inadvertently raised his cup to his lips, took a sip, and immediately replaced it sharply on the table with a grimace.

'Shall I order some fresh coffee?' Jess suggested, with a grin.

'That would be a very good idea,' Ben replied.

'Mr Schroeder,' Little said, as Jess was pushing her chair back and getting to her feet, 'Mr Davis tells me that we might not be able to call Joan as a witness. Is that true?'

Jess sat back down quietly. Little paused.

'I don't understand it. We were close. We were planning to get married. I know she must be upset about the charge, but I would have expected her to give me the benefit of the doubt, you know, to stand by me. At least she could come to court and tell the jury that we are... were... engaged to be married. I mean...' His voice trailed away miserably.

Ben exchanged a quick glance with Barratt Davis.

'She is not refusing to come to court,' Ben said. 'But whether or not we call her is something we can decide nearer the time, when we have a better idea of how the case looks. Try not to worry about that for today. As I say, once we have the prosecution evidence from the committal proceedings, we will have a much better idea of where we stand.'

A waiter passed by. Jess picked up the coffee pot and waved it in the air. The waiter nodded, took the pot from her hand and marched smartly away towards the kitchen.

Little sat back and closed his eyes. After some time, he stood.

'I'm going to All Saints for a while,' he said, 'to pray before the hearing. Would you mind picking me up there when it's time for court?'

'It's just across the street,' John Singer said, pointing to the front window of the lounge. 'Beautiful parish church, fifteenth century, some parts even older. Oliver Cromwell was baptised there.'

'Ah yes,' Barratt Davis smiled. 'Local boy made good, or bad, according to your point of view.'

'Yes,' Singer replied. 'He was born just a bit farther down the High Street, and the grammar school where he was educated is opposite the church, just across the square.'

He stood and looked at the retreating figure of Ignatius Little, which had almost reached the front entrance of the hotel.

'I think I will join Ignatius in prayer for a few minutes, if you don't need me.'

'By all means,' Barratt replied. If he was surprised, he did not show it. 'We will pick you up just before 10 o'clock. It never does any harm to be at court in good time.'

He waited until Singer had left the hotel. They could see the pair walking across George Street towards the church.

'Well, he is the solicitor for the Diocese' he said, 'and I suppose a few prayers can't do any harm. We need all the help we can get with this, don't we? All right, it is the boy's word against his, but somehow, that reflection is not yet making me feel particularly relaxed about the case. I have every confidence in you, Ben, but if God wants to weigh in and lend a hand, He's going to get no opposition from me.'

'Absolutely, Mr Davis,' Ben smiled. 'I make a point of never turning down a bit of divine intervention – as long as it's on my side.'

'Quite right,' Barratt replied. 'Oh, and by the way, I will be calling you Ben from this point, and I want you to call me Barratt. No more of that Mr Schroeder and Mr Davis stuff, except in front of clients and in Chambers, obviously. You're one of the stable of Bourne & Davis counsel now, and we prefer first names, even if, as a member of the Bar, you are exalted in rank above us mere solicitors.'

'He means that as a compliment,' Jess said confidentially, leaning across the table towards Ben.

'And it is accepted as such,' Ben replied.

'A nice piece of evasion, if I may say so,' Barratt resumed, with a grin. 'About the fiancée, I mean. The last thing we need today is a conversation about whether he can get it up with her, and whether there might be some section of humanity he fancies more than attractive young women.' He turned to Jess. 'You did report that she was attractive, didn't you? Did I get that right?'

'Yes,' Jess replied, 'she is attractive, and a very nice girl, as far as I could judge from one meeting. And she doesn't seem to be inhibited sexually.'

'So, no reason not to lust after her then, is there?' Barratt mused quietly, as if to himself. 'Well, "sufficient unto the day is the evil thereof".' He raised his voice to its normal level again. 'And speaking of that, how are you feeling about being prosecuted by your former pupil-master?'

Ben laughed. 'I nearly passed out when he first told me,' he replied. 'It is a bit daunting. But, on the other hand, I think it will be daunting for Gareth, too. He knows he won't be able to get away with anything. I know too much about the ways he works.'

'Well said,' Barratt nodded.

He turned and gazed through the window in the direction of the church.

'He's not entirely on our side, of course.'

'Who? God?' Ben asked.

Barratt laughed. 'No. John Singer.'

Ben nodded. 'He has a potential conflict of interest.'

'Yes. He may be supporting Mr Little for now, but if the good vicar is convicted, the Diocese will be running for cover. They will drop him so fast it will make our heads spin. I only hope we can rely on the witnesses Singer is summoning up for us.'

'Well, they must be concerned about being sued,' Ben replied. 'But I don't think we have to worry about the witnesses. The Diocese will work with us for now. It's not in their interests to jettison Little unless, and until, he is convicted.'

Barratt nodded thoughtfully.

'Do you think they have a form of prayer for this?' he asked.

'What?' Jess queried, looking puzzled.

'In the Book of Common Prayer. They have forms of prayer for everything, don't they? For harvest home, for those in peril on the sea? I was just wondering if they have a form of prayer for vicars charged with touching up choir boys.'

'Barratt!' Jess protested.

'Don't ask *me*,' Ben grinned.

'I think they must. It would go something like this, wouldn't it?'

He spread his arms out wide and looked up towards the ceiling.

'"Oh, most gracious and most bountiful God, we beseech thy

blessings on A, (or he may say, the Vicar of wherever it is) who this day stands in peril from a jury of his peers. Or, actually, if possible we would prefer a jury of people who are not his peers. Defend this, thy servant, we pray, against every false allegation, and preferably also against every true one. In thy mercy, strengthen the hands of his most able solicitors and counsel, that they may safely deliver him from the peril aforesaid, and may get him off, to the greater glory of thy holy name and to the greater glory of Bourne & Davis and of Mr Ben Schroeder of counsel."'

Jess was pointing at him.

'There is no hope for you, Barratt. You are going straight down when you die,' she said through her laughter.

'I don't doubt it for a minute,' Barratt replied.

The waiter returned with hot coffee and fresh milk. Jess thanked him and poured. Suddenly, Barratt became more serious again.

'I'm sure Merlin has told you about our next case from this holy part of the world?'

'The St Ives murder?' Ben replied. 'Yes. I was going to ask if we could have a word about it once the committal is over.'

'Yes, as much fun as the Reverend Little's case may be, that's going to be a different affair altogether. Did Gareth do a capital case when you were his pupil?'

Ben shook his head. 'No. He has done a few, one or two on his own. But he would very rarely talk about them.'

'That's the way of it,' Barratt replied. 'You don't talk about them much once they are over. You want to forget and move on.'

He paused for a sip of coffee.

'Martin Hardcastle will be leading you. Do you know him?'

'By reputation,' Ben replied cautiously.

'Yes, quite,' Barratt replied. 'I'm sure Merlin filled you in on the rumours.'

'Well, I...'

'He drinks,' Barratt said, matter-of-factly. 'Always has. But he's bloody brilliant in court. Merlin would prefer me to go to someone in your Chambers, of course. Well, he's the clerk. That's his job. But you've only got the one Silk, haven't you? And this isn't a case for Bernard Wesley, Ben. Horses for courses, that's all it is. In a civil dispute or a messy divorce, no one better. I would go to Bernard every time. But not for crime. I would go to Gareth, if he was in Silk. Is he going to apply?'

Ben nodded. 'I'm sure he is, either this year or next,' he replied.

'Good. I'm sure he'll get it.'

He looked up at the ceiling with a smile.

'All the same, Barratt,' Ben said. 'The rumours have been pretty persistent. I don't know Hardcastle myself, and I'm not saying you should be thinking of anyone in my Chambers. But aren't you taking a chance? I mean, in a case like this…'

'Martin Hardcastle,' Barratt intoned reflectively. 'Have you heard of Ulysses S Grant?'

'Yes, he was President of the United States, after the Civil War, wasn't he?'

'Yes. But before he was President, he was a general in the Union Army under Lincoln. By reputation he was the most competent and fearless of all the Union commanders. He won the decisive engagement at Shiloh, which split the Confederacy in half and shortened the war by a good while. Now, *there* was a man who had a reputation for drinking too much. Do you know what Lincoln said when that rumour reached him?'

'No,' Ben admitted.

'He said: "If drink makes fighting men like Grant, then find out what he drinks and send my other commanders a case!" That's the way I feel about Martin. The rumours are grossly exaggerated, as they were in Grant's case – he suffered from migraines, which some mistook for hangovers, deliberately or otherwise. They can talk all they like, but Martin is a good man in a fight, just like Grant. He has been through this kind of case with me before, Ben. I want him by my side again.'

'I understand,' Ben replied.

'I will book a consultation through his clerk once I know a little more about what the prosecution have. You, Jess, and I will have to go through everything thoroughly before the consultation. Martin will expect us to be prepared.'

He took another drink of coffee.

'I'm hoping, *entre nous*, that our friend Mr Singer will bow out of that,' he said with a nod of the head in the direction of All Saints church. 'I don't mind him praying for divine assistance in the vicar's case, if he thinks it will help, but he will be no bloody use to us in a capital murder. He will just get in the way.'

'Oh, and by the way,' he added, after a brief pause, 'don't expect Martin at the committal. He will expect you to handle that. Sort of thing juniors ought to do. You will understand when you meet him.'

16

THEY WALKED TOGETHER without a word along the narrow path that led from the main door of the George, through the graveyard in front of All Saints Church, where Singer and Little joined them, in the shadow of two large oak trees, into Market Square; then across the square to the fine eighteenth-century Town Hall, where the County magistrates sat. As they entered the small entrance hall, Ben saw Gareth Morgan-Davies leaning against the wall to his right, in conversation with a man he did not know. A black-gowned usher, tall and dignified, with short silver hair and matching eyebrows, carrying a clip-board and a pencil, greeted them.

'You will be the defence side, then?' he asked cheerfully. 'The prosecution is already here, Mr Morgan-Davies, of Counsel. And you are the Reverend Mr Little, are you, sir?'

Little nodded reluctantly. The usher made a careful note on the sheet of paper he had on his clipboard.

'My name is Barratt Davis, Bourne & Davis, with John Singer, solicitors for the defence. Mr Ben Schroeder, of Counsel, and my assistant, Jess Farrar.'

'Thank you, sir.' Another careful note.

'The magistrates will be sitting in Court 2 today, sir. That's just through that door to your right. The grand jury room, where they sit most of the time, is upstairs, but we are expecting quite a crowd today, including some gentlemen of the press, so they decided they wanted more room. The clerk today is Mr Philip Eaves, local solicitor, very good on the law, so I'm told. There's a conference room through the door on your far left, which you will have all to yourselves today. It's right next to the cells, but don't let that bother you. It's not a big building, so we have to make use of the space. My name is Paul, by the way. Let me know if you have any questions.'

'Thank you,' Ben replied. He turned to Barratt. 'Why don't you take Mr Little and Mr Singer to the conference room. I'm going to have a quick word with the prosecution.'

Barratt nodded. He shepherded his charges to his left and through a low wooden door.

Gareth seemed disconcertingly cheerful.

'Ah, good morning, Ben. Do you know Philip Martineau, prosecuting solicitor for the County? Philip, this is Ben Schroeder, who is defending Mr Little.'

Ben shook Martineau's hand.

'Let's have a word,' Gareth said, putting a hand on Ben's shoulder and taking him aside, while Martineau sat and busied himself with a file. They both leaned against the wall.

'Have you thought about advising your chap to plead?' Gareth asked. 'He could ask to be dealt with by the justices today, instead of going up to Quarter Sessions. It's his first offence, and the prosecution are prepared to tell the court that the boy is making a full recovery, and has probably suffered no lasting harm. I doubt they would send him inside: especially as his plea would spare Raymond the ordeal of giving evidence.'

Ben shook his head.

'Have you seen what the local papers have been saying about this case? They might feel they have no choice but to send him inside. Besides, Gareth, he's a clergyman. It's not just a question of whether he goes inside. He will be defrocked, or whatever they call it. His life will be over.'

'His life as a clergyman is over already,' Gareth said. 'This will follow him around for the rest of his life. There's no point in making things worse than they already are. Martineau says the boy is going to be a good witness. A jury is going to believe him.'

'I'm not so sure,' Ben replied. 'And even if they do, the judge will have to tell them that it is dangerous to convict in the absence of corroboration. It's his word against Raymond's, and he *is* a vicar.' He smiled. 'It's a case for the Morgan-Davies credibility index, isn't it? Vicars win against most other witnesses – anyone except bishops, nuns and...'

'And War widows. I knew I shouldn't have taught you so bloody much,' Gareth returned the smile. 'Now it all gets turned back on me and used against me, doesn't it?'

'Certainly,' Ben replied.

Gareth nodded, smiling.

'Well, that's fair enough, I suppose, and you have a point,' he conceded. 'But, in fairness, I should warn you that you are not completely up to date with the evidence. We do actually have some corroboration, as it happens.'

Ben was taken aback. He had asked Little in detail about the events of the evening, and had detected nothing which offered the prosecution case support from a source other than Raymond. Without such evidence, the case was legally uncorroborated.

'I'm sure you will call the organist, Sharples,' Ben ventured tentatively. 'That puts Raymond in church on the Wednesday evening, perhaps even in the vestry. But it doesn't implicate Little in the commission of an offence.'

'I quite agree,' Gareth replied. 'But that wasn't what I was referring to.'

'So…?'

Gareth turned his head away slightly.

'I'm sure your client knows all about it,' he said, 'and he will hear it once we start the evidence. So, what's it to be? Last chance.'

Ben took a deep breath.

'No, Gareth, I can't deal with it like that. You've got to tell me what to expect. You can't expect me to talk to him about a plea unless I have the full picture. If it's something that takes me by surprise and my solicitors have to make further inquiries about it, I will have to apply for an adjournment. I don't think either of us wants this case to drag on longer than it has to.'

Gareth appeared to hesitate, but then turned back to face Ben.

'Your client as good as admitted it to the boy's father that same evening,' he said. 'That's why the father called the police. He wasn't sure he would, just based on what Raymond told him when he got home. And it wasn't because he didn't believe him. The Stones are church-going people and it goes against the grain for them to make a complaint against a minister. So Stone phoned Little and told him what Raymond had said.'

Ben exhaled heavily and looked away.

'And what did Little say, according to Stone?' he asked.

Gareth made a show of opening the file he was carrying and finding the right document though, knowing Gareth as well as he did, Ben was quite sure that he had no need to refresh his memory. Whatever had been said he would have memorised, word for word.

'He said: *'I'm sorry. If anything happened, I didn't intend it. I don't know what came over me.'*'

For some time, Ben stared into space, then he recovered himself.

'And you were going to ambush us with that?' he asked quietly.

'Not at all,' Gareth said. 'I'm calling Stone to give evidence about it this morning. I assumed that your client would remember speaking to Stone on that evening and would have given you instructions about it.'

He paused.

'But I will tell you this,' he added confidentially. 'Don't blame Martineau for not telling your solicitor about it. If you cross-examine Stone or the officer in charge at some stage, you will find out that Stone only came forward with this evidence rather late in the day.'

'How late in the day?' Ben asked.

'Monday. Three days ago,' Gareth replied.

'That doesn't make sense,' Ben pointed out. 'If that was his reason for going to the police in the first place, why wouldn't he…?'

'A point that you will no doubt explore with him and hammer home to the jury, as I would in your shoes,' Gareth said. 'It's more of a frustration for us than for you, believe me.'

Ben shook his head.

'Thank you for telling me, Gareth,' he said. 'I won't be cross-examining anyone today. We will be reserving our defence for trial.'

'I'd have you drummed out of Chambers if you did anything else,' Gareth smiled.

As Ben was walking away, Gareth called him back.

'Ben, just a moment. Martineau tells me you are going to be junior counsel for that chap they arrested for the house-boat murder.'

'Yes.' He paused. 'Martin Hardcastle is leading me.' He paused again. 'I know. I have spoken to Barratt Davis about it, but…'

Gareth nodded. 'Look, I've known Martin for years,' he said. 'I've been against him a number of times, and it is never an easy assignment. He's quite a force in the courtroom and the prosecution will underestimate him at their peril. It is a bit of a risk these days, but Barratt knows him as well as anyone, and if he is happy with him I wouldn't worry too much. It's Barratt's responsibility, after all. Just keep your eyes open. Prepare everything thoroughly. Martin is obsessive about that. And don't get upset when he treats you as if you don't exist. It's just his way.'

'Very reassuring, Gareth,' Ben replied. 'Thank you.'

Gareth laughed.

'Oh, Ben, one other thing. I expect you've heard that I'm taking on Clive Overton as a pupil?'

'Yes, Donald Weston told me. He and Clive are good friends. Donald wouldn't say much else, but wasn't there…?'

'A scandal? Yes, there was. I don't know all the details. Clive was involved in some kind of prank at college that went wrong, and resulted in the death of another undergraduate. No charges were brought, but Clive's father, the fearsome Miles Overton QC, sent him abroad, to America, until it had all died down. Bernard Wesley got involved in bringing him back, and Bernard asked me to take him as a pupil once he had been called to the Bar. He's passed all his exams, and he is being called this month. I just wondered whether I could send him to court for a day or two so that he can see a murder – assuming I don't have one myself. I think it's something he ought to see. I will tell him to make himself useful, take a note, do any research you may need, and so on.'

'Yes, of course,' Ben said, 'as long as Hardcastle has no objection.'

'Much appreciated,' Gareth said.

Ben moved to leave, but suddenly turned back.

'Gareth, why did Bernard get involved in bringing Clive into Chambers?' he asked. 'I always heard that he and Miles Overton were not exactly close. Harriet Fisk and I heard rumours that it was somehow connected to our being asked to join Chambers. I don't want to pry, but…'

Gareth was silent for some time.

'I will tell you what I know about that at another time, Ben,' he promised. 'I have always intended to. I think it's only fair that you should know. But I'm not sure I know the whole story, and I may have to insist on your confidence as to what I do know.'

'Of course.'

'Also,' Gareth added, 'I would need the fortification of several glasses of wine to get started on that.'

'Now I *am* intrigued,' Ben said.

* * *

The group in the conference room looked around expectantly as Ben opened the door. The conference room was small and cramped. There was barely enough room for them all to stand.

'Did you learn anything useful?' Barratt Davis asked.

Ben ignored him, and walked straight up to Ignatius Little, looking him straight in the face.

'Is there anything you would like to tell me, Mr Little?' he asked. 'Something you may not have told Mr Davis or myself until now? Have we not made it sufficiently clear to you that you make it very difficult for us to defend you if you are not completely frank with us?'

'I don't understand,' Little's voice was quiet, hesitant. 'What kind of thing are you talking about?'

'Something like having a conversation over the phone with Raymond's father on the evening in question,' Ben replied. 'That kind of thing.'

Ben heard the sharp intake of breath to his right.

'What's this?' Barratt asked.

'Prosecuting counsel has told me that he intends to call evidence from Mr Stone,' Ben explained, 'to the effect that Mr Stone phoned Mr Little later on the Wednesday evening, after Raymond had returned home and given his father his account of what happened. I am told he will say that, when confronted with the allegation, Mr Little replied: *"I'm sorry. If anything happened, I didn't intend it. I don't know what came over me."* Does any of that sound familiar to you?'

Little sat down heavily.

'Well,' Barratt said, in exasperation, 'that's their corroboration, isn't it?'

'Assuming that Mr Stone's evidence is true,' Ben replied. 'Is it true, Mr Little?'

Little buried his head in his hands for some time. Eventually he looked up.

'Yes… no… I mean… yes, Stone did phone me. It was very late, 11 o'clock or even later. I was about to go to bed. I was very tired.' He paused.

'What was said between you?' Ben asked. 'Leave nothing out.'

He turned towards Barratt to ask for a note to be made, but Barratt already had pen and notebook in hand.

'He sounded totally confused,' Little replied. 'He was saying something about touching, but he wasn't making any sense. He was almost incoherent. I believe now that he was angry. To be frank, at the time, I thought he must have been drinking. I'm afraid I didn't take him seriously. I knew nothing had happened. I assumed it was some kind of misunderstanding. The call ended. I went to bed, and thought no more about it.'

'Until the police arrived on your doorstep the following morning,' Ben commented.

'Yes.'

'What, if anything, did you say to Stone? Think hard, Mr Little. This is very important. Your words, as precisely as possible.'

'What is it he is claiming I said?'

'"*I'm sorry. If anything happened, I didn't intend it. I don't know what came over me.*"'

Little shook his head. 'I may have said that if anything happened, it was not intentional. It can happen that you brush up against someone when you are putting the vestments away or stowing supplies of communion wafers or wine in the cupboards. The vestry is not very big; there's not a lot of room to move. So, yes, I may well have said something like that. But I didn't say "*I don't know what came over me*". I would have no reason to say such a thing.'

'Can you remember anything else about the call, anything at all?' Ben asked.

'No,' Little replied. 'It didn't last very long at all, and Stone was doing most of the talking. He was talking, and then he suddenly disconnected, and that was that.'

Barratt had concluded his note. He looked up.

'And you didn't tell Counsel or myself about this earlier because…?'

Little shook his head. 'I should have,' he admitted. 'I can see that now. For some reason it escaped me. If it had stuck in my mind as important, I'm sure I would have told you. I'm sorry.'

Ben looked up to the ceiling.

'Well you have told us now,' he said. 'So at least now we know what we are up against. Unless there is something else you haven't told us?'

Little shook his head silently.

There was a knock on the door and Paul put a discreet head into the room. 'Sorry to disturb, sir. But the bench has asked for everyone in the case of Ignatius Little to come into court, if you please.'

They followed the usher across the entrance hall to the entrance to the court. Paul took Ignatius Little by the arm and steered him towards the dock, where a uniformed dock officer took charge of him. Ben hastily took his seat in the front row reserved for counsel. Gareth Morgan-Davies sat to his right, with Philip Martineau behind him. Barratt Davis, John Singer, and Jess Farrar slid into the row behind Ben. The courtroom had changed little since its original construction in 1745. It was built of an elegant light-stained pine. The magistrates' bench was at the front of the court, opposite the small dock. The jury box was to his left, the witness box to his right. Above them, on the first floor of the building, a long narrow public gallery ran along the left side and back of the court, its protective rail painted a glossy white. Looking around the gallery, Ben noted that every seat was occupied. Such was the public interest in the case, that you would have had to be at court early to have a chance of getting in, and a few seats had clearly been reserved for the press.

Ben glanced up at the three magistrates, their bench elevated slightly above the rest of the court. The chairman was an elderly man wearing a dark grey suit and blue tie. He had short white hair, and the suggestion of a white moustache protruded above his lower lip, almost as if he had forgotten to shave it off. To his right, a younger man with dark hair, his suit lighter in colour and, to Ben's eye, indicating rather more money than taste. He wore a very large Swiss watch on his left wrist. To the chairman's left, a quiet-looking woman in a dark two-piece suit, and a small dark blue hat tilted slightly forward and to the left. The magistrates' clerk, Philip Eaves – local solicitor and very good on the law, so Paul was told – a youngish man wearing thick glasses, sat in front and slightly lower.

'Your worships,' Eaves was proclaiming, 'this is the case of Ignatius Little.'

He looked towards Little.

'Stand up please. Is your name Ignatius Little?'

'Yes, sir.'

'Sit down please.'

Gareth stood immediately.

'May it please you, sir. I appear to prosecute in this case. My learned friend Mr Schroeder appears for the defendant. My learned friend has been good enough to indicate to me in advance that the defendant will be electing trial. The prosecution is prepared to proceed with the committal today.'

'Thank you, Mr Morgan-Davies,' Eaves said. 'Stand up again, please, Mr Little. Ignatius Little, you are charged that on or about the 22nd day of January 1964, at St Ives in the County of Huntingdon, you indecently assaulted Raymond Stone, a male under the age of sixteen years. On this charge, you have the right to be tried by a judge and jury at Quarter Sessions. But if you wish, you may be tried by the magistrates in this court. I must caution you that, if you elect to be tried in this court by the magistrates and you are convicted, the court may commit you to Quarter Sessions for sentence if they consider that the offence merits greater punishment than they have power to impose. Where do you wish to be tried?'

A momentary hesitation only.

'I wish to be tried by a judge and jury.'

'Very well. Please be seated.'

The committal proceedings took the rest of the court day – but not because of the volume of the evidence. To prepare the depositions of the prosecution witnesses, Eaves had to record the evidence verbatim in longhand as it was given, a process which ensured that the hearing proceeded at a snail's pace. Gareth opened the case to the magistrates in a matter of two or three minutes, outlining for them what the case was about, before calling Raymond Stone to give evidence. At Gareth's request, the magistrates excluded anyone not involved in the case from court during his evidence, and made an order prohibiting any public identification of Raymond, and any reporting of the case which might have that effect. Knowing that the evidence would not be challenged until trial, and that the defence would not be opposing the committal, allowed Gareth to limit his witness to what was strictly necessary to establish a legally sufficient case. The full trauma of re-living every detail was postponed – for the moment. Raymond was smartly dressed in his school uniform, a dark blue blazer, grey trousers and a red-and-blue striped tie. His hair was immaculately brushed and combed.

Ben turned around to Barratt Davis.

'Barratt, would you mind taking a note, so that I can watch him?'

'Will do,' Barratt whispered.

As Ben watched Raymond Stone during his short evidence, his anxiety about the case increased. He knew that it would be difficult for an average jury to imagine a boy of that age making up the details of the kind of offence about which he was giving evidence. Ben scrutinised him carefully for any hint that he had been coached, or told what to say. The boy did not seem intimidated by the courtroom or by the evidence he had to give, and he did not strike Ben as a witness who had been coached. It was a worrying sign.

John Sharples gave evidence that both Ignatius Little and Raymond Stone had been on the church premises on the evening of Wednesday 22 January, and that Raymond had gone into the vestry after choir practice to help the vicar with preparations for the Sunday services. Sharples himself had not entered the vestry. Having locked the organ and put away his music, he had left the church to return home.

Next, Gareth called Godfrey Stone, Raymond's father. He described Raymond's return home from choir practice on the occasion in question. The boy had gone upstairs to his room immediately, and without saying a word to his parents, which was unusual. He had followed him upstairs to talk to him and had noticed that he seemed upset. His son had given an account of being indecently touched by the vicar in the vestry. Raymond's mother had then come upstairs to comfort him. Ben noted that Stone's description of what Raymond had said was very general and consisted of little more than an allegation of 'touching'. After discussing the situation with his wife, he had been concerned enough to phone Little to demand an explanation. Asked how Little had responded, Stone said: 'he apologised and said he didn't know what had come over him'. He may have said that it was unintentional, Stone added. Asked by

Gareth whether he could be any more precise about what had been said, he stated that he could not.

Lastly, Gareth called PC Willis to deal with his arrest of Ignatius Little the following morning, after Mr Stone had attended St Ives police station to make a formal complaint. He had cautioned Mr Little, who had exercised his right to remain silent. Later, Little had been charged.

At the conclusion of the case, the clerk asked Little whether he wished to give evidence, call witnesses, or say anything in answer to the charge. Ben replied on his behalf. Mr Little did not wish to say anything or call evidence. He would reserve his defence until trial. Without retiring, the magistrates found that there was a case to answer. Ben stood again.

'Before you commit, sir,' he said, 'while there is no objection to the committal, the defence does have some concerns about the case being committed for trial in Huntingdonshire. This case has attracted considerable local publicity, and it would be difficult to assemble a jury which has no knowledge of the case. I am concerned that the defendant may not receive a fair trial, and I would ask that the matter be committed farther afield, perhaps to Cambridge Quarter Sessions.'

To Ben's surprise, Gareth stood immediately.

'If I might indicate, sir, the prosecution has no objection to the application. We do not concede for a moment that a Huntingdon jury would be unable to try the case fairly, but we do accept that justice must not only be done, but must be seen to be done, and if the court feels, perhaps after consulting Cambridge, that it would be more prudent to move the case in the light of any local notoriety, we would not oppose that course.'

The magistrates conferred briefly.

'We have heard what has been said,' the chairman declared. 'As the prosecution has stated, a Huntingdon jury will be quite capable of putting any publicity out of their minds and of giving the defendant a fair trial, as we would ourselves if the case were to be tried before us in this court. The case will be committed for trial to Huntingdon Quarter Sessions. The defendant's bail is extended until the time of trial.'

'Well, that's all right then,' Barratt commented as they left court.

'No problem with a fair trial in Huntingdon. I'm sure we are all relieved to hear that. I'm sure you all noticed the representatives of the fourth estate in court today, plying their trade.'

Ben nodded. 'Let's continue to keep track of their efforts. We can always renew the application at Quarter Sessions.'

'I will make sure we have all the press reports available,' Singer said. 'The Diocese keeps copies of everything of that kind for its own purposes.'

'Anything else you need us to do today, Mr Schroeder?' Barratt asked.

Ben turned to Ignatius Little.

'Yes. Since we are in the neighbourhood, I would like to make a short detour to St Ives and take a look at your vestry,' he said.

17

IT HAD NOT been easy for Eve to travel from Fenstanton to Bedford. The two towns were no very great distance apart. Someone with a car could have made the journey comfortably in an hour. But Eve did not have the luxury of a car, and she had to thread her way cross-country by sooty local trains and fume-filled buses. Her appointment was for noon, which had meant that she had to leave home early. She could not afford to miss a connection. The prison authorities were very clear that, if she did not arrive promptly, her visit would be cancelled. By the time she arrived at Bedford Gaol she felt tired and headachy, and she was sure that her clothes showed all the dirt she had accumulated during the journey. She had baked Billy some small sponge cakes and brought him some tobacco, but they were confiscated by the guards as failing to comply with rule so-and-so, the result of failing to complete form something-or-other not less than so-many days in advance of her visit. Eve had no comprehension of the details, but she was canny enough to suspect that the cakes would find their way to the prison officers' tea room during the course of the afternoon. She asked several times to have the tobacco back, but a senior officer told her that it had been classified as contraband and could not be returned.

It was the first sight she had had of her brother since the officers had taken him from her living room nearly a month earlier, and she found herself deeply affected. The sight of him constrained by bars and impenetrable glass, when he should have been out of doors at his lock, by his river, was at first almost too much for her to bear. She knew what he was accused of doing, but it did not make sense to her. She had always suspected, in a dark part of her mind, that what Billy did with her, what her father had done with her, was wrong. But Billy had never done her harm. She could not understand how anyone could think of him as a violent man. She had always trusted him. He provided for her and looked after her. There was no reason not to trust him. But there was a coldness around her neck and on her chest, where Jennifer Doyce's gold cross and chain had briefly hung. There was something not right about it. She had sensed it when the police officers had taken it away from her. Something had changed in that moment in her feelings towards Billy.

'How are they treating you?' she asked. 'I think you've lost weight. Are you all right?'

They were in a cold, cheerless visiting cell without natural light. A single bare bulb, set high in the ceiling, provided barely adequate illumination. A small metal table and two chairs, their metal dented, their white paint chipped, were the room's only furnishings. They had been left alone, but an officer, stationed in the corridor outside, kept them under constant observation through a dark window.

'Yes, I'm all right,' he replied. 'The food isn't too good, but I don't expect I will be here very long.'

'I hope not, Billy,' she said. She paused. 'Did you see your lawyers today?'

Billy brightened up noticeably.

'Yes,' he replied. 'Some of them. That's why I don't think I will be here very long.'

Eve looked doubtful. 'Is that what they told you?' she asked.

He laughed. 'No, no, they don't say things like that. But they don't have to, do they? They know what they are doing, that's the important thing.'

'Well, who are they?' she asked. 'I met Mr Singer, but…'

'No,' Billy replied. 'It's not Mr Singer. He doesn't do cases like this, and besides, he's from St Ives, isn't he? No, these gentlemen are from London. I have my solicitor, Mr Davis, who came today, and my barrister, Mr Schroeder – both from London.'

'From London,' she echoed.

'Yes, and that's not all, either.'

'Oh?'

'No. Because it's a serious case, I not only get a barrister, I get a main barrister.'

'A main barrister? What do you mean?'

'Well, my barrister, Mr Schroeder, does most of the work getting the case ready, with Mr Davis. But then there's another barrister, Mr Hardcastle, and he's a very important gentleman, and he will argue my case in front of the judge and jury. So he is my main barrister.'

'That sounds very good,' she conceded. 'It sounds as though they are looking after you.'

He nodded. 'This Mr Hardcastle is so important,' he said, 'that apparently I won't see him until the trial starts, except possibly once. He's too busy, see.'

Eve was looking doubtful again.

'Well that can't be right, Billy, can it?' she asked. 'How is he going to argue your case unless he comes and talks to you and finds out what happened, and…?'

'That's where Mr Davis and Mr Schroeder come in,' Billy explained patiently. 'It's their job to tell Mr Hardcastle all about the case, so that he can prepare himself to argue it. That's the way they do it in London, these important barristers.'

'Well, all right,' she said. She thought for some time. 'If you say it's all right, I'm sure it is. But did they tell you what they are going to do? I mean, you said they know what they are doing. Did they…?'

'Yes,' he replied emphatically, leaning forward towards her across the table. 'I have – what did they call it? – an alibi.'

'What's that?' she asked.

'It's a legal term,' he explained. 'It means I wasn't on that boat, so I couldn't have killed that man, or… well, I couldn't have done whatever else they say…'

'Well, if they know that…'

'No, well, the police don't know it, or they don't believe me. So…' He hesitated.

'What?' she asked.

'So you and I have to tell the jury that I wasn't there. Both of us. Mr Schroeder was very insistent about that, Eve, Mr Davis too. If we both tell them, it will be much better than just me telling them. So Mr Davis will take a statement from both of us when he comes next time, to show to Mr Hardcastle so that he knows what questions to ask us.'

She stared at him blankly.

'But Billy, I don't know where you were,' she said quietly, as if concerned that the prison officer might overhear.

The same thought occurred to Billy. They continued to speak in lowered voices.

'Of course you do,' he insisted.

'No. I don't. Not really. I know you went out to work at the pub like you always do. But you know I go to bed early, before closing time. I know you were in your bed when I woke up the next morning.'

And you didn't come to me during the night, she added, in the silence of her own mind. *And I don't know what you do on those nights when you don't come to me.*

'Well, there you are, then,' he said. 'I came home from work. I didn't want to wake you. Where would I go at that time of night?'

'Well, I will tell them what I know, Billy, but I can't... you know...'

Billy pushed himself back into his chair.

'Eve, look, I have to get out of here...'

'I know, Billy.'

'All I'm saying is, perhaps you will remember something. Perhaps you heard me come in, when I turned my key in the door, or walked upstairs, you know. Perhaps you left your bedroom door open and saw me going to my room. You could have woken up for a moment and just forgot about it.'

Eve didn't respond – she seemed to be thinking hard.

'Eve, you must be worrying about money with me not working.'

She nodded.

'It's hard, Billy,' she said. 'I'm worried about all the bills, and things that have to be done around the house, you know. There's the roof needing some new slates and there are pipes that need lagging, and you're not there, and there's no money to pay anyone to come in and do it.'

'Well, there you are then...'

'And there's another thing, Billy.'

'What?'

'The River Board say I wouldn't be able to stay on in the house if you... well, if you are away a long time. They would have to find someone to take over the lock, you see.'

'Are they seeing to it properly?' he asked. 'Are they keeping the lock up, cutting back the rushes?'

'Yes, they send somebody,' she replied.

'Because if you let it go, if you let it get out of hand, it's the devil's own job to get it back under control after.'

'Yes, I know,' she replied.

There was a long silence between them.

'If I did remember something,' she said, 'should I tell Mr...?'

'Mr Davis. Yes. But wait until he comes to see you.'

'All right. If I do remember...'

'And Eve,' Billy added. 'Don't tell Mr Davis anything about us, you know, you and me. It wouldn't help the case, and it's got nothing to do with it anyway.'

She stared at her brother for a long time, feeling the coldness around her neck. Her hand moved instinctively as she traced the outline of the missing chain on her skin.

'Billy, you did find that girl's cross and chain, didn't you?'

'Of course I did,' he replied, a little too quickly.

She nodded.

'And you do have... what was it? An alibi?'

'Of course I do.'

'All right, Billy,' she said. 'I'm going to go now.'

'And you will make a statement to Mr Davis?'

'I remember you being in bed the next morning,' she said, 'but I will try to remember more, Billy. I will try very hard.'

18

'MR SINGER AND I are not staying long, Ben,' Barratt Davis said, as Merlin showed the two men and Jess Farrar into Ben's room in Chambers. 'We are dropping off some paperwork for you and Jess to look through and organise before we see Martin Hardcastle on Tuesday. I've sent copies to Martin's Chambers, of course, but he's not going to read it before the consultation, knowing him. So you're going to have to explain it all to him.'

Alan, the junior clerk, in his shirt-sleeves, carried a large box into the room with obvious effort, and dumped it unceremoniously beside Ben's desk.

'That's it,' Barratt said. 'Should be enough to keep you busy for a while.'

'Should be,' Ben replied, gesturing to his visitors to sit. 'Thank you, Alan.'

'Tea or coffee, anyone?' Merlin asked.

'A cup of tea would go down very well,' Singer replied. 'I had to leave St Ives rather too early this morning. Milk and one sugar, please.'

The others declined, and Merlin disappeared discreetly.

'I do also want to bring you up to date with what we have been doing,' Barratt said. 'John has been visiting Billy Cottage at Bedford Gaol regularly since he was remanded. But we did not want to begin the process of taking instructions until we were fairly sure we understood the prosecution's case against him. In addition, John thought he wasn't ready...'

'He appeared to be in shock for the first week or two,' Singer said. 'He couldn't concentrate very well. It was almost as if he didn't believe what was happening – as though he thought that any moment they would simply open the gates and let him out, so that he could go home and attend to his lock.'

'I've seen the same reaction before, in other defendants in his position,' Barratt said quietly. 'There's nothing you can do except wait for them to adjust to their new reality. You can't rush it. You just have to wait until they are able and ready to talk to you.'

'Has he been able to give you further instructions?' Ben asked.

'Yes. John let me know as soon as he thought we might make some progress. We have had two conferences with Cottage since then, within the last two weeks. You will find his signed proof of evidence among the papers. I am sure that, when you read through it, you will see a number of points at which his account of the facts seems rather…'

There was a knock and the door opened. Merlin entered, bearing a cup of tea for Singer.

'Can Miss Fisk pop in just for a second, sir?' Merlin asked. 'She needs a book.'

'Of course,' Ben replied.

Harriet entered hurriedly, apologetically.

Everyone stood, and Ben raised a hand towards Harriet.

'May I introduce Harriet Fisk? We joined Chambers together, and we share this room. Harriet has graciously allowed me to take it over to some extent today. Harriet – you know Barratt Davis, of course, his legal assistant, Jess Farrar, and John Singer, a solicitor from Huntingdonshire.'

'Nice to meet you all. Sorry, Ben,' Harriet smiled. 'Must have my copy of the County Court Practice. I didn't realise you'd started.'

'No problem,' Ben replied. 'Jess and I will be on our own, poring over papers, most of the day. It's not going to disturb us if you come and go.'

Harriet quickly selected the volume she needed from her desk.

'Ah, the Green Book,' John Singer smiled. 'I've spent many happy hours immersed in that tome.'

'Mr Singer doesn't have much of a life, Miss Fisk,' Barratt said.

'Neither do I,' Harriet smiled. 'Especially when I have pleadings due.'

She left as quickly as she had come.

'Does Miss Fisk ever do ecclesiastical law?' Singer asked.

Jess reached out an arm and pushed him in the shoulder.

'You would have to ask Merlin,' Ben smiled. 'Now, you were saying – about Cottage's proof of evidence?'

'He puts forward an alibi,' Barratt replied. 'But it doesn't account for all the prosecution's evidence. That is something we are going to have to talk about once you have been through all those papers. The good news is that the alibi is supported by his sister, Eve, as far as it goes. Essentially, they say, Billy was working an evening shift at a local pub. That wasn't unusual. He did it to supplement his income from the lock. He left just after closing time and made his way home. He remained at home the rest of the night and didn't go out until the next day. If the trial began tomorrow, I would say he would not make a great witness. His education is limited and he gets frustrated easily. It wouldn't surprise me if he has quite a temper. But his demeanour may improve a bit once the trial gets closer.'

'What about the sister?'

'Barratt asked me to interview her,' Singer replied. 'She has the reputation locally of being a bit slow. So we thought it would be better to have someone from St Ives talk to her.'

'Good idea,' Ben nodded.

'I'm not at all convinced she is slow,' Singer said. 'I spent a long time with her. I had to, just to gain her trust. She didn't understand who I was or what I was doing, to begin with. At first, she seemed concerned that I had something to do with the police. I had to explain to her that I was there to help Billy. But at least that gave me time to observe her and, based on what I saw, I think her mind is fairly normal. She hasn't had much by way of an education – neither of them did, according to local people who know the family – so she speaks in a rather simple way, almost child-like at times. But she understood my questions, and she did corroborate her brother's alibi to some extent. She says he was at home in bed when she woke up the next morning. The only thing is…'

'Go on,' Ben encouraged.

'Well… she does have a tendency to agree with what is being said to her at any given time. I would put things to her and she would agree, almost as if she felt she had to. I deliberately put one or two things to her to see if she would contradict herself, and once or twice she did, though she corrected herself when I pointed it out. I am not sure what may happen when she is cross-examined, to be honest.'

Ben nodded. 'Well, that's a useful thing to know in advance,' he said. 'We will have more questions to put to both of them when we have been through the prosecution's papers.'

Barratt stood.

'Ben, John has indicated that he does not wish to be involved in this case indefinitely. I quite understand that. He is busy with diocesan matters, and…'

'And I don't have the stomach for it, to be quite honest, Mr Schroeder. Mr Little is about the limit for me as far as criminal work is concerned,' Singer said. 'So Barratt will be Mr Cottage's solicitor of record from Monday.'

Ben stood also.

'Quite all right,' he said. 'Thank you for everything you have done. But I am going to ask one thing. If we need to interview Eve again, it would be best for you to do that. You have her trust, and it sounds as though that is important. It wouldn't help if someone else had to start again from the beginning.'

'I'd be glad to do that,' Singer said, as they shook hands.

'Call the office if you have any questions,' Barratt said, on his way out. 'And let's talk before we go to see Martin on Tuesday.'

When they had gone, Ben and Jess looked at each other.

'Where do you want to start?' she asked.

Ben took off his jacket, put it on a heavy wooden hanger, and hung it on the coat rack which stood behind the door. He undid his tie and threw it deftly on to his desk. He pointed in the direction of the bottom shelf of the huge bookcase which occupied most of the wall to the left of his desk.

'There are files and assorted office supplies over there. First, I want to find out what is in that box. Then I want to get all the paperwork organised, filed and labelled. Then we can actually start reading it and finding out what this case is really about.'

'I'm good at cross-referencing,' Jess volunteered. 'I helped the librarian re-arrange every book the school had when I was in the sixth form.'

'All right. We will put that talent to good use. Let's drag the box into the middle of the room. We will probably have to sit on the floor, I'm afraid.'

'My natural habitat,' she smiled.

'Would you like some coffee? I can have Alan make some.'

'Yes, actually that would be good. No milk, just a little sugar.'

Together, they dragged the box from the side of Ben's desk.

'Not too far,' she suggested. 'So we can lean against the back of your desk and still reach it.'

Ben left to make arrangements for the coffee. When he and Alan returned a few minutes later with coffee for both of them and a plate of ginger biscuits, Jess had removed her shoes and was sitting, cross-legged, between the box and his desk, a pencil between her lips and a sheaf of papers on her lap. Two large empty files and a pile of labels and dividers were within easy reach of her left hand. Ben sat down beside her.

'Why don't I glance at each document we come to?' he suggested. 'I will start to build up a picture of the case, and we can devise a filing system for them according to subject matter.'

'And according to date,' Jess added. 'Chronology matters too, yes?'

'Yes, indeed,' Ben replied. He reached up and seized a blue notebook from his desk. 'I will start making some notes as we go along.'

The time was 10.15.

* * *

By 3.30 that same afternoon the box Barratt Davis had brought had been emptied and an impressive array of files, labelled, indexed and cross-referenced, was spread across the room. Two plates, which had held sandwiches, supplied by Alan from a café on Fleet Street and consumed hastily during a short lunch break, lay pushed up against the bookcase. Jess was leaning back wearily against Ben's desk. She slowly untangled her legs from their crossed position, and stretched them out in front of her.

'I'm not sure I can get up,' she said. 'I may have to stay here until my legs start working again. I don't think they have any blood going through them.'

'My legs are all right,' he said. 'But my back is aching.' He sat up, straightening his back as much as it would allow. 'Well, at least we have something to show for it, don't we? It all looks very different from that pile of paper we were handed this morning.'

'I think we should both get medals.'

'We should. And we have definitely earned our weekends.'

Her head dropped. 'Don't remind me,' she said.

'What?'

'The weekend. Don't remind me.'

'Not looking forward to it?'

She sighed, tentatively rotating her ankles and flexing her toes to see if they were working.

'Oh, it's just that it's nothing special – again. Having nothing else to do, I will take the train down to darkest Sussex and while away the hours with my parents, as usual. I really need to spend more time arranging things to do in London – or anywhere. It's not as though I don't have friends. But since I've been working for Barratt, the working week is such a whirlwind that I never seem to get around to planning anything. If I keep it up much longer, my friends are going to forget who I am.'

Ben twisted round to face her.

'Would you like to do something different – really?'

'Yes.'

'Have you ever been to a football match?'

She smiled at him in surprise.

'Well, I used to watch my brothers play for their school.'

Ben returned the smile. 'That's not what I mean,' he said. 'I mean a *real* football match, in the First Division.'

'What, in a big ground, with thousands of people shouting at each other?'

'Exactly.'

'No. Never.'

Ben took a deep breath.

'Well, why don't you give it a try tomorrow afternoon. My family is from the East End, and we are all West Ham supporters. My father can usually get tickets. Sometimes I take a young friend with me. His name is Simon Dougherty; he has just turned eleven, and he is the step-son of a member of Chambers, Kenneth Gaskell. Simon grew up in Walthamstow and has supported the Hammers all his life. I often take him to a match if his father can't take him for some reason. We've arranged to go tomorrow. We are playing Manchester United at home, Upton Park. You would be very welcome to join us.'

Ben's stomach tightened into a knot as he spoke. He suddenly felt exposed, vulnerable. He had been stupid, he had spoken without thinking. He had offended her. He began to search his mind for any graceful way to withdraw. He had been presumptuous. He was…

'That sounds like fun,' she was saying. 'That gives me the perfect reason to stay in London for the night, and I will have a new experience tomorrow.' She experimented with pushing herself up. 'Oh, thank God, I think my legs have started responding. I might even be able to stand up.'

Ben rose to his feet and stood in front of her. He offered both hands. She accepted. He pulled her to her feet and brought her shoes. She put a hand on his shoulder to support herself as she put them on.

'I usually meet Simon at Waterloo at midday,' he said. 'Kenneth and Anne live down in Surrey, so they put him on the train. I pick him up, we have lunch, and it gives us plenty of time to get to Upton Park. But I can arrange to pick you up later along the way, if you prefer.'

'No. Waterloo at twelve would be fine,' she said. 'Let's meet under the clock. I look forward to it.'

She walked slowly towards the door, then suddenly stopped, and turned to face him. Her face suggested concern.

'Oh, there is just one thing I think you should know…' she began. Ben's heart began to sink again. He felt his anxiety return.

'What's that?'

'My father and brothers support Arsenal,' she replied. 'Is that a problem?'

'Only if you do,' he smiled.

Harriet Fisk passed Jess in the doorway, as she was coming in and Jess was leaving.

'My word, you two have been busy,' Harriet said, with approval. 'It seems you had a more productive day than I did, trying to get a county court registrar to listen to me.'

'Yes, I think we did rather well,' Ben replied with a smile.

19

THEY STOOD TOGETHER at the end of Platform 9, and waved to Simon until his train was almost out of sight. She took his arm and they turned to leave the station. He was still crestfallen.

'I'm sorry, Ben. They had an off-day, didn't they?'

'They certainly did. Losing 2-0 at home to that lot. I don't know what the world is coming to.'

She laughed. 'I'm sorry,' she said. 'I know it's not funny. But you and Simon were such a pair. I've never seen two such glum faces.'

Ben grinned ruefully. 'I know,' he said. 'It's the price you pay for being a fan. But apart from that, did you enjoy it?'

'I did, actually. Honestly, I wasn't sure I would. But it was really exciting, all those people cheering their team on when they were attacking, groaning when the other side scored. I got quite carried away. I would do it again. And the least I can do is try to cheer you up – unless you have other plans?'

Ben shook his head. 'No, none at all. What do you have in mind?'

She tucked her arm more tightly under his. 'We're going to start with a brisk walk over Waterloo Bridge – unless you have had enough of cold, damp fresh air for one day?'

'No, that sounds good.'

'It will blow the sad thoughts away, and remind you that there is always next week.'

'Never was a truer word spoken,' Ben groaned. 'We are playing Manchester United again next week, in the Cup.

'Exactly my point,' she said. 'The Hammers have every incentive to make sure it doesn't happen twice.'

They walked slowly together out of the station and along the approach to Waterloo Bridge. It was after 7 o'clock and already growing dark. A cold breeze was blowing across the river; there was a very slight mist and the suggestion of rain in the air. As they approached the bridge, the lights of the buildings on the far side of the river twinkled through the gathering gloom. St Paul's Cathedral loomed into view to their right, the Houses of Parliament almost tucked away in a corner to their left as the river took a sharp turn. Traffic was light, and only one or two pedestrians passed them on the bridge.

'How did you come to meet Simon?' she asked.

'It was while his mother was getting her divorce,' he replied. 'Kenneth was acting for her.'

He sensed Jess turn her face towards him.

'And now Kenneth and Anne are...?'

'Yes,' he replied. 'It was rather quick. There were all kinds of rumours. But they had known each other years before. I suppose it all re-kindled. Anyway...'

'Anyway...'

'Anyway, I was in Chambers on a Friday afternoon. I can picture it exactly. It was the same afternoon Merlin gave me Bourne & Davis's brief for Sergeant Mulcahy.'

'Your first case.'

'My first case. I was about to go home for the day. But I was passing the clerk's room, and I saw this little boy sitting in the waiting area, looking completely forlorn. He was wearing a West Ham scarf. So I approached him and talked to him. Anne was in conference with Kenneth, or she was in his room, anyway. I didn't find out the details of the case until much later, but Simon was having a terrible time of it. Anne's husband was violent towards her when he was drunk, which was almost every night, and Simon saw a lot of the violence. I didn't know any of that when I first saw him. He just struck me as sad, and he seemed so lost, so alone, sitting there.'

She squeezed his arm.

'So I asked him if he would like to come to Upton Park with me for the next home game. Anne didn't seem to mind, so we went. Once the divorce was final, and the husband had some access to Simon at weekends, I thought that would be that. But he can't take Simon to all the games, so now we work it out between us.'

'Well I think it's really wonderful that you do that for him,' she said. 'I could see how much it means to him. He seemed really happy – except when Manchester United scored the two goals, of course. Sorry, won't mention that again.'

Ben laughed. 'I'd already forgotten about it,' he said. He paused. 'I'm glad I can do something for Simon. But I get a lot out of it, too. It takes my mind off work. If I go to a game on my own I'm usually pre-occupied with some problem in a case, but with Simon I have to concentrate on what's going on here and now. It's good for me. It also reminds me of how lucky I am to have my family.'

'Do you have a big family?'

'Not huge, but more than enough. They all live in Whitechapel, near the family business.'

'Oh?'

'Yes, Schroeder's Furs and Fine Apparel in Commercial Road. The family has been in the business for generations, but we are originally from Vienna. We moved to London at the turn of the century, settled in the East End, and started up the business again, just as it was in the old country.'

'Tell me about your parents. Do you have brothers and sisters?'

'One of each. Larry is almost seventeen and Ella is thirteen. My father, David, is the main partner in the business. He runs it with my uncle Eli. My mother, Ruth, worked there too for a long time, but she stayed home with Larry and Ella. She is a fantastic cook, among other things. Then there is my grandfather, Joshua. He actually came to court for Sergeant Mulcahy's case, without telling me. He sat in the public gallery and didn't announce himself until it was over.'

She laughed. 'Good for him.'

'Yes. Then there are all kinds of uncles and aunts and cousins who descend on us at Passover and Hanukkah. To be honest, I don't know who all of them are, or how they are related to us, but no one seems to mind. It can be a bit chaotic at times, but it has always been a warm, loving home.'

He paused.

'The family has done quite well financially. But we have – I don't quite know how to say it – something of an identity crisis. We are not sure who we are: Austrian, English, Jewish, all of those things.

So we have always tried hard to be part of the community. Part of that is the synagogue, of course. The family is observant, but my parents didn't bring us up to be too strict, certainly about food. We keep away from pork, but we are not kosher. But we also try hard to be English and Londoners, specifically East Enders, so we support West Ham and all the rest of it. And…'

'And..?'

'And I never talk this much. I must be boring you to death.'

'Not in the least. Talk to me all you want. It's interesting.'

They had crossed the river and were walking the few yards towards the Strand and Aldwych.

'Are you hungry?' she asked.

'Starving. It seems a long time since lunch.'

'Do you like Indian food?'

'I've never tried it. There are one or two Indian restaurants open now in Commercial Road. I keep meaning to try it, but I never have.'

'Ah,' she said. 'Well, it's high time you did. We don't have to go as far as the Commercial Road. There is one not far from here, within striking distance of the Temple. Barratt introduced me to it. People from the firm go there for dinner quite often.'

They turned right on to the Strand. The restaurant was unobtrusive, apparently part of a small commercial hotel, its presence marked only by a small, dark sign. They had to climb three flights of stairs to reach it. The restaurant was dim and sparsely furnished, with small framed chairs and tables with chipped formica tops.

'It dates back to 1946,' Jess smiled, as they were seated, 'and I don't think they have altered, or even decorated the place at all since then. It's one of London's better-kept secrets. You wouldn't be likely to find it if you didn't know it was here. And if you didn't know how good the food is, you would probably think twice about staying, even if you did find it.'

A waiter brought menus, and they ordered beers.

'Why don't you let me order for you?' she suggested. 'Indian food can be quite spicy and it's best to start off with something fairly mild until you get used to it.'

Ben sipped his beer happily.

'Order away,' he replied. 'I'm sure I'm in good hands.'

'Are you the first in your family to go to the Bar?' she asked, as the waiter retreated towards the kitchen with their order.

Ben nodded.

'They must be very proud of you.'

He sighed, and leaned forward with his arms on the table.

'I think so. I know my mother and my grandfather are. It was a problem for my father.'

'Why?'

'Because, as the oldest son, I am supposed to take over the business when he dies. Which means that I was supposed to work in the business as soon as I was old enough.'

She sat back, nodding.

'Yes, I see. A long tradition?'

'Long enough. But I just could not see myself doing it. I knew before I left school that I wanted to come to the Bar. But I had to persuade...' He stopped and laughed. 'If I tell you this, you are going to think we are all very strange. I'm sure you do already.'

'No. Go on.'

'Well, before anyone in the family takes a major decision, it has to be the subject of a round-table conference, with all available adult family members present. I used to call it the family council. My decision to become a lawyer was discussed several times. I am sure you can imagine. My father would be talking about how I was betraying the family. But my grandfather and my mother, and even my Uncle Eli, stood up for me. My grandfather gave me the money to join the Middle Temple and find a pupillage. But not before we had discussed every aspect of my becoming a barrister, including how it might be the end of civilisation as we knew it.'

Jess's eyes had opened wide. 'That sounds terrifying!'

'Actually,' Ben replied, 'it was good practice for the Bar in a way. I had to argue for what I wanted; I had to explain it, justify it.' He laughed. 'They would not have minded half as much if I had decided to become a solicitor.'

'Oh?'

'That might have been useful to the business.' On an impulse, he mimicked his father, holding his hands out wide, the voice with its modulated East End accent pitch perfect. 'Do you know how much we pay Morton Levenson year after year?'

She laughed, then became serious.

'So, that's quite a burden you've taken on yourself.'

'How do you mean?'

'To prove to your father that you have done the right thing, even if it means breaking with tradition; to show the family council that they were right to give you that opportunity. Don't you feel that as quite a responsibility?'

Ben thought for some time.

'Perhaps,' he replied. 'But they have never held it over my head. I'm sure it still rankles with my father, but he has never brought it up. They all take a keen interest in what I'm doing. And I've always had confidence in myself. For me, the real question is...'

The waiter returned with chapatis and condiments, hot pickle, and a dish of chopped onions. Jess could sense Ben's hesitation. She wanted to reassure him that he did not have to open up to her.

'Ben...'

'For me, the question is whether I fit in. Barristers generally come from very different backgrounds to mine. They mostly went to public schools and either Oxford or Cambridge, they belong to the right clubs, they...'

'Most of them are not Jewish kids from the East End,' she said, matter-of-factly. 'No, they are not. And that's why it is so good that you have made it to the Bar. You are breaking two traditions, not just one.'

'I felt it when I was taken on in Chambers. I know that there is at least one member who didn't want me.'

She nodded.

'But here you are.' She paused. 'Ben, you have been very frank with me, which I really appreciate. In return, I want to tell you something which you probably don't realise.'

He nodded enquiringly.

'Do you know why Barratt Davis likes you so much?'

Ben shrugged. 'I've always thought it was because I won that case for Sergeant Mulcahy.'

She shook her head. 'That is part of it. But all the barristers we use get good results in court. That's why we go to them.' She sat up straight. 'No, he respects the way you have fought your way into the profession, as well as how good you are in court. He knows you have had to stand up and assert yourself, both in and out of court. That's something Barratt admires – because it's something he could never do himself.'

Ben opened his eyes wide.

'It's true. Barratt is very good at what he does. He is a model solicitor. He is wonderful with clients. They trust him, they talk to him, they give him information, often without even knowing it. He is also well organised and efficient. But if he lives to be a hundred, he will never stand up in court and do what you do. He won't even appear on his own in the magistrates' court to do a guilty plea. The very thought of speaking in public terrifies him. His partner, Geoff Bourne, does it. He is in the magistrates' court and the county court all the time. But not Barratt. Oh, he has a good line of banter about being a mere solicitor, and about barristers being superior, which I am sure becomes irritating after a while. But the thing is, he actually means it. He is in awe of the Bar – and of you. He will never say that to you, not in a million years, but that doesn't mean I can't say it.'

Ben sat back in his chair.

'What I mean to say, Ben,' she continued, 'is that the very thing you fear may go against you can also be your greatest strength. I don't doubt for a moment that you are going to succeed at the Bar, and neither should you.'

20

'SUMMARISE THE CASE for me, Schroeder, please,' Martin Hardcastle said, lighting a cigarette.

Ben was seated in front of Hardcastle's desk, to his right. Next to Ben sat Barratt Davis, and next to Barratt, Jess Farrar. Ben had the feeling that his life was, for the time being, composed of an endless series of new and uncomfortable experiences, each no doubt designed to enable him to learn, and each hugely disconcerting. He had attended consultations with Silks as a pupil with Gareth Morgan-Davies, but always as an observer. Silks, he knew, had high expectations. They took for granted that their juniors would know the case inside out, and would take control of the mundane research and paperwork which was a necessary part of every case, leaving the Silk free to spend his time in the intellectual stratosphere, in profound contemplation of the law, strategy, and tactics. Gareth, who was close to taking Silk himself, and who was in any case senior enough to allow such pretension to flow over his head with an amused detachment, was able to hold his own, and insist on a realistic division of the work. But Ben, as junior as he was, would put himself at Hardcastle's disposal.

Sometimes the preparation and paperwork could be done at leisure, but not in a capital murder case. From the day the defendant was charged with capital murder, there was a relentless pressure to get the case ready for trial with as little delay as possible. The pressure affected prosecution and defence alike, with the result that all participants became extremely fraught. Ben had done what he could to master the papers he and Jess had worked their way through. Now these would be subjected to the critical eye of a leading criminal Silk.

He found Hardcastle a strangely imposing figure. He was not a large man, but he made up for any lack of size by a certain presence, the source of which was hard to define. It was partly due, no doubt, to his immaculate appearance. A dark grey three-piece pin-stripe, the pin-stripe judged to perfection – any whiter and it would undermine the serious greyness of the suit, any bolder and it would betray the wearer's lack of height. The tie, a lighter grey with white dots, was tied firmly, yet did not look tight and had not a single crease. His room was unusually decorated for a room in Chambers. No dark colours and racing prints. Instead, the walls were painted in the palest of greens, and the modern artwork featured lines and boxes in the style of Mondriaan.

But what disconcerted Ben most was his desk. Save for a large cut-glass ashtray, a silver cigarette box and a matching tabletop lighter, the desk was almost empty. Barratt Davis's brief lay unopened, its contents neatly tied together under the back-sheet by lengths of pink ribbon. No notebook, no pen was visible, and Hardcastle himself sat still, his eyes nearly closed, as if to absorb everything said to him by the force of his concentration, without any need for an aide-memoire. He had greeted Barratt Davis warmly enough when they entered his room, but a brief nod of the head sufficed for Ben and Jess.

'*Silks don't actually live in a different world,*' Gareth had once remarked after a particularly trying afternoon. '*They just think they do.*'

Ben was trying hard to hang on to that thought.

'At about 10.30 on the evening of 25 January of this year, a Saturday night,' Ben began, 'a young courting couple, Frank Gilliam and Jennifer Doyce, were seen to leave the Oliver Cromwell pub, in St Ives, Huntingdonshire, together. The pub is very close to the north bank of the River Ouse. They walked in an easterly direction through some meadows along the river bank. A witness, Mavis Brown, who works in her father's corner shop close to where the meadows begin, sold them two packets of Woodbine cigarettes. They were never seen alive again. The same witness, Mavis Brown, says that, just a few minutes after the couple left the shop, she saw a man walking in the same direction. She had a clear view of him and gave a detailed description. She did not know the man, but she heard him singing a song to himself, the *Lincolnshire Poacher*. This was just before 11 o'clock.

'At about 8.30 on the morning of 27 January, Archie Knights, a retired army officer, was walking his dog further downstream, by Holywell Fen, when he passed a houseboat called the *Rosemary D*. The *Rosemary D* had been owned by a couple called Douglas who are wanted by the police in connection with fraud. It seems they had to leave St Ives in something of a hurry, and they left the boat in place with all its effects. It has since been used fairly regularly by courting couples who want a private place to be together. The police surmise that is why Frank and Jennifer would have been there. Knights noticed something odd – something about the door. Something did not look right to him. He boarded the craft to take a look.'

Ben took a slow breath as he turned a page in his notebook.

'He found Frank Gilliam dead. He was lying on the floor. His skull had been fractured by multiple blows with a blunt instrument. Jennifer Doyce was lying on the bed, her dress pulled up, her underwear pulled down, exposing her genitals. She also had trauma to the head from a blunt instrument, and she had been raped. But she was alive – just about. There was blood everywhere. Subsequently, police recovered a winch handle from the river, which had formed part of the equipment of the *Rosemary D*. It is stained with blood, somewhat degraded, but identifiable as stains of blood of two different groups: group A, Jennifer's blood group; and group O, Frank's group. The scene of crime officer also lifted a fingerprint from the inside ledge of a window, which is identified as that of Billy Cottage. The fingerprint is next to a blood stain, identified as blood of group A.'

Ben flicked over the pages of his notebook and continued.

'Jennifer Doyce has told the police that the man who assaulted and raped her, and who assaulted and killed Frank Gilliam, was singing a song under his breath while raping her. It was the *Lincolnshire Poacher*. When she went to the *Rosemary D* with Frank that night, Jennifer was wearing a heavy and expensive gold cross and chain that had belonged to her grandmother. There were marks on her neck suggesting that it had been forcibly removed. When the police went to Cottage's house to interview him on Thursday 30 January, they found his sister, Eve, wearing the same cross and chain. She said her brother had given it to her. When interviewed, Cottage admitted that he had given it to her. He said he had found it but, unfortunately, he gave the police several conflicting accounts of where and when he had found it. He also denied ever being on board the *Rosemary D.*'

Ben closed his notebook.

'The other point of interest is that Billy Cottage has a previous conviction for indecent exposure. An officer found him masturbating in a garden while watching a young woman undress in her bedroom. When arrested...'

'When arrested, he was singing the *Lincolnshire Poacher* to himself.' Hardcastle had listened to Ben's presentation without a word, eyes closed, inhaling deeply from his cigarette, otherwise motionless. Now, he suddenly came to life, his eyes opening wide, sitting forward, his hands folded in front of him. 'Which means we can't challenge Mavis Brown or Jennifer Doyce about their ability to recognise obscure folk tunes when people hum them – not without bringing in the previous conviction.'

Hardcastle lit another cigarette.

'What is Cottage's blood group?'

Ben looked at Barratt Davis, who shook his head.

'I will find out,' he replied, making a note.

'Where exactly was Cottage's fingerprint found?' Hardcastle asked.

'On an interior window ledge, opposite the bed, in the aft cabin.'

'The cabin where Frank and Jennifer were found?'

'Yes.'

'Do we know whether the fingerprint was on top of or underneath the blood stain, or perhaps mixed with it?'

Ben reached for a file from the pile he had placed by the side of his chair. Hardcastle held up a hand.

'Let me save you the trouble. The answer is "no, we don't know",' he said. 'There is not a word in the fingerprint examiner's report that tells us one way or the other. It may be that he does not know. That would be excellent news.' He looked at Ben. 'Because...?'

'Fingerprints can't be dated,' Ben replied. 'If we can't answer that question, we can't rule out the possibility that the fingerprint was already on the window ledge before the evening of 25 January.'

Hardcastle pointed the cigarette approvingly.

'Very good. That would mean that Cottage is a liar, but not necessarily a murderer. What is Jennifer Doyce's condition and prognosis?'

'She has made a remarkable recovery. When she first arrived at Addenbrookes they didn't think she would last into the next day. Then they thought she would have permanent brain damage. But she woke up and confounded everyone. She is still in a wheelchair. But the doctors don't think there are any more internal injuries. She is likely to make a full recovery, but of course, they are not sure how long that will take. She is expected to be able to give evidence, at trial, if not the committal.'

'Which is both good and bad for Mr Cottage,' Hardcastle said. 'It is bad because it means that she will give evidence against him, *Lincolnshire Poacher* included. On the other hand, it is also good because it means that the prosecution will only have one indictment for murder. Of course, they are proceeding on the Gilliam murder first.'

'Yes,' Ben replied. 'There is a second indictment waiting in the wings, alleging the attempted murder and rape of Jennifer Doyce and the theft of the gold cross and chain.'

'All of which also comes into evidence on the murder indictment, unless we can find a very ingenious reason to keep it out,' Hardcastle observed.

He paused.

'Why is this a capital murder? There was no use of a firearm, and Frank Gilliam was not a police or prison officer killed in the line of duty.'

'The prosecution will argue that the murder was in the course or furtherance of theft,' Ben replied. 'The girl was wearing a distinctive gold cross and chain, quite valuable, which was found in Billy Cottage's possession. Marks on her neck suggest that it was taken from her forcibly at the scene.'

'But *she's* not dead, is she?' Hardcastle insisted. 'It was *her* cross and chain, but it's the *boyfriend* who is dead. If he stole from her, and she's alive...?'

Ben nodded and continued the thought.

'Then how can the murder of *Gilliam* be in the course or furtherance of theft? Yes. That occurred to me too. It may be that we can argue that the judge should order the prosecution to amend the indictment to one for non-capital murder.'

'What's the argument against that?'

'He could have killed Frank to enable him to steal from Jennifer. He doesn't have to kill the person he steals from. A bank robber kills a security guard. But he steals from the bank. It's still capital murder.'

'Yes,' Hardcastle agreed quietly. 'Still, the motive they really want to put before the jury is rape, not theft, isn't it? What if the theft was an afterthought? What if he kills Gilliam so that he can be free to rape Jennifer Doyce? Only when he's finished with her does he notice the cross and chain, and thinks, "that might fetch a bob or two down the market" or "that would look good on my sister", so he takes it as an afterthought. By that time, Frank is already dead.'

Ben nodded and made a note.

'Look at every case you can find,' Hardcastle instructed brusquely. 'Not just under the Homicide Act. Go back to the common law felony-murder rule. If you can't find any helpful cases here, try the main Commonwealth jurisdictions. The intent to steal ought to be formed before the murder is committed. If the prosecution can't prove that, it shouldn't go beyond non-capital murder.'

Hardcastle stubbed his cigarette out firmly.

'Very good, Schroeder,' he said. 'Now, Barratt, what does Mr Cottage have to say for himself?'

Barratt had opened his file. 'He worked at the Oliver Cromwell that Saturday evening. He did not notice Frank and Jennifer in particular, though he has no reason to doubt that they may have been there. It was a fairly busy night. He did not leave the pub until well after 11 o'clock. He can't be exact about the time, but whatever time it was, he went straight home, and stayed there, in bed, until the next morning. He didn't follow Frank and Jennifer, and he had no reason to know that they were aboard the *Rosemary D*. She is moored on the opposite bank of the river, so he would have had no reason to be there. Mavis Brown is mistaken and, in any case, she doesn't identify him.'

'Yes, she does, unfortunately,' Hardcastle responded quietly. 'So does Jennifer Doyce. What about the gold cross and chain?'

'He found it in some long grass by the river bank on the Tuesday, when he was in the area cutting back reeds and grass to keep the river clear of obstructions to navigation. It's part of his job. It was some distance from the crime scene area, which is why the police would have missed it. He admits that he lied to the police about where and when he found it, but he says he was frightened and panicked. He also accepts now that he should have handed it in, but it looked nice and it was obviously worth a bit.'

'Talking of lying to the police,' Hardcastle asked, 'how does he account for his fingerprint being found on the window ledge?'

'He now admits that he did board the *Rosemary D* on one occasion, probably two or three weeks before the murder. He was worried that she was a hazard to river traffic, and he wanted to see whether there was any information he could find to hand over to the River Board. He was hoping they would move her.'

'No good reason not to tell the police about that,' Hardcastle observed.

'No,' Barratt agreed quietly.

'I hope he's telling the truth about that,' Hardcastle said, after a pause. 'I really do. Because if the prosecution were ever able to prove that the blood stain got on to the window ledge before the fingerprint, or even at about the same time, Billy Cottage would hang. I don't think there would be anything we could do about it.'

21

ARTHUR LUDLOW HAD left the long brown envelope undisturbed on the telephone table by the front door, where his mother had placed it, in accordance with Ludlow family tradition, on the day it arrived. He left it there to preserve the memory; so that it would be waiting for him every day on his return from work; so that every day, he could re-live the moment when his life changed for ever. As he gently lifted the envelope from the table, feeling the familiar touch of the coarse brown paper, he would remember the heart-stopping moment when he carefully teased the top of the envelope open. He would read, as if for the first time, his name and address, written in black ink by someone with a neat hand: Arthur Ludlow Esq, (*'Esq'*, no less) 23 Borough View Road, Blackburn, Lancs; and above his address, at the top of the envelope, the printed capital letters: OHMS – On Her Majesty's Service. It was a daily pleasure that never grew old, never lost its sheen.

The letter written to Arthur 'On Her Majesty's Service' was no longer enclosed in the envelope in which it had arrived. It had long since hung, encased in an austere black frame, on the wall of the front room, next to a photograph of the family on holiday at Morecombe, circa 1938, and a commemorative plate depicting the Queen and Prince Philip on their wedding day. Arthur had placed it there so that he was free to gaze at it more or less at will, at any time of the day or night because, as custom dictated, the front room of the terraced house, while the most formally and expensively furnished, was used only when guests were expected on such special occasions as Christmas and funerals. At other times, it remained unoccupied, silent and aloof, a place of superiority far removed from the unassuming dullness of the rest of the house. Over the course of time, Arthur had gazed at it so often that he knew every word by heart. It was dated 25 November 1958, typed on Home Office stationery, his name and address repeated, top left, in the correct official manner.

Dear Sir,

I am directed by the Home Secretary to inform you that following your application and your interview and training at HM Prison, Pentonville, your name has been added to the list of persons competent for the office of executioner. You are reminded that, as the list of persons competent is in the possession of High Sheriffs and Governors, it is unnecessary to apply for employment in connection with an execution. Any such application may be regarded as objectionable conduct and may lead to the removal of your name from the list. You are also reminded that it is expected that the conduct and general behaviour of a person on the list will be respectable and discreet, not only at the place and time of execution, but before and subsequently.

A memorandum of the conditions to which any person acting as executioner is required to conform is enclosed for your attention. Any inquiry should be directed to the undersigned.

Yours Faithfully,

(Illegible handwritten signature)
James Milburn
Assistant Permanent Secretary

* * *

The chain of events which had led to the letter's arrival began early on a Saturday evening in a pub called the Anchor Inn, in Darwen. The Anchor was within reasonable walking distance from Ewood Park, home of Blackburn Rovers Football Club.

Life at 23 Borough View Road had continued, interrupted only by service in the world wars, for the lifetimes of two generations of Ludlows before Arthur. His father and grandfather had lived almost identical lives, working as assistant brewers at the Thwaites Brewery, a local landmark and valued contributor to the economy of the town. After an all-too-brief youth each had courted a local girl and brought her to the house as his bride; and each had a son, an only child. Arthur left school at 16 and, about four years before he could legally drink the product, was duly apprenticed in his turn to learn the trade of brewer at Thwaites. When he made his application to the Home Office, Arthur was 25 years of age, and a fully-qualified brewer. His father had been dead for three years. His mother looked after him and, although she was in robust good health, fretted constantly about the lack of a bride prepared to take her place when her time came.

Arthur's social life consisted of visits to Ewood Park; the occasional game of crown green bowls during the light summer evenings, a public green being conveniently situated just across the road from the house; and Saturday nights. Saturday night was spent at one or more pubs in the company of his two best friends, Sam Shuttleworth and Terry Pickup. The three young men had been at school together, and Sam now worked alongside Arthur at Thwaites. Terry drove a Blackburn Corporation bus. On Saturdays, when the Rovers were playing at home, they started with an afternoon at Ewood Park, from where they would adjourn to the Anchor Inn for a few pints to celebrate or drown their sorrows, as the case might be. It was during such an early autumn evening in 1957, after a dispiriting loss, that Arthur Ludlow saw the rest of his life staring him in the face from the dregs at the bottom of an empty pint glass. This was it. It was never going to change. He would follow in the footsteps of his father and grandfather; work as a brewer all his life as they had; die too young, as they had; live in the same house as they had; marry the same kind of woman as they had; and have nothing to look forward to except watching the Rovers and endless nights spent downing pints with Terry and Sam. Arthur loved and respected his parents and grandparents. He found no fault with their choice of lifestyle in the times in which they had lived. But the world was changing. There were opportunities available which past generations could not have dreamed of. He was in danger of letting them pass him by. He would leave the world having made no impression on it. And it was then that Arthur Ludlow decided that it was not enough; that he had to make some change, that he had to aspire to something more.

But however long he gazed into the dregs of his beer, he found no inspiration about what he was looking for, much less how he might go about attaining it.

He drained the glass and walked slowly to the bar. The depressing display at Ewood Park seemed to have sucked the life out of the supporters, and the Anchor Inn was relatively quiet. Only a scattering of blue and white scarves lay desolately on tables in front of groups of men of all ages who were making little conversation.

'Same again, Arthur?' the landlord asked.

'Aye, same again, Joe, thanks.'

'Where are your mates tonight? Didn't you go to t' match?'

Arthur tossed his head back in disgust.

'Aye, and a right bloody waste of time it were, an' all. If they get any worse, we'll be in't third division before long. Terry and Sam went home for tea. They'll be in for a pint later, happen.'

Arthur paid for his beer and was about to return to his seat.

'You can take a look at this while you wait, if you want,' Joe offered sympathetically, reaching for a copy of the *Daily Express* he had folded up at the side of the till behind the bar. 'It might take your mind off t' Rovers. It's yesterday's mind, but still...'

'Aye, I will, thanks,' Arthur replied.

He spread the newspaper out on the table and sipped his pint as he scanned stories about politics with little interest. He flipped through the pages quickly. Towards the end of the paper, just before the sports pages, were several pages of official announcements and advertisements for jobs. And there it was.

The Home Office

Additions to the List of Approved Executioners

The Home Office proposes to add a number of names to the list of persons competent to conduct executions. The list is provided to High Sheriffs and Governors of Prisons who are responsible for the carrying out of judgments of execution, and who may invite persons on the list to conduct a particular execution. Selection for the list is by interview and training. Candidates must be persons of exemplary character and in sound health. The Home Secretary wishes to emphasise that any evidence of prurient interest, or disposition towards

publicity seeking or sensationalism, will be regarded as disqualifications for the
position. Applications in writing should be sent to the address given below, giving
full details of the applicant's educational background and record of employment.
Full disclosure must be made of any disability.

Arthur had never thought very much about capital punishment. He
had accepted it as a part of British life. To the extent he had ever
considered the matter, he approved of it as a form of natural justice.
'An eye for an eye' was a lesson which had been drilled into him at
chapel every Sunday when he was a child, and he saw no reason to
question it. He supposed that there must be men who carried out
executions, but it had never before occurred to him to ask who they
were, or to imagine that such a position could be applied for. But
suddenly, everything became clear. He could be of service to High
Sheriffs and Governors. He could occupy a respected position in
public service. He could take the first steps towards a different life.
He did not, for one moment, doubt his ability to be a hangman, or
his temperament for the job.

When Terry and Sam made their way into the bar some forty
minutes later, the *Daily Express* was still open at the announcements
page on the table in front of him. Looking up, Arthur smiled brightly.

'What will it be, lads? A pint of the usual?'

'I don't know what you've got to be so bloody cheerful about,'
Terry replied. 'We played like a right bunch of old women.'

'It's just a game, Terry,' Arthur said brightly. 'Happen we'll win
next week.'

'Get home,' Sam said wearily. 'No bloody chance. Any road, after
this afternoon you shouldn't be looking that happy until you've had
at least three pints. What's up? Did somebody die and make you
rich?'

Arthur began his walk to the bar.

'No,' he replied. 'But I've made a decision about my future.'

Terry and Sam exchanged looks.

'Oh, aye?' Terry said.

'Aye. I'm going to be t' public hangman.'

Sam and Terry looked at each other for a moment, then burst out
laughing.

'Get home, you daft bugger,' Sam said.

'I bloody am, an' all,' Arthur insisted, as he made his way to the bar. 'You'll see if I don't.'

'Right,' Terry replied. 'You're a grand lad, Arthur. A pint of the usual it is, then.'

22

'YOU BLOODY DIDN'T,' Sam said, shaking his head incredulously.

'I bloody did, an' all,' Arthur insisted.

'Give over, the two of you,' Terry intervened. 'You sound like summat' out of a pantomime.'

'Well, that's Sam's fault for not believing me,' Arthur replied.

There was a silence. Without taking his eyes off Arthur, Terry took a first sip of his pint.

'Did you though, Arthur?'

'Aye.'

Sam snorted before taking a long drink.

'So what you're saying is: you answered an advert in the *Daily Express* to be a hangman; you filled in t' form; and they asked you to go to London for training.'

'That's what I said.'

'Just like that?'

'No, not just like that. I told you. They interview you first. You go to the nearest big prison to be interviewed by the Governor. So I went to Strangeways, you know, in Manchester. Then, if they are satisfied with t' interview, they might invite you to Pentonville Prison in London for training for a couple of days.'

'What kinds of things did the Governor ask you?'

Arthur shook his head.

'All kinds of things. About my education; how I heard about the job; why I was interested in it; did I have any relatives who had applied in the past; was I in good health; had I ever been in trouble with the law; what did I do when I wasn't working at Thwaites. You would have thought I wanted to work for MI6 or summat.'

'They wanted to know if there were owt strange about you,' Terry suggested.

'We could have bloody told them that,' Sam said sullenly. 'No need to go all t' way to bloody Strangeways.'

'Well, they can't be too careful, I suppose,' Terry said. 'You can't have the public hangman running amok and going on t' rampage, can you? No telling what might happen if he got out of control with a noose in his hand.'

Arthur smiled. 'Aye, they have to have the right man for the job. They made that clear enough. Any road, when I came out of the interview, I had no idea how it had gone, really. But a couple of weeks later, they said I should come to London for the training.'

'What were it like, the training? Did you actually hang anyone?' Terry asked.

'Get home, you daft bugger,' Sam replied. 'They wouldn't let you do that while you were training… at least I bloody hope not. Would they?'

'No,' Arthur said. 'Of course not. No, you have to wait after the training. If they think you can do it, they put you on the list, and then you can act as assistant to the chief executioner. You do that a lot before they put you in charge of an execution yourself.'

'I should bloody hope so, an' all.' Sam muttered, raising his pint to his lips.

23

1964
13 April

BEN WALKED BRISKLY across Market Square to the Huntingdon Town Hall. He paused briefly and took a deep breath before entering the building and making his way across the small entrance hall to the conference room. He had asked Barratt Davis and Jess Farrar to go on ahead of him after a hasty breakfast in the George Hotel, where they had each taken a room for the duration of the trial of Ignatius Little. He wanted to sit quietly for a while in the hotel lounge, re-reading his notes, going over the case in his mind, trying to bring his nerves under control. His first jury trial at the Old Bailey had been a case of rape. Ben, thrust into it as a pupil, had secured his client's acquittal, earning praise from all concerned, including the judge; but it had been a nerve-wracking experience, and its memory lingered. Since then there had been one or two short trials, for house-breaking and receiving stolen goods; the defendants had long records and little to hope for, and the trials had been far less stressful. The memory had receded. Now, the prospect of defending against his former pupil-master, in a case in which the stakes were high, had brought the bad memories back into sharp focus. He needed a few minutes alone with his thoughts.

In the conference room he shook hands with Ignatius Little, and tried to assess his mood. The vicar was understandably nervous, but Ben did not sense any resignation or any hint of the kind of near-paralysis which afflicted some clients at the beginning of a trial. He was smartly dressed in a dark grey suit, with a pale green tie, borrowed from Barratt Davis for the occasion.

Little had wanted to wear his clerical collar throughout the trial, but Ben had forbidden it.

'It's too assertive,' he had cautioned. 'And it will attract some awkward questions from the prosecution. Let's not forget that you are suspended from exercising your ministry at present.'

Ben left the conference room to find Gareth Morgan-Davies. Barratt followed him into the hall, touched his arm as he turned towards the robing room, and walked a few steps with him.

'Jess talked with Joan Heppenstall this morning,' he said confidentially. 'She is willing to come in case we need her to give evidence. She understands that it will be your decision whether to call her or not, but she felt she owed it to Mr Little to be here. I told her she would not be needed until tomorrow, so she is taking a train from York later this afternoon. Jess will pick her up from Peterborough station and take her straight to the George. We have a room booked for her. There's no need for her to see him before she comes to court. We don't want her deciding it was all a terrible mistake and jumping on the first train back to York.'

Ben nodded.

'Good. We will see how it goes. Hopefully Jess will get a sense of how she is feeling towards him. She's a calculated risk, but we may need her, especially if he wobbles in cross-examination. What about the character witnesses from the Diocese?'

'Also booked for tomorrow. John Singer is in charge of getting them here. He has two or three possible witnesses lined up, led by a Canon, no less – the ecclesiastical sort, I mean, not the kind they used at Balaclava. John promised to let me have proofs of evidence from them all this afternoon.'

'We don't want to overdo it,' Ben said. 'I will call the Canon, and perhaps one other, depending on how it goes, but that's it. We don't want the jury to think the Diocese is mounting its own defence rather than Little's.'

In the robing room Ben found Gareth Morgan-Davies, already in wing collar and bands, his gown and wig laid casually on the table in front of him. His white-ribboned prosecution brief lay unopened on top of a blue notebook nearby.

'Good morning, Gareth,' Ben said, as brightly as he could manage, hoping that he sounded more confident than he felt. 'You look cheerful.'

'I am extremely cheerful,' Gareth replied. 'Another Five Nations under our belt this year, marred only by the fact that we could only draw with England and had to rely on the Scots to beat them for us. But Wales is on top once again.'

'Congratulations,' Ben smiled. 'I hope the result was celebrated in suitable style.'

'Of course,' Gareth replied. 'Speaking of which, your lot are not doing too bad, are they? Aren't you in the Cup Final?'

'We are,' Ben said, 'against Preston North End. We have high hopes.'

'Good. Now, to business. Any last-minute change of heart by the vicar? I would still be glad to put in a good word to the court if young Raymond doesn't have to give evidence.'

Ben shook his head.

'Sorry, Gareth. But there is still time for the prosecution to confess its error and allow this good man of the cloth to leave the court without a stain on his character.'

Gareth picked up his pack of Dunhills and a box of matches from the desk, selected a cigarette, lit it, and drew on it thoughtfully.

'Ah, so we are still some distance apart, then?'

'Afraid so.'

'Well, so be it. Look, Ben, I will call Raymond first as soon as I have opened the case. I am going to ask them to close the court to the public during his evidence. I'm not entitled to that. It is a matter of discretion for the court. It is a public trial. But…'

'I won't oppose the application,' Ben replied immediately.

Gareth nodded. 'Much appreciated.'

'And we can take a break before cross-examination. If you want, we could even leave it until after lunch.'

'No need. He may need a short break, but on the whole it is probably best for him to get it all over and done with as soon as possible. I will call his parents next, father first. Mother can take him out for something nice to eat until his father has finished, and then they can take him home.'

'I'm not going to be too long with any of them,' Ben said.

'Good,' Gareth grinned, pushing himself up from his chair. 'I'm glad you learned something from me.'

'From you and Arthur Creighton,' Ben replied. 'You both drummed it into me. Don't cross-examine unless you have to. If you have to, get what you need, then shut up and sit down.'

'And never was better advice given,' Gareth said. 'Well, you must excuse me. I must find Martineau and make sure we have everybody in place. Good hunting.'

* * *

It was 10.30. The trial was listed in Court 1, the Assize Court. Court 1 was not a great deal bigger than Court 2, where the committal proceedings had been held, but it was somehow far more imposing. The judge's bench was elevated far above the floor of the courtroom, giving the impression that the judge was a superior being who had come from some higher place to preside and, unlike Court 2, the dock in Court 1 had a door which led directly to the cells. Philip Eaves, who had acted as clerk at the committal, had been assigned to act as clerk of court for the trial.

The public gallery on the floor above the court was packed, as was a smaller gallery to the left of the dock. Ben noted the strong press presence, including some whom he recognised from the committal proceedings. Paul, the usher, who had greeted Ben and Gareth as if they were long-lost friends, called on those present to stand. The chairman of Quarter Sessions, His Honour Judge Gerald Peterson, entered the courtroom and took his seat on the bench. A slightly built man, wearing barrister's robes over a dark pin-striped three-piece suit, he moved lightly and quickly, his keen grey eyes darting around the courtroom, giving the impression of missing nothing. Moments later, the members of the panel from which the jury would be chosen at random, twenty in all, every one clad in a suit and tie, walked cautiously into the courtroom under Paul's watchful eye. They congregated around the jury box, holding coats and hats, shuffling their feet, looking around them at the judge and barristers in their wigs and gowns, waiting for something to happen, and anxious not to do anything out of place.

'Where are the women?' Ben heard Jess whisper in the row behind him.

'It's not unusual to have a panel of men only,' he heard Barratt whisper in reply. 'The jurors are selected from the register of property owners, who are mainly men. You do get the odd woman occasionally.'

Ben heard Jess's snort of disapproval and grinned.

'Ignatius Little,' Eaves was saying, 'the names I am about to call are the names of the jurors who may try you. If you wish to object to them, or to any of them, you must do so as they come to the book to be sworn and before they are sworn, and your objection shall be heard.'

Ben turned around to the dock to nod at Little, just to remind him that any objections were for Ben to decide on. He had chosen not to renew his application for a change of venue, and there was no ground to challenge the array of jurors as a whole. But he had asked Little to signal to him immediately if he thought he recognised any member of the panel. Little shook his head briefly, and Ben acknowledged this with a nod. So there was to be no challenge for cause. But Gareth had always impressed on him the wisdom of using at least one peremptory challenge, just for effect – the defence was entitled to challenge up to seven jurors as of right, without assigning any cause. Ben looked closely at the panel. He was searching for any hint that a juror might be unduly conservative or closed-minded. Sometimes dress and general appearance gave such indications but, to his dismay, he could find no inspiration at all. No one juror looked either particularly intimidating, or particularly sympathetic. They all seemed to look much the same, a sea of anonymous bank clerks in grey suits. He sensed that Gareth was aware of his dilemma, and felt, rather than saw, the smile to his right. He shook his head in frustration.

'Members of the jury in waiting,' Eaves continued, 'as I call your name, please answer audibly and take your seat in the jury box.'

Ben challenged two jurors whose look did not appeal to him. Two fresh jurors wearing similar suits replaced them. The jurors took the oath one by one; each swore to faithfully try the defendant and give a true verdict according to the evidence. The clerk dismissed the members of the panel who had not been chosen. Ben deliberately diverted his attention from the two he had challenged, but felt their questioning glances as they left court.

'Members of the jury,' Eaves said, 'the defendant, Ignatius Little, is charged in this indictment with indecent assault on a male. The particulars are that on or about the 22nd day of January 1964, at St Ives in the County of Huntingdon, he indecently assaulted Raymond Stone, a male under sixteen years of age. To this indictment he has pleaded not guilty and it is your charge, having heard the evidence, to say whether he be guilty or no.'

Judge Peterson looked down towards counsel's row.

'Yes, Mr Morgan-Davies.'

Gareth rose, nodded briefly to the judge, and turned to face the jury. He had his notebook in front of him on a folding lectern that accompanied him everywhere.

'May it please you, sir, members of the jury, my name is Gareth Morgan-Davies and I appear to prosecute this case. My learned friend Mr Schroeder appears for the defendant, the Reverend Ignatius Little.'

He held out a hand in Ben's direction. Ben half rose from his seat, and inclined his head towards the jury.

'Members of the jury, I must tell you at once that you will no doubt find some of the evidence in this case unpleasant and disturbing. The charge is one of indecent assault on a ten-year-old boy and I am quite sure that you will find some of what you hear distressing. But you are jurors and, later in the trial, the learned judge will tell you that you are the judges of the facts. As judges, it is your duty to weigh the evidence dispassionately, which means that you must put aside any feelings of discomfort you may have and look at the evidence objectively, clinically, to decide whether the man accused did in fact commit this offence. The learned judge will also tell you that it is a fundamental principle of our law that no man is liable to be convicted unless the prosecution proves the case against him beyond reasonable doubt, on the whole of the evidence. What I say, what my learned friend may say, is not evidence. The evidence will come from the witnesses who come into court and give evidence from the witness box. My task now is simply to give you a short summary of what I expect the evidence to be.'

For the first time, Gareth donned his reading glasses and glanced down at his notes.

'The 22 of January, gentlemen, was a Wednesday. At St Martin's Church in St Ives, Wednesday evening is set aside for choir practice. Raymond Stone, the victim of this offence, was a member of the choir, and he attended choir practice on that evening, as did the organist and choir master, John Sharples. Also present in the church, although he was not directly concerned with the choir, was the vicar of St Martin's, the Reverend Ignatius Little, the defendant in this case. You will hear that choir practice began at about 7 o'clock and ended a little after 8 o'clock. When it ended, most members of the choir went home immediately. But you will hear that the vicar sometimes asked a boy to remain behind for a short time, to assist him with some preparations for the coming Sunday services. Sometimes hymn and psalm numbers had to be displayed in the wooden holders attached to the pillars inside the church. But some of the preparation was done, not in the church itself, but in the vestry, a small room to the left of the altar at the front of the church, used to store the vicar's vestments, items such as the chalice and plate used during communion, objects such as candlesticks for the altar, and supplies of communion wine. You will hear that the defendant asked Raymond Stone to assist him with such preparations in the vestry. Raymond had helped the vicar in this way before, and he agreed to do so on this occasion. It should have taken no more than ten to fifteen minutes, at most. John Sharples was at the rear of the church, the opposite end to the vestry, locking up the organ, after which he left for the evening. No one else was left in the church. All that was quite usual. There was nothing surprising about any of that in itself.'

Gareth removed his glasses.

'But on the 22 of January, something happened in the vestry which took Raymond Stone very much by surprise. Raymond will tell you about it himself. His vicar, the Reverend Ignatius Little, had more in his mind that evening than making preparations for Sunday services. You will hear that, in a dreadful breach of trust, Mr Little indecently assaulted Raymond, a ten-year-old boy who was a member of his choir, and the child and grandchild of members of his congregation. You will hear that the vicar unzipped his own trousers, took out his penis, and invited Raymond to touch it.'

A ripple ran around the public gallery. Paul rose to his feet and sternly called for silence. Gareth waited for the shock to subside.

'The defendant then touched Raymond's penis through his trousers. Fortunately, members of the jury, matters went no further, because Raymond had the presence of mind to turn and run out of the vestry. He ran all the way home at top speed, not stopping until he reached his home, just a few hundred yards from the church. On arriving home, he immediately ran upstairs to his bedroom, without a word to his parents. His parents, loyal members of the defendant's congregation, will tell you that this was unusual. Generally, Raymond would have come into the living room to tell them he was home. They were concerned. They went to Raymond's room separately to talk to him. They will tell you that Raymond was very upset. It took them some time to get the boy to tell them what had happened. But, eventually, he disclosed that the defendant had touched him. Mr Stone will admit to you that, at first, he was loath to believe his son. He thought there must have been some mistake, some misunderstanding. He telephoned the defendant – it was by now late, about 11 o'clock – and asked him what had happened. Gentlemen, you will hear that the defendant replied that he did not know what had come over him, and he apologised to Mr Stone. The prosecution say that the defendant, in effect, admitted his guilt of this offence to Mr Stone.'

Ben had been watching Gareth out of the corner of his eye, and had noted some hesitation in his voice as he came to the father's evidence. He noted that Gareth dealt with it briefly and in no great detail. It was something Gareth himself had taught Ben to look out for. Gareth lacked confidence in his witness; he was not entirely sure what he would say. Ben made a note to himself to press the father even harder on that part of the case than he had intended.

'That, in outline, is the case you will hear, members of the jury. At the end of the case, the learned judge will sum up the case to you on the law, and you must take the law from him. But I anticipate that the direction he will give you about indecent assault will be consistent with the prosecution's case, and I anticipate that he will tell you that a boy of Raymond's age cannot give consent to being touched for the purposes of an indecent assault. Bear in mind that, as I have said, the prosecution must prove the case beyond reasonable doubt if you are to convict.'

He turned back towards the judge.

'Sir, my first witness will be Raymond Stone. Given his age, and the matters with which he will be dealing, I ask that the court be closed to the public and press for the duration of Raymond's evidence. It is a matter for your discretion, sir, but my learned friend has been good enough to indicate that he has no objection.'

Ben stood immediately. 'That is correct, sir.'

Judge Peterson considered briefly. 'Very well,' he ordered. 'The public gallery and press box are closed until further order. All those not involved in the case will please leave court.'

Without turning round, Ben was aware of the frustration of the onlookers and reporters. They filed out of court slowly and noisily, as if hoping that the judge might think he had made a mistake, and change his mind to allow them to hear the gory details. An elderly lady who volunteered for such things had been looking after Raymond until it was time for his evidence. She now walked him slowly ahead of her into the courtroom. As before, he was dressed in his best school uniform, his hair cut short – a picture of innocence. Ben felt his anxiety start to rise, and had to take several deep, slow breaths to control it.

24

'RAYMOND, WHAT IS your full name?' Gareth asked quietly.

'Raymond Godfrey Stone, sir.'

'Do you live in St Ives with your parents?'

'Yes, sir.'

'Do you have any brothers or sisters?'

A shake of the head.

Gareth smiled. 'You have to say something. You see that nice lady with the notepad? She is taking notes. She can't write anything down if she can't hear you. Let's try again. Any brothers or sisters?'

A tentative smile in return.

'No, sir.'

'Do you and your parents go to church on Sundays?'

'My parents and grandparents all go. I go with them.'

'Is that to St Martin's Church in St Ives?'

'Yes, sir.'

'Who is the vicar of that church, Raymond?'

Hesitation. Ben stood.

'Sir, there is no dispute about any of this. My learned friend can lead until the incident itself.'

Judge Peterson nodded. 'Thank you, Mr Schroeder, most helpful.'

'I am much obliged to my learned friend. Raymond, is the vicar the Reverend Little, and is he the gentleman over there in the dock?'

Raymond looked around the court. Ben noted that his gaze rested on Little for some time. Raymond nodded.

'Again, Raymond, you have to…'

'Sorry, sir, yes.'

Effortlessly, Gareth led Raymond through a description of the church, the composition of the choir, the arrangements for the weekly choir practice, the role of John Sharples, the various tasks that had to be done to prepare for Sunday services. Ben found himself losing focus momentarily as he listened with admiration to Gareth's easy, polished flow, as he had so often as a pupil. With an effort he forced his mind to concentrate.

'Now, Raymond, would Mr Little sometimes ask a boy to help him after practice, for a few minutes, with the various things you told us have to be done for the Sunday services?'

'Yes, sir.'

'Did he ask you to help sometimes?'

'Yes.'

'What kinds of things would he ask you to do?'

'Getting his vestments ready for Sunday, fetching the communion wine.'

'Where would you go to do that?'

Hesitation.

'Raymond…?'

'In the vestry, sir.'

'Is the vestry a small room at the front of the church, up by the altar, where the vicar keeps things like vestments and supplies for services?'

'Yes, sir.'

'Did Mr Little ask you to do anything on the evening of 22 January?'

'Yes, sir.'

'What did he ask you to do?'

'He asked me to come into the vestry to put out his vestments, and the chalice, and the communion wine for Sunday.'

'Were those tasks you had done before?'

'Yes, sir.'

'What time was it when Mr Little asked you to do that?'

'I'm not sure exactly…'

'No, of course, roughly what time?'

'It was after 8 o'clock.'

'Did you go to the vestry?'

'Yes, sir.'

'Who else was in the vestry?'

'Just me and Mr Little.'

'Where was Mr Sharples, do you know?'

'In the church, I should think, unless he had gone home.'

'Did he come into the vestry at all?'

'No, sir.'

'Now, the vestments and so on he asked you to put out, where were they kept?'

'There is a big cupboard against the wall, sir, opposite the door. It's more like a wardrobe, really. That's where all the vestments and different things for the altar are kept. The wine is kept on a shelf. It's a bit high up. I could only just reach it.'

'Did you go to the wardrobe?'

'Yes, sir. I opened the doors and reached up for the wine. I thought I would get that out first.'

'Then what happened?'

Silence. A suggestion of a tear. Ben felt his throat tighten.

'All right, Raymond, it's all right... let me ask you this. Where were you going to put the wine?'

'There is a big table in the middle of the room. That's where we put the wafers, the wine, the candlesticks, and any stuff for the altar. The vestments have to be hung on a coat rack behind the door.'

'So when you took down the wine, did you turn around towards the table?'

'Yes, sir.'

'Where was Mr Little when you turned around?'

'He was standing...'

'It's all right.'

'He was standing between me and the table.'

'Facing towards you, or away from you?'

'Facing towards me.'

'What happened next? Did Mr Little do anything?'

Silence. Gareth allowed some time to go by. Ben glanced up at the judge, and noted that he was looking at Gareth as if to suggest a break. But Gareth showed no sign of having noticed. Ben guessed that he would prefer to avoid prolonging the evidence unless it proved absolutely necessary.

'Well, let me ask you this, Raymond. Did you notice anything different about Mr Little when you turned around, about his appearance?'

Quietly.

'Yes, sir.'

'What did you notice?'

Hesitation.

'It's all right.'

'I noticed he had undone his trousers at the front, sir.'

'And as a result of that, could you see anything?'

'Yes, sir.'

'What could you see?'

'His…'

Silence.

'Do you know the word for it?'

'I am not sure, sir.'

Ben saw Gareth turn towards the judge. He was going to ask permission to ask a leading question, and the judge would almost certainly allow him to lead Raymond on such a sensitive subject. Ben calculated quickly and decided on a pre-emptive strike. He rose quickly to his feet.

'I have no objection to my learned friend leading,' he said, 'as long as the jury understand that we do not accept the evidence.'

'I'm much obliged to my learned friend,' Gareth said. He turned towards Ben with a look – apparently hurt, but with the hint of a smile – which Ben understood immediately.

It said: *'You got that trick from me, didn't you? And you turned it against me.'*

Ben gave him an innocent look in return. Gareth turned back to his witness.

'Raymond, was it his penis?'

Raymond nodded.

'You have to…'

'Yes, sir.'

'Do you understand what the penis is?'

Hesitation.

'Yes, sir.'

'Did Mr Little do anything?'

'Yes, sir.'

'What did he do?'

Hesitation.

'He asked me to touch his…'

'His penis?'

'Yes, sir.

'Do you remember exactly what he said?'

'No, sir.'

'All right. What did you think he wanted you to do? How did he want you to touch him?'

'With my hand.'

'Did you touch it?'

'No, sir.'

'How many times did he ask you to touch him?'

'Once or twice, sir.'

'But you didn't?'

'No, sir.'

'Did Mr Little say or do anything else?'

Silence.

'Raymond…?'

'He touched me, sir.'

'He touched you? Where did he touch you?'

Hesitation.

Quietly. 'The same place, sir.'

'Your penis?'

'Yes, sir.'

'Did he touch you through your trousers?'

'Yes, sir.'

'Did he say anything while he was touching you?'

'No, sir.'

'What did you do then?'

'I ran, sir. I ran out of the vestry as fast as I could.'

'Did Mr Little follow you?'

'No, sir.'

'Where did you go?'

'I ran home.'

'How long did it take you to run home?'

'I'm not sure, sir. Not long. Just a few minutes.'

'All right, Raymond. Now, when you got home, what did you do?'

'I ran upstairs to my room.'

'Without speaking to your parents?'

'Yes, sir.'

'Did your father come upstairs to see what was going on?'

'Yes.'

'And did you tell him…?'

Ben stood quickly.

'I would ask my learned friend not to lead on this, sir.'

The judge nodded.

'Of course,' Gareth said. 'What did you say to your father?'

'I told him that Mr Little had touched me.'

'Do you remember exactly what you said?'

A shake of the head.

'I can't remember now, sir.'

Gareth hesitated, as if unsure whether to press. After some time he nodded, as if to himself.

'Thank you, Raymond. I have no more questions to ask you. Mr Schroeder will have some.'

Ben stood quickly.

'Sir, I'm entirely in your hands. If Raymond would like a break, we can certainly take one now. But I am only going to be a few minutes, and he may prefer to get it over with.'

The judge nodded.

'Raymond, what would you like to do? Would you like a break, or would you like to go on for just a few more minutes?'

'We can go on, sir,' Raymond replied politely.

* * *

'Raymond, can I ask you first about the vestry? It's a very small room, isn't it?'

'Yes, sir.'

'You could fit three or four vestries into this courtroom at least, couldn't you?'

Raymond smiled. 'Yes, sir.'

'And the table in the middle of the room, that's a rather large, round wooden table, isn't it?'

'Yes, sir.'

'A bit too big for the room, really, don't you think?'

Raymond nodded. 'Much too big.'

'Yes. And there's not much room between the table and the

wardrobe, is there?'

'No, sir.'

'In fact, there's hardly room to open the wardrobe doors without banging them into the table, is there?'

'There is not much room, sir, no.'

'So, if you were taking something out of the wardrobe, and someone else was standing behind you, by the table, you could easily bump into them by accident, couldn't you?'

'I suppose so, sir.'

'Is it possible that's what happened – that you bumped into Mr Little as you were turning round to put the wine on the table?'

Hesitation.

'I don't think so, sir.'

Ben paused.

'You don't think so. All right. Raymond, how long have you been singing in the choir?'

'Since I was seven, sir.'

Ben smiled.

'You started young, didn't you?'

Raymond smiled back.

'Yes, sir. My parents started giving me singing lessons when I was just five or six.'

'They wanted to encourage you, didn't they?'

'Yes, sir.'

'Do you like singing?'

'I love it, sir.'

'Would you like to go on singing when you grow up?'

'Yes, sir. I hope so.'

'So do I,' Ben said. 'I understand you are very talented musically, a very good singer?'

'Well...'

'It's all right. Don't be shy.'

'Yes, sir, I think so.'

'You go to school in St Ives, don't you?'

'Yes, sir.'

'Do you have music lessons there?'

Hesitation.

'Yes, sir... well, sort of...'

'Not very good?'

'Not as good as my parents, sir.'

'No. I understand. You would probably have preferred to go to the King's School at Ely, the cathedral school, wouldn't you? Do you know about it?'

Ben saw Gareth rise.

'Sir, I'm not sure where my learned friend is going with this. Is it relevant to the case before this jury?'

'Mr Schroeder?' the judge inquired.

'It is, sir. That will become clear with a subsequent witness, if the court will allow me a little leeway.'

Gareth shrugged and sat down.

'Very well,' the judge said.

'Much obliged, sir. Raymond…?'

'I think any boy would, sir.'

'Yes, of course. Because you can sing in the cathedral choir, and perhaps even go on to Cambridge University as a scholar when you are older, can't you?'

'Yes, sir.'

'But there are not many places for choristers, are there?'

'No, sir.'

'And you have to get in quite young, don't you? By the time you are your age, it's almost too late, isn't it?'

A look of sadness.

'Yes.'

'Your parents did apply to send you to the King's School, didn't they?'

'Yes.'

'But you were not accepted, were you?'

'No.'

'Did they tell you why?'

Resentful now, arms folded across his chest, a frown on his face.

'Mr Sharples didn't think I was good enough.' Then, suddenly. 'But I was. I *was*. What does he know?'

Ben nodded.

'You knew you were good enough, Raymond, didn't you?'

'Yes. I was.'

'Your parents knew too, didn't they?'

'Yes.'

'If Mr Sharples didn't recommend you, was there any other way to get in?'

Hesitation.

'If Mr Little had asked them to take me…'

'That's what your parents said? If the vicar asked them, they might take you, even if Mr Sharples didn't agree?'

A nod.

'You have to…'

'Yes.'

'But Mr Little wouldn't ask them, would he?'

Quietly.

'No. He wouldn't ask.'

Ben allowed a few moments to pass.

'Were you angry about that?'

Silence.

'All right. Raymond, Mr Little didn't touch your penis, did he?'

The frown still on the face, the arms still folded tight.

'He did.'

'And he didn't expose his penis to you, did he?'

'He did.'

'Thank you, Raymond. I have no more questions.'

'Thank you, Mr Schroeder,' Judge Peterson said. 'If there is nothing further…'

Gareth shook his head.

'It's a bit early, but the jury has had a long morning. We will adjourn until 2 o'clock for lunch. The public and press will be re-admitted to court after lunch.'

The jury left court. Bows were exchanged between Bench and Bar, and the judge was gone.

Out of the corner of his eye Ben saw a folded note being pushed across counsel's bench towards him. It read: 'nicely done'. Ben turned, but Gareth was already on his way out of court.

* * *

Lunch was a hurried sandwich at the George. Jess was preparing to set out for Peterborough to meet Joan Heppenstall, and John Singer had left for Ely to ensure that the church witnesses were in place and prepared for the next day.

'So far, so good,' Barratt Davis observed.

'Yes. I'm glad to have that behind us,' Ben replied. 'We may make some headway with the father this afternoon, and then it's up to Little tomorrow.'

'I've been trying to read the jury, but they're an expressionless bunch, aren't they? They are not giving anything away at all. I thought there might be some reaction to the boy's evidence, but not even a flicker, that I saw.'

'They are straight out of jury central casting,' Ben replied. 'I couldn't even make a clear choice about who I wanted to challenge.'

'I noticed that. How did you decide, just out of interest?'

'I picked the two I thought were wearing the most expensive suits.'

Barratt laughed out loud.

'Well, if Little does well in the box, and if the Canon gives him a ringing endorsement, and if we decide we can call Joan, we may be in with a chance, don't you think?'

Ben nodded.

'The trouble with this case, Barratt, is that I'm not entirely sure what our defence is. It seems to be that *someone* made this story up because Little wouldn't recommend Raymond for the King's School. But the problem is, I'm not sure *who*.'

'What does your gut say?' Barratt asked.

'The father,' Ben replied immediately.

'Mine too.'

Ben finished his coffee.

'All right. Let's go and find out what he has to say for himself.'

25

'PLEASE GIVE THE court your full name,' Gareth began.

'Godfrey Stone.'

'Are you the father of the previous witness, Raymond Stone?'

'That is correct.'

'Mr Stone, where were you on the evening of 22 January this year?'

'I was at home with my wife.'

'Where was Raymond, to your knowledge?'

'He left the house at about ten minutes before seven to walk to the church for choir practice.'

'Was that a regular occurrence on Wednesday evenings?'

'It was, yes.'

'What time did you expect Raymond back?'

'Some time after 8 o'clock; not later than 8.30.'

'At what time did Raymond actually get home on this particular evening?'

'A little after 8.30.'

Gareth paused, as if consulting a note.

'How did you become aware that he had returned?'

Ben suddenly sat forward and concentrated hard on the witness. He seemed ill at ease. He had his hands behind his back, but the pose did not seem relaxed. Ben felt sure that the hands were tightly clasped together. He was shifting his weight from one foot to the other.

'I heard the back door open.'

'Did Raymond have a key?'

'No. We would leave the back door open for him.'

'Did you hear him come in?'

'Yes. But then...'

'Go on, Mr Stone.'

'Instead of coming into the living room and saying "hello" to his mother and me, as he usually did, and telling us about choir practice, he ran straight upstairs to his room and closed the door.'

'And that was unusual for him, you say?'

'Very. In fact, I don't think he had ever done that before.'

'I see,' Gareth said. 'What, if anything, did you do?'

Ben glanced at Gareth. It was a very cautious question, as non-leading as it could be. He turned his head back and watched the witness hesitate.

'I didn't do anything at first. I thought perhaps he needed the toilet, or there was something he wanted in his room. So I was expecting him to come downstairs. But he didn't. I left it for five or ten minutes, then my wife and I looked at each other, and said…'

'Well, you can't tell us what was said, but what did you do?'

'I went up to Raymond's room.'

'What did you find?'

'I went in and found him crying. He was sitting at the desk that he uses for his homework, he had his head down on it, and he was crying his eyes out.'

'It may be an obvious question, Mr Stone. But I want you to tell the jury as precisely as you can what state Raymond appeared to be in.'

'He was very distressed. Almost hysterical, I would say.'

'I see. What did you do?'

'I tried to comfort him, and I asked him what was wrong. At first, I thought he might have been hurt, but I couldn't see any sign of injury. He was just very upset.'

'Did he tell you what was wrong?'

Ben hesitated. He noticed the judge glance down at him. He had, of course, prepared for this moment in his mind. He could venture a technical objection on the ground that whatever Raymond said was hearsay and inadmissible. But Gareth would argue that it was a recent complaint – a complaint by a victim of a sexual crime shortly after the event – and so was admissible. The probability was that the judge would allow the evidence, and the probability was that he would be right to do so. Ben quickly decided to follow his instinct, and remained in his seat.

'Eventually.'

'What do you mean by that?'

'I had to ask him several times. He did not want to talk about it. I didn't want to force him. But I didn't know what was wrong, and I felt that I had to find out.'

'What, if anything, did he tell you, eventually?'

Ben noted the form of the question again. The witness hesitated for some time; when he finally answered, he blurted his answer out quickly, without pausing for breath.

'He told me that the vicar had touched him, in the vestry, after choir practice.'

'What did you understand Raymond to mean by that?'

Ben shot to his feet.

'Sir, my learned friend knows very well that he cannot ask that.'

'Mr Morgan-Davies…' Judge Peterson began.

Gareth held up a hand. 'My learned friend is quite right.' He looked down at his notes, flashing Ben a grin, which Ben pretended to ignore.

'What did he say, as precisely as you can, please?' Gareth asked. His tone suggested that he did not expect a useful answer.

'He said that the vicar had exposed his penis to him and had touched his penis through his clothes.'

Gareth and Ben exchanged glances.

'I see. What did you do after Raymond had told you all this?'

Stone raised his eyebrows.

'I went downstairs and told my wife what had happened. She immediately went up to see Raymond, to comfort him. She was up there with him for at least half an hour. Then she came down, made him some cocoa, and we put him to bed. Once he was in bed, we talked about what to do. At first, I didn't want to do anything.'

'Why was that?'

'Well… Mr Little was our vicar, you know. The whole family are members of his congregation. I was shocked. To be honest, I thought that Raymond might have imagined it. I didn't want to tell anyone until I was more sure. So we talked about it, and we decided that I should telephone Mr Little and ask him about it.'

'What time was it by then?'

'It was late, close to 11 o'clock, I should think. We talked about it for a long time, going back and forth.'

'Did you then phone Mr Little and talk to him?'

'I did.'

'What was said between you?'

'I told Mr Little what Raymond had said. I asked him about it.'

Hesitation.

'What, if anything, did Mr Little say?'

'He apologised and said something like, he didn't know what had come over him.'

'Something like? Can you tell the jury precisely what was said?'

'Not really. I was very shocked that night. I can't give it to you word for word, but that was what he said.'

Gareth nodded.

'Did you telephone the police the following morning?'

'Yes, I certainly did.'

'And did you go to the police station to make a formal complaint?'

'I did.'

'Thank you, Mr Stone. I have no further questions.'

* * *

'Raymond told you that the vicar had exposed his penis to him, did he, Mr Stone?' Ben asked.

'He did.'

'In so many words?'

'Yes.

'Using the word "penis"?'

Hesitation.

'Yes.'

'He came out with that very word himself, did he? You didn't have to prompt him?'

'I don't know what you mean?'

'Well, boys have different words for it, don't they? "Penis" is a grown-up word, isn't it? I just wondered whether "penis" was the word he used, or the word you are using for what he said?'

'No, he used the word himself.'

'I see. And he told you that the vicar had touched his penis?'

'He did.'

'Again, using the word "penis" himself, without your suggesting it?'

'That is correct.'

Ben looked down at the documents laid out in front of him and selected one with no particular haste.

'Mr Stone, do you remember giving evidence at the magistrates' court on 13 February, when your deposition was taken?'

The witness unclasped his hands, brought them around to the front of his body, and folded them across his chest. The gesture was so similar to Raymond's stance in the witness box that Ben could not resist a smile.

'I do.'

'Do you remember my learned friend Mr Morgan-Davies asking you about what Raymond had said to you in his room?'

'Yes.'

'You can see your deposition if you wish. Your evidence was that Raymond had said that Mr Little had "touched" him? You were unable to remember any more than that, is that not correct?'

'If you say so.'

'No, Mr Stone. The jury must hear what *you* say about it. Is it not the case that you said only that Raymond said he had been touched? You gave no details at all, did you? Nothing about touching his penis?'

'No. Not then, no.'

'Do you remember my learned friend pressing you and asking you, as he has today, whether you could recall the precise words Raymond used?'

'Yes.'

'And did you reply that you could not remember?'

'I believe so, yes.'

'Is it also true that, in your deposition, you said nothing about Mr Little exposing himself to Raymond?'

Silence.

'I can ask the usher to show you your deposition, if you would like to see it.'

'No. I did not say that specifically.'

'No. Mr Stone, would you care to explain to the jury why you have given these details today, although you were unable to recall them during your deposition?'

The witness shifted position miserably in the witness box.

'I suppose no one asked.'

'My learned friend will correct me, if I am wrong' Ben said. 'But he asked you to describe in detail everything Raymond had said. Is that not true?'

Stone looked at Gareth for support, but Gareth remained impassive in his seat. Silence.

'Let me move on to something else,' Ben said. 'You phoned Mr Little at about 11 o'clock that evening, as you have said. There is no dispute about that. But he did not say anything about not knowing what had come over him. That's complete nonsense, isn't it?'

'No. That's what he said.'

'Really? Well, if he did say that, that would be quite important, wouldn't it?'

'What do you mean?'

'Well, your vicar would have been admitting that he had behaved indecently towards your son, wouldn't he?'

'Yes.'

'That would be quite shocking to you, wouldn't it?'

'It *was* quite shocking.'

'And yet you did not mention that phone call to anyone until 10 February, almost three weeks later, and only three days before the committal proceedings? Is that not correct?'

'Yes.'

'Not a word to the police when you phoned them the morning after?'

'No.'

'Not a word when you went to the police station?'

'No.'

'Did it just skip your memory?'

'It must have.'

Ben paused.

'Yes. It must have. Raymond is a gifted singer, isn't he, Mr Stone? Exceptional for his age?'

Ben watched the sudden change of subject take the witness by surprise. He turned towards Ben with a startled look.

'Yes, he is,' he replied defensively.

'And you and your wife wanted his talent to be recognised, so that he could go to the King's School at Ely, did you not?'

Hesitation. Stone turned to appeal to the judge.

'I don't see what that has to do with this case.'

'Answer the question, please, Mr Stone,' Judge Peterson replied.

'Well, yes, we did. Why shouldn't we?'

Ben shook his head. 'I'm not criticising you at all for that, Mr Stone. On the contrary, choir boys at the Cathedral School have many advantages, don't they? Their talents are on display. They can begin musical careers. They may win scholarships to Cambridge colleges as choristers, or even organ scholars. Isn't that right?'

'Yes.'

'Yes. Of course you would want that for your son. And you believed he was good enough, didn't you?'

For the first time, Stone looked assertive.

'We *knew* he was good enough. We had been to Ely Cathedral. We had heard the choir many times. My wife and I have musical backgrounds. We started him off singing. We *knew* he was at least as good as some of those other boys.'

'Yes,' Ben said. 'But the clock was running, wasn't it? Usually choristers start by the age of eight, so that their voices can be properly trained, don't they? Eight or nine is about the limit. Raymond was ten. So, unless he was accepted more or less immediately, his chance would have gone forever, wouldn't it?'

Stone nodded unhappily.

'I'm sorry, Mr Stone. Please answer audibly.'

'Yes.'

'You approached Mr Sharples, as the choir master, for a reference, didn't you?'

'Yes.'

'But Mr Sharples wouldn't give Raymond a reference, would he?'

Stone became animated, rocking backwards and forwards, his hands in front of him, gripping the rail of the witness box.

'Sharples didn't know what he was doing. He didn't take the time and the trouble to...'

'I'm not concerned with the rights and wrongs of that, Mr Stone,' Ben said. 'I am sure you believe that Mr Sharples was wrong. That's not my concern. My point is that, once Mr Sharples formed that view, Raymond's only hope was Mr Little; because if the vicar recommends a boy, the school will generally audition him – at least take a look at him. Isn't that right?'

'Yes.'

'You asked Mr Little for a reference, didn't you?'

'Yes.'

'You needed it desperately because time was running out?'

'We had to do something quickly, yes.'

Ben paused.

'Mr Little refused, didn't he?'

Despondent, now.

'Yes.'

'How did you feel about that?'

The simple question, the invitation to express himself, seemed to take Stone aback. To Ben's surprise, he answered quietly.

'What hurt us was that he didn't even think about it,' Stone replied. 'He didn't even listen to Raymond sing, except in the choir on Sundays, and you can't tell much with the service going on, people coughing and moving around, and so on. You have to be there for choir practice. He didn't even consider it. We not only asked him, we begged him. But he just said that Sharples was a better judge than he was, and that was the end of it. And our family have been members of that congregation for three generations. We have been churchwardens, and...'

'I quite understand,' Ben said. 'He didn't treat you as you deserved to be treated. As your vicar, he let you down.'

'He did.'

'And you were angry about it, weren't you?'

The witness folded his arms again, and considered.

'I was very upset. We all were.'

'*Upset*?' Ben asked incredulously. 'You weren't upset, Mr Stone. You were angry. You were furious, weren't you?'

'I wouldn't say...'

'And that's what this is all about, isn't it?'

'I don't know what you mean by that.'

'Yes, you do. This is about revenge, isn't it? Mr Little thoughtlessly ended your son's musical career before it had even begun. And in return you, or Raymond, or both of you, have made up these stories about him, haven't you? To get your own back?'

Stone pointed a finger at Ben, spluttering.

'You can't say things like that,' he shouted. He turned to the judge. 'You tell him. He can't say things like that.'

'Counsel has a duty to put his case to you, Mr Stone,' the judge said quietly. 'You don't have to accept it. What do you say about it?'

'It is not true,' he shouted.

'I have no further questions,' Ben said dismissively, resuming his seat.

* * *

Gareth then called Raymond's mother, Angela Stone. All she could say was that she had gone up to Raymond's bedroom after his father had talked to him. The boy was very upset. She made him cocoa and settled him down in bed. Her husband had told her what Raymond had said but, before she could pass it on to the jury, Ben successfully objected that it was hearsay, and Gareth did not press the matter. Gareth did not ask her about the King's School. After a moment's hesitation, Ben decided not to cross-examine.

Lastly, Gareth called PC Willis, to deal with the arrest of the Reverend Little at his vicarage. He gave evidence that he had interviewed Little under caution later that same day, and that Little had stoutly denied any wrongdoing from first to last.

'Officer,' Ben asked, 'what was the defendant's reaction on being arrested?'

'He was extremely shocked, sir', Willis replied.

'How did that shock manifest itself?'

'When I told him he was under arrest, he almost collapsed into a chair, sir. I'm not sure he even heard me caution him. I repeated it two or three times, to make sure. I allowed his housekeeper to make him a cup of tea before I took him to the station. I had to leave it for several hours before I could interview him.'

'Thank you, officer.'

'His solicitor, Mr Singer, also witnessed his distress, sir,' Willis added, unprompted. 'He spent some time with Mr Little before he was interviewed.'

'Thank you very much officer,' Ben said. 'Nothing further.'

Gareth stood.

'May it please you, sir, that is the case for the prosecution.'

Judge Peterson looked up at the clock, which indicated that the time was 3.30.

'I think that's as far as we will go today,' he said. 'Members of the jury, we will resume at 10.30 tomorrow morning.'

'I will extend the defendant's bail overnight,' the judge said to Ben, after the jury had left court. 'But your client should be aware that I will not necessarily do so once the jury has retired.'

In the robing room, Gareth was hurriedly donning his tie and jacket.

'Fifteen minutes to catch my train,' he said. 'I think I can just make it.'

'You're not staying? You're going back to London and coming out here again tomorrow morning?' Ben asked.

'Oh, God, yes,' Gareth replied. 'You know me well enough, Ben. I don't like to be away from home unless I'm in Wales. Besides, I'm outnumbered here. I will see you tomorrow.'

He hesitated at the door and looked back at Ben.

'There's still time to plead.'

'Goodnight, Gareth,' Ben replied, smiling.

* * *

Barratt Davis was waiting for him outside the Town Hall. They stood together silently for a while, enjoying the fresh air of Market Square. The exertions of the day were catching up with them and, despite a light drizzle, they were grateful to be out of the stuffy atmosphere of the courtroom. At length, Barratt began the slow walk across the square to the George.

'I tried to get Little to hang around to talk to you, but he really wanted to get away,' Barratt said. 'He is a bit on edge, as one might expect. I told him to meet us at the hotel not later than 9 o'clock tomorrow, so you will have time to give him a few last-minute tips about giving evidence. I've explained that once he begins his evidence, he won't be able to talk to us until it's finished. He understands that.'

'Was he happy with the way things went today?'

'Yes, he seemed to be. He enjoyed your cross of Stone Senior – as did I, by the way.'

Ben smiled.

'Thank you. Yes, I think we scored a couple of points there. I don't think Gareth was happy with him. And he hardly pressed the mother at all, did he? It seemed to me that he wasn't sure what she might say.'

'And it was a good decision not to cross her,' Barratt replied. He stopped just outside the front door of the George. 'I have the impression that Little thinks we are doing well so far. He does have one concern, though, and he seems quite worried about it.'

'What's that?'

'It was what the judge said, just before he rose – about withdrawing bail once the jury retires. Little says he is extremely claustrophobic. The idea of being locked up while they decide his fate is making him anxious.'

Ben sighed.

'Barratt, if he is convicted…'

'Yes, I know,' Barratt said. 'I did remind him of that. But, for some reason, the idea of being locked up for this particular period of time is worrying him. I said you would mention it to the judge tomorrow. Can you do it before he gives evidence?'

Ben shook his head.

'That's not a good idea,' he replied. 'There is a good chance that the judge will be against us. It's not unusual for bail to be withdrawn at that stage in a serious case. If the judge tells him that before he gives evidence, he will be worrying about it more than he is now. I need him to be able to concentrate on his evidence. He's going to need his wits about him when Gareth cross-examines. Better to leave him with some hope of bail being extended and, if not, cross that bridge when we come to it.'

Barratt nodded.

'Fair enough.'

They entered the George. Jess had already taken possession of their favourite corner table. She stood as they approached.

'You both look like men who need a drink,' she smiled. 'I am happy to take orders to the bar. How did it go this afternoon?'

'I think it went as well as we could have hoped,' Barratt replied. 'Ben did quite a bit of damage to the prosecution witnesses. Hard to read this bloody jury, though. They are not giving anything away.

But at this point, I would say we are in with a chance. Mine's a pint of bitter – and then you can tell us about Joan Heppenstall.'

'Same for me, Jess, thanks,' Ben said.

The bar was quiet, and Jess returned quickly with drinks and dinner menus. She resumed her seat.

'Joan is in her room,' she said. 'She said she was tired, and would have room service. But she is here, and she has every intention of being in court tomorrow.'

Ben glanced across at Barratt.

'Jess, I'm depending very much on your judgment in this. You have talked to her. If anyone has a sense of whether we can trust her as a witness, it's you. It's a big decision. If we call her and she does well, there is no doubt it will help.'

Jess ran her hands through her hair nervously.

'What does "doing well" mean?' she asked.

'Ideally,' Barratt replied, 'we would like her to say that they spent days at a time in bed and they were at it like rabbits.'

Ben laughed. 'If she's going to say that, Barratt, let's make sure we call the Canon first,' he said.

'I will make a note of that,' Barratt grinned.

Ben became more serious. He leaned forward across the table.

'Jess, look, it's my decision whether or not to call her. I don't want you to worry about it. No one is going to blame you – certainly not me. But I need you to tell me honestly what you think. I trust your judgment. I'm not worried about her sinking him without trace out of malice. She would not have left York if that was how she felt. I'm sure of that, based on what you have told us before. She is obviously a woman of integrity. However much she may feel betrayed, I don't believe she would do that. But I am concerned that she might damn him with faint praise, if you get my point.'

Jess nodded thoughtfully.

'We talked quite a lot on the way from the station. I think she was being honest with me. She is here to help Ignatius. She is intelligent enough to know what that means.' She paused. 'I would call her.'

Ben smiled.

'Thank you,' he said. 'Then, that's what I will do. And now, to dinner.'

26

'I AM GOING to keep my examination in chief as short as I can,' Ben said. 'I can't guarantee how long cross-examination will last, but Mr Morgan-Davies is not one of those barristers who go on and on. He is usually short and to the point. The important thing, Mr Little, is that you concentrate on the questions. Answer the question and then stop. Don't try to make a speech. Don't try to defend yourself. That's my job. Keep it short. That way, you will give the jury the impression of confidence – and it will get you out of the witness box as quickly as possible.'

Ben was relieved that Little did not seem as nervous as he had feared. He was tense, but that was to be expected. Anything less and the jury might even be suspicious. Little nodded.

'I will be all right,' he said. 'I was very relieved to know that Joan was here. Suddenly I felt more confident.' He paused. 'I wish I could have seen her last night.'

'It wasn't advisable,' Ben replied quickly. 'She is going to give evidence for you. We don't want the jury thinking you have discussed your evidence together. Mr Morgan-Davies would be entitled to ask you about what you discussed. Much better to keep you apart until after you have both finished your evidence.'

'And on the other matter, Mr Schroeder, you will…?'

'Yes, I will ask the judge to extend bail while the jury is out,' Ben replied. 'I don't know what he will say, I can't promise anything, but I will ask. Don't think about that now, Mr Little. This is the most important moment of the trial. Everything may depend on your evidence. Concentrate on your evidence, and we will worry about everything else later.'

* * *

'Tell the jury something about yourself,' Ben said. 'Where did you grow up?'

Little seemed composed in the witness box, standing still and, as Ben had instructed him, speaking directly to the jury as he gave his answers.

'I grew up in Suffolk, not far from Ipswich,' he replied. 'My father was a vicar in a country parish. My mother helped him in the parish.'

'Brothers or sisters?'

'No. I'm an only child.'

'After school, what did you do?'

'I got a place at Selwyn College, Cambridge, to read Classics. I got an upper second.'

'What else did you do at college?'

'I helped the chaplain in chapel in various ways. But I also rowed a bit. Not in the first eight or anything like that, but our boat did reasonably well in the summer and Lent bumps.'

'No oar to put on the wall, though?' Ben asked, smiling.

Little smiled back. 'No, I'm afraid not.'

'When did you decide you wanted to be a clergyman?'

Little looked away from the jury for a moment, then back again. He took his time with his answer.

'I think I have always known. Certainly, since I was a boy. Of course, the church has always played a part in my life because of my father. But it always seemed natural to me to follow in his footsteps. I never really wanted to do anything else.'

'After Selwyn, you went on to theological college?'

'Ridley Hall in Cambridge, yes.'

'When were you ordained?'

'In 1959.'

'Just before we move on,' Ben said, 'when a man puts himself forward for ordination in the Church of England, does the Church make any inquiries about his character?'

'Very much so,' Little replied. 'They interview you in depth, they speak to your family, friends, everyone.'

'The jury will hear more detail about that from Canon Williams later,' Ben said. 'But let me just ask you this. Did anyone ever suggest to you that there was any problem about your being ordained? Any question about your character?'

'Never once,' Little replied firmly.

'What was your first posting after you were ordained?'

'I was curate at St Anthony's, Great Shelford. I stayed there for about three years – until last year, when I was appointed vicar at St Martin's in St Ives.'

'While you were curate at Great Shelford, did you have any particular responsibilities?'

'Several. One – which is quite a common thing for curates to undertake – was the church youth club.'

'Tell the jury about that. How many young people came to the club?'

'We might have anywhere from five or six up to twenty or more, depending on the time of year, and what kind of activities we planned.'

'Were there both boys and girls?'

'Yes.'

'What ages?'

'From ten up to seventeen. We didn't have a big enough congregation to have different clubs for different age groups, as they might in a bigger parish. They all joined in together.'

'Was any complaint ever made about your conduct in Great Shelford?'

'Never. On the contrary. I believe I was well liked. When I left, the youth club gave me a leather-bound volume of the Psalms and Proverbs.'

Ben paused. 'I suppose I should ask you this formally, though it is really quite obvious. Have you ever been convicted of any criminal offence?'

'Never.'

Ben paused again.

'Mr Little, did you indecently assault Raymond Stone?'

Little looked directly into the eyes of the jury.

'I did not.'

'Did you expose your penis to him?'

'I did not.'

'When Mr Stone telephoned you on the evening of 22 January,

did you say to him that you didn't know what came over you, or any words to that effect?'

'No. I had no reason to say any such thing.'

'Did you say that you were sorry about anything?'

'I may have said something like that, yes.'

'Why would you have said that?'

Little shook his head.

'Mr Stone was not making sense. It was late at night. He was talking very rapidly. He kept saying something about touching, but I didn't understand what he meant. I assumed he was saying that Raymond had somehow been hurt at church. I might very well have brushed up against Raymond in the vestry, of course. It's a small space and people are always getting in each other's way. But I had no recollection of Raymond complaining about anything. It never even occurred to me that he was referring to anything... you know... improper. Never, for a moment. The man was barely coherent. To tell you the truth, I thought he might have been drinking. I probably should have taken more time to ask questions and try to understand but, as I said, it was late, I was tired, I had a funeral service to conduct the next morning. I just wanted to get rid of him. I may well have said I was sorry but, if so, I was only talking about some accidental contact.'

Ben nodded.

'Mr Little, I am sorry to have to ask you this, but I must. Do you have any sexual interest in boys?'

'Absolutely not,' Little replied firmly.

'Who is Joan Heppenstall?' Ben asked.

'She is my fiancée.'

'You are engaged to be married?'

'Yes. But for this case, we would be planning our wedding now.'

'Do you still hope to marry her in due course?'

'Yes, I do,' Little replied without hesitation.

Ben smiled.

'Wait there, Mr Little. There may be some more questions for you.'

* * *

'So, Mr Little,' Gareth Morgan-Davies began, 'this ten-year-old boy has made all this up, has he?'

'He has.'

'He has made up a story involving exposure of the penis, the touching of a penis. He has got all that from his imagination, at the age of ten, has he?'

'I cannot say where he got it from.'

Gareth smiled.

'No, of course. But does it not follow from the questions put on your behalf that the boy either made all this up himself, or was fed the story by his father?'

'Yes, I suppose it does.'

'Yes. And all this, you say, is because you refused to give him a recommendation for a place at the King's School, is that right?'

'I cannot say.'

'That was the suggestion made on your behalf,' Gareth pointed out.

Ben stood.

'Sir, with all due respect to my learned friend, it is not for the defendant to speculate about why a story may have been made up.'

Judge Peterson looked puzzled.

'That was what you put to the witnesses, Mr Schroeder.'

'It was, sir. I have a duty to explore the evidence. But the defendant has no burden of proof. It is not for him to prove why witnesses may have lied.'

Before the judge could reply, Gareth intervened.

'Sir, I will be happy to re-phrase my question. Mr Little, you watched Raymond Stone give evidence to this jury. Did it seem to you that it was easy for him?'

Ben stood again.

'Sir…'

'The jury will draw their own conclusions about that, Mr Morgan-Davies,' the judge said.

'Very well, sir. Mr Little, is it your evidence that he lied to the jury?'

'Yes, it is.'

'This ten-year-old boy lied to this jury by saying that you exposed your penis to him?'

'Yes.'

'And by telling them that you touched his penis through his trousers? All lies?'

'Yes.'

'And while you cannot say why, you are not aware of any grudge or ill-feeling on his part, or his father's part, except for the matter of the King's School, is that right?'

'Yes.'

'If the family were to be angry with anyone about that, it should have been John Sharples, should it not, rather than you? After all, he was the organist, the choir master – he was the one who judged Raymond's talent as a singer?'

Little spread his arms out in front of him.

'I agree. But I was told that I had some influence in the matter.'

'Mr Sharples was alone in the church on the evening of 22 January, just as you were alone in the vestry, wasn't he? It would have been just as easy for him to accuse Mr Sharples falsely if he had chosen to do so. Is that not correct?'

'I cannot say. Sharples may have been alone in the church at some point, but I had asked Raymond to come to the vestry to assist me, and he agreed to do so.'

'Is it right that the Stone family have been loyal members of the St Martin's congregation for at least two generations?'

'To my knowledge, yes.'

'You are not telling the truth, are you, Mr Little? You have a sexual interest in boys which you did, perhaps, keep hidden until recently?'

'That is not true...'

'You found Raymond impossible to resist?'

'No.'

'You had the perfect opportunity, having him all to yourself in the vestry, with no one else around, didn't you?'

'No.'

'And you no doubt believed that even if he did complain, no one would believe him, no one would take his word against that of the vicar. Was that what you thought, Mr Little?'

Little had turned deathly pale. He rocked back and forth in the witness box.

'I did not hear a reply to my question, Mr Little.'

The reply was shouted, at the top of his voice. It was so shocking, after the quiet exchange which had preceded it, that the entire courtroom seemed to wake up from a reverie. The effect on the jury was palpable. The members of the jury sat up sharply in their seats, and stared at the witness.

'No!' He brought his fist down hard on the top of the witness box. 'That is not true. It is a pack of lies. I cannot say what has made them say these things against me. Perhaps I ought to have been more sensitive about the question of the school. But I had just arrived in the parish; it was my first living as vicar. I had a great deal to do, a great deal on my mind. Sharples had said that Raymond was not good enough for King's, and I thought no more about the matter. Perhaps I should have questioned him, but I did not. I regret that now. But I did not touch that boy or expose myself to him. I am a man of the cloth, a man of God. I am not guilty of this offence.'

Gareth seemed as taken aback as the jury. He sat down abruptly. Ben stood. He was not for one moment tempted to re-examine.

'Unless you have any questions, sir?'

Judge Peterson did not.

* * *

Canon Anselm Williams of Ely Cathedral gave evidence that before Ignatius Little had been admitted to Ridley Hall Theological College to study for ordination, the Diocese had carried out a thorough background check. It was standard procedure. In addition to establishing that he had never been in trouble with the law, an experienced Archdeacon of the Diocese had interviewed members of his family, his university tutor, his college chaplain, his headmaster and house master, and as many of his friends as they could find – all with the willing cooperation of Ignatius himself. No one had given the slightest hint of any unsuitability for the ministry, and there was no suspicion of any sexual interest other than towards women who were potential marriage partners. Since being ordained, Ignatius Little had been an effective and well-regarded clergyman. No complaints had been made about his behaviour. He had run a successful youth club for both boys and girls while serving as curate of St Anthony's, Great Shelford. The Diocese had great hopes for his future.

'Canon Williams,' Gareth asked, rising to his feet slowly, 'is it not true that, despite the careful inquiries which every diocese makes about its ordinands, there are occasionally cases in which clergymen come before the courts, and are convicted of criminal offences, including offences of dishonesty, even sexual offences?'

'That is true,' the Canon conceded.

'Does it not follow from that fact that those who make the inquiries are fallible, and that men are sometimes ordained who have a propensity to commit such offences?'

'All men, and all human endeavours, are fallible,' the Canon replied.

'Quite so,' Gareth said, sitting down.

* * *

Ben took a deep breath.

'May it please you, sir, I call Joan Heppenstall.'

As the usher led Joan into court, every eye turned towards her. She was dressed in a dark blue dress with matching shoes and handbag, a light blue hat worn slightly forward. She seemed composed as she walked unhurriedly to the witness box, pausing to turn and smile at the defendant in the dock. Ben turned behind him just enough to catch Jess's eye and mouth his thanks. Jess had spent the morning with Joan and had assured Ben that she was ready. Ben smiled as he looked across at Joan.

'Please don't be nervous, Miss Heppenstall. Please give the court your full name.'

'Joan Louise Heppenstall.'

'What is your relationship to the defendant, Ignatius Little?'

'I am his fiancée.'

'You are engaged to be married?'

'Yes.'

'When did you become engaged?'

'Just after Ignatius was ordained. But we agreed that we would not marry until he had his own living as a vicar.'

'I see. How did you meet?'

She smiled.

'My father is a canon at York Minster. Ignatius was one of a group of ordinands who came to York for a conference at which my father was presiding. We spoke, and a few days later he asked if he might come to York to see me again. I said "yes". He came to York several times, and I went to Cambridge several times to visit him. We fell in love. He asked me to marry him, and I said "yes".'

Ben closed his eyes for a moment. The moment which had kept him awake at night before and during the trial had arrived.

'*Most people think,*' Gareth had once told him during his pupillage, '*that success as a barrister comes from what you do in the courtroom. It doesn't. It comes from the late nights you spend working and from the nights you spend without sleep because you know that you are going to do something the following day which will make or break the case. You are going to do something which may get your client off, and which may sink him without trace and send him to prison for ten years. There is no way to tell which in advance. You can only rely on your gut, your instinct. Success at the Bar comes from being right when you take that kind of decision. And, Ben, there is no way to take that kind of decision without lying awake at night, sometimes night after night. Being in court is the easy part, once you get used to it. It's what goes on in your head and in your heart before you get to court, during the wee small hours, that really matters.*'

It had been 4 o'clock that morning before Ben had snatched a couple of hours of fitful sleep. He was about to ask questions which might result in victory, but which might equally send the defence into a death spiral. He had rehearsed the questions he was about to ask over and over in his mind. But he was most concerned, not about what he was going to ask her, but about what he was *not* going to ask her, and about what Gareth might ask her. Jess had persuaded him that he had nothing to fear from the answers Joan would give to him, but he knew instinctively that there was no way to predict what she might say if Gareth pressed her hard in cross-examination. Whether or not that happened might depend on how he asked the questions. He had finally decided on a bold approach.

'Miss Heppenstall, I am sorry that I have to ask you this. I would not do so if I had any alternative. Have you and Mr Little had full sexual intercourse?'

Joan blushed slightly, but answered without hesitation.

'No, we have not.'

'May I ask why not?'

'The Church does not approve of sexual intercourse before

marriage. Given the position that Ignatius holds in the church, we agreed that it would be wrong.'

'Of course. Again, I have no wish to embarrass you. I am not going to ask for details. It may be that my learned friend will do so. But for my purpose, I am content if you will answer simply "yes" or "no". Have you and Mr Little engaged in any sexual activity falling short of full sexual intercourse during the quite long period of your engagement?'

The answer, again, was immediate.

'We have, on a number of occasions.'

Ben nodded. 'Thank you, Miss Heppenstall. Please wait there. There may be further questions.'

Ben sat down and made a pretence of looking at some notes – anything not to betray his concern by looking at Gareth. Gareth took his time getting to his feet. He looked at Joan, then at Ben, finally at Joan again. There was a pause which seemed to Ben to go on for ever.

'I have no questions, sir,' he said, resuming his seat.

27

'THE QUESTION YOU have to decide, members of the jury,' Gareth said, 'is whether this ten-year-old boy, Raymond Stone, has come to this court to lie to you – to make false allegations against his vicar. If so, it was a wicked thing for this young boy to do, was it not? But is that what has happened here?'

Ben had closed his case. There would be time for closing speeches before lunch; the judge would sum up in the afternoon and the jury would then retire.

'You saw Raymond Stone give evidence, and you heard what he had to say. Do you remember how difficult it was for him? Do you remember how he had such trouble using the word "penis"? Did he subject himself to this ordeal, to the ordeal of making such shocking allegations against his vicar, to the ordeal of having to repeat them both before the magistrates and in this court, to the ordeal of being robustly cross-examined by my learned friend – very properly and ably cross-examined, let me add – when he knew they were untrue? Did his father, a loyal member of the defendant's congregation, put him up to it? What reason does the defence suggest for such treachery? That the family were angry because Mr Little had not supported Raymond's application to become a chorister at the King's School in Ely.'

Gareth paused and shook his head.

'Does that make any sense, members of the jury? Let us assume that Raymond wanted to go to King's, and that his family wanted that for him. Let us assume that it was a strong wish. But is that really a motive for this young boy and his father to exact such terrible revenge against this defendant – to ruin his career, indeed his life? It doesn't make sense, does it? Surely, if they wanted revenge against anyone it would have been against John Sharples, the choir

master. You may think that it would have been his decision to refuse
to recommend Raymond – the decision of a man who knew what he
was talking about in the world of music – that would have weighed
most with the school. John Sharples was available to be the victim
of a desire for revenge on the evening of 22 January, just as much
as Mr Little, was he not? He was alone in the church after choir
practice, locking the organ and arranging his music for the coming
Sunday services. Would it not have been just as easy for Raymond to
accuse Mr Sharples, if he wanted revenge? Just as simple and, you
may think, far more logical.'

Gareth paused to look towards the dock for a moment.

'No one wants to believe that a man of the Church would behave
in this way. We would all prefer to believe that clergymen are the
very model of virtue and, for the most part, they are so. But sadly,
as Canon Williams agreed, there will always be the exceptional
case. This is that case, members of the jury. The defendant might
well have reflected later, as he admitted to Raymond's father, that
he did not know what had come over him. But it is not difficult to
understand, is it? Mr Little has a weakness for young boys. Perhaps
in the past he had resisted it successfully. Apparently even those who
knew him best were unaware of it. But temptation overcame him on
the evening of 22 January, and he allowed his desires to overcome
his judgment. It is a tragic case, but your duty is to find him guilty of
an offence which is proved by the evidence.'

* * *

Ben stood at once.

'Different things are important to different people,' he began.
'Isn't that what life teaches us? To most of us, gaining a place at
a Church of England choir school may not be a matter of great
importance, or even of great interest. I confess, it certainly would
not in my case.'

Judge Peterson was frowning, but the members of the jury smiled
broadly. One or two chuckled aloud and, glancing to his right, Ben
saw that Gareth was also smiling.

'But to the Stone family, a place at King's would have made a
huge difference to Raymond's future, wouldn't it? School fees paid,

scholarships to be won, the prospect of a scholarship to a Cambridge college, the prospect of a bright future in the world of music – all of this was tantalisingly close, wasn't it? And Raymond is a gifted singer. Yes, John Sharples had his reservations about how good he was, but you heard evidence that the last word could have been that of the vicar of Raymond's parish – this defendant, Ignatius Little. Logical or not, the family believed that their vicar had the power to make it happen. He did not make it happen. He did not even try to make it happen. Mr Little admitted to you that he should have taken the matter more seriously, but he had just arrived in the parish, he had all manner of things to do, and it failed to engage his attention. You and I might have shrugged it off, members of the jury, got on with our lives. But remember that this was a family which had supported this church loyally for at least two generations. Is it beyond belief that they thought the parish – and the vicar – owed them something? Is it so hard to believe that they felt that their vicar might have taken the trouble to write just one letter, to make at least some effort to help them reach a goal that was so important to them?'

Ben turned over a page in his notebook.

'I disagree with my learned friend about that. But I also disagree with him on a more fundamental matter. This case is not about whether the King's School affair caused these false allegations to be made. I say that because it is not for the defendant to prove why false allegations have been made against him. When he directs you about the law this afternoon, the learned judge will tell you that the defendant does not have to prove his innocence. He does not have to prove anything. Under our system of law it is for the prosecution to prove the defendant guilty, if you are to convict, and they must prove him guilty beyond reasonable doubt. Anything less than that, and you must acquit. You can only find guilt proved if it is proved by the evidence. So let us turn away from speculating about motives, and examine the evidence.'

Ben paused to let his eye run swiftly over his notes.

'This case turns on what you make of the evidence of Raymond Stone, doesn't it? The learned judge will also direct you that it is dangerous – yes, dangerous, members of the jury – to convict on the evidence of such a young child, unless his evidence is corroborated, that is to say, supported by evidence independent of Raymond. The prosecution set out to prove that Raymond told his father what had happened when he arrived home. But you heard that, as recently as the committal proceedings before the magistrates in February, Mr Stone could not remember Raymond saying that Mr Little had exposed his penis, or that he had touched Raymond's penis. He said not a word about that, even though my learned friend pressed him. Yet he tells you now that Raymond did give those details to him. How could he not have remembered that before? It is simply not credible, is it? And even if it were, members of the jury, the learned judge will tell you that what Raymond said to his father could not be corroboration, because it was not independent – it was evidence coming from Raymond himself.'

Ben leaned forward, stretching his hands out on the bench in front of him.

'So the prosecution falls back on what was billed as the decisive evidence. Mr Little, it is said, admitted the offence to Godfrey Stone during that late-night phone call. You have heard Mr Little's account of that phone call, members of the jury, and you may think that it had the ring of truth. Members of the jury, do you really think that, if Mr Little had said to Mr Stone, *"I don't know what came over me"*, Mr Stone would have kept quiet about that until just before the committal proceedings? And that was the evidence, wasn't it? He said nothing to the police when he phoned them the next morning; nor did he mention it when he went to the police station to make his complaint. Don't you think that, if Mr Little had admitted such an offence, that would have been the first thing he told the police? Could it be, members of the jury, that he had suddenly realised that the evidence was not going to be enough unless he helped the prosecution out with something more? There may be more than one reason, gentlemen, why Raymond Stone had difficulty in saying the word "penis". It could simply be that he was reluctant to lie to you, but felt that he had no choice, once matters had been taken this far.'

Ben put his notebook aside and stood up straight. He glanced towards the dock.

'Members of the jury, like all defendants, this defendant is entitled to the benefit of the doubt. But I submit that you do not need to rely on the benefit of the doubt in this case. The evidence is not nearly enough to convict, and it is essentially uncorroborated, making it dangerous to convict. Ignatius Little is a man of good, even of exemplary character. He is a man of the cloth. Such a man is not to be convicted on evidence such as this. Restore him to his church; restore him to his fiancée. Return the only verdict open to you on the evidence – one of not guilty.'

28

PAUL HAD SUGGESTED that they retire to the George while the jury was out. He would telephone the hotel when they were needed back at court. The jury had retired at 3.15 after a summing up which both Ben and Gareth thought fair and balanced. But, to Ben's disappointment, the judge had ordered Ignatius Little to remain in custody while the jury deliberated. Little looked pale and shocked as the prison officer took him to the cells. But they could do nothing now except wait in the hotel lounge. Jess had ordered coffee. John Singer had been invited to join them, but had withdrawn to All Saints church to confer with Canon Williams.

'Where is Joan?' Ben asked. 'I saw her in court during the closing speeches and summing-up, but I lost her when we came out of court. I wanted to introduce myself properly and thank her.'

Jess took a deep breath.

'She left for the station as soon as the jury retired,' she replied.

'What?'

'I told her we would take her back to Peterborough later if she wanted to wait for the verdict. I said she could spend another night here if she wanted to. But she said she wanted to catch a train and go home as soon as she could.'

They were silent for some time. Barratt raised his coffee cup.

'Well, Ben, bloody good job, win, lose or draw,' he said. 'Any predictions?'

Ben looked up at the ceiling.

'We have a chance. But I'm afraid the jury might agree with Gareth about the Stone family's motive for fabricating something like this. It does seem a bit far-fetched when you sit back and look at it objectively. So I think we are not out of it, but we have to be prepared for the worst.'

'Likely sentence?'

'Twelve to eighteen months.'

Barratt exhaled heavily.

'On the other hand,' he insisted, 'you demolished the father's evidence. How could he not have remembered what Raymond said until trial? How could he not have remembered a confession over the phone?'

'So, your prediction is…?'

Barratt grimaced. 'Guilty, if I had to bet on it,' he conceded. 'Despite all that. Somehow, I just can't picture that boy lying about things like that. He may have; but it's just hard to picture.'

Jess was smiling.

'What do you think?' Barratt asked.

'Not guilty,' she replied firmly.

'You sound very confident,' Ben smiled.

'I was watching the jury when Joan gave her evidence,' Jess said simply. 'They liked her.'

* * *

The call to return to court came just after 6 o'clock. The long day had not diminished the enthusiasm of the public or the press, and Ben had to push his way through the throng of expectant spectators to take his seat in counsel's row. Gareth was already in court and smiled as Ben opened his notebook.

'What do you say? Half a crown?'

Ben smiled back. 'Done.'

He turned to look towards the dock as the officer brought Little into court. He looked ghastly. Ben confined himself to a nod – a smile might raise his hopes unfairly. They all stood as Judge Peterson entered court. Finally, Paul led the jury back to the jury box. The foreman was a portly man in his fifties, his dark three-piece suit enlivened by a red and white dotted handkerchief fluted casually in his top pocket. Philip Eaves curtly ordered the foreman and the defendant to stand.

'Mr Foreman, has the jury reached a verdict on which you are all agreed?'

'We have, sir.'

'On this indictment, charging the defendant, Ignatius Little, with indecent assault on a male under sixteen, do you find the defendant guilty or not guilty?'

The foreman looked directly at Judge Peterson.

'Not guilty,' he replied firmly.

'You find the defendant not guilty, and is that the verdict of you all?'

'It is.'

Ben glanced to his left as he stood and caught Gareth's whispered congratulation.

'Told you so,' he heard Jess whisper behind him.

'Sir, may the defendant be discharged?'

The judge was about to reply when there was a loud crash from the dock. Ben turned, just in time to see the dock officer lunge forward in an effort to prevent Ignatius Little from collapsing. He was too late. With surprising dexterity, Paul ran to the dock to lend a hand. After a glance at the floor of the dock, he turned to the judge.

'Sorry, sir, but is there a doctor in the house?'

The foreman was already making his way from the jury box.

'There is,' he replied. 'Let me through, please.'

Judge Peterson ordered the court to be cleared, and left the bench. By the time the courtroom had emptied, the foreman had administered smelling salts and Little was beginning to sit up. The usher brought him a glass of water.

'Just fainted,' the foreman said. 'The stress of the occasion, most likely. He will be all right tomorrow. It would be a good idea for him to take it easy tonight – go home, draw the curtains and spend a restful evening, drinking water, but nothing stronger.'

He began to make his way from the dock.

'I would definitely advise leaving the communion wine where it is,' he added, turning his back.

Little looked around him. Ben was leaning on the rail of the dock, Barratt and Jess immediately behind him. John Singer and Canon Williams stood several feet away, looking uncertain as to what to make of the situation.

'You are free to go sir, whenever you feel up to it,' the dock officer said. 'But if I were you, I would sit there for a while till you get your breath back. There's no rush.'

Little sat quietly for some minutes, before allowing the dock officer to help him to his feet. He adjusted his tie.

'How are you feeling now?' Barratt asked.

'I'm all right,' Little replied shakily. 'Thank you, Mr Schroeder, Mr Barratt, everyone. I can't thank you enough.'

'We are pleased that it worked out well,' Barratt replied. 'I'm sure Mr Singer will give you a lift home to St Ives. You will have some things to discuss with him in connection with the Diocese, but I would recommend leaving that for a day or two until the stress has worn off a bit.'

Little suddenly smiled.

'I will feel better as soon as I speak to Joan,' he replied. 'Where is she? Is she outside?'

Ben walked quietly back to counsel's row to collect his papers, leaving Barratt and Jess to field that particular question. Looking back a moment or two later, he saw Little sit down again in the dock, holding his head in his hands. Glancing down at his brief, he saw a small hand-written note lying on top. *'Well done,'* the note read. *'See you back in Chambers.'* On top of the note was a gleaming half crown.

29

DESPITE THE LATENESS of the hour, Ben returned to Chambers to leave his robes and check for messages from Merlin. Once John Singer had taken charge of ferrying a disconsolate Ignatius Little back to St Ives, he had enjoyed a couple of beers with Barratt and Jess on the train back to London. He was ready to go home and get some rest, but duty called. To his surprise, there were lights burning in Chambers. He looked at his watch – almost 10.30 – and he took a curious walk through the corridors. Perhaps just the cleaners. But he found Gareth Morgan-Davies in his room, a glass of whisky before him on his desk. On seeing Ben, he stood cheerily.

'Ben, come in my dear boy. You found your half crown, I hope?'

Ben grinned. 'Yes. Thank you.'

'Papers for next week,' Gareth confided. 'I had to come in and take a quick look. What's your excuse?'

'Habit, I suppose,' Ben replied. 'Merlin has drilled it into me so often – always check in. By the time the jury came back it was too late to call Chambers.'

'Quite right, too. Drink?'

'I don't mind if I do,' Ben said. 'I'm exhausted.'

Gareth poured him a glass of whisky and waved him into a chair. 'You did well, Ben,' he said. 'Did he do it?'

Ben savoured his first taste of the whisky, warm and mellow.

'I hope not,' he replied.

'It was the girl who made the difference,' Gareth said. 'It was the right thing to call her. I thought he came across as a bit wooden, but she was very human. It must have been hard for the jury to imagine him interfering with little boys when he had her in his life.'

Ben nodded. 'Yes, that was our assessment of it,' he replied. 'How did you get on with the prosecuting solicitor? Will he be sending more work to Chambers?'

'Yes, I think so,' Gareth replied. 'He seemed happy. I don't think he expected too much of this case, what with Little being a clergyman of good character. It was always going to be an uphill battle, and I don't think the verdict came as a complete surprise. Yes, I think he is serious about coming to us, and I should think Merlin will be able to sell you to him without too much trouble after your work for Mr Little.' He smiled. 'In fact, I have already put in a good word.'

'Thank you,' Ben said, raising his glass.

'Ben, you said some time ago that you wanted to talk about your being taken on in Chambers. What was it you wanted to know, exactly?'

Ben put his glass down on the small side table by his chair. He hesitated.

'I suppose I wanted to know why, how it happened.'

Gareth smiled.

'It happened because you were elected unanimously by the members of Chambers.'

Ben returned the smile. 'Yes. But it was all so odd – or so it seemed to me. There was a time when you seemed sure that Chambers wanted to take on both Harriet and me, that there would be enough work for all of us. And then something happened, and you didn't talk about it for a long time, and I got the sense that it would be just Harriet. It wasn't until Merlin came through to the pupils' room after the Chambers meeting that I knew I had been elected, and at that point I was in shock. I had been sure it was over. I was all ready to gather up my things and move on. I didn't know whether it was Anthony Norris, or something to do with whatever was going on in Chambers.'

Gareth nodded. He stood and re-filled both their glasses.

'I quite understand your confusion,' he replied. 'It was a confusing time.' He paused. 'All right. I will tell you what I know. But I don't know everything. The only person who knows everything is Bernard Wesley, and if he hasn't told me, he won't tell you. And it's probably right that he should not tell either of us the whole story. It involves some rather delicate matters. If the full story were known, even now, it would not do Chambers any good. So, be discreet with this.'

'Of course,' Ben said.

'You know about Clive Overton, of course – his history at Cambridge. We talked about it the other day.'

'Yes.'

'So you know that his father, Miles, had sent him to America, with instructions not to darken our shores again. But then Kenneth Gaskell got himself involved in a messy divorce case, Bernard leading him and Miles Overton leading Ginny Castle on the other side.'

'Yes. I know the case settled rather abruptly. Kenneth and Anne were married, and the husband got access to Simon, which was what he really wanted out of it.'

'All perfectly true,' Gareth agreed. 'What you probably didn't know was that Kenneth and Anne had known each other for years. They grew up close to each other in Surrey, and there was apparently some mutual attraction between them, which rekindled during the case.'

Ben sat back in his chair.

'Yes. I need hardly tell you that this is the part that you should be discreet about. They began a relationship, assuming that they had an overwhelming case against the husband and that he would fold, and the case would go away, very quickly. Unfortunately, they reckoned without Miles and Ginny and a rather enterprising local solicitor who set a private detective on them.'

Ben exhaled sharply.

'Yes, photographs and all, so I understand, though I haven't seen them, of course. Anyway, to make a long story short, Miles and Ginny drafted a cross-petition, alleging adultery against Anne and Kenneth, which they threatened to serve and proceed with, unless Bernard agreed to capitulate. They gave him seven days to think about it. Bernard's instructing solicitor was Herbert Harper of Harper, Sutton & Harper. You met Herbert a number of times when you were my pupil; you know how much work he sends to Chambers, so you can imagine how he reacted to it.'

'Bernard told him everything?'

'Of course. He had no choice. Herbert knew what a strong case of cruelty they had against the husband. There could be no explanation for caving in and giving him everything he wanted. Predictably, Herbert wanted Kenneth's head on a silver platter and he was on the point of removing all his work from Chambers.'

Ben shook his head. 'That would have been...'

'A disaster, yes. It would have been the end of Chambers. It wasn't just a question of Herbert's work, though God knows that alone would have been a huge blow. But if Herbert removed his work it would only be a matter of time before all our other solicitors asked themselves why, and the whole story would have leaked out sooner or later – probably sooner. It would have been the end and, of course, Miles Overton knew that only too well.'

Gareth saw that Ben had almost finished his whisky and, without asking, refilled both their glasses.

'From that point forward, Ben, my knowledge is patchy. I know that Bernard went up to Cambridge to see Harriet's father. Both he and Miles had been at his college, of course, as had Clive, until his university career ended so abruptly. Bernard did not tell me what they discussed, but I remember that when he got back, his spirits seemed to have revived. He had been completely devastated after his meeting with Herbert, almost ready to give up, it seemed to me. But when he returned from Cambridge he was a new man. He wouldn't tell me what was going on. But he asked me – well, ordered me, would be a better way of putting it – to do two things. The first was that, when he asked me, I was to accept a pupil without question. He wouldn't tell me who, at the time, but...'

'Clive Overton,' Ben said.

'Yes.'

'What was the second thing?'

Gareth took a long time to reply.

'Bernard ordered me to make sure Harriet was offered a tenancy in Chambers, regardless of what I had to do to make it happen.'

'Regardless...'

'Ben, I swear, I didn't think there would be the slightest difficulty. Chambers had been talking about taking you both on for some time. I had been pushing the idea that there was more than enough work – and I was right. Aubrey didn't object as long as Harriet got in, of course. Kenneth had been banished from London with instructions to do whatever Bernard told him to do. Peter and Roger could be persuaded easily enough. But I ran into a problem...'

'Anthony Norris,' Ben said quietly.

'Yes. Ben, it wasn't what you think. It wasn't because you were

Jewish. He had talked about that in the past, but that was before your win at the Old Bailey. For some reason, he seemed to have set his face against taking you both. But he actually told me that, if it came to a choice, he would choose you over Harriet. Of course, that put me in the position of having to speak out for Aubrey's pupil instead of my own. I had a drink with Aubrey and Anthony at the Club, and I still remember the look they gave me when I told them where I stood: that I preferred to take you both, but that if it came to a choice, I would have to choose Harriet. I remember desperately wanting to tell them why, to tell them what was going on. But I couldn't. Bernard had demanded total confidentiality. And there it was. It was agreed.'

He paused to take a deep draught of his whisky.

'I hated doing it, Ben, I want you to know that. I told Bernard that we had to find you a place elsewhere if we couldn't take you, and I want you to believe that he agreed immediately, and that we would have done so. It was just that…'

'You had other concerns,' Ben replied in a matter-of-fact tone. 'I understand that, Gareth. Of course, you had to do whatever it took to save Chambers.'

'After I had secured agreement for Harriet, Bernard had a meeting with Miles and everything was resolved. In due course Clive arrived in Chambers as my pupil.'

He sat back in his chair.

'And that, Ben, is all I know.'

Ben stared, open-mouthed.

'But in that case, how was I elected? How…?'

'I honestly haven't the faintest bloody idea,' Gareth replied. 'Bernard proposed you himself immediately after we had elected Harriet. I was stunned. I hadn't expected it, and I am quite sure that no one else expected it. Bernard didn't give me any warning. But he proposed you, and made it fairly clear that he would regard it as unacceptable if you were not elected. I seconded the motion, of course, and it was carried unanimously. I can only assume that, for whatever reason – whether because he was intimidated by Bernard on the day, or because he thought it was the right thing to do or, knowing Anthony, just on a whim – Anthony changed his mind. I remember that there was a kind of collective sigh of relief when he put his hand up. But as to why, Ben, your guess is as good as mine.'

He drained his glass.

'I'm sorry that I have had to tell you such an awful tale, Ben – especially on a day when you have had such a notable success. But perhaps it's the best day to tell you because, after all, none of that matters now. All that matters is that you are a member of Chambers and you are doing well. And the next time we meet to decide whether to take on a new tenant, you and Harriet will be there voting with us.'

Ben nodded. He put his glass down and left after wishing Gareth a good night.

30

21 June

MARTIN HARDCASTLE CHECKED into his room at the George Hotel in Huntingdon at about 4 o'clock on Sunday afternoon, the day before the trial of Billy Cottage was due to begin. He was aware that Ben Schroeder and Barratt Davis were not planning to arrive until early evening, bringing with them all the case papers and a supply of notebooks and pens. He preferred to establish himself in his room before they arrived, so that he could make the arrangements he needed to make with the hotel staff without the risk of being overheard. A young man called John was assigned to carry Martin's bags and robes upstairs to his room. Martin had requested this particular room because it was situated at the far end of the corridor, to the right on the first floor of the hotel. As a result, instead of overlooking the High Street or the courtyard, the view was limited to a short terrace of rather ugly cottages on George Street. The view was of no concern to Martin Hardcastle. What mattered was that he was away from the hustle and bustle of the hotel, the endless comings and goings of guests and staff.

John was 18 years of age. He had short ginger hair and an unprepossessing appearance. His nose was short and stubbed and his face had not yet quite shed the last pimply blotches of adolescence. He was slightly built, but the effortless manner in which he carried heavy items up and down the steep staircase bore witness to a strength which the awkward angular shape of his body did not suggest. John trained hard in his spare time. He was a promising amateur inside right, and still harboured dreams of playing at a higher level. Martin noted the strength as he watched John carefully deposit the bags by the large wardrobe which stood against the wall opposite the bed.

John was turning to leave. Martin already had the ten pound note in his hand and, without actually offering it, was making no effort to conceal it.

'The name's John, is it?'

'Yes, sir.'

'How long have you worked at the George, John?'

The answer appeared to require some thought. 'About a year, sir.'

'A year. I see. Then you probably know by now the importance of discretion. You look like a trustworthy young man to me. Can you be trusted to be discreet, John?'

John grinned. 'Yes, sir.' It was true. John had kept quite a few secrets during his time at the George, all related to finding people in rooms who should not have been there and who, when found, were not wearing much by way of clothing. And at his football club he was practising discretion by keeping quiet about the thing between his coach and the centre half's wife, which was now entering its second season.

Martin extended his arm slightly, bringing the ten-pound note into clearer view. John could not keep from grinning.

'I know what you're thinking. But it's nothing like that, I assure you. What I would like from you, John, is room service. I shall take my breakfast and dinner in my room each day during my stay, and I should like you to bring my meals to me. In addition, I will sometimes require a bottle of Bell's whisky, for which I shall pay in cash. I require a bottle this evening, and there may be other evenings when I require the same. In addition, I require that you bring it to me without attracting any attention either to me or to the bottle. Finally, I require your discretion in not answering any questions you may be asked about me, by other members of staff or anyone else, and in reporting to me any questions that are asked. I have a number of associates who will be checking into the hotel later. Naturally, I will spend some time downstairs with my associates, and I will be in and out of the hotel during the day. Do not pay any special attention to me at those times.' He paused. The grin had vanished. 'Do you understand everything that I have said?'

'Yes, sir.'

Martin extended his arm fully, proffering the ten pound note.

John's hand closed around the note but, as he tried to pull it towards him, Martin tightened his grip.

'One moment,' he said. 'This is for you, and there will be others where that came from, but first I need to know whether we have an agreement.'

John put a finger over his lips. 'Yes, sir. We have an agreement.'

Martin smiled brightly and released his grip on the note.

'Excellent.' He reached into his pocket for a further note. 'Then you may bring the bottle now, and I will arrange dinner later.'

31

'WHERE'S MY MAIN barrister?' Billy Cottage asked. It was a reasonable question. Billy had met his QC only once, on the occasion of a conference at Bedford Gaol. Barratt Davis had assured him repeatedly that Martin Hardcastle would be fully attentive to the case. Yet, here he was at the Huntingdon Summer Assize; his trial was about to begin; and so far he had seen only his junior counsel and his solicitor. It was not helping that the cell in which Billy was confined was small and claustrophobic. It was on the outside wall of the building in a small corridor at the rear of Court 1. Paul, the usher, who liked to think of himself as a friend and confidant of Ben Schroeder and Barratt Davis now that they were in their second trial in his court, had cleared the corridor for them so that they could confer with Billy through the bars, and not make matters worse by crowding into the cell.

'Mr Hardcastle will be here shortly,' Barratt replied. 'It's the first day of the assize and he has a ceremonial duty to perform as Queen's Counsel.'

'The assize begins with a service at the parish church,' Ben added, 'with everyone in full regalia. After the service, the judge processes across the square to the court with his chaplain, the mayor, the sheriff, and Uncle Tom Cobley and all. The judge asked Mr Hardcastle to join the procession. As a QC he could not really say "no". There's nothing unusual about it. There is always a lot of fuss on the first day of the assize. Don't worry, he will be here to see you once all that is over. The trial won't begin straight away, in any case. There are some more ceremonial things to do in court, and then the judge has a plea of guilty to deal with, and a civil matter which has settled. They also have to sort the jury panel out, so it will be some time before they are ready for us. I know it's not very comfortable here. It's an old building...'

Billy had stopped listening. His understanding of the world had reached its limits with all the talk of church services and full regalia, processions in which his QC was obliged to join with his judge, the mayor and all the rest of them. These were things which did not impinge on his world. His only previous experience of court was his appearance before the magistrates, which had lasted less than half an hour. What had this to do with a trial in which they would decide whether or not he would hang? For that matter, what did Ben Schroeder's wig and gown have to do with it? It was all a million miles away from the Fenstanton lock. The lock, he understood – understood it better than any man living. He understood Eve and he understood his house. Beyond those limits he was a stranger. And being a stranger was an uncomfortable feeling. All he wanted was to get back to his lock and his house; to get back to Eve. Why couldn't they just get it over with instead of having services and processions? He had been waiting months already. Get it over with. Suddenly those words brought back the reality of his situation in sharp focus. His vision narrowed. He started to sweat and felt faint. He sat down on the narrow bench at the back of his cell. It seemed to have become darker, and the old refrain filled his head again...

When I was bound apprentice in famous Lincolnshire,
Full well I served my master for nigh on seven years.

'Let's see if we can get him some water', Barratt said. 'I will be back in a moment, Billy. Sit forward and hold your head down as low as you can between your hands.'

'Do you think he will be all right in court?' Jess asked.

'He will have to be. It's always the same in a case like this. They sit in jail pretending it's never going to happen, and then, suddenly, one day it does. The reality hits them. We will take care of him, Ben, if you want to go outside to wait for Martin.'

Ben nodded and they walked together along the short corridor to the door which led out into the foyer of the Town Hall. Barratt turned to speak to the two prison guards who had taken up their positions outside the door at Paul's request. Ben saw a familiar figure in wig and gown looking through a window at the front of the building, as if to see whether there was any excitement in the square yet. He smiled and walked over to Andrew Pilkington.

'Andrew. I see you are prosecuting me again.'

Pilkington turned with a smile. He cut an elegant figure. Well over six feet in height with piercing blue eyes, he eschewed the standard barrister's three-piece suit with its inhibiting waistcoat in favour of a black double-breasted jacket and dark grey trousers with the suggestion of a white pinstripe.

'Indeed I am. Ben Schroeder. The rape case at the Bailey, wasn't it? What was his name?'

'Harry Perkins.'

'Perkins, that was the chap. And you got him off after telling Milton Janner to bugger off and stop interrupting you. I've been dining out on the story ever since. So has the judge, I believe. How are you, Ben?'

Ben laughed. 'Very well, thanks. I'm not planning on doing anything similar in this case. I have leading counsel to make sure I don't misbehave – or get out of my depth.'

'Ah yes, the formidable Martin Hardcastle, no less. Where is Martin? Not running late, I hope, if you know what I mean. You'll have to keep an eye on him, Ben, you know.'

'As a matter of fact, Andrew, at this very moment he is attending church, fully robed and ready to process across the square with the judge.'

'Really? Well, good for him.'

There was a silence.

'I didn't know they let you Treasury Counsel types out of the Old Bailey to visit the provinces,' Ben said. 'Are you being led, or are you on your own?'

Andrew took a deep breath. 'I'm flying solo. I've done several capital murders as junior, led by more senior Treasury Counsel. But this is the first time they have let me loose on my own. It is easier away from home, and they thought this case... well, you know...'

'It's a strong case,' Ben interjected. 'Yes, I know. You don't have to tell me.'

'Even I shouldn't mess this one up,' Andrew added.

'There's no question of your messing anything up, Andrew,' Ben smiled. He was remembering Andrew Pilkington's grasp of detail and his pleasant, understated, but precise manner with witnesses and the jury – a potentially lethal combination. 'And I'm sure they know that about you already. They wouldn't have sent you otherwise.'

'Thank you for the vote of confidence, Ben,' Andrew replied, returning the smile. 'I hope I can live up to it. I don't expect you to hope for that, needless to say.' He turned back towards the window. 'Oh, look, I think the procession is getting ready for the long trek. I am seeing a number of people in very silly fancy dress.'

* * *

Mr Justice Lancaster was not particularly fond of pomp and ceremony. Before his appointment as a judge of the Queen's Bench Division of the High Court some seven years earlier, Steven Lancaster had practised in Silk at the commercial bar. He accepted a judicial appointment at the third time of asking. On the first two occasions he had declined because, having two sons still at expensive schools, he preferred to avoid the reduction in income that the judicial salary would entail. But on the third occasion, the Lord Chancellor made it clear that the offer would probably not be made again, and he duly accepted the reduced income, albeit with the considerable compensation of the prestige of the High Court and a knighthood. He accepted the complicated formal dress as part of the job, though he was sure that, without his clerk Simon, who had a thorough understanding of such mysteries, he would never have sorted out the various robes appropriate to criminal and civil cases, summer and winter sittings. Simon could be relied upon to have the correct dress laid out for him in his Chambers, whether in London or on circuit. Like most High Court judges, when he was first appointed, Lancaster's knowledge of criminal law was almost non-existent. It was a field into which most likely candidates for the High Court bench rarely strayed. But, unlike many of his colleagues, instead of trying to bluff his way through until he got the hang of it by sheer dint of experience, Steven Lancaster took a more practical approach. At his first sitting in a criminal case, which happened to be at the Old Bailey, he called counsel into his Chambers, admitted his almost complete ignorance of criminal law and practice, and asked for their help. It was given without hesitation and induced respect, rather than contempt, in the eyes of the barristers practising before him. Within three years, he was generally held to be as good as any judge of the Division in criminal cases.

It was still a bit of an ordeal getting dressed up in his formal robes, including full-bottomed wig, tights, and black buckled shoes, and walking in procession in public. But at least at Huntingdon the walk across Market Square was a short one, and once in court he could revert to his everyday robes, shorter wig, and normal footwear. He had already sat through a rather tedious service in a chilly All Saints Church, and listened to the traditional sermon on the virtues of justice given by his chaplain for the assize. As he waited for the procession to form, he felt some impatience. He knew, of course, that a capital murder case awaited him. He had dealt with such cases before. He had no particular views for or against capital punishment in principle, though he was sceptical about its claim to act as a deterrent. The persistently constant murder rate seemed to suggest that it was not.

On the other hand, perhaps there was a certain justice about it. But the physical reality of it all disturbed him. The process of pronouncing the death sentence wearing the black cap was grotesque, its effect on the defendant and his family devastating. Facing a man he was to sentence, knowing that he would almost certainly be dead within a few weeks, was something no judge relished – even though the public and press sometimes entertained speculations to the contrary – and most were heartily glad when the moment passed and they could escape from the bench to the sanctuary of their Chambers. He forced his mind away from the subject while he waited. At last they were ready.

Philip Eaves, acting today as clerk of assize, led the way in formal morning dress, bearing a box perched on a small cushion. The box contained the Queen's Commissions of Assize, Oyer and Terminer, and Gaol Delivery, which authorised the judge to sit on circuit. Behind Eaves walked the chaplain in clerical garb; behind the chaplain, the High Sheriff, wearing a morning coat resplendent with medals, breeches and buckled shoes, a ceremonial sword hanging from his belt on the left side; behind the Sheriff, Simon in morning dress; behind Simon, Mr Justice Lancaster in his summer criminal robes. Behind the judge came the Mayor of Huntingdon, wearing his chain of office and, behind him, the Town Councillors. Behind the Councillors walked Martin Hardcastle, Queen's Counsel, fully robed. Uniformed police officers flanked the procession on both sides.

As the judge entered the Town Hall, Ben and Andrew bowed respectfully. Martin Hardcastle detached himself from the procession and walked over to join them. Mr Justice Lancaster was conducted to his Chambers, where someone from the office was making him a nice cup of tea.

Martin nodded briefly to Andrew.

'Pilkington, a word outside, if you please. Schroeder, would you please go into court and make sure that our instructing solicitor has brought all the necessary papers with him? Please make sure you have all the documents in place in front of you to hand to me when needed. Mr Davis may place my brief, unopened, in my place on the Silks' bench.'

Smiling, Andrew raised his eyebrows towards Ben.

'Certainly,' Ben replied. 'Are you coming to see Mr Cottage before we begin?'

Hardcastle waved the question away.

'Later. I have a number of matters to discuss with Pilkington and I am not sure how long we may have before the judge is ready to start the trial.'

He placed an arm around Andrew Pilkington's shoulders and ushered him quickly outside. Turning to make his way into Court 1, Ben saw Martin light a cigarette as he stood close to Andrew, the two engaged in an animated conversation. In court, Barratt Davis and Jess Farrar were unpacking the documents from the boxes in which they had travelled and placing them on the second row, reserved for junior counsel, and the third row, in which they would sit. The courtroom was a hive of activity. The public gallery was filling up, resulting in constant movement and a hubbub of conversation. Simon, assisted by the High Sheriff's secretary, was busy arranging the judge's papers on the bench. Philip Martineau, prosecuting solicitor for the County, was talking to a representative of the Director of Public Prosecutions. Paul was conferring with

Philip Eaves, who was doing his best to talk to him while at the same time tying the ribbons of his bands securely behind the back of his head. Counsel appearing in the matters listed before the trial of Billy Cottage were jealously guarding the small space they had been able to claim in counsel's row as Philip Martineau and Barratt Davis gradually encroached on it with their mountain of papers. The courtroom looked as though it had shrunk, and had suddenly become very small.

'He wants his brief placed, unopened, in front of his place in the Silks' row,' Ben said, with more than a hint of frustration.

'I know,' Barratt replied. 'I've been through this before with His Majesty. Where is he, by the way? I thought the procession had finished.'

'He is talking to Andrew Pilkington outside. I tried to get him to see Cottage, but nothing doing. He said he would see him later.'

Barratt shook his head. 'He doesn't like talking to clients during a trial. He says it breaks his concentration. He will be as good as his word – he will go to see him later.' Seeing Ben's look, he smiled. 'Don't worry. You will get used to it.'

Before he could reply, Philip Eaves called for silence and asked whether everyone was ready for the judge to make his entrance. Mr Justice Hardcastle entered court in his red robes, flanked by the High Sheriff and the chaplain – another relic of the assize. They would quietly disappear after lunch, by which time the real work of the assize would have begun.

32

BILLY COTTAGE'S CASE was called on just after 11.15. A jury panel had been assembled and was waiting outside Court 1. Martin Hardcastle had asked that they remain outside until he had addressed the judge on a point of law. This was it, Ben thought. The battle for the life of Billy Cottage begins here.

'My Lord, before the jury is sworn,' Martin said, rising to his feet, 'there is a point of law I must raise, and it is one which must be dealt with now, as a preliminary point.'

'Yes, Mr Hardcastle?'

'My Lord, your Lordship has seen the indictment. The Crown proposes to try William Cottage for capital murder, the allegation being that he murdered Frank Gilliam in the course or furtherance of theft. While there is some evidence that whoever attacked Frank Gilliam later stole a gold cross and chain from Jennifer Doyce, it is the Crown's case that Cottage raped Jennifer Doyce, and that he killed Frank Gilliam to facilitate that crime. Moreover, I do not think my learned friend will dispute that the evidence he proposes to call will show that Frank Gilliam was already dead by the time the attacker, whoever he was, stole the cross and chain. The killing could not, therefore, have been in the course or furtherance of the theft; and it is clear that he stole from Jennifer Doyce, not from Frank Gilliam. I invite your Lordship to direct the Crown to prefer an indictment which alleges non-capital murder, and to quash the present indictment.'

Mr Justice Lancaster had been listening intently, scribbling notes as Hardcastle spoke. Now, he looked up.

'But Mr Hardcastle, it will surely be a matter for the jury whether they find that the murder was committed in the course or furtherance of theft. If they are not sure of that they will convict, if at all, only of non-capital murder. They are entitled to return that alternative verdict, are they not?'

'They are, my Lord.'

'Then, it would seem to me that your application is premature.'

'My Lord, with respect, no. This is a case where it would not be possible for a jury, properly directed, to return a verdict of capital murder. The evidence does not allow it. I submit that your Lordship would be obliged to withdraw the question of capital murder from them at the close of the prosecution case. Nothing but prejudice to Mr Cottage can result from allowing them to consider it until that point, and then have it withdrawn from them on what may seem to them to be technical grounds. The right course is to deal with the matter now, and withdraw that question before the trial begins.'

The judge nodded.

'I see. Yes, thank you, Mr Hardcastle. Mr Pilkington, what do you say about that?'

'My Lord, in my submission, a jury, properly directed, would be fully entitled to convict of capital murder. Grateful as I am to my learned friend for telling me what the Crown's case is, perhaps I may be permitted to explain that to your Lordship myself?'

Both the judge and Hardcastle smiled.

'My Lord, I do propose to adduce evidence that William Cottage raped Jennifer Doyce. I do contend that he killed Frank Gilliam to facilitate that crime. But I do not concede that the rape was the only purpose in his mind on that night. Indeed, the evidence shows that Cottage also stole the gold cross and chain she was wearing...'

'Mr Hardcastle says that he stole it from her, not from Frank Gilliam, the person he killed.'

'With respect, my Lord,' Pilkington replied at once, 'that makes no difference at all. I am sure your Lordship is familiar with section 5(5)(e) of the Homicide Act 1957, to be found in chapter twelve of *Archbold*, which provides that: *"theft includes any offence which involves stealing or is done with intent to steal"*. There is no suggestion that the person who is killed must be the victim of the theft. Take, for example, a case in which a bank robber kills a security guard in the course of a robbery. The robber is not stealing from the guard, he is stealing from the bank. But surely my learned friend would not argue that a charge of capital murder would be misconceived under the Act? It is the very mischief Parliament had in mind when the Act was passed and the categories of capital murder were defined.'

Mr Justice Lancaster was nodding.

'Will the evidence show that Frank Gilliam was dead before the cross and chain was stolen?'

Pilkington hesitated.

'My Lord, we cannot say exactly at what time Frank Gilliam died. But I am prepared to accept that the jury could very properly draw that conclusion, and I would not seek to resist it. Nonetheless, it is also open to the jury to conclude that the killing of Frank Gilliam facilitated whatever offences Cottage intended to commit, or did commit, on that evening, and if they draw that conclusion, the killing was in the course or furtherance of theft. There is no language in the Act which prevents that result. It is a matter for the jury.'

He paused to observe the judge's reaction. Mr Justice Lancaster thought for some time, his head down over his notebook, before looking up again.

'I am against you, Mr Hardcastle. There is evidence from which the jury could conclude that the killing was in the course or furtherance of theft. I will direct them carefully about that, and about the alternative open to them. And, of course, let us not forget that before they convict of anything, they must be sure that it was William Cottage who was the attacker.'

Hardcastle stood and bowed.

'As your Lordship pleases. In that event, may I invite your Lordship to rule that the Crown should not be permitted to adduce evidence of rape? If the underlying crime is really theft, the allegation of rape can have no effect but to prejudice the jury against him.'

Pilkington leapt to his feet.

'My Lord, I have already made it clear that the Crown does not suggest that the theft was the only...'

But the judge was holding up a hand.

'Mr Hardcastle, I am rather surprised by your submission. It sounds rather macabre, but is it not in Cottage's interest to have the jury focus on the rape, rather than the theft?'

Hardcastle smiled broadly.

'I don't press the point, my Lord,' he conceded.

'Very well,' the judge said. 'Let's proceed.'

Throughout this exchange Billy Cottage had sat impassively in the dock, but now Philip Eaves ordered him to stand.

'William Cottage, you are charged in this indictment with capital murder. The particulars of the offence are that you, on the night of the 25 to the 26 of January 1964, in the County of Huntingdon, murdered Frank Gilliam, and the murder was in the course or furtherance of theft. How say you? Are you guilty or not guilty?'

Billy looked around the court before replying.

'Not guilty.'

Martin Hardcastle had already decided that, unless his professional instincts literally screamed otherwise, he would not exercise any peremptory challenges. This would be a trial about the merits of the case, not about lawyers' games. The defence would accept the first twelve citizens selected at random and trust them to do their duty. The result was an all-male jury, but with three generations represented and with dress varying between the most formal business suits and sports jackets with grey slacks. Running an experienced eye over them, Martin concluded that they were as good as he was likely to get.

33

MR JUSTICE LANCASTER nodded in Andrew's direction.

'Yes, Mr Pilkington.'

Without undue haste Andrew placed his notebook on his podium and turned slightly to his left to face the jury.

'Much obliged, my Lord. May it please your Lordship, members of the jury, I appear for the Crown in this matter. My learned friends Mr Hardcastle and Mr Schroeder appear for the accused, William Cottage.'

Hardcastle remained staring fixedly ahead. Ben, however, turned slightly and gave an almost imperceptible nod of the head in the direction of the jury.

'Mr Cottage is the man seated in the dock at the back of the court.'

The jury glanced nervously to their right. Billy Cottage sat motionless beside the prison officer, his eyes apparently fixed on the floor of the dock.

'You already know, members of the jury, that the accused is charged with capital murder. His Lordship will direct you as to the law later in the trial but, with his leave, I will make it clear now that it is no part of your duty to consider the consequences of your verdict. That is a matter for the law. Your duty is to consider the evidence and to say by your verdict whether or not the Crown has proved its case beyond reasonable doubt. Under our system of law, no accused has any obligation to prove his innocence. It is always for the Crown to prove his guilt. His Lordship will direct you later in the trial and, with his leave, I make it abundantly clear now that you may not convict Mr Cottage unless the evidence proves his guilt beyond reasonable doubt. The Crown contends that the evidence does so, and does so very clearly, but that is a matter for you to decide.'

Pilkington gestured to Paul, who was sitting quietly but attentively beside Philip Eaves.

'With the usher's assistance, I would like to provide you with two documents. The first is the indictment, which is the formal statement of the charge against the accused and which you have already heard read to you by the learned clerk of assize. The second has two pages, and I am grateful to my learned friends for their agreement that you may have this exhibit now, so that you can see the various places to which I shall refer during my opening speech. The first page is an Ordnance Survey map, showing the town of St Ives and the section of the Great Ouse river between St Ives and Holywell Fen, which lies about a mile to the east of St Ives. The second page is a street plan of the centre of St Ives. There will be one copy of each document between two.' He turned briefly towards the bench. 'My Lord, the map and street plan will be Exhibit One.'

'Yes,' the judge replied.

Paul briskly distributed the documents and resumed his seat.

'If you will look at the indictment with me,' Andrew continued, 'you will see that it alleges that the murder of Frank Gilliam occurred during the night of the 25-26 of January of this year. It occurred at Holywell Fen in the County of Huntingdon.'

He paused for a sip of water.

'Members of the jury, you will hear from Charles Edwards, the licensee of the Oliver Cromwell public house in Wellington Street in St Ives, that a young couple came into the pub during the evening of Saturday 25 January. Mr Edwards noticed them because the Oliver Cromwell is a mainly male establishment, and it was rather unusual for young women to be drinking there. He was able to recognise them later from photographs shown to him by the police. The man was Frank Gilliam. Frank was twenty-three and he was training to be a bank manager. The young woman was his girlfriend, Jennifer Doyce. Jennifer survived the events of that night, and you will hear evidence from her either tomorrow, or the day after tomorrow. But she was badly beaten, she was raped, and you will hear that she is very lucky to be alive. You will see, when she gives evidence, the effect her ordeal has had on her. Jennifer Doyce is twenty-one years of age and, before that night, was training to be a librarian here in Huntingdon.'

'Members of the jury, the accused, William Cottage, was employed by Mr Edwards as a part-time barman, and he was working at the pub on the night of the 25 of January while Frank and Jennifer were there. His full-time daytime employment was as the lock keeper on the river at Fenstanton, but he worked at the Oliver Cromwell at night to earn some extra cash.'

Andrew paused to turn and glance briefly at Cottage, drawing the jury's eyes with him.

'Frank and Jennifer had plans for that night. They were going to walk the mile or so along the river to Holywell Fen. If you will look with me at the St Ives street plan, you will see that Wellington Street ends at its junction with Priory Road.'

He waited for the members of the jury to spread their plans out in front of them.

'You will see the Oliver Cromwell marked on the plan with the letter A. If you turn left on leaving the pub and walk to Priory Road you will come to a small corner shop. It is marked with the letter B. The shop is the last building on Priory Road, and if you continue you will come to a gate with a turnstile, which leads into the meadow. The gate is marked with the letter C. Once you pass through the gate, you are free to walk along the bank of the river towards the Fen. If you look at the Ordnance Survey map, you will see the Fen marked with the letter D.'

Andrew looked up from his notes to smile at the jury.

'Members of the jury, at first blush it may seem strange that Frank and Jennifer were going to walk almost a mile to Holywell Fen along the river late on a bitterly cold night. But there is no mystery about it. They were in love. They wanted some solitude to be together, and Holywell Fen offered them that opportunity, because moored by the river at the Fen is a houseboat called the *Rosemary D.* The boat belongs to a couple called Douglas. Mr and Mrs Douglas abandoned her quite some time ago when they had occasion to leave the country rather suddenly. When they did, they left behind all her fixtures and fittings and all her domestic contents, leaving her habitable and rather comfortable. You will hear that the *Rosemary D* had become a favourite haunt of courting couples. The boat was not locked, so it was easy to climb on board and enter the living quarters. That is where Frank and Jennifer went when they left the Oliver Cromwell.

Jennifer will tell you, quite frankly, that it was their intention to have sexual relations with each other for the first time, and that they had begun to do so before they were attacked.

'We know that they walked in that direction because, on the way, they stopped briefly at the corner shop, letter B on your plan. The shop was not generally open at that hour, but Mavis Brown, whose father owns the shop, was doing some late-night stock-taking when she saw Frank and Jennifer looking in through the shop window. She opened the shop for them and sold them two packets of Woodbine cigarettes. Members of the jury, police officers later found those two packets in their clothing with three cigarettes missing from each, stubs of two Woodbine cigarettes were found in an ashtray in the sleeping quarters of the *Rosemary D*. Miss Brown was later able to identify Frank and Jennifer from photographs. I will return to Mavis Brown in just a moment, because she provides another important piece of evidence.'

Andrew paused and sipped more water.

'William Cottage left the Oliver Cromwell shortly after Frank and Jennifer, even though his evening shift had not actually finished. It is the Crown's case that he followed the couple as they walked towards the *Rosemary D*. It would not have been difficult to follow without being seen. They had left the street lights of St Ives behind. There might have been some moonlight, but it was a damp, cloudy night, probably quite dark. The Crown say that William Cottage followed Frank and Jennifer all the way to Holywell Fen. He waited until they were aboard the *Rosemary D*, and distracted by their passion for each other.'

Andrew again gestured to Paul.

'Members of the jury, I will now show you another document. Again, I am grateful to my learned friends for indicating that they have no objection. This, with your Lordship's leave, will be Exhibit Two.'

'Yes,' the judge said.

Paul walked across to Andrew, took the copies with him and distributed them to the jury.

'Members of the jury, again, one between two. This is a floor plan of the *Rosemary D*. You will see that as you board her, you have the forward deck, and then to your right a door. If you go through that door, you are in the living quarters, with a small kitchen, a lounge area and a toilet. The living quarters are marked A on the plan. Then, if you make your way further aft, you walk through a narrow door into the sleeping quarters, marked B on the plan.'

Andrew allowed the jury to take in the other details shown on the plan while he refilled his water glass from a carafe.

'I am now going to jump ahead somewhat. You will notice, members of the jury, that the plan also has some shapes marked on it. These shapes reflect what was found on the morning of Monday 27 January. At about 8.30 on that morning, a man called Archie Knights, a retired Army officer, was walking his dog along the river bank by the Fen, as he often does at that time of day. Mr Knights will tell you that he noticed something out of place, that the door leading to the living quarters was ajar. He decided to investigate. He will tell you that what he found shocked him. It was the scene of a frenzied, violent attack. He hurried to the nearest phone and called the police. Shortly afterwards two officers, PC Willis and PC Hawthorne arrived, and also observed the scene. Frank Gilliam was lying on the floor by the side of the bed. The position of his body is illustrated by shape F. He was dead. You will hear from the pathologist who performed the autopsy that he died from a fracture of the skull and internal bleeding resulting from massive head injuries. The evidence will be that those injuries were caused by repeated blows from a large and heavy blunt instrument. Lying on the bed on her back was the apparently lifeless body of Jennifer Doyce. She had also suffered severe head trauma, almost certainly inflicted by means of the same weapon. Her dress had been pulled up and her underwear pulled down, and there were injuries to her genital area which suggested that she had been violently raped.'

Andrew saw the jury tightening their lips, and paused to allow them to breathe under cover of drinking some water.

'Mr Knights had thought that Jennifer was also dead, so he had reported two deaths to the police. But when PC Willis looked at Jennifer more closely, he noticed a slight movement of her eyelids, and he realised that she was still alive. She was taken to Addenbrookes Hospital, where she underwent surgery, and made what her doctors say has been an almost miraculous recovery. You may think, members of the jury, that she may well owe her life to PC

Willis's attention to detail and quick thinking. During the course of the investigation, the police sent frogmen to dive in the river alongside the boat, just in case the assailant had thrown his weapon overboard, and in due course, the divers recovered a heavy metal winch handle, which would have been kept on the forward deck of the *Rosemary D.* When the winch handle was tested, it was found to be stained with blood matching the groups of Frank's blood and of Jennifer's; group A for Jennifer, group O for Frank. The Crown say that this was the murder weapon. You will see the winch handle later in the trial.'

'It is the Crown's case, members of the jury, that the man who murdered Frank Gilliam, and who raped and viciously assaulted Jennifer Doyce, was this accused, William Cottage. Why do we say that? We say that there are three chains of evidence that put the case beyond any reasonable doubt, indeed beyond any doubt at all.'

'Firstly, a police scene of crime officer found a fingerprint on a window ledge in the sleeping quarters. The fingerprint was mixed with a small quantity of blood of group A, Jennifer Doyce's blood group. The fingerprint was that of the accused, William Cottage. When interviewed by Detective Superintendent Arnold and Detective Inspector Phillips, Cottage lied to the officers by denying that he had ever been on board the *Rosemary D.*'

'Secondly, when police officers went to Cottage's home, the lock keeper's house at Fenstanton, to arrest him in connection with this matter, they saw his sister, Eve, wearing a distinctive and quite valuable gold cross and chain, which she claimed had been given to her by her brother, the accused. Members of the jury, that gold cross and chain has been identified by Jennifer Doyce as the one she was wearing when she left home to accompany Frank Gilliam to the *Rosemary D* on the night of the 25 January. She will tell you that she was still wearing it when she boarded the boat. When the police searched the boat, there was no sign of it, but marks on Jennifer's neck suggest that it was taken from her neck during the assault on her. The Crown say that William Cottage stole that cross and chain in addition to assaulting and raping Jennifer Doyce, and that the theft was part of a crime spree in the course and furtherance of which he murdered Frank Gilliam. When interviewed by the police, Cottage said that he had found the cross and chain, but he gave several mutually inconsistent accounts of where and in what circumstances he found it, and I anticipate that you will have no hesitation in concluding that he told the police a pack of lies about it. He had that cross and chain because he took it from Jennifer's body in the course of his violent and frenzied attack on her, and on Frank.

'Thirdly, and finally, I return to Mavis Brown. She, you recall, was the young lady who kindly opened the corner shop late at night to sell Jennifer and Frank their Woodbines. She will tell you that a minute or two after they had left the shop, walking in the direction of the meadow, a man walked in the same direction, pausing briefly under a street light near the shop. The man was wearing a hat, and she was not able to see his face. But Mavis is able to say that in the stillness of the night, she distinctly heard him singing a song to himself, and she was able to identify the song as the well-known folk song, the *Lincolnshire Poacher*. Why does that matter? Well, members of the jury, you will hear from Jennifer Doyce that her assailant was singing that same song softly as he was raping her, and you will hear from the police officers who arrested William Cottage that they also heard him sing that song to himself in the back of the police car as he was being transported to St Ives police station.'

Andrew paused for effect.

'There is also no dispute that, in September 1961, William Cottage pleaded guilty before the Huntingdonshire Magistrates' Court to an offence of indecent exposure. He was conditionally discharged for twelve months. The facts of that case are that PC Willis, by coincidence one of the arresting officers in this case, found Cottage standing in the front garden of a house, late at night. His penis was exposed and he was masturbating while he watched a young woman who lived in the house getting undressed for the night. As he approached, PC Willis noted that Cottage was singing the *Lincolnshire Poacher* to himself *sotto voce*.'

Ben had been taking a careful note of the opening, but his hand froze on the pen. He waited for Martin Hardcastle to jump up to protest, to demand that the jury be discharged because of the improper admission of the accused's bad character. He felt, rather than saw, a similar reaction from Barratt Davis, sitting behind him. But his leader remained seated and displayed no reaction. Ben tried to make himself write a note, but his fingers were not yet cooperating. A hand tugged on his gown from behind. A folded note landed on his desk, bearing the single word *WHAT!?* in Barratt's handwriting. Ben turned around and shrugged helplessly.

Andrew Pilkington was closing his notebook.

'Members of the jury, the Crown say that that evidence identifies William Cottage as the perpetrator of the attacks on Frank Gilliam and Jennifer Doyce just as surely as if he had been seen by an eye-witness. It is as if he left his calling card at the scene. After lunch, I will begin calling the evidence. As I said before, the Crown brings this case and the Crown must prove it. But I anticipate that, when you have heard the evidence, you will have no doubt that it was this accused, William Cottage, who murdered Frank Gilliam, and you will say so by your verdict.'

He turned to Mr Justice Lancaster.

'My Lord, it is almost 1 o'clock. Would this be a convenient moment?'

The judge nodded.

'We will adjourn for lunch until 2 o'clock', he replied.

All in court stood as the judge and the High Sheriff left the bench. Billy Cottage was immediately whisked away to the cells by the prison officers.

* * *

Ben seized his notebook and strode out of court, pushing his way through the crowd of spectators leaving the public gallery, to the lobby of the Town Hall, and then out into the fresh air of Market Square. Martin Hardcastle had turned to his left and was lighting a cigarette by the corner of the building which faced the old Falcon Inn on the south side of the square.

'What's going on?' Ben demanded.

Hardcastle inhaled deeply from his cigarette.

'In what sense do you ask?' he countered.

Ben found himself almost speechless.

'In what sense…? Andrew Pilkington told the jury about his previous conviction,' he blurted out eventually.

'Yes, Schroeder, I know that. I was listening to the opening.'

'Well, why didn't you… why didn't you object? Why didn't you ask the judge to discharge the jury?'

Barratt Davis had fought his way out of the Town Hall to join them.

'Schroeder, Andrew Pilkington is junior Treasury Counsel. He knows better than to mention previous convictions when it's not allowed. He mentioned it because I invited him to do so.'

Ben and Barratt stared at him in silence.

'You told him he could bring it up?' Ben asked, after some time.

'Of course,' Hardcastle replied. 'It was the only realistic course to take.'

'And I assume you will explain why to Mr Cottage later?' Barratt asked. 'He looked rather disturbed when they took him back to his cell.'

'Certainly,' Martin replied with a thin smile. 'And, if really necessary, I will explain it to both of you now – though, I must say, I am surprised that it should be necessary; it seems obvious enough to me.'

There was another silence. Martin exhaled deeply, expelling a cloud of grey-blue smoke.

'Very well. By letting it in, I have purchased the right to challenge the evidence about the *Lincolnshire Poacher* without having to tread on eggshells. That evidence, together with the gold cross and chain, is going to kill Cottage unless we can discredit it. There is not much we can do about the cross and chain, except to hope that the jury finds his story about finding it more probable than we do. But I think we can make some progress on the *Lincolnshire Poacher*, which is far more deadly evidence, but vulnerable to attack through cross-examination. The moment I challenge that evidence, with Mavis Brown, or with Jennifer Doyce, or with the police officers, Pilkington will demand that the conviction go in. He will be right, and the judge will agree with him. I achieve nothing by trying to keep it out except watering down my cross-examination to the point of ineffectiveness. Putting the conviction in now removes all our inhibitions, and may gain us some credit for frankness with the jury. Besides, indecent exposure is a minor, non-violent offence, which bears no relationship to murder. It may even point away from Cottage if the jury can be made to see him as a peeping Tom, and nothing more.'

He inhaled deeply from his cigarette and then exhaled. 'That is why I invited Pilkington to mention it.'

Ben and Barratt looked at each other.

'You might have told us beforehand,' Barratt replied sheepishly.

Hardcastle dropped the butt of his cigarette on the ground and stamped on it half-heartedly.

'I'm sorry, Barratt,' he replied. 'It was all a bit frantic this morning, what with having to go to church and march in procession, and then talk to Pilkington. Skipped my mind, I'm afraid. Please understand that I have to take the lead on these things and make decisions. In this case, it was a rather last-minute decision.' He raised a hand. 'I'm sorry. I should have said something. I probably should have asked you what you thought.'

He took out another cigarette and lit it.

'Allow me to redeem myself by asking your advice about something else. I am confident that I know the answer, but it is an important point. This afternoon, or tomorrow morning, the scene of crime officer is going to give evidence about finding Cottage's fingerprint on the window ledge. We know that he cannot date the fingerprint and there is not a word in his report about how its position relates to the blood stain of Jennifer Doyce's group found in the same place. In other words, the prosecution cannot prove whether the print got there before the stain, or the stain before the print, or whether both got there at the same time. My question is: do we leave that point unspoken, so that we deny the prosecution the chance to close that door on us? Or do we question him directly to establish the point beyond doubt, in which case he may try to finesse the issue and make the question come alive in the jury's minds? There is always a case for letting sleeping dogs lie, but in this case...'

'You must ask him about it directly,' Ben replied, without hesitation. 'It is not the kind of point the jury can follow unless we make it clear for them. He may try to finesse it, but it's not in his report, and the science is against him. The text-books are on our side on this. I looked at them all. He can't win that point.'

'I agree,' Barratt added.

Hardcastle nodded. 'Then we are all agreed.'

Jess appeared from the direction of the George, walking quickly.

'Sandwiches,' she announced. 'I've got roast beef, ham, or cheese.

They wrapped them up for me, so I'm not quite sure which is which. There isn't much time. Should we eat them out here?'

'Well done, Jess,' Barratt said. 'How was Cottage when you left him?'

'Not very good,' Jess replied, with a glance at Hardcastle. 'I told him we would *all* go to see him after court this afternoon.'

'And we shall,' Barratt said, unwrapping a ham sandwich. He took an appreciative bite. 'It's hard to believe, isn't it, that murder is capital when it's in the course or furtherance of theft, but not in the course or furtherance of rape?'

Hardcastle had selected cheese and was inspecting the sandwich carefully before committing himself to a bite. 'Yes,' he agreed. 'Of course, Parliament intended that provision to deal with cases of armed robbery, not cases of snatching a trophy as an afterthought during another crime. But unfortunately, the wording they used fails to make that distinction.'

'That doesn't seem fair,' Jess protested. 'Especially in a case like this, when it's obvious that the motive was rape, not theft.'

'It's not fair,' Ben agreed. 'But at least it gives us something to talk about in the Court of Criminal Appeal.'

'Quite right,' Hardcastle said. 'But let's hope it doesn't come to that.'

34

AFTER LUNCH, ANDREW Pilkington began with his evidence about the crime scene. First came Archie Knights who told the jury in graphic detail about what he had seen on board the *Rosemary D*. The jury sat grim-faced as he relived his shock and distress. Next came PC Willis and PC Hawthorne, who recounted the work they had done at the scene. PC Willis told how he had first assumed that Jennifer Doyce was dead but, as he was about to make his way back on deck to summon the forensic team, thought he saw the merest flicker of her eyelids. It had been difficult to see in such poor light, and he had wondered whether his eyes were deceiving him. But he had moved closer to Jennifer, and felt for a pulse. After some seconds her eyelids flickered again. He sent for the river ambulance, and she was taken to Addenbrookes Hospital in Cambridge. Martin Hardcastle asked no questions of any of these witnesses.

Pilkington had agreed that PC Willis would be recalled later to deal with the arrest and subsequent investigation, to maintain the chronology for the jury. At that time, Martin would have a number of questions.

'My Lord, I now call Nathaniel Harding,' Pilkington said.

Nathaniel Harding was a small, wiry man with prematurely greying hair and the faintest suggestion of a wispy moustache. He wore a navy blue blazer and dark grey slacks, a light grey tie with a printed anchor emblem in red. He took the oath in a low voice. The judge reminded him to keep his voice up. Slightly more loudly, he supplied Pilkington with his name and address.

'What is your occupation, Mr Harding?'

'I am now a freelance diver. I provide services to various commercial companies, as well as to the police, when required.'

'What kinds of services do you provide?'

Harding shrugged. 'It can be a lot of different things. If the owners of a vessel suspect damage to the hull, I may go down to take a look. Sometimes an anchor gets stuck and we have to find out why. Sometimes, I am asked to search for a particular item.'

'What is your experience in this kind of work?'

'I was a Royal Navy diver for almost twenty years. I retired with the rank of Chief Petty Officer.'

'Did you see some service as a diver during the War?'

'I did, sir, but you understand, I can't talk about...'

'No, no,' Pilkington reassured him. 'I was asking only for some background about your experience. I assume you have had extensive experience in the private sector since the War?'

'I have, sir.'

'Thank you. Now, coming to the present case, did the Huntingdonshire Police ask for your assistance in the course of their investigation?'

'They did.'

'And what were your instructions?'

'I was asked to search an area of the river bed around a houseboat called the *Rosemary D.* She was moored on the north bank of the Great Ouse river about a mile east of St Ives, at a place known locally as Holywell Fen.'

'When was this?'

'The dive took place on Wednesday 29 January, in the afternoon.'

'What were you asked to search for?'

'I was asked to look for a heavy object which might have been used as a weapon on board the *Rosemary D* during the commission of violent crimes four days earlier.'

'Did the police describe the item you were looking for in any more detail?'

'No, sir. They just said it would be heavy. If I found anything answering to that general description I was to bring it up for further inspection.'

'Did you have anyone working with you?'

'Yes, we never dive alone. I would always have one colleague on board the vessel, and perhaps one in the water with me. In this case, my colleague Ivor Rees was with me. We took turns, one in the water, one controlling from on board.'

'Did you find anything answering the description of the item you were asked to look for?'

Harding nodded. 'I did, sir. To my surprise, I found something after quite a short time.'

'Why was that surprising?'

'Well, there are fairly strong currents around Holywell Fen. Ivor and I thought that even a heavy object might have drifted some distance downstream over a period of four days. So we were thinking it might take a day or two. But in fact, we got lucky.'

'What do you mean by that?'

Harding smiled. 'Within half an hour, or forty minutes, we found an object which had become entangled in the anchor line and had then sunk into the silt. It wasn't going anywhere.'

'With the usher's assistance...'

Paul rose at once from his seat in front of the bench, and took an item wrapped in a heavy plastic bag from the clerk's table.

'If you would please examine the item the usher is handing you, and tell me whether you recognise it? If you need to remove it from the bag let me know and the usher will do it for you wearing gloves. It may still have some chemicals on it from the forensic examination.'

Harding held the bag up to the light and peered through the plastic wrapping.

'That is not necessary, sir. That is the item I found. It is a winch handle.'

'My Lord, may that please become Exhibit Three?'

'Exhibit Three,' Mr Justice Lancaster confirmed.

'I should have asked you this: how deep was the water you were searching by the boat?'

'Not very deep at all, sir, five to six feet, I should estimate. But of course, it is very dark. We have to use powerful searchlights to see anything down there.'

'When you brought the winch handle to the surface, did you notice anything about it?'

'Yes, sir. I noticed some dark stains.'

'The jury will see those with another witness. Finally, this: what did you do with Exhibit Three when you brought it on board?'

'I gave it immediately to PC Willis, and I saw him place it in a heavy plastic bag like the one it is in today.'

'After discovering Exhibit Three, were you asked to search any further?'

'No, sir. The officers seemed happy with the result of the search.'

'Thank you, Mr Harding. Please wait there. There may be some further questions.'

'No questions, My Lord,' Martin Hardcastle replied at once.

'My Lord, I also have Ivor Rees, but unless my learned friend wishes me to do so...'

'No, thank you,' Hardcastle replied.

* * *

'I shall not call him. My Lord, I now call Dr Joseph Wren,' Andrew Pilkington announced.

Dr Wren was about sixty years of age, dressed in a dark brown tweed suit with a light blue shirt and a brown bow tie with white polka dots. He wore his tortoise-shell half-moon spectacles around his neck on a thin silver chain. Under his arm he carried a blue file folder. He placed the folder on the small working surface of the witness box in front of him, recited the oath without looking at the card Paul handed to him, and nodded politely to the judge.

'Dr Wren, what is your profession?'

'I am a medical doctor, and I have the usual qualifications as such. If anyone wants to hear them, I would be glad to oblige...'

Martin Hardcastle rose to his feet.

'My Lord, Dr Wren is a well-qualified pathologist. The defence has no objection to his expertise.'

Dr Wren nodded in Hardcastle's direction with a smile.

'I am very much obliged to my learned friend,' Pilkington said. 'Dr Wren, in short then, you are a forensic pathologist of some twenty-five years' experience. You have performed post-mortem examinations and you have given evidence as an expert witness in many cases during that period, on behalf of several police forces including those of Cambridgeshire and Huntingdonshire, is that correct?'

'It is.'

'You lecture regularly on forensic pathology for the Department of Medicine at Cambridge University, and you are the joint editor of a leading textbook on the subject?'

'That is correct.'

'Thank you, Doctor. Do you have a report, or notes you would like to consult?'

'Yes, if I may, I would like to refer to my report and to my notes as necessary, to refresh my recollection.'

'No objection,' Hardcastle said.

'Much obliged. Doctor Wren, on the 29 of January this year, were you asked by Cambridgeshire Police to examine and perform a post-mortem examination on a body?'

Dr Wren put on the half-moon spectacles which sat happily on a prominent ridge about half way down his nose. He opened the file folder and found his report.

'I was. The body was that of a male, who was identified to me by his parents and by documentary evidence as that of Frank Gilliam, date of birth 8 October 1940, a resident of St Ives. The body was that of an adequately nourished white male, consistent with the stated age, and was unremarkable except for the presence of serious trauma to the head.'

'Let us come to that,' Andrew Pilkington said. 'What precisely did you observe about the head?'

'The deceased had suffered several blows to the head. Because of the degree of damage to the skull and the brain tissue, I was not able to determine precisely how many blows had been struck, but I can say with some confidence that it was either three or four.'

'Why do you say that, Doctor?'

'There was one blow,' Dr Wren replied, demonstrating the position by running his hand through his own thinning hair, 'to the back of the head, apparently struck from directly behind him and from some height above. That is clearly identifiable as a single blow. You then have a blow to the left side of the head, again identifiable as a single blow, and then you have either one or two blows to the front of the head, the forehead and the right part of the front of the head, which caused the most extensive damage of all. It is possible that this damage was caused by a single blow. The extent of that damage may be due to the shape of the weapon used. But it is also possible that it was the result of two separate blows. If it will assist, I have prepared a diagram showing the locations of the injuries, and I have prepared copies for his Lordship, counsel, and the jury, if you wish.'

Andrew glanced towards Martin Hardcastle, who nodded briefly. Paul immediately stood, took the copies from Dr Wren and distributed them in a matter of seconds to the judge, the jury, and to Martin Hardcastle.

'Exhibit Four,' the judge noted.

'Much obliged, my Lord. Dr Wren, the jury will see that you have marked your diagram with the letter A to indicate the injury to the back of the head, the letter B to indicate the injury to the right side, and the letter C to indicate the one or two injuries to the right front of the head, is that correct?'

'Yes it is.'

'Dr Wren, based on your examination of the body and your professional experience, did you form an opinion as to the type of object that might have been used to inflict the kind of damage you observed to the head of Frank Gilliam?'

'I did, sir.'

'Would you please tell his Lordship and the jury what your opinion is in that respect?'

Dr Wren carefully removed the spectacles and allowed them to fall back against his chest, held by the silver chain.

'The damage I observed in this case is as severe as any I have ever seen to the head in all the years of my experience. There were extensive fractures to the skull in each area, and there was significant displacement of brain tissue also. I can say, not only that this was the result of an exceptionally frenzied attack, but that the blows must have also been struck using a heavy blunt object.'

'Did you find any fragments or other evidence to indicate of what material that object would have been made?'

'I did not.'

'May Dr Wren please be shown Exhibit Three?'

Paul lifted the winch handle, still in its packaging, from the clerk's bench and, with a deliberate show of its weight, placed it on the edge of the witness box.

'Dr Wren, please look at the object you have been handed.'

Dr Wren picked up the winch handle and held it in front of him, feeling its shape and testing its weight by raising and lowering it slightly in his hands.

'Dr Wren, are you able to say whether that object is capable of inflicting the kind of damage you have described to the jury?'

Dr Wren considered for a few seconds.

'Undoubtedly it would be capable of doing so. It also seems to me that the shape of this object would be consistent with the uncertainty about one or two blows to the right front of the head, position C on the diagram. Used in a certain way, this would provide the attacker with a quite broad area of contact across the head.'

Andrew glanced down at his notes.

'Finally, Dr Wren, have you formed any opinion about the cause or causes of Mr Gilliam's death?'

'I have. The cause of death was massive intracranial haemorrhaging resulting from severe head trauma caused by blows inflicted using a heavy blunt object. The attack caused multiple fractures of the skull, irreversible brain damage, and uncontrollable internal and external haemorrhaging. The first blow would have rendered Mr Gilliam unconscious, and may have been fatal in itself. The second blow would certainly have been fatal. Death would have followed within a very short time of the attack.'

'Dr Wren, there may be some further questions. Please wait there.'

* * *

Dr Wren nodded in agreement. For the first time in the trial, Martin Hardcastle seemed to come to life. He sprang to his feet, though his thick brief still remained unopened, the pink ribbon tied securely around it, on the bench beside him.

'Dr Wren, you spoke of the wound to the back of the head being the first wound. Did you intend to say that it was the first in time? Can you say with any certainty which was the first wound caused to Mr Gilliam?'

Dr Wren hesitated.

'Not with any certainty, no.'

'Do you have any basis whatsoever for saying so?'

'I have no medical reason.'

'Was it an assumption? The result of trying to reconstruct the event?'

'Yes, I daresay it was.'

'You made the not unreasonable assumption that the attacker approached Mr Gilliam from behind; that the blow was struck to the back of the head by someone standing above him. Would that be fair?'

'Yes.'

'The blow to the back of the head caused him to fall off the bed on to the floor, which gave the attacker the opportunity to inflict two further blows?'

'I thought that to be a reasonable interpretation of the events which might have led to the injuries I saw.'

Hardcastle nodded.

'Quite so. And would it also be a reasonable assumption, given that the blow was struck to the back of the head from above, that the attacker may well have struck the blow while Mr Gilliam was lying down, having or being about to have sexual intercourse with Jennifer Doyce?'

Andrew Pilkington was on his feet immediately.

'My Lord, that question is quite improper,' he protested. 'My learned friend is inviting the witness to speculate about the sequence of events.'

'My Lord,' Hardcastle replied, 'the witness has already speculated quite liberally on that subject. I am merely inviting him to do so a little more precisely. And my learned friend has, I think, been realistic enough not to pretend to the jury that Mr Gilliam and Miss Doyce were on board the *Rosemary D* for the purpose of playing charades.'

Several members of the jury permitted themselves a brief smile.

Mr Justice Lancaster looked across at the witness.

'Dr Wren, you may answer if you have a reasonable scientific basis for an opinion. If you do not, you must say so.'

Dr Wren took a deep breath.

'Again, there is no medical reason for supposing that, but I would agree that it is a possible interpretation of my findings.'

'Thank you, Doctor,' Hardcastle said, sitting down.

Andrew Pilkington stood slowly, turning slightly to give himself a view of the clock on the wall behind him, above the dock. It was approaching 3.30.

'My Lord, it is somewhat earlier than usual, but may I invite your Lordship to rise? I had hoped to be able to call Dr Walker to deal with the injuries to Jennifer Doyce. But I understand that he had a medical emergency at Addenbrookes earlier in the day, and has asked if he might come tomorrow morning. In the circumstances...'

The judge glanced up at the clock. 'Yes, very well, Mr Pilkington.' He turned to the jury. '10.30 tomorrow morning, members of the jury please. Make sure you do not discuss the case with anyone outside court.'

35

THE PRISON OFFICERS led Billy Cottage through the door at the rear of the court, across the narrow corridor, and into his cell. He had understood some of the day's proceedings, but the evidence seemed to be given so quickly that he barely had time to digest an answer before the next question was asked. Often he found himself distracted by the judge's red robes, and found himself staring at them as if mesmerised. In one way the robes seemed absurd, totally removed from reality. What did they have to do with his trial? He was facing the threat of being hanged. Why was the judge dressed up like this, as if he were on his way to a fancy dress party? His own barristers' robes were strange enough, but at least they were a sober black and white. The judge's robes were so brilliant, so striking that they seemed absurd, yet also terrifying, in some way he could not quite define. He had not dared to look at the jury. But he was aware of their eyes turning in his direction at various times, especially when Andrew Pilkington mentioned his previous trouble with the law. Why had that come up? When he was first charged, John Singer had assured him that no one was allowed to mention that. Now the jury knew, and they had looked at him. The cell seemed even smaller than it had before; more claustrophobic.

A prison officer opened the door leading to the entrance hall. The harsh metallic sound of the turning key jolted Billy back to the present.

When I was bound apprentice in famous Lincolnshire,
Full well I served my master for nigh on seven years,

'We will take him back to Bedford for the night as soon as you've finished with him,' he heard the officer remark cheerfully.

Billy's legal team filed slowly into the corridor, and stopped outside his cell.

'Well, so far so good,' Martin Hardcastle said. 'Nothing to link you to the offence yet. The real work begins tomorrow.'

'Did you want to ask Mr Hardcastle anything, Billy?' Barratt Davis asked.

Till I took up to poaching as you shall quickly hear,
Oh, 'tis my delight on a shiny night in the season of the year.

'Yes,' Billy replied. He had been sitting on the narrow wooden bench at the back of the cell. Now he stood and walked slowly to the front, holding on to the bars of the door with both hands. 'I can't understand why you let them tell the jury about my other trouble.'

'It's all to do with the evidence about the song...' Hardcastle began, but Billy cut him off.

'If they think I'm the kind of man who goes around doing that all the time, it's going to look as though I'm guilty.'

'They won't think that, and even if they do...'

'It's not fair. I only did that once, and now...'

'Mr Cottage, listen to me...'

'No, you listen. If they find me guilty, I'm going to be hanged...'

But then he was suddenly quiet. His determination to confront Hardcastle seemed to melt away into nothingness.

'Even now, look how long I've been away from my lock, look how long I've been away from Eve...'

Success to every gentleman that lives in Lincolnshire,
Success to every poacher that wants to sell a hare,

Hardcastle was becoming irritated, and he had been about to demand that Billy listen to him. But the abrupt change in mood and tone took him aback. He was silent for some time, conscious of the eyes of Ben Schroeder and Barratt Davis on him.

'I'm doing all that I can to get you back to your lock, and back to Eve,' he replied quietly. 'But to do that, I need you to trust me. Just as you would trust a surgeon if you needed an operation. I'm asking you to place yourself in my hands, although I know that is a difficult thing to do.'

Billy was returning very slowly to his bench at the rear of the cell.

'The reason I allowed the jury to know about your previous trouble is that they would have had to find out eventually. It was just a question of when, and I preferred to do it on my terms rather than the prosecution's terms.'

Billy had resumed his seat. He looked up.

'The reason I had to do it is this. Tomorrow, they are going to try to prove that whoever killed Frank Gilliam and raped Jennifer Doyce was singing the *Lincolnshire Poacher*. I have to challenge that. I have to create a doubt in the jury's minds about it. Once I do that, prosecution counsel is going to want to call PC Willis to say that you were singing that same song when you were arrested before. I have no way of resisting that. If I seem to resist it, it will look a lot worse to the jury than it does now. So we put it in now. We say to the jury: "we have nothing to hide. Billy Cottage spied on a woman *once*. But he's not a killer".'

Billy's head had dropped back down again. Martin Hardcastle exhaled heavily.

'I hope you understand that,' he said. 'But whether you do or don't, I need you to trust me. That's the only way this is going to work.'

He turned away towards the door.

'You're my main barrister,' Billy replied. 'I just hope you know what you're doing.'

Bad luck to every gamekeeper that will not sell his deer,
Oh, 'tis my delight on a shiny night in the season of the year.

By the time Ben and Barratt had reassured Billy Cottage as much as they could, Hardcastle was nowhere to be seen.

'He's gone back over to the George,' Jess said, meeting them at the door of the Town Hall. 'He said he would have dinner in his room to prepare his cross for tomorrow. He doesn't want to be disturbed.'

'Par for the course,' Barratt commented cheerfully, feeling Ben's eyes on him. 'He always does that during trial. If he's in London, he goes straight home after court. I think it's because he needs his solitude to concentrate.'

He looked at his watch.

'I'm off too,' he added.

'What, to your room?' Ben asked. 'It must be catching.'

'No,' Barratt replied with a smile. 'I'm going into town. Suzie is having a party at the boutique to entertain all kinds of important people in the world of fashion. I promised her I wouldn't miss it. God knows, she's turned up at any number of terminally boring Law Society shindigs over the years as a favour to me. It's the least I can do. I'll be back on the early train tomorrow. Enjoy your dinner.'

He set out quickly across the square.

Ben and Jess were left staring at each other. Spontaneously, they both burst out laughing.

'Feeling abandoned?' Jess asked.

'Decidedly,' Ben replied. 'First my leader, now my instructing solicitor.'

'Well, at least you still have me,' she said.

'And I am glad of your company' Ben smiled.

Without too much haste they crossed Market Square and entered the George.

'Drink in an hour?' Jess suggested. 'I feel the need to change. I got very hot this afternoon.'

'So do I,' Ben smiled. 'A full day in court wearing a stiff collar and studs is bad enough without being strangled all the way through dinner.'

They began to walk together up the dark wooden staircase which led to their rooms.

'I'm glad to hear someone admit it's not a comfortable way to dress,' Jess replied. 'It looks awful.'

'It's not in the least comfortable,' Ben said, 'especially for those of us who didn't go to Eton and get used to it at a young age. It seems that the ability to perform well in uncomfortable dress is one of the qualities needed for professional success in England.'

'Ah, the old stiff upper lip principle.'

'Or the old stiff collar principle. There are those who say that things like collar studs won us the Empire.'

'If so, they are losing it rather rapidly now,' she replied.

He suddenly laughed.

'What?' she asked.

'Oh, nothing. It's just that I have a standing joke with my grandfather about becoming Viceroy of India. When the family council was talking about my becoming a barrister, and they were saying I wouldn't be accepted because of being Jewish, I was going to tell them about a Jewish barrister who became Lord Chief Justice of England and Viceroy of India. But before I could say a word, my grandfather told them for me. He already knew all about it.'

She smiled. 'Rufus Isaacs,' she said. 'Later Marquess of Reading.'

Ben stared at her in surprise. 'I am impressed,' he said.

'I'm an historian, remember?' she replied. 'The Raj was one of my subjects.'

'Hence the taste for Indian food?'

'Perhaps.'

'Well, my grandfather took great delight in sharing his knowledge about Rufus Isaacs, and there wasn't much anyone could say after that. But he has never let me forget it. He still calls me "Viceroy" sometimes.'

They laughed.

'But please believe me. I have no ambitions for Empire,' he said. 'The stiff collar just comes with the job.'

They had reached her room. She had her key in her hand and opened the door. She looked towards the end of the corridor.

'And, sadly, difficult Silks come with the job too,' she said, smiling and closing the door.

* * *

Two hours later they had done justice to the George's passable steak and kidney pie and were sipping coffee.

'Have you thought of becoming qualified?' Ben asked.

'Becoming a solicitor?'

'Yes.'

She leaned back in her chair, threw her head back, and looked up at the ceiling, smiling.

'Just recently, as a matter of fact. I've been wondering about it.'

He was nodding encouragingly.

'When I first started with Barratt, it was just a job, something to do while I was deciding what to do with my life – while I considered all the glorious opportunities open to history graduates from Bristol University. I never thought I would want to be a lawyer. But now… watching him work, seeing how the firm helps its clients, seeing how interesting the cases are, I am beginning to think it's something I might want to do.'

She leaned forward towards him.

'There are drawbacks, obviously, such as dealing with people like Martin Hardcastle.'

Ben laughed.

'You really don't like Martin, do you?'

'No, I don't. I wouldn't say anything in front of Barratt, obviously, but no, I don't like him. I think the way he treated Billy Cottage today was horrible. The man is charged with murder. He may be facing a death sentence, and Hardcastle is coming across as though it's just another case, something of technical interest – a game almost. I couldn't treat a client like that, and neither could you, Ben. Don't give me the speech about Silks being different, because I don't buy it. I know you will never treat a client that way – even when you get Silk.'

'I hope not,' he replied.

'You won't,' she said definitively.

'There is nothing we can do about Martin,' Ben said. 'There will always be people like that, especially at the Bar. So the only thing that matters is how *you* treat people. It's particularly important as a solicitor, because you have far more to do with clients than barristers – especially Silks. You *have* to be good with clients. And I know you would be good, because I've already seen evidence of it.'

'Oh?'

'I watched you with Joan Heppenstall when we did the Reverend Little's case,' he replied. 'I watched you hold her hand, reassure her, encourage her, get the most out of her. It's because of you that she gave evidence at all, and it's because of you that she gave evidence so well. That's what brought the jury over to our side.'

He finished his coffee.

'So if you decide to do it, I will be the first to applaud.'

'Well, I'm still pondering,' she said.

They both sat in silence for some time.

'Can I ask you something? You don't have to tell me.'

'Of course.'

'Do you have a girlfriend?'

He was taken aback by the question, and stared at her for some time. She did not flinch or divert her eyes.

'Why do you ask?'

'I'm curious. And if I'm going to be a lawyer I have to get used to asking questions.'

He sat up in his chair and leaned forward to be closer to her.

'Not since university,' he replied, after some time. 'You know, with taking my bar finals, then doing pupillage, and now beginning practice…'

She cut him off, shaking her head.

'That's not it,' she insisted. 'You're the kind of man who would make time for things you care about, however busy you may be – as you do when you take Simon to watch West Ham. It's not time. It must be something else.'

He took a deep breath and looked away across the dining room towards the church.

'Ben, you don't have to say. Just tell me to mind my own business. I don't…'

'I had my heart broken,' he said suddenly. 'I fell in love during my second year of university. Utterly and completely in love. Unfortunately, she didn't feel the same way. There was some boy she knew at home in Kent. I think they are married now. In any case, she made it clear that we could have no future together.'

'This was at university?'

'Yes.'

'So, three or four years ago?'

'Yes.'

'And the world ended?'

'Yes. The world ended.'

'That's a lot of power for one girl to have, to make the world end.'

He shrugged.

'I'm sorry. I didn't mean to be flippant. I know you've been hurt. Will the earth start spinning around its axis again one day?'

'I don't know.'

She stood and walked around the table to stand at his side. To Ben's amazement she took one of his hands in hers and then kissed him on the cheek, not a light sympathetic peck, but a warm kiss, with depth.

'I really hope it does,' she said gently.

She released his hand, but not hurriedly.

'I need an early night,' she said. 'I will see you for breakfast. Goodnight.'

36

'MAY IT PLEASE your Lordship, I call Dr Christopher Walker.'

Even at 10.30, as Andrew Pilkington called his first witness, the promise was of a warm day. Paul had opened a window in the courtroom, but Ben already felt the atmosphere oppressive as his robes and collar began to cling to him. Martin Hardcastle did not seem to notice. As ever, he was sitting impassively, barely moving, appearing to be totally focused on the evidence. He had still not opened his brief. Ben's papers were spread far and wide on the desk top in front of him, but Martin's lay in a single precise pile, the pink ribbon tied securely around them.

Ben was relieved to see that his leader seemed to be in a better mood today. He had even volunteered to see Billy Cottage before court and had been encouraging, while still reinforcing the need to remain impassive and give nothing away to the jury on a day when the evidence was going to hit closer to home.

Dr Walker began by telling the jury that he was an experienced doctor, head of internal medicine at Addenbrookes Hospital in Cambridge, and that he was in charge of the care of Jennifer Doyce.

'When was Miss Doyce admitted to your hospital?'

Dr Walker glanced up at the judge. 'If I may refer to my notes?'

Mr Justice Lancaster looked at Martin Hardcastle, who gave the briefest of nods.

'Please do so, Doctor.'

'Thank you, my Lord.' He opened a large brown file and allowed his finger to move slowly down a page. 'She was admitted at about 11.30 on the morning of 27 January. I saw her at about 12.45, after she had been stablilised and received some initial treatment from a junior member of my staff and, of course, from the nursing staff.'

'What was her condition when you first saw her?'

Dr Walker did not seem to need his notes for that question. 'She was unconscious and barely able to breathe without assistance. Her vital signs were very weak indeed. She had received very serious injuries to the front and right side of the head, indicative of blunt force trauma, which had resulted in a suspected fractured skull. She had two broken ribs, and she had numerous bruises and lacerations to her face and arms. There was bruising in the area around the vagina, and the nursing staff said that there had been some bleeding in that area on admission. She was critically ill and it appeared to me that she was unlikely to recover.'

'Could you explain that conclusion to the jury in more detail?'

'The fact that she was unconscious and that there was such severe head trauma suggested that there would have been some degree of internal bleeding. We had no way to control it. She was too weak even for exploratory surgery – she would never have survived any attempt to intervene surgically. My staff had taken X-rays of the skull which revealed evidence of at least one fracture line, but they were inconclusive as to the extent of the damage. But all the indications were that, if there was internal bleeding, it would probably be fatal. All we could do was make her comfortable. We had her on drips to rehydrate and feed her, but it was just a holding operation – everything we were doing was to keep her stable and prolong her life as far as we could. I informed Jennifer's mother of the situation.'

Pilkington smiled.

'In the light of that first impression, Doctor, the events of the next few days must have come as a considerable surprise to you?'

Dr Walker returned the smile, shaking his head.

'Surprise doesn't even begin to describe it', he replied. 'Medically speaking, it is quite remarkable that she survived. It is even more remarkable that she appears to have done so without catastrophic brain injury. None of the doctors with whom I have discussed the case could relate any similar case within their experience in which that was the outcome. It was not predictable in medical terms at all.'

'A fortuitous combination of circumstances?'

'Indeed so. I can only conclude that her initially profound level of unconsciousness suggested the presence of more serious internal injury than had actually been caused. It also suggests that we, and the emergency crew who treated her at the scene, were highly successful in immobilising her head, and that the portions of the skull where the fractures were did not move relative to each other. This would hold out the possibility that the fracture lines might be stable in themselves, and had not caused significant injury to the brain. In that case, provided that they remained stable, they would gradually heal.'

He turned over several pages in his file before continuing.

'Either she has someone watching over her, or she is a very lucky young woman,' he added, 'depending on your point of view.'

Pilkington nodded.

'She owes a great deal to you and your team.'

'She owes a great deal to the emergency crew, and to the police officer who realised that she was still alive,' Dr Walker replied. 'But for them, my team would never have had the opportunity to do anything for her. She would probably have been dead on arrival.'

'Yes. Doctor, I know that you are not a forensic expert...'

'No, I am not.'

'...so I do not propose to ask you about her injuries in general. But I do want to ask you about one matter. You said that you observed some bruising in the vaginal area, and that you were told that some bleeding had been observed, yes?'

'That is correct.'

'From your own observation, or from anything in your records, are you able to say whether Jennifer Doyce had had sexual intercourse recently, prior to her admission?'

The judge looked at Martin Hardcastle, as if anticipating an objection. But Martin made no move to get to his feet.

'It is my medical opinion that her injuries were consistent with recent forceful sexual intercourse,' Dr Walker replied. 'But it is my understanding that such injuries cannot be regarded as definitive as to whether the act of sexual intercourse was, or was not, consensual.'

'Was there any other evidence that sexual intercourse had taken place?' Pilkington asked.

'A junior doctor and a nurse recorded the presence of what might have been sperm in the outer vaginal area. They took swabs, which

I understand confirm the observation that sexual intercourse had taken place, but were inconclusive as far as any identification was concerned.'

'Doctor Walker, was there also a red mark, about one inch in length, to the left side of Miss Doyce's neck?'

'Yes.'

'In your opinion, was that mark consistent with...?'

'Really, my Lord,' Martin Hardcastle interrupted. 'It is not for this witness to speculate about that.'

'I agree, Mr Pilkington,' the judge said.

'As your Lordship pleases,' Andrew replied smoothly. 'Dr Walker, were Miss Doyce's personal possessions inventoried at the time of her admission?'

'Yes, of course, that is routine.'

'Do you have that inventory with you?'

'I do, sir.' Dr Walker turned over several documents in quick succession. 'Yes.'

'Does the list include any items of jewellery?'

'One silver ring from the right third finger.'

'Anything else?'

'No, sir.'

'Lastly, Doctor, you know that the prosecution intends to call Jennifer Doyce as a witness tomorrow?'

'Yes.'

'Can you confirm for the jury that, in your opinion as her treating physician, she is medically fit to give evidence?'

Dr Walker closed his file.

'Yes, subject to certain conditions,' he replied. 'She is still moving around in a wheelchair and wearing a neck brace. She will travel to court by ambulance with an attending nurse. You understand, we are still monitoring her closely. Skull fractures take some time to heal, and we have not intervened surgically. We may yet have to do so. We continue to take X-rays, which are encouraging, but her recovery is far from complete. Something could still go wrong. A sudden movement could yet cause internal damage. It may be several more months before it would be safe to say that she can lead a fully normal life though, if all goes well, we hope that she will be well enough to return home in a few weeks from now.'

He looked up at Mr Justice Lancaster.

'But I do wish to make clear, my Lord,' he added, 'that the main consideration in allowing her to give evidence is her own wish to do so. I have explained the possible risks, but she is adamant that she wants to tell the court what she remembers. Were it not for that, I would have done everything in my power to keep her out of court. I have no desire to hinder the court in its work, of course. I am speaking as a medical man. I must ask the court to bear in mind that, in addition to her fragile physical condition, giving evidence in this case, reliving the events, will inevitably be a traumatic experience for her. I do ask the court to allow her to pause in her evidence if she wishes to do so. And I consider it important that I should be present in court with her.'

'I am sure that there will be no objection to that,' the judge replied.

Martin Hardcastle jumped to his feet. 'None whatsoever, my Lord... The defence will gladly comply with any directions the court may give in accordance with Dr Walker's advice.'

'I am much obliged,' Pilkington said. 'Wait there, please, Doctor Walker. There may be some further questions for you.'

* * *

'Only one or two,' Hardcastle said. 'Doctor, is it your experience that serious head trauma may result in some inability to remember with clarity the events which led to the trauma?'

Dr Walker shook his head. 'That's not really my area.'

'No, of course. But is it not a general medical observation that head trauma may cause some degree of amnesia? Not in all cases, of course, but in some?'

'There are cases in which the patient does not recall everything at first. Sometimes the memory comes back over time.'

'And in a very serious case, it may not return at all, isn't that right?'

'I am aware that there have been such cases. I have not myself encountered a case in which there was no memory at all. And that is not true of Jennifer's case.'

Hardcastle glanced in the direction of the jury.

'Ah, well, that is why I ask, Doctor,' he said. 'You remember, of course, that because of her medical condition, you did not think it advisable for Miss Doyce to attend the magistrates' court for the committal proceedings in this case.'

'That is correct. It would have…'

'No, no, I mean no criticism,' Hardcastle insisted. 'I am sure you had perfectly good medical reasons for giving that advice, and there was no reason why the committal proceedings could not continue without her. But, as a result, we have no deposition from her, as we do in the case of the other witnesses.'

'No.'

'She has spoken to others – to her medical advisers, the police, even her family. We have an informal statement from her, but we have no deposition against which to test the evidence she will give tomorrow. So I must ask you this, Doctor. Tomorrow, the jury must bear in mind, must they not, that Miss Doyce's recollection of events may not, or may not yet, be quite accurate?'

Pilkington was on his feet before Dr Walker could reply.

'My Lord, that is quite improper. Miss Doyce's evidence is for the jury to evaluate. It is not for this witness to comment on it.'

'I am not asking him to comment on her evidence,' Hardcastle replied. 'I am simply asking him whether there is a medical basis for the jury to be cautious about it. The witness is a medical man, and there is nothing improper about asking his opinion on that question.'

'I see no objection to the question,' the judge said. 'Doctor Walker, you may answer if you can do so based on your medical expertise. If you cannot, just say so.'

Walker took a deep breath.

'Jennifer has not talked to me about the incident in detail at all,' he said. 'I have no personal knowledge of the state of her memory. All I can say is that, in general terms, head trauma sometimes causes some degree of amnesia, which usually goes away in time. Whether that is true in Jennifer's case, I cannot say.'

'Thank you, Doctor,' Hardcastle said, resuming his seat.

'Doctor Walker,' Pilkington asked, 'in medical terms, is it possible that the emotional trauma of giving evidence in a courtroom may help to bring back a memory which the patient had lost?'

For a moment, Hardcastle seemed poised to object, then he settled back into his seat without getting to his feet.

'I believe so,' Doctor Walker replied. 'As I say, it is not really my field, but I am aware of such cases as a result of discussions with colleagues.'

'Unless your Lordship has any questions…?' Pilkington said.

'Dr Walker,' the judge said, 'has Miss Doyce been receiving any treatment or counselling from a psychiatrist or psychologist?'

'My Lord, I know that she has seen Dr Bushell, our staff psychiatrist, several times. Dr Bushell consulted me before prescribing a sedative and fixing the dosage. I do not know how much he has discussed the events with her, but I am sure that he must have done so to some extent.'

'Yes, I see,' Mr Justice Lancaster said. 'Thank you, Doctor. You are released for today. If you want to bring anything to my attention about Miss Doyce's evidence tomorrow, please let the clerk know.'

'I will, my Lord. Thank you.'

37

'MY LORD, THE next witness is Gerald Harlow.'

Harlow, a small, rather untidy figure, took the oath rapidly and without expression. He was dressed in a grey sports jacket and slacks, and wore a crumpled yellow tie over a white shirt. Several pens of different colours were visible in the top pocket of the jacket. He was carrying a tattered brown leather briefcase, which he placed with a conspicuous gesture on the floor of the witness box. He turned confidently towards the judge.

'Gerald Harlow, my Lord. I am a scene of crime officer employed by Cambridgeshire Police, based at Cambridge.'

'Thank you, Mr Harlow,' Pilkington said. 'Could you begin by explaining to the jury what a scene of crime officer does?'

'Certainly, sir. My first job is to attend the scene of a crime on being instructed to do so by the senior investigating officer, and to make sure the scene is intact and is preserved, as far as possible.'

'As far as possible?'

'It is always possible that the scene may have been contaminated before my arrival. This may occur because of ambient conditions, including weather, or because of careless intervention by a member of the public, or even a police officer, or sometimes just because of the passage of time since the crime was committed. If I may continue...?'

'Please.'

'Once the scene is secure, I then examine the scene as carefully as I can, searching for material capable of being subjected to forensic analysis.'

'What kinds of material do you look for, particularly?'

'First, any pieces of tangible evidence which may relate to the offence, for example an implement used to commit the offence, something left at the scene, or anything that may be relevant. Of course, the investigating officers will usually have picked up anything obvious and, hopefully, placed the item carefully in an evidence bag to preserve it for examination. But they can miss smaller items. It is my job not to miss things. I then proceed to look for latent fingerprints and for stains indicating the presence of blood or other bodily fluids.'

'If you find any material of that kind, do you take impressions or samples for analysis at the forensic science laboratory by yourself or your colleagues?'

'Yes, sir.'

'In this case, did you attend a crime scene on a houseboat called the *Rosemary D* berthed at Holywell Fen on the afternoon of 27 January this year?'

'Yes, sir, I did, on the instructions of Detective Superintendent Arnold.'

'Please describe the scene to the jury as you saw it on your arrival.'

'If I may refer to my notes, sir?'

Pilkington glanced across at Hardcastle, who inclined his head. 'Yes.'

Harlow made a show of producing a large spiral notebook from his briefcase. 'The scene I was asked to examine was a cabin at the back of the boat. I think they like to call that "aft", sir.'

'Yes,' Pilkington agreed, suppressing a smile.

'I was given to understand that this was the sleeping quarters, which was confirmed by the presence of a bed. Other officers had been assigned to the front cabin, and the deck of the boat, and I confined my attention to the aft cabin. I immediately noticed the presence of several large stains which appeared to be blood.'

'By this time, I take it, Mr Gilliam's body had been removed by other officers, and Miss Doyce had been taken to hospital?'

'Yes, sir.'

'Thank you. Please continue.'

'The largest area of staining was on the floor. It was immediately adjacent to an area marked out by another officer in chalk, which I understood to represent the position in which Mr Gilliam's body had been found. The position of the stain was consistent with a loss of blood from Mr Gilliam's head.'

'Did you take a sample from this stain for analysis?'

'I took several swabs, sir, and placed them in individual evidence bags, each marked with an exhibit number consisting of my initials, GH, and a number. On sealing each bag, I signed a label which I then attached to the bag, indicating that it was my exhibit.'

'Is that standard practice? And, to save time, can the jury take it that you followed the same procedure with each exhibit you took from the scene?'

'Yes, sir.'

'Thank you. And – I think there is no dispute…?'

Hardcastle shook his head.

'I am grateful. There is no dispute that the swabs taken from the position adjacent to Mr Gilliam's head were later analysed, and found to be stains of human blood of group O. Is that right?'

'That is correct, sir.'

'Thank you. What was the next item that attracted your attention?'

'I also noticed what appeared to be significant blood staining on and behind and to the right side of the bed. The pattern of staining here was very different, because there were numerous smaller areas of staining, some on the bedclothes and some at different positions on the floor. There were also some very small spatter stains adjacent to the large stains, which it was unnecessary to try to deal with separately, even if it had been possible to do so.'

'What did you do in relation to the larger stains?'

'I carefully removed each item of bedclothes from the bed, and placed each in a separate large plastic container, which I then sealed for identification. I took several swabs from each area of staining on the floor and placed them in evidence bags, sealing and marking them as I explained previously.'

Pilkington picked up the forensic report from the desk top in front of him. 'And if I can summarise the findings when these items were analysed which, again, is not in dispute. The stains on the bed linen proved to be human blood of group A, with the exception of one stain of about one square inch on the right-hand edge of the top blanket, about three inches from the bottom of the blanket, which was found to be human blood of group O. Is that right?'

'It is, sir.'

'And the stains on the floor were all found to be human blood of group O. Yes?'

'Yes, sir.'

'And I think there is no dispute. Is it right that Jennifer Doyce's blood group is group A, and that Frank Gilliam's is group O?'

'That is correct, sir.'

'All right. Now, just before we go any further with the crime scene, I want to ask you about another matter. Did you, in the course of your examination of the scene, find anything which might have been used as a weapon in the assaults?'

'No, sir. I did not.'

'But at a later date, was an item brought to you for analysis, and was it your understanding that it had been recovered from the river bed, close to the *Rosemary D*?'

'Yes, sir.'

'My Lord, may the witness please be shown Exhibit Three?'

Paul quickly found Exhibit Three and held it up in front of the witness box.

'Is that the item you were given?'

'Yes, sir.'

'It has been described as a winch handle from the *Rosemary D*. What was found on analysis of this item?'

'Despite the degradation caused by its being immersed in water for some time, it was possible to identify a number of small stains, which on analysis proved to be human blood of both group A and group O, for the most part mixed or partly mixed together. I cannot, of course, say what the extent of staining was, or what the pattern of staining was before the contamination caused by the river water. In my opinion, sir, it would not be safe to draw any conclusions about those matters.'

'Thank you. Did you examine an ash tray in the sleeping quarters?'

'I did, sir.'

'What, if anything, did you find?'

'I found two cigarette stubs, sir.'

'Were you able to establish by observation what brand of cigarettes they were?'

'Yes, sir, they were Woodbines.'

'Was any other evidence of Woodbine cigarettes discovered on board the *Rosemary D* to your knowledge?'

'Yes, sir, one of my colleagues discovered two packets which would have contained ten Woodbines cigarettes, one in the right-hand pocket of Mr Gilliam's jacket, the other in Miss Doyce's handbag. Each packet contained seven cigarettes.'

'Was there any other evidence to suggest who might have smoked any of these cigarettes?'

'Yes, sir. One of them had traces of lipstick of a colour which appeared to be identical to that worn by Miss Doyce.'

Pilkington paused to consult a note.

'Thank you. Now, lastly, on a window ledge in the same cabin, did you find a further piece of evidence?'

'I did. I found a latent fingerprint which I was able to lift for the purpose of comparison.'

'When you say comparison, do you mean comparison of a latent print with known fingerprints you have on record, for the purpose of identifying a particular individual?'

'Yes, sir.'

'Would you tell the jury whether there is a generally accepted minimum number of distinguishing characteristics which allow a valid comparison to be made?'

'In general, no expert would venture an opinion about identification by fingerprints unless he finds at least eight matching characteristics.'

'How many such characteristics were there in the case of the print you found on the window ledge?'

'Twelve, sir. '

'Before I come to the results of the comparison, did you find anything else at the site of the latent fingerprint?'

'Yes, sir. At the site of the print I found a red stain, measuring about one inch by a quarter of an inch. I took a swab of this stain, and when analysed it proved to be human blood of group A.'

'Did the blood stain in any way prevent the fingerprint from being examined?'

'No, sir, even though the stain was to some degree mixed with the print, the ridges were perfectly clear.'

'I see. And, again, I think it is not disputed, when a comparison was made, was it found that the fingerprint found on the window ledge was that of the accused, William Cottage?'

'That is correct, sir.'

'I have nothing further, Mr Harlow, please wait there.'

* * *

Martin Hardcastle was already on his feet.

'Mr Harlow, is it correct that there is no known method of determining at what time a fingerprint is left on a surface?'

Harlow smiled in the direction of the jury. If he had a pound for every time he had been asked that question…!

'That is correct, sir. It is sometimes possible to tell in general terms whether a print has been somewhat degraded, but that does not assist in assigning a date to the print.'

Hardcastle paused. The answer he wanted to his next question did not necessarily follow from the last answer. But Harlow had not made any claim to the contrary in his report. If he went the wrong way, Hardcastle would hammer him about why he had omitted such an important matter from the report. But the only guaranteed result of that line of questioning was that the expert would be embarrassed. The evidence would still be there for the jury to accept and act on. It was the first critical moment of the trial for the defence of Billy Cottage.

'Is it also correct, Mr Harlow, that you cannot say whether or not the latent fingerprint was deposited on the window ledge at the same time as the blood stain?'

Harlow bit his lip.

'I cannot say that with any acceptable degree of scientific certainty.'

'You don't know?'

'Scientifically, I don't know.'

'And you cannot exclude the possibility that the fingerprint was deposited on the window ledge on an occasion before the blood was deposited?'

'I would have to concede that,' Harlow replied reluctantly.

'Thank you, Mr Harlow,' Hardcastle said, sitting down.

Andrew Pilkington was rising to his feet, but the judge intervened.

'I am sorry, Mr Pilkington, but I have other duties to perform as the Assize Judge. We will adjourn for lunch until 2 o'clock.'

Pilkington smiled. By 'other duties' Mr Justice Lancaster meant that he would be having yet another formal lunch with civic dignitaries. If the trial lasted long enough he and Martin Hardcastle might be invited to take lunch with the judge but not, apparently, today. After the ritual bows between bench and bar the morning's session of the court was over.

38

THEY ASSEMBLED AGAIN at Martin Hardcastle's preferred spot for smoking, just around the corner and to the left from the entrance to the Town Hall. Jess had been assigned to make sure that Billy Cottage had no urgent questions about the morning's proceedings, after which she met John who, at Martin's insistence, had undertaken to bring their daily sandwiches from the George. The weather was warm but fresh, a welcome relief from the stifling atmosphere of the courtroom. They were hungry, and conversation flagged while they did justice to their sandwiches. It was a rather public lunch. Despite the uncomfortable cramped conditions, public interest in the trial showed no signs of flagging. The public gallery had once again been full, and small clusters of reporters, as well as curious onlookers who had spilled out on to the street, surveyed the group from a distance across the square, wondering what they could be discussing, how well they thought they were doing.

'So, what about Dr Bushell?' Barratt asked, once the sandwiches were almost gone. 'Do we ask the prosecution for details of any notes or statements he may have made?'

Hardcastle crumpled the wrapping paper from his sandwich into a tight ball and lobbed it successfully into a litter bin which stood against the wall to his left. He lit a cigarette.

'Ah, yes. What has Jennifer Doyce been saying to her psychiatric counsellor? What do you think, Schroeder?'

'Dangerous,' Ben replied immediately. 'If there was anything which undermined the prosecution's case, or gave us any help at all, Andrew Pilkington would have provided it to us without being asked.'

Barratt Davis was looking doubtful, but Hardcastle jumped in immediately on Ben's side.

'Treasury Counsel,' he said. 'You can take it to the bank. It's the code. It would be automatic. There is nothing there to help us.'

'Which doesn't mean there is nothing there,' Ben continued. 'And if we cross-examine Jennifer about anything she may have said since the attack, the prosecution will re-examine and bring every word of Dr Bushell's notes in. They may even apply to call Dr Bushell, and we won't get any sympathy there. I think we have to challenge her evidence as it is given without worrying about what she may have said to Dr Bushell.'

Hardcastle pointed towards Ben with his cigarette.

'Absolutely right,' he said. 'Out of the mouths of babes and sucklings.'

Ben remained impassive, but Jess could not suppress a look and snort of disgust. Hardcastle raised his eyebrows, as if belatedly reflecting on his comment. He continued hurriedly.

'We are going to assume that Jennifer Doyce told Dr Bushell exactly what she is going to say when she gives evidence tomorrow. Dr Walker was quite helpful. He has done some of our work for us. With a little prompting, he has already planted in the jury's mind a question about whether they can rely on Jennifer's memory after everything she has been through. We don't need to attack her at all, so we are not going to have to risk alienating the jury by being aggressive. We can be nice to her and still get what we want.'

He threw the butt of his cigarette on to the ground and stamped on it.

'But that is for tomorrow. This afternoon we have to worry about Mavis Brown.'

He turned abruptly and walked back into the Town Hall. Barratt stared after him for a moment before following. Jess turned to Ben.

'I'm sorry, Ben. I'm surprised you didn't hit him. How can he be so offensive?'

'Apparently it's a natural gift,' Ben replied. 'Jess, I don't know why people in my profession feel obliged to act like that, but apparently they do. It's something you just have to shrug off. You will be used to it by the time you become a solicitor.'

'I may be changing my mind about that,' she said. 'I'm not sure I could just shrug it off. Life's too short.'

They turned towards the entrance.

'Did Cottage have anything to say?' Ben asked. 'Anything in

particular we need to talk to him about after court?'

'He is getting anxious about giving evidence again,' Jess replied. 'He was asking when it would be his turn, and when it would be Eve's turn. I told him it would be a day or two, and that we would have plenty of time to talk to him about it before he goes into the witness box. But he seems a bit agitated.'

'Well, that's not surprising,' Ben said. 'I'll mention it to Martin.'

'He'll like that,' she replied sullenly. 'Something else out of the mouths of babes and sucklings.'

Ben patted her sympathetically on the arm as he opened the door for her.

* * *

'My name is Charles Edwards.'

'Are you the landlord and licensee of the Oliver Cromwell public house at St Ives?'

'Yes, sir.'

'For how long have you been the landlord of that house?'

Edwards was a stout man, rather too stout for his age, which was about fifty. He was dressed in a blue blazer, light grey trousers and a blue and white striped tie. He clearly felt nervous about giving evidence, but it was not for any want of experience. He had given evidence before the licensing justices at the magistrates' court on many occasions during his long career as a pub landlord. He ran a good house, always had. He had never been refused a license, and his impeccable record should have put his mind more at ease. But it was an aspect of the job he had never quite got used to. As a result, he pretended thought about the reply he gave to each question asked, even when none was necessary.

'Oh, about seven years, sir.'

Andrew Pilkington looked up at Mr Justice Lancaster.

'My Lord, with the usher's assistance, may the witness be shown Exhibit One? The jury have copies. It is the ordnance survey map and street plan of St Ives.'

'Yes,' the judge replied.

Paul took the exhibit from the clerk's desk and handed it to the witness.

'Mr Edwards, if you will please look at the second page of the exhibit you have been given, you will see that it is a street plan of St Ives. Can you point out to the jury where the Oliver Cromwell is on this page?'

Edwards held the plan at arm's length. His eyes were no longer quite as cooperative as they had been, but he had always taken his good eyesight for granted and was stubbornly resisting the thought of spectacles.

'Yes, sir, it is here,' he replied, pointing to a spot on the page.

'Can you please hold it up so that my Lord, the jury and my learned friends can see it?'

Edwards complied.

'Thank you. I think you are indicating where the letter A is marked on the plan, which would mean that the house is situated in Wellington Street, close to where that street ends at its junction with Priory Road. Is that right?'

'Yes, sir.'

'And perhaps you can help us with this. If you turn left on leaving the Oliver Cromwell and walk to Priory Road, you will come to a small corner shop, marked with the letter B, which is Mr Brown's shop, is it not?'

'Yes, that's correct.'

'It seems that the shop is the last building on Priory Road, and if you continue you will come to a gate with a turnstile, letter C, which leads into the meadow beside the river. Yes?'

'Yes, sir.'

'Thank you. That is all I want to ask about that, so you can put the exhibit down. Now, do you know the accused, William Cottage?'

Edwards looked into the dock, where Cottage sat impassively, staring straight ahead.

'Oh, yes, sir. I've know Billy for – oh, it must be three years, at least.'

'In what capacity?'

'Well, he's quite a well-known character in St Ives. He's the lock keeper at Fenstanton, of course, and you'd see him around town a lot, minding his own business, doing this and that.'

'Yes. But...'

'You can lead him,' Martin Hardcastle was whispering from his left.

'I'm much obliged. Have you employed Mr Cottage at the Oliver Cromwell?'

'Yes, sir. For a good two years. He's an assistant barman, part time. It's because there's not so much traffic on the river as there used to be, sir. There's not as much work for the lock keepers, so Billy wanted to make an extra quid or two in the evenings, and I was happy to take him.'

'I see. And how many evenings a week did Mr Cottage work for you?'

'He was usually with us Friday and Saturday nights, which is when we are the busiest; he would start at 5.30 and work until an hour after the last customer leaves when we close. I believe he may have done another evening in the week somewhere else.'

'Now, did there come a time when the police asked you to cast your mind back to a Saturday evening earlier in the year, the 25 January?'

'Yes, sir, they did. It was just after the two bodies had been discovered up at the Fen. They wanted to know whether I remembered the young man and young woman being in my pub on that Saturday evening.'

'And did you remember?'

'I did, sir. They showed me their photographs and I did remember them being with us.'

Pilkington glanced across at the jury.

'Mr Edwards, no doubt you have a lot of people in the Oliver Cromwell, especially on a Saturday night. The jury may be wondering how you can be sure that you remember Frank Gilliam and Jennifer Doyce being there on that particular Saturday. What do say about that?'

Edwards smiled.

'You don't get many young couples in the Oliver,' he replied. 'Time was you didn't get many ladies at all. That's changing now, of course, and there are one or two pubs in the town centre where it's not at all unusual to see couples – hotels like the Golden Lion, for example. These days, you might even get girls on their own, which would have been unheard of a few years ago. I'm not much in favour of that myself and, as I say, we don't get it so much at the Oliver. We are still mostly a men's pub. Oh, you will get the odd old biddy who comes into the snug for her bottle of Guinness. But we don't even see couples that much. I also remember that they seemed a bit – I don't know – apprehensive. They didn't talk very much, as I recall. It was almost as if they were miles away.'

'Thank you,' Pilkington said. 'Do you remember at what time they arrived?'

Edwards shook his head.

'I'm afraid not. I didn't serve them, and I only noticed them once they were sitting down. It wasn't very early, and I don't think they stayed very long. I do remember we were quite busy when I noticed them.'

'Who did serve them, do you remember that?'

'Billy Cottage, sir.'

'And do you remember at what time they left?'

'Again, I couldn't give you an exact time. It wasn't long before closing time. But how long before, I couldn't say. I remember they had left when I began to call time.'

'Do you remember when Billy Cottage left the Oliver Cromwell that night?'

Edwards snorted and jerked his head back.

'Oh, I remember that well enough. He left before some of the customers. He is supposed to be there for an hour after the last customer leaves, so that we can collect the glasses, tidy the house up, wash the glasses and put them back in place. But on that evening, he just buggered off and left me and Alf to do it all.' He looked up at the judge. 'Excuse my language, my Lord. I haven't seen him since, but he would have got a right piece of my mind if I had done.'

Pilkington smiled.

'Yes, I'm sure. But I want to press you a bit more about the time, if I could. What time was closing time?'

'We close at 11 o'clock on Saturday evenings.'

'And can you relate Billy leaving either to 11 o'clock or to Frank Gilliam and Jennifer Doyce leaving?'

Edwards put his hands on his hips and thought for some time.

'It can't have been long after they left. I'm sure they were gone when I started to call time, and I always look for Billy and Alf once

I've made the first call, so that I can make sure they are getting started on collecting the glasses and don't serve any more drinks. I remember speaking to Alf, but Billy was nowhere to be seen. I thought he might have gone down the cellar for some reason, but he hadn't. As I say, I didn't see him again. So he must have left somewhere around 11 o'clock, and it can't have been very long after the couple. I'm sorry, sir. That's all I can tell you.'

'Mr Edwards, do you by any chance remember what Billy Cottage was wearing on that evening?'

Edwards bowed his head for some moments.

'Not in any great detail. He was wearing a red shirt, or a red and white check – it was something he wore quite often. What I remember most is his shoes – he always wore the same ones. They were filthy. They looked as though they hadn't been cleaned since before the War.'

'Thank you, Mr Edwards. Wait there, please.'

* * *

Hardcastle stood.

'Did you see Frank Gilliam and Jennifer Doyce leave?'

'Not that I remember, sir, no.'

'Did you see Billy Cottage leave?'

'No.'

'Mr Edwards, it doesn't always take an hour to collect the glasses and tidy the house, does it? Not with three of you doing it?'

'Not always, sir.'

'And if it took less than an hour, you would not expect your assistants to stay until the end of the hour for no reason, would you?'

Edwards smiled.

'Well, no, obviously, once they have finished...'

'Of course. It wouldn't make for good employee relations to keep them from their homes unnecessarily, would it?'

'No.'

'The Oliver Cromwell has a fairly small bar area in front of the bar as you come in from Wellington Street, and a longer, quite thin seating area running away from the street, is that right?'

'You've been there, sir, have you? If so...'

'I will ask the questions, Mr Edwards, thank you,' Hardcastle said.

'Yes, sorry, sir. I didn't mean…'

'My question is whether the house has a longer, thinner seating area running away from the street?'

'The lounge, yes.'

'You also have a garden, I believe, but presumably it would not be open in January?'

'Correct.'

'And where were you when you called time?'

'I was behind the bar.'

'And Alf must have been either behind the bar, or in the bar area, if you remember speaking to him?'

'Yes.'

'Is it not possible that Billy Cottage was clearing up in the lounge at that time?'

'No. I would have seen him. I looked for him, believe you me.'

Hardcastle nodded, glancing at the jury.

'Mr Edwards, let me make clear that I am not trying to avoid the fact that Mr Cottage left work before he was supposed to. I concede that he did, and it was not the first time, was it?'

'No, it wasn't.'

'No. But what I am suggesting is that he may well have been clearing up in the lounge, at least for a few minutes, and perhaps that he did go down the cellar for a short time. My point is that he did not leave immediately after Frank Gilliam and Jennifer Doyce. Think carefully, Mr Edwards. You cannot exclude that possibility, can you?'

Edwards raised his hands.

'I didn't see him leave. All I know is, I looked for him and he wasn't there.'

'Could that have been because he left by the back door?'

His recollection of the misconduct of Billy Cottage had been incensing Edwards throughout his time in the witness box. The idea of yet a further breach of the house rules moved him to anger. His face turned a bright red.

'He's not supposed to do that,' he insisted, a little too loudly. 'He's supposed to come and check with me after he's finished clearing up, and I tell him when it's time to leave, and when he leaves it is through the front door.'

'We can agree, then, Mr Edwards, that Mr Cottage is not a very satisfactory employee?' Hardcastle asked quietly.

'No, he most certainly is not,' Edwards replied vehemently. He stared briefly at Billy Cottage, then crossed his arms and looked defiantly at Martin Hardcastle, awaiting the next question with relish. But it never came. Hardcastle had resumed his seat and seemed to be examining his fingernails.

39

Mavis Brown wore her best frock for the occasion, pale green with small white dots, and a darker green hat she had worn to her cousin Freda's wedding the year before, and plain brown shoes with a low heel. She had been apprehensive about this moment ever since the police had first interviewed her, but her father had reassured her that she had nothing to fear as long as she told the truth. The judge in his red robes and the barristers in their black and white seemed intimidating at first, but Mavis had a ready sense of humour and it was not long before she began to find the scene rather funny – a bit of a giggle, as she might have said to her friends – and the thought relaxed her. Andrew Pilkington had been asking her about the stock-taking she had been doing on the night of 25 January.

'Does the front window of your shop overlook Priory Road?'

'Yes, sir.'

'And, as the jury will be able to see from the street plan, can you also see some distance along Wellington Street towards the Oliver Cromwell?'

'Yes.'

'Did there come a time on that evening,' he asked, 'when you looked through the window and saw one or more people outside the shop?'

'Yes, sir. I was a bit taken aback to see anyone outside the shop at that time of night. But there they were, a young couple, standing outside, trying to get my attention by waving to me.'

'Of course, the shop was closed?'

'Oh, yes, we close at 5 o'clock on Saturdays.'

'What did you do?'

'Well, I wouldn't usually have opened the door once we had closed, but they were smiling, they looked very nice, and I thought it wouldn't do any harm. So I opened the door.'

'Did they say what they wanted?'

'They had run out of cigarettes. They seemed a bit desperate. So I asked them to come in, opened the till, and I sold them two packets of ten.'

'Do you remember what brand of cigarettes they wanted?'

Yes. Woodbines, sir, both of them.'

'A few days later, did the police show you photographs of these two young people?'

'Yes, sir.'

'And were you able to identify them as the couple to whom you had sold the cigarettes?'

'Yes, sir.' There were suddenly tears in her eyes. She reached into her handbag for a small, white lace handkerchief. 'I can't believe what happened. They were a really nice couple.'

Pilkington nodded and gave her a few moments before continuing.

'When they left, did you notice in what direction they walked?'

'Yes, sir, towards the meadow.'

'I see. Again, as the jury can see, that would have meant turning left out of the shop to walk towards the river?'

'Yes.'

'Thank you. Miss Brown, did you see anyone else outside your shop on that evening?'

She nodded vigorously. 'A man. Just a minute or so after the couple had left.'

'Was the man someone you knew, or had seen before?'

'No, sir.'

'Can you describe him for the jury?'

'I couldn't see his face. He was wearing a dark woolly hat which was pulled down to his eyes. He wasn't very tall.'

'What else was he wearing?'

'The main thing I noticed was that he was wearing a raincoat, but he had it open. It was a very cold night and I thought that was strange. Underneath the raincoat I thought I saw a dark jacket of some kind and a red and white checked shirt. He had dirty brown shoes.'

'Thank you,' Pilkington said. 'How clear was your view of this man? Where was he in relation to you?'

'I was at the shop window. I had just locked the front door again. He was just standing there under the street light on the corner of Wellington Street. I had a clear view.'

'Did you see from which direction he had come?'

'No, I'm afraid not. When I noticed him, he was standing still. I didn't see where he came from.'

'In which direction was he facing?'

'Towards the meadow, sir.'

'Do you remember anything else about this man at all?'

Mavis suddenly laughed.

'Yes, sir. I heard him singing.'

'Singing?' Pilkington asked, smiling. 'What was he singing, can you tell us?'

'Yes, sir. He was singing the *Lincolnshire Poacher*.'

'The *Lincolnshire Poacher*. "*When I was bound apprentice...?*"'

He stopped abruptly. Martin Hardcastle had jumped to his feet.

'My Lord, I really must ask my learned friend not to lead on this. It is of the utmost importance.'

Mr Justice Lancaster nodded.

'Mr Hardcastle is quite right, Mr Pilkington. Re-phrase, please.'

'Of course, my Lord. Miss Brown, how do you know it was the *Lincolnshire Poacher*? Was it because of the words, the tune...?'

'I didn't know the words. I recognised the tune. Shall I explain?'

'Yes, please.'

'I had heard the same song a few days before. I was listening to a folk music concert on the radio with my father. It was late one evening, just before bedtime. The singer was Steve Benbow, and he sang that same song.'

'Have you any doubt that it was the same song, the one that you heard on the radio, that the man was singing?'

'No, sir, it was the same one.'

'For how long did he continue singing?'

'Oh, just a few seconds. But I heard it clearly.'

'Yes. What did the man do when he finished singing?'

'He walked off in the direction of the meadow, sir.'

'Did you see him again after that?'

'No, sir.'

'Finally, Miss Brown, can you tell the jury what time it was when you sold the Woodbines to the young couple?'

'I can't tell you exactly. All I remember is that, as I was switching off the lights after the man had walked away, I looked up at the clock on the wall at the back of the shop. It said a quarter to eleven. But I can't be sure that was the correct time.'

'No, of course. Thank you very much, Miss Brown,' Pilkington said. 'Please wait there. My learned friend may have some questions.'

* * *

Hardcastle stood slowly and without fuss, as if trying to appear reassuring.

'Miss Brown, do you have a particular interest in folk music? I know a lot of young people do, today.'

She smiled. 'No, sir.'

'Are you musical generally? Did you take piano lessons, sing in the church choir, anything like that?'

She nodded. 'I took piano lessons. I started when I was seven. But I didn't really take to it. I stopped when I was eleven or twelve.'

'How was it that you happened to be listening to Steve Benbow late at night?'

'Oh, it was just by chance. We didn't know what was going to be on. I always have a cup of cocoa with my dad before bed, and he usually has the radio on. It could be anything. Sometimes we listen to the news. But on this evening…'

'It happened to be Steve Benbow. Yes, I see. For how long was this man singing outside your shop?'

'How long?'

'Yes. You have told the jury that he was singing the *Lincolnshire Poacher*? I believe the *Lincolnshire Poacher* has several verses. Is that correct?'

'I'm sure I couldn't say, sir.'

'Well, never mind. However many there are, how many of them did he sing? One? Two? Perhaps part of one?'

Mavis was staring ahead blankly.

'Well, can I ask you this?' Hardcastle continued. 'Can you tell the jury any of the words of the song that you remember him singing?'

Andrew Pilkington rose to his feet.

'My Lord, I must object. Where is my learned friend going with this? Perhaps he would like Miss Brown to sing the *Lincolnshire Poacher* for the jury?'

The jury sniggered.

'Well, my Lord,' Hardcastle rejoined, 'it was only a few minutes ago that my learned friend was trying, until your Lordship rightly restrained him, to remind the witness of the words by reciting them to her. But I can put his mind at rest. I would not dream of having Miss Brown transform your Lordship's court into a musical theatre...'

The jury now laughed openly and loudly.

'I am merely seeking to explore the witness's recollection.'

Mr Justice Lancaster was trying, not entirely successfully, to suppress a smile.

'Perhaps you could do so in another way?' he suggested.

Hardcastle smiled towards the jury. 'Certainly, my Lord. Miss Brown, when the man had gone and you had locked up the shop, you went upstairs to join your father, didn't you?'

'Yes, sir.'

'And I would like to understand this, and I would like the jury to understand this too. Were the two of you drinking cocoa together as usual?'

'Yes, sir.'

'And did you say anything to your father about what you had seen and heard?'

'Yes, of course.'

'You did? What did you tell him, exactly?'

'Well, I told him about selling the cigarettes to the young couple, and about seeing the man outside the shop.'

'What about the man singing? Did you tell your father about that?'

'Yes.'

'What did you tell him?'

'I said that the man was singing, and how strange it was, and I said I thought I recognised the tune.'

Hardcastle paused and turned towards Ben, his eyebrows raised. Ben nodded.

'As the *Lincolnshire Poacher*? Did you tell your father that you recognised it as the *Lincolnshire Poacher*?'

'No, sir. Just that I recognised it.'

'I see,' Hardcastle continued. 'Then what happened?'

She smiled. 'My dad asked me to hum the tune for him. I hummed it. I had to do it twice, I think. And then he said, "I know what that was. We heard it the other night, you know, when Steve Benbow was on. It's called the *Lincolnshire Poacher*".'

Hardcastle turned to Ben with a look of triumph. Ben smiled broadly. Andrew Pilkington had lowered his head, appearing to concentrate on a sheet of paper.

'So, Miss Brown, what actually happened is this, is it? You heard a man singing a song? You cannot say for how long, and you do not know any of the words? You thought you recognised the tune after hearing Steve Benbow sing it a few nights earlier? You hummed it twice for your father? And he – not you – *he* identified it as the *Lincolnshire Poacher*? Have I summarised your evidence fairly?'

She nodded. 'That's what happened, sir.'

'Thank you very much, Miss Brown. Nothing further, my Lord.'

40

WITH A SHAKE of his head, Pilkington stood.

'My Lord, I call Helen Doyce.'

Mrs Doyce wore a black dress, hat and shoes, an outfit she might have appropriately worn to a funeral; and she had, in fact, worn the same clothes when Frank Gilliam was buried. She regarded the day's proceedings as an extension of that sad occasion in St Ives. She was softly spoken, so much so that the jury had to strain to hear.

'Mrs Doyce, are you the mother of Jennifer Doyce?'

'I am.'

'I would like you to look at something, please.'

After gesturing to Paul, Pilkington handed the usher an object wrapped in a clear plastic cover.

'The usher will unwrap this for you, Mrs Doyce. Would you please tell the jury whether you recognise it?'

Mrs Doyce took the gold cross and chain from Paul, held it in her hands for some moments, and began to cry, almost inaudibly, but with tears flowing copiously down her cheeks. Martin Hardcastle and Ben Schroeder did their best to look straight ahead.

'Take your time, Mrs Doyce,' Andrew Pilkington said. 'There is no rush.'

'Would you like a break?' Mr Justice Lancaster suggested.

Mrs Doyce shook her head. She took a handkerchief from her handbag and dried her eyes.

'No, thank you. This is a gold cross and chain which belonged to my mother, Jennifer's grandmother,' she replied. 'My mother gave it to Jennifer when she was confirmed.'

'I see. And can you tell my Lord and the jury, based on your own observation, whether Jennifer wore it and, if so, how often?'

Mrs Doyce smiled.

'I don't think she has ever taken it off,' she replied, 'except perhaps to have her bath or go to bed. She wears it everywhere she goes. She adored her grandmother, and she adores this cross and chain. She has been asking when she can have it back. I tell her, "when the case is over", but she is very distressed. She...'

She began to cry again.

'My Lord, I have nothing further,' Pilkington said. 'May this be Exhibit Five?'

'Exhibit Five,' the judge confirmed.

'No questions, my Lord,' Hardcastle said, hardly rising from his seat.

* * *

'My Lord, I now recall PC Willis. I don't know whether your Lordship or my learned friend requires him to be re-sworn?'

'Yes, please,' Hardcastle replied immediately.

Willis duly took the oath.

'Officer,' Pilkington began, 'you have already told the jury about your discovery of the body of Frank Gilliam on board the *Rosemary D*, and about your observing that Jennifer Doyce was alive and having her transported to Addenbrookes. I want now to ask you about one or two other matters. Firstly, on the morning of the 30 of January, with Detective Superintendent Arnold and Detective Sergeant Phillips, did you go to the lock keeper's house at Fenstanton?'

Willis turned towards the judge. 'If I may refer to my notebook, my Lord?'

'When did you make your notes?' Pilkington asked.

'On my return to St Ives police station, about an hour later, my Lord. The events of the morning were fresh in my memory.'

Pilkington glanced at Martin Hardcastle.

'Did he make them on his own, or with the other officers?' Hardcastle whispered.

'Did you make your notes on your own, or with the other officers?' Pilkington asked.

'I made them on my own,' Willis replied.

Hardcastle nodded.

'Then you may refer to your notes, officer.'

'Thank you, sir. Yes, I did go the Fenstanton lock keeper's house on that morning.'

'Whose house is that?'

'The accused, William Cottage, lives there, sir, together with his sister, Miss Eve Cottage.'

'What was your purpose in going to Mr Cottage's home on that morning?'

'We wished to question him regarding this case, sir.'

'I see. Was Mr Cottage at home when you arrived at the house?'

'No, sir. He arrived about twenty minutes after we did.

'Was anyone at the house when you arrived?'

'Yes, sir. Miss Eve Cottage. We identified ourselves as police officers and told her that we wished to speak to her brother. She said he would be back before too long, and invited us into the house to wait.'

'Yes,' Pilkington said. 'While you were waiting, did you notice anything in particular about Miss Cottage's appearance?'

'I did, sir.'

'What was that?'

'I noticed that she was wearing a heavy gold cross and chain.'

'And why was that of interest to you?'

'I was aware that a piece of jewellery of that description was alleged to have been stolen during the events on board the *Rosemary D* on the night of 25 January, sir. I had been shown a photograph of the item in question, which I believe was taken for insurance purposes.'

'With the usher's assistance, officer, please look at Exhibit Five.'

Willis nodded instantly as Paul approached him with the cross and chain.

'That is the piece I saw Miss Cottage wearing, sir.'

'Thank you. What did you do when you saw it?'

'Detective Superintendent Arnold questioned her about how she had come by the piece, sir. She said...'

Hardcastle was already half way to his feet when Pilkington interrupted Willis.

'We can't have what Miss Cottage said, officer. But, yes or no, did she give Superintendent Arnold an explanation for having it?'

'Yes, she did, sir.'

'What did you do next?'

'Superintendent Arnold explained that he had reason to believe that the cross and chain belonged to someone else, and asked her to surrender it to him, which she did without objection, sir.'

'Did anything else happen on that morning?'

Willis turned over a page of his notebook.

'Yes, sir. Shortly afterwards, Mr Cottage returned home, and after a brief conversation Detective Inspector Phillips arrested him on suspicion of larceny.'

Pilkington surveyed his own notes for several moments.

'I will deal with the arrest with Superintendent Arnold and Inspector Phillips,' he said. 'But if my learned friend has any questions about that, are you prepared to answer them now?'

'Yes, sir,' Willis replied.

'Actually,' Pilkington continued, 'there is one other matter. I think there is no dispute about it. In September 1961, was there an occasion when you arrested the accused, William Cottage, for indecent exposure near a house in St Ives?'

'Yes, sir.'

'Did you observe that offence being committed?'

'I did, sir.'

'What did you see?'

'Mr Cottage was hiding in some bushes outside the house and was masturbating while he watched a young lady getting undressed in an upstairs room of the house, sir.'

'Thank you. Officer, was there any aspect of the incident you found unusual?'

'There was, sir. As I approached, Mr Cottage appeared not to notice me. I was able to get within touching distance before he saw me. I distinctly heard him humming or singing a tune.'

'Indeed. Did you recognise the tune?'

'I did, sir. It was the *Lincolnshire Poacher*.'

'What happened after you arrested Mr Cottage?'

'I took him to St Ives police station, sir. He was detained overnight. The following morning he appeared before the magistrates and pleaded guilty to indecent exposure. He was conditionally discharged for twelve months.'

'Has Mr Cottage been convicted of any other offence?'

'No, sir, he has not.'

'Yes, thank you, officer, wait there, please.'

* * *

Martin Hardcastle glanced at the jury with the suggestion of a smile, as if to confide in them, a calculated intimacy. '*You know what's coming, don't you? We have been down this road together before.*'

'Are you a musical man, officer?'

Willis laughed briefly. 'No, sir, not at all.'

Another glance towards the jury.

'Really? You disappoint me. You sound as though you might be a useful baritone. No singing in the police choir, for instance?'

'I don't think there is any such thing in Huntingdonshire, sir.'

'Oh? What a pity. Well, perhaps the church choir, then? No…? Well, regardless, you said that when you arrested Mr Cottage in 1961 he was humming or singing the *Lincolnshire Poacher*?'

'That is correct, sir.'

'Well, which was it? Was he humming or singing?'

Willis puffed out his cheeks and exhaled heavily.

'I really can't recall, sir. It has been more than two years.'

'But you do recall after two years that it was the *Lincolnshire Poacher*?'

'Yes, sir.'

'Even though you are not a musical man?'

'Yes, sir.'

'So we don't know whether you recognised the words or the tune, do we?'

'No, sir.'

Hardcastle paused. Seeing Andrew Pilkington ready to spring to his feet, he extended a hand in his direction.

'No reason to be concerned. I am not going to risk the ire of his Lordship or my learned friend by asking you to sing it – or even to hum it, for that matter.'

Willis ventured a weak smile. 'I am relieved to hear that, sir.'

'Yes, I am sure you are. It's a rather convenient memory to have in the context of this case, isn't it?'

Now Pilkington was on his feet.

'Really, my Lord, that is quite improper. My learned friend knows better…'

But Hardcastle had already resumed his seat and evidently had no intention of insisting on an answer. Mr Justice Lancaster did not intervene.

'My Lord,' Andrew Pilkington said, once Willis had left the courtroom. 'The Crown's next witness is Jennifer Doyce. I am sure your Lordship will appreciate that we want to complete her evidence in one day, rather than keep her waiting this afternoon and having to come back tomorrow. So I have not asked her to be here this afternoon. I have taken the liberty, after consulting with Dr Walker, of asking them both to be present for 10.30 tomorrow morning. I hope that will meet with your Lordship's approval.'

'Yes, of course,' the judge replied.

'I have no other evidence to call today,' Pilkington said.

The judge smiled at the jury.

'Then that is all for today. Please be back in time to resume at 10.30 tomorrow morning, members of the jury.'

* * *

'Well, I thought that went as well as we could have hoped this afternoon, Mr Cottage,' Martin Hardcastle said.

The team had once more gathered outside the small cell at the back of Court 1 and had, as usual, only a few minutes before the prison officers took Billy Cottage back to Bedford for the night.

'What did you think?'

Billy nodded. He did not really know what to think, but if his main barrister thought it had gone well, then that was a good sign. He did not understand why. The mention of his previous conviction had unnerved him, and so had the repeated references to the *Lincolnshire Poacher*. Every time the song was mentioned, the words ran through his head like some kind of endless tape he was powerless to control. The words stayed in his mind. It was almost as if he could form no other thought while they were there. Once or twice, he had felt that he might just blurt them out, start singing aloud, right there in the courtroom. He knew how mad that would be, but once or twice he was not sure that he could stop himself. The urge was particularly strong during the moments when he thought Martin Hardcastle was going to invite a witness to sing. How could he avoid joining in? That thought unleashed another train of thought. What would happen when his turn came to give evidence, when he had to speak in court? Would he be able to control the words then? And what about Eve? What would she say when the prosecuting barrister asked her hard questions? What might she tell him? And that brought back the spectre of being hanged.

'Can I ask you something, Mr Hardcastle?'

'Of course.'

'When will I be giving evidence?'

Martin knew that Ben and Barratt had both answered that same question more than once. It struck him that Cottage could not quite come to terms with it.

'Not tomorrow. Very likely the day after. We've got Jennifer Doyce tomorrow, then Superintendent Arnold and Inspector Phillips. They are going to take some time. Don't be anxious about it. We will have the chance to talk to you before you give evidence. For now, let's worry about the prosecution's case. We have made some progress, and we may be able to make more tomorrow. One step at a time.'

Cottage nodded. There was a silence.

'Do I have to give evidence? Does Eve have to?'

Martin looked to his right and saw Barratt raise his eyebrows in apparent frustration.

'Yes. I think you will have to,' he replied. 'So will your sister. This is not a case where I can invite the judge to stop the case at the close of the prosecution case, so it will go to the jury. You have an alibi, but the only way we can put that before the jury is for you and Eve to give evidence about it. These were brutal crimes, Mr Cottage, and there is some evidence against you. The jury will need a basis to find you not guilty, and it is our job to provide it to them. Mr Schroeder and I are persuasive fellows, but even we can't persuade anyone without evidence.'

He looked directly at Ben.

'I agree,' Ben said at once. 'The jury needs to hear from you. They need to hear your side of the case.'

'Can I do it without Eve having to say anything?'

Martin shrugged.

'You could. But obviously the jury would want to know why Eve had not come to support you when she was at home at the relevant time. It would not look good.'

The answers took away the spark of light which had briefly ignited in the mind of Billy Cottage. The spectre returned. He turned his back and walked to his seat at the back of the cell, waiting for the words to return.

Success to every gentleman that lives in Lincolnshire,
Success to every poacher that wants to sell a hare,
Bad luck to every gamekeeper that will not sell his deer,
Oh, 'tis my delight on a shiny night in the season of the year.

41

'How did your training go this afternoon?'

John smiled. 'Very well, sir, thank you. I took a knock to the ankle in the game last week and I wasn't sure how long I would last, but I came through fine.'

'So you will be fit for the weekend?'

'Looks like it, sir.'

'Good.'

John had left the tray with his dinner on the small table by the window of Martin Hardcastle's room. The steak and kidney pie was still on the menu and there was a bottle of the house *vin ordinaire* to wash it down. Martin settled the white napkin, lifted the metal dish cover, and looked doubtfully at the food on his plate. It did not look particularly appetising; certainly nothing to write home about, but then again, he was in the country, and what could you expect? This wasn't London.

'Ring down if you fancy a pudding, sir,' John said. 'It's apple crumble tonight. Not bad.'

'I will,' Martin replied. 'Did you manage to get…?'

'In your dressing table, sir, middle drawer. I thought I wouldn't leave it out. You never know. One of the girls might come in to pull down the bed covers and, between you and me, sir, you can't always trust them not to gossip.'

Martin smiled as he handed John a note.

'Good man. Keep the change.'

'Thank you, sir,' John said, with a bright smile. 'Will there be anything else?'

'I'll ring if there is,' Martin replied.

He locked the door as soon as John had left. He opened the middle drawer of the dresser, took out the bottle of Bell's, and placed it on the table behind his dinner tray. John was a bright lad, he reflected, and dependable. Not many lads of his age would have thought of doing that. He would put in a good word for him with the manager of the hotel. He deserved a leg up. He placed a finger on top of the bottle of whisky. Reward time was drawing near, and he had earned his reward today. But he would have to eat something first. He contemplated the steak and kidney pie for some time. Unappetising as it looked, it was a long time since his lunchtime sandwich, and he was hungry. The wine had been opened, and he poured himself a large glass. With the help of the wine he managed to force down most of the pie, with some dry mashed potatoes barely relieved by a thick brown gravy, and some overcooked green beans. He replaced his knife and fork on the tray. He could have eaten something more but, after some thought, he decided that he could not face the apple crumble. He lifted the wine bottle from the tray, replaced the metal cover over the plate, carried the tray to the door, and set the tray on the floor just outside. He hung the 'Do not Disturb' sign on the door handle, closed and locked the door. It was a signal to himself that the day was over, that he did not have to deal with anyone until the next morning, that he had some time for himself. He could feel confident that he would spend the remainder of the evening without any further intrusion.

He had left his briefcase on the bed. He now opened it and took out his blue barrister's notebook. Moving to the wardrobe he took a pen from the inside pocket of his jacket, and settled back down at his table. He opened the notebook and wrote a heading in bold letters. 'Cross of Jennifer Doyce'. He underlined it for effect, once, then twice. He had gone over this cross-examination in his mind many times, but now the time had come to focus his thoughts and decide exactly what line to take. He re-filled his wine glass. He had to be gentle, no doubt about that. Jennifer was a victim, and the jury was bound to feel for her. Martin would have pounded her without a second thought, victim or not, if the case required it, but the case did not require it. Billy Cottage could afford to have nothing but sympathy for Jennifer Doyce. She had been savagely beaten and raped by someone other than Billy, and he could condemn that brutality just like any other half way decent member of society. What was important – essential even – was that Jennifer had been raped, and that the rape must appear to the jury to be the central event of the night of the 25 January – the prime, if not the sole reason, for the killing of Frank Gilliam.

Although it seemed bizarre, it was essential for both judge and jury to keep the rape in the forefront of their minds, and to push the gold cross and chain to the back. If convicted of murder, Billy would get the death penalty if he had killed in the course or furtherance of theft, but life imprisonment if he killed in order to rape. Martin drained his wine glass. It was a strange universe in which that could be true, but you could only play the hand you were dealt, and in some ways it made his task easier. There was no reason to be anything other than kind to Jennifer Doyce – as long as he could get her to concede the possibility that she was mistaken about the *Lincolnshire Poacher*. That was the problem. He was about to write something, but suddenly put his pen down on the table. He had done well today with Mavis Brown. It had been an unexpected break. What if he could re-think the problem?

The thought focused his eyes on the bottle of Bell's. The thoughts which were creeping into his mind demanded a real drink. He replaced the cork in the wine bottle. Somewhere between half and three-quarters empty, he noted. That was respectable enough. He would leave it on the table, as a record of his official drinking for the evening. He twisted the top of the whisky bottle sharply, and unscrewed it. There was a clean tumbler on the dressing table. He poured a glassful and allowed it to swirl in the glass before taking an appreciative sip. The familiar feeling of warmth and reassurance ran through his body as he settled in his chair. What was he thinking? Had something shifted today? Was he being too pessimistic? He had started the trial with the assumption that nothing could be salvaged except life imprisonment rather than a death sentence. The evidence against Billy Cottage was circumstantial, but it was compelling. To have a chance of achieving more, he had to undermine three pieces of evidence: the blood-stained fingerprint; the *Lincolnshire Poacher*; and the gold cross and chain. He had already undermined the fingerprint. The prosecution's forensic officer had been forced to concede that it could not be dated. The *Lincolnshire Poacher* was a deadly detail which no jury was likely to write off as a coincidence, but he had made progress today. If Jennifer Doyce could be challenged as he had challenged Mavis Brown and PC Willis, the case was suddenly looking rather different – there might be some doubt. There was a chance – apart from the gold cross and chain; apart from the one aspect of the case he needed to go away. But Cottage's frantic and contradictory efforts to explain away the cross and chain to Detective Superintendent Arnold were not credible. The jury had not heard all that yet, but they would soon. There was no obvious way around that. But he had raised a question about whether the mark on Jennifer's neck was necessarily the result of the cross and chain being removed forcibly from her body. Was she wearing that piece of jewellery at the time of the attack? Her mother thought that she wore it all the time, but had she worn it that night? She had intended to yield her virginity to Frank Gilliam on board the *Rosemary D*. Would she have taken her grandmother's memory to bed with her that night? Might she have taken it off before they started, perhaps even before she boarded the boat? In which case, might it have been lost, just as Billy Cottage claimed? Jennifer would not want to admit that, but the point could be made. If that worked, the prospect of the death sentence began to recede.

Then he had the problem of Cottage's alibi. His conversation with Cottage that afternoon was fresh in his mind. Cottage did not want to give evidence, and he did not want his sister to give evidence. That much was obvious. But was it a simple and understandable nervousness? Or was it something more worrying? Martin had the proofs of evidence of Billy and Eve, carefully put together by Barratt Davis after more than one long meeting with each. The alibi stood up on paper. Barratt was an excellent solicitor with a good eye for detail, and the proofs of evidence read well. But the proofs of evidence would not go before the jury. Billy and Eve had to go into the witness box, give evidence, and subject themselves to Andrew Pilkington's cross-examination. Martin doubted that the orderly story set out in Barratt's proofs of evidence would stand up to that. The alibi was technically adequate, but desperately short on detail. Nothing about how Billy had got home, or what he had done on arriving home, except for having a drink and going to bed. Eve could say only that he was at home in bed when she awoke at around 7 o'clock the following morning – nothing about the time of his arrival home, how he looked, how he behaved. She had been in bed since early evening. It was the kind of cross-examination he would love to conduct. He would be disappointed if he left a single brick standing. Andrew Pilkington was Treasury Counsel. He would do it just as well. The chances were that the alibi would unravel, taking with it the last vestige of hope for a 'not guilty' verdict.

Yet, strangely, after today, Martin could not help feeling that his prospects had improved a little. He took a deep drink. How exactly had the world changed? He was pleased with the way he had holed the prosecution case today. If, by some miracle, he could repeat that result with Jennifer, the case might be holed below the waterline. He smiled as the phrase went through his mind, thinking how apt it was to a case which had begun on the water. Case sinking. Case sunk without trace. Martin Hardcastle, pirate, strikes again and hoists the Jolly Roger to the top of the mast. He poured more whisky. What if he could get to that point? What if he could in fact dispense with the probably disastrous alibi evidence? What if the prosecution case did not call for a response?

He was entering murky waters now – another apt phrase, another smile. God, he was on form tonight. Ideas were flowing. A bigger picture of the case was forming in his mind. Then a distraction. Memories of other cases in which he had done damage to the prosecution case, sufficient to mean that no response was called for from the defence. What a luxury that was! How often had it happened that Martin spent days chipping away at the prosecution case, using every skill at his command, winning the admiration of judge and counsel alike, only for all the good work to be utterly undone by thirty minutes of cross-examination of the defendant? Many such cases came to mind. God, practice at the Bar would be so easy if it were not for clients. It was almost unbearably frustrating to lose a case because the client lacked the basic intelligence to get his story straight and stick to it. The prosecutor's cross-examination was usually like shooting fish in a barrel. There was no real doubt in Martin's mind that such would be the case with Billy Cottage. He could picture Billy treating the court to a rendition of the *Lincolnshire Poacher*. The picture made him laugh aloud. He had not met Eve. Barratt described her as quiet. That could mean many things, almost all of them unhelpful. Billy Cottage and Barratt Davis no doubt saw the alibi evidence as the main hope of salvation.

Increasingly, Martin was seeing it as the resource of last resort.

He was getting tired. He should make some notes for his cross of Jennifer Doyce. He drained his glass. One more, to keep himself awake. Then another distraction. The young waitress who had served him at breakfast. She had worn a short black dress and a frilly white apron, with black stockings and shoes with a bit of a heel. Perhaps she would be willing. Perhaps John could arrange something. She would be all right for a night. Not that he could actually contemplate it. Far too much of a risk But there was no harm in thinking it. With all the stress he subjected himself to, he deserved some release. In London, sometimes, he had found ways and means late at night. But here in the country, it was not realistic. So the procession of former partners through his mind began again. He tried to force his mind to focus on his cross-examination of Jennifer Doyce, but he was aroused now, and could not ignore it. Eventually he gave in, undressed, and got into bed, switching off all the lights except for the bedside lamp on the far side of the narrow bed.

He dozed off for some time in the aftermath and, when he awoke, his pocket watch told him that it was almost 1 o'clock. He made his way to the bathroom, washed his face and body with warm water, and put on his dressing gown. He had failed to make any notes for his cross-examination of Jennifer Doyce. Switching on the lamp on his table, he gazed at the heading in his notebook. What was it he had been thinking about? He must set his alarm clock for the morning. He would do that as soon as he had made a few notes. There was really nothing to the cross and chain, when it came right down to it. After what she had been through, how could anyone expect her to know the *Lincolnshire Poacher* from Beethoven's Fifth? And if she wavered on the *Lincolnshire Poacher*, he would be satisfied. All he needed was some rest. But after the sexual rush and his unplanned nap he felt disconcertingly awake. He would drink another glass of whisky to help him drift off. During that glass, the problem of the gold cross and chain returned. He had had a good thought about that, an insight, earlier. What was it? He finished the glass and poured another. Something to do with...? Yes, of course. Would she really have worn the gift her grandmother had given her when she was confirmed when she intended to lose her virginity to Frank Gilliam? How to put that to her without causing offence?

He dozed off again. When he awoke it was 3.30. He had made no notes, but it all seemed clear. He really must take himself to bed. But not just yet, not for a few more minutes. He still needed to reward himself for what he had done today. When he finally fell on to the bed, it was almost 5.15.

42

24 June

WHEN THE REPEATED knocks on the door and the sound of Jess Farrar's anxious voice eventually broke into his uneasy sleep, Martin Hardcastle looked at his alarm clock and saw that the time was almost 10.15. He suddenly felt very cold. He pushed himself up off the bed and into a standing position at the second attempt and tried to speak. No words came. He cleared his throat roughly and tried again.

'Just a minute.' The words were painful to speak, raspy, barely audible.

He began to walk towards the door, but abruptly diverted to the bathroom, where he threw up violently into the toilet. After wiping his mouth on the sleeve of his dressing gown, he sat down on the floor as the reality of what had happened swept over him. He closed his eyes. No. This couldn't be happening. It wasn't fair. All he had done was to stay up and plan his cross-examination of Jennifer Doyce. He was always so careful. He didn't deserve this. Not in a capital murder case. Not on the day when such an important witness was to be called. How could he have allowed this to happen? Summoning all his strength he hauled himself to his feet and made his way to the door.

'Jess, I'm sorry. I was taken ill during the night. Food poisoning, I think. I overslept. I will be with you in a couple of minutes.'

But there was no reply. Jess was no longer there. And in any case, Martin Hardcastle would not be with anyone in a couple of minutes. No sooner were the words out of his mouth than he had to rush back to the bathroom, and by that time he was quite aware of his situation. He knew from experience that he was not going to recover before the next day. This was another day when he would not appear at court. The last such day, of course, the last time ever. He would never do it again. But today, he was going to have to deal with it.

* * *

'I can't get any reply,' Jess reported, the frustration in her voice obvious. 'He's either dead or out for the count. Either way, we may have to get the hotel staff to open the door.'

Ben and Barratt had been ready to leave for court for almost an hour. Martin Hardcastle should have been with them long before. But calls to his room had gone unanswered, and eventually Barratt had dispatched Jess to his room with instructions to wake him. They were standing in the small foyer of the George, near the door, getting in the way of other guests and pacing impatiently.

'All right,' Barratt replied. 'I'll handle it. Ben, why don't you and Jess go on ahead? You might want to sound the judge out about sitting late, and let Jess have a word with Cottage so that he doesn't think we have abandoned him.'

Ben nodded.

'Yes, all right, but for God's sake get a message to us as soon as you know what's going on. It's already twenty past. If I ask for a late start, the judge is going to ask why, and for how long.'

But Barratt was already half way up the stairs.

'Jess, come straight back and find me once you have seen Cottage, and I will give you an update to pass on to Ben. I will either be in Martin's room or down in the foyer.'

Throwing on his wig as he fought his way past a group of spectators into the courtroom, Ben managed to scramble into counsel's row just as Mr Justice Lancaster entered court. Jess had had a matter of a couple of minutes in which to try, unsuccessfully, to reassure Billy Cottage that he was still legally represented, after which she took off running to the George. Now Billy Cottage was in the dock, the jury was seated, Andrew Pilkington was looking at him inquiringly from his right, and Ben was facing a High Court judge in a capital murder case without a leader. For several seconds, no one spoke. Then Ben rose cautiously to his feet.

'My Lord, I'm sure your Lordship has noticed that my learned friend Mr Hardcastle is not yet here.'

'I had noticed that, Mr Schroeder,' the judge replied, not unpleasantly. 'No doubt you are about to explain why.'

Ben swallowed hard.

'My Lord, I regret that I am not in a position to do so at this precise moment. He did not come down from his room this morning, and those instructing me are trying to ascertain why. It may be that he is unwell though, as I say, I cannot confirm that. In the circumstances, may I ask your Lordship to rise for a few minutes so that I can find out one way or the other, and make any further application I may have to make to your Lordship?'

Andrew Pilkington stood.

'I rise simply to remind your Lordship that we have an extremely vulnerable witness here today, who is being kept waiting.'

'Yes, I am obliged to my learned friend,' Ben said pointedly. 'That is why I invited your Lordship to rise for a short time so that I can take instructions and inform the court about what is happening. I am quite sure that Mr Hardcastle does not wish to keep Miss Doyce waiting, any more than I do, or my learned friend does.'

Ben thought he caught a look exchanged between Mr Justice Lancaster and Andrew Pilkington. For some time the judge seemed to stare into space.

'I will rise for fifteen minutes,' he announced. 'At the end of that time, Mr Schroeder, I expect to be told precisely what the situation is.'

Ben nodded. 'I am much obliged, my Lord.'

As soon as the judge had risen, he ran from the courtroom. There was no one in the foyer. He left the building and ran towards the George.

***

Barratt Davis stood, leaning against the door of the bathroom in Martin Hardcastle's room, while Martin sat on the floor beside the toilet. The vomiting had become more spasmodic now, but Martin still looked deathly pale and he had a severe headache. It had taken Barratt several minutes of banging on the door to induce Martin to open it. When he eventually stepped into the room and sized up the situation, he asked Jess to find Ben and tell him that they would need an adjournment, at least until 2 o'clock, rather than a late start.

'It was that bloody steak and kidney pie,' Martin complained, making every effort to sound suitably outraged. 'I thought it didn't taste quite right. I shouldn't have eaten it, but I was starving and I was working on my notes for the cross of Doyce. I convinced myself it would be all right. I'm going to make a complaint, and I may sue them in the county court. That will bloody teach them to do this to a Silk.'

Barratt left the door and walked slowly to the table by the window, where he noted an empty whisky bottle, an empty wine bottle, and a blue barrister's notebook open at a page which bore a heading suggesting notes for the cross-examination of Jennifer Doyce – but with no notes below it. He turned and walked back to the bathroom.

'We can talk about that later, Martin,' he said. 'At the moment I have Ben asking the judge for a late start, and I don't know how that is going. So I need to go over to court. I need to know whether you will be able to come to court today, and if so, how long you will need. Can you tell me that?'

Martin looked up miserably and contemplated getting dressed for court. The thought of a tight stiff collar brought his nausea flowing back.

'Possibly 2 o'clock,' he replied, after some time. 'But I would prefer the whole day. The judge should be understanding about it. He knows how important it is to have the leader present in a case like this. Tell Schroeder to hammer that home to the judge. I am sure it will be all right.'

Barratt made for the door.

'Please call down and leave a message at the desk before lunch,' he said. 'I am sure the judge will want to be updated.'

He met Ben and Jess in the lobby. Ben had just arrived.

'The judge has given me fifteen minutes,' he said, 'which is just about up. What can I tell him?'

Barratt bit his lip. 'He says it's a case of food poisoning,' he said. 'He is blaming it on the steak and kidney pie. He says possibly 2 o'clock, but he would prefer tomorrow.'

Ben swore under his breath.

'What do you think, Barratt?' he asked. '*Is* it food poisoning?'

'If you think of whisky as food, then yes.' Barratt replied. He paused. 'All right, I suppose I should give him the benefit of the doubt. In any case, I assume we will give the judge the official version as related to me by Martin himself.'

Jess was shaking her head.

'There was nothing wrong with the steak and kidney pie,' she muttered, 'apart from it being a bit tasteless. We all had it.'

'There is no time to worry about that now,' Ben said. 'We can hold an inquest later. Let's get back to court and tell the judge he has to keep Jennifer Doyce waiting for a day because Martin had a bad helping of steak and kidney pie.'

'I'm sure he's going to like that,' Barratt replied.

* * *

'My Lord, I am very grateful for the time you have given me,' Ben began.

The judge did not react.

'I can now tell your Lordship that Mr Hardcastle is unwell, quite ill. I am instructed that he may have eaten something for dinner yesterday evening which has brought on a bout of food poisoning. I understand that he may be well enough to attend court this afternoon, but those instructing me doubt that he would be well enough to conduct an important part of this very serious case by then. In the circumstances, I am reluctantly compelled to seek an adjournment until tomorrow morning.'

Andrew Pilkington leapt to his feet.

'Oh, really, my Lord...'

Mr Justice Lancaster cut him off with a wave of his hand.

'I need not trouble you, Mr Pilkington. Mr Schroeder, it is unfortunate that Mr Hardcastle is unwell, of course. But it is of the highest importance that the jury should hear Miss Doyce's evidence today, and that she should not have to come back tomorrow. We will proceed with the evidence, and if Mr Hardcastle recovers sufficiently to join us, then so much the better. But Mr Cottage has two counsel, and one of the reasons for that is so that, if one of them has to be absent for some sufficient reason, the other can continue without loss of time to the court.'

'My Lord...'

'No,' the judge said. 'We have lost enough time already. Let us proceed. We will take a short break after examination in chief, Mr Schroeder. I am sure the witness would welcome it, and you can have a few minutes to pull your thoughts together for cross-examination – if Mr Hardcastle has not appeared by then.'

Ben bowed to the judge and resumed his seat. He turned behind him to look at Barratt, who was rolling his eyes.

'I swear to God, I'm going to bloody kill him for this,' he whispered.

'Tomorrow,' Ben replied. 'Today I need you to take notes for me.'

43

'MY NAME IS Jennifer Doyce.'

Dr Walker had steered Jennifer Doyce into court in her wheelchair, bringing it to rest in front of the bench, so that she could be seen by judge, jury and counsel, as well as by the crowd of reporters and onlookers in the public gallery. The trial had been building momentum in the media. All the daily newspapers were giving it extensive coverage, and a BBC television crew had been spotted outside the Town Hall just as she was arriving. She was dressed in a beige sweater and brown slacks, a blue scarf around her neck, and clutching a white handkerchief. Jennifer was still only twenty-one years old but she looked at least twice that age. She was pale, gaunt and haggard, and the very last thing on earth that she needed was to re-live the events on board the *Rosemary D* in front of an audience – any audience, let alone an audience of journalists. Dr Walker had offered to tell the judge that the pressure would be too much, that it was not advisable for her to give evidence, but she would not hear of it. What Jennifer was about to do was not about her. She was giving evidence for Frank. It was a trial for his murder, and it was the last and the only act of love she could now perform for him. She could have turned her gaze on Billy Cottage with a slight movement of her head, but she did not once acknowledge his existence.

'I believe you have written your address down for his Lordship, and you need not give it to us. But is your home in St Ives?'

Her voice was quiet, but steady and determined. Ben had taken Martin Hardcastle's seat in the front row, pushing aside Hardcastle's unopened brief, so that he could sit alongside Andrew Pilkington. Unobtrusively, he ran his eyes over the jury. They were tight-lipped, obviously moved by Jennifer's appearance, and hanging on her every word.

'Yes.'

'How old are you?'

'I am twenty-one.'

'Do you have a job?'

'Yes, I am a trainee librarian. I work in Huntingdon.'

Suddenly, Ben looked at the jury again. They looked like men who might use a public library, or at least have children who would use one. Was there any chance that...? But he caught no glimpse of recognition.

'When did you first meet Frank Gilliam?'

The question prompted the first use of the handkerchief. Ben gazed fixedly at the note he was making. It was going to be a long morning. Andrew Pilkington was giving her whatever time she needed. Dr Walker had taken his seat behind Andrew and would tell him if Jennifer needed a break; otherwise, he would continue at whatever pace Jennifer wanted. That was all right, Ben thought, initially; the longer the examination in chief lasted, the more chance there was that Martin Hardcastle would put in an appearance. But the thought did not last long. The problem was that Barratt Davis had been absolutely specific about Martin's condition, and Ben quickly concluded that his appearance now might not be in anyone's interests. Unlike Martin Hardcastle, Ben did have some notes for a cross-examination of Jennifer Doyce. Like any junior, part of his role was to understudy his leader, and to be ready with his suggestions when his leader consulted him. He had not been consulted. Ben was no longer surprised by that. But it meant that he would probably be responsible for the cross-examination on his own. It was a disturbing thought and he had to fight to subdue his nerves. Still, he was confident that he knew the points he would have to make, and he had anticipated correctly that he would have to tread gently. He could now see exactly how gently.

'I met him about three months before this happened, some time in October.'

'How did you meet?'

'Through friends. I would go out with my friends on a Saturday night and someone introduced us.'

'And how did your relationship develop?'

She smiled thinly.

'He asked me out. We started going out together. We would go to see a film, go out for coffee, go dancing sometimes.'

'Yes, I see,' Andrew said. 'I believe that Frank was training in management at Lloyds Bank in St Ives, is that right?'

'Yes.'

'How old was he?'

The handkerchief came up to her eyes again. There was a pause.

'He was twenty-three.'

'Did you love him?'

'Yes.'

Pilkington paused again, this time for a prolonged period. He glanced over his shoulder at Dr Walker, but the doctor shook his head, and he waited. At length the handkerchief moved down again from the eyes to the lap.

'Miss Doyce, I don't mean to embarrass you, but I must ask, for the jury, about the events leading up to the 25 of January.'

'I'm not in any way embarrassed,' she replied.

Ben looked up again. She was angry now, but controlling it. Well, she had every right to be angry. He followed her eyes. They were strong, and fixed on Andrew Pilkington.

'Thank you. During the early part of January, did you have a conversation with Frank about sexual matters?'

'Yes.'

'Had you had a sexual relationship of any kind before that?'

'Not really. We had kissed and cuddled, that kind of thing.'

'I see. During January, what did you discuss?'

She sat up in her chair.

'We agreed to exchange our virginities.'

'To exchange...' Andrew smiled, momentarily thrown off balance. 'I'm sorry, I haven't heard it put that way before.'

Some of the tension was broken. The judge and jury permitted themselves a chuckle. Jennifer smiled also.

'That's the way we thought of it. People usually say that the woman surrenders herself to the man, but it wasn't like that for us. It wasn't just me surrendering myself to him. It was something we both wanted.'

'Yes. Was there some discussion between you about where the... exchange... would take place?'

She smiled again. 'Yes. Frank told me he had heard about this boat which was moored up at Holywell Fen.'

'*The Rosemary D*?'

'Yes. The word had spread that it was used by couples who wanted somewhere to make love. A girl who worked with Frank had been there with her boyfriend. We thought there wouldn't be many people who wanted to go there during the cold weather. We didn't have anywhere to go, you see. We were both living with our parents.'

'Yes, I see,' Andrew said.

She continued as if she had not heard him.

'Of course, now, I wish I had just asked someone, one of my friends. I'm sure I could have arranged...' She seemed to come back from a distance. 'I'm sorry. What were you asking?'

'No, that's all right. Did you make plans to go to the *Rosemary D* on the night of the 25 January?'

'Yes. It had to be a Saturday night, because that's when we always went out. We didn't have much chance during the week.'

'How did you plan to get to the boat?'

'We planned to walk from St Ives. It's the only way, really.'

'All right. Please tell the jury about the earlier part of the evening, before you got to the *Rosemary D*.'

'Frank picked me up from my house at about... I think it was about 8 or 8.30, and I seem to remember that we went to Jack's Café and had something to eat.'

Ben paused in his writing and looked up.

'You *seem* to remember...?' Andrew was asking.

She shook her head in frustration. 'There are some parts of the evening I am still blank about,' she replied. 'It's been coming back to me in patches. I remember getting dressed before leaving home, choosing what I was going to wear and so on. I remember leaving the house with Frank. I think the police checked with Jack's... but anyway, I think that is what happened.'

Pilkington nodded. 'What do you remember after leaving your house?' he asked.

'I remember being with Frank in the Oliver Cromwell,' she replied. 'I remember that because it was something we had talked about when we were planning the evening. We had to walk past the

Oliver Cromwell to get to the meadows, and we thought we might need a couple of drinks before we set out, just to steady our nerves, so we planned to call in there on the way.'

'Do you have any memory of what time you arrived at the Oliver Cromwell?'

She shook her head.

'No. It wasn't all that long before it closed, I do remember that. We didn't stay very long, and I remember Frank saying it was getting on towards closing time and we should be on our way.'

'Please describe where you went when you left the Oliver Cromwell.'

'We turned left outside the pub and walked to the end of Wellington Street, then we were about to turn right into Priory Road, when we realised that we had both run out of cigarettes. We must have smoked our last ones in the Oliver Cromwell.'

'What did you decide to do?'

'We were about to go back to the pub because they had a vending machine, but I noticed there was a light on at the corner shop in Priory Road, and there was a girl who seemed to be working. The door was locked, but we knocked on the window, and she heard us and she let us come in to buy cigarettes.'

'What kind of cigarettes did you buy? How many?'

'Woodbines. We each bought a packet of ten.'

Andrew Pilkington nodded.

'Thank you. Now, before we come on to your walk to the *Rosemary D*, there is one other matter. May the witness please be shown Exhibit Five?'

Jennifer was lost in a torrent of tears before Paul had even reached the witness box. Dr Walker reached forward and tapped Andrew on the arm. He instantly nodded his agreement, and turned towards the bench.

'My Lord, I wonder whether we might have a short adjournment?'

'Certainly, Mr Pilkington,' Mr Justice Lancaster replied. 'Fifteen minutes, members of the jury, please.'

* * *

'I don't envy you this one, Ben,' Barratt observed, as they left Court

1 and found a haven in the Square away from the prying eyes of the press and public. 'And it will be you, by the way, won't it, Jess? She has just come back from the George.'

'He's stopped throwing up, at least for now,' Jess replied matter-of-factly. 'But he is still in a bad way, and I don't see that changing significantly in the near future.'

'I'm sorry, Ben,' Barratt said quietly. 'I didn't realise how bad things had got. I shouldn't be doing this to you.'

'Don't worry about it,' Ben replied. 'Oddly enough, if this had to happen on one day of the trial, today was probably the right day. We don't need very much from Jennifer, and we can do it all wearing kid gloves. I have my notes. I am ready.'

'I know that, Ben,' Barratt said. 'But it is still not something that should have happened. I was too loyal to Martin. I can't say I wasn't warned. You mentioned it, Merlin told me. God knows, there has been enough gossip going around about him for the last year or two. I didn't pay enough attention. I was too loyal. It is a weakness we solicitors have.'

Ben grinned. 'I'm not sure that's necessarily a weakness, Barratt,' he said. 'I'm all in favour of loyalty in the right circumstances.' He paused. 'And actually, I have to say, Martin was handling this case pretty well until today.'

'That's all very well,' Barratt replied. 'But when I retain a Silk, I prefer him to do the whole case pretty well.'

Ben took a deep breath.

'I suppose what I'm trying to say is that we need to postpone the inquest on this situation until after the trial. I know you are going to have a few things to say to Martin, and to his clerk, no doubt. But we need to have him with us for the rest of the trial, Barratt – if only for the sake of appearances. It wouldn't look good if leading counsel suddenly disappeared half way through. We have to present a united front to the jury.'

Barratt smiled. 'It's all right,' he said. 'I'm not going to cause a scene. I can wait. But I'm not going to take any more of that "I'm-a-Silk-and-you're-not" nonsense any more, and I hope you won't either.'

'I am officially emancipated, as from today,' Ben grinned. He turned to Jess. 'How is Billy today?'

'Very quiet,' she replied. 'I only had a minute with him, but I couldn't get a word out of him. He seemed to be lost in some little world of his own.'

Barratt nodded. 'Wonderful. Just what we need when he's about to give evidence. Well, I suppose we ought to get back. We are not going to get to cross before lunch, are we?'

Ben shook his head. 'Not at this rate. And I don't think there's any need for Jess to keep running back and forth to the George. Let's just leave him alone until this evening.'

'Thank you, Ben,' Jess said gratefully.

* * *

'It's my gold cross and chain, which was given to me by my grandmother,' Jennifer said, handing the piece back to Paul.

'Can you think back, Miss Doyce, and tell the jury whether you were wearing that gold cross and chain when you left your house on the night of the 25 of January?'

'Yes, I was.'

'This may seem an odd question. But how is it that you can remember that?'

'Because I always wear it, wherever I go. I always have, ever since my grandmother gave it to me, and I will wear it again as soon as it is returned to me.'

'Thank you,' Andrew said. 'Now, please tell my Lord and the jury where you and Frank went after you had bought your Woodbines.'

'We walked a few yards to the end of Priory Road, through the little gate on to the meadows. Then we walked along the river until we came to the boat.'

'How long did the walk take?'

'It must have been almost an hour,' she replied. 'It's a good walk up to the Fen.'

Andrew smiled. 'Forgive me for asking this, Miss Doyce. But it was a freezing cold night, and no doubt it was going to be very cold on the boat. Did you think…?'

She smiled back. 'We just wanted to do it,' she replied simply. 'We were determined. We had heard that there were good blankets on the boat, and a paraffin heater. We were wearing jumpers and heavy coats, and we had flashlights. We thought we were well enough prepared. We couldn't get the paraffin heater to work, though. I think it must have run out of fuel.'

'If you can now picture yourself arriving at the *Rosemary D,*' Andrew said. 'What did you do?'

'We both got our flashlights out. Frank climbed on board first and helped me to jump on to the deck. He opened the door. The first cabin is like a living room and a kitchen. Then you come to the bedroom. Fortunately, there was no one there. We had been worried about finding another couple there and having to either wait for ages out in the cold, or go back home.'

'I'm sure,' Andrew said. 'What did you do once you were in the bedroom?'

'As I said, we tried to get the heater to work, but it wouldn't. So we decided to keep all our clothes on. We were a bit nervous, so we each smoked a cigarette. We may even have smoked more than one, just talking, you know, waiting for one of us to start things off.'

'Yes.'

Again, it was as if she did not hear him. 'And I remember…'

'Yes. Go on.'

'I remember Frank making a joke. He had just taken his rubbers out of his coat pocket, you know, and we were a bit nervous still, and he said he hoped he would be able to… you know… in such a low temperature…'

The jury shared a smile. But the handkerchief was up at her eyes again, and Andrew allowed her another pause.

'Then what happened?'

'I undid my coat and went to lie on the bed. I remember that suddenly, I didn't feel nervous any more. I unfastened my stockings at the top and pushed my knickers down. Frank came and lay down, partly on top of me, partly by my side. I helped him unbutton his trousers…'

'It's all right,' Andrew said. 'Please go on.'

'I found his… his penis, and I started rubbing it. We were still giggling and I was teasing him, saying I hoped he would be up to it. I remember… I remember Frank saying he should get his rubbers, and I remember saying to him, "no, let me touch you for a little while before you put it on", and he was saying, "all right then, but not too long", and we were still giggling, and I could feel him getting hard, and then…'

She fell silent, seeming to have lost all contact with the courtroom. After some time, she returned.

'I'm sorry.'

'That's quite all right, Miss Doyce. You had just said that Frank had begun to get an erection.'

She had been looking across the courtroom, somewhere above the jury's heads. But she suddenly turned back and stared at Andrew.

'And then it happened.'

'What happened?' he asked.

'I heard this noise. It sounded like someone opening the door to come into the first cabin. I thought, "well, it's probably just the wind". But then I heard someone walking very fast through the first cabin, bumping into the furniture, then this shadow appeared…'

Andrew glanced behind him. Dr Walker was sitting back, not indicating the need for a break, yet.

'Miss Doyce, I know this is difficult. When you say a shadow…?'

'A man – well it could have been a man or a woman at that stage – but it was a man. A man wearing a coat had come into the cabin. I called something out, I don't remember what. Then I saw the man raise his arm to its full height above his head. He was holding something, but I couldn't see what it was. He hit Frank from behind, and I heard Frank make a little grunting sound, and… it's funny what you remember… I remember just for a second or two feeling his penis go soft again, before…'

Andrew paused again, leaning back against his chair, arms folded. Eventually she looked up.

'Before…?' Andrew prompted.

'Before the man hit Frank again. And this time, the man was pulling him up and off me by the back of his coat, and he hit him again on the head with all his force. I actually heard the blow as well as seeing it. It was like… it was like… no, I'm sorry, I can't say it…'

'It's all right, you don't need to,' Andrew said. 'What happened to Frank after…?'

'It sounded like a perfect cover drive,' she said.

'What?' Andrew gasped.

'You know, when the batsman hits one through extra cover for four and gets it right in the middle of the bat. You know how it sounds? It was just like that.'

The court was totally silent.

'I'm sorry. I didn't want to say it, but I can't get it out of my mind. I… I get nightmares about it…. I follow the cricket, you see…'

She broke down then, weeping hysterically.

Andrew looked up at the bench.

'We will break for lunch,' the judge said. 'I will rise until 2 o'clock.'

* * *

Outside court, Andrew Pilkington took Ben aside.

'Ben, what's going on with Martin?'

Ben shrugged. 'Food poisoning, courtesy of the George's infamous steak and kidney pie.'

'No, seriously. We both know what the source of the poisoning is. When will he be back?'

Ben exhaled heavily.

'I'm told tomorrow, Andrew. I have no reason to think otherwise.'

'I can't agree to an adjournment. I need to get Jennifer out of the witness box and back to Addenbrookes this afternoon. Dr Walker is pretty insistent about that after this morning.'

'I understand. I'm not asking for an adjournment. I'm going to cross her, but I can promise you I won't take very long, and I'm not going to beat her up.'

'I know that,' Andrew replied. 'I just needed to make my position clear, that I am not going to back down and agree to an early day to help Martin out of this.'

'I wouldn't expect you to,' Ben replied.

Andrew was turning back towards the robing room.

'I wouldn't be surprised if the judge takes the matter up,' he said. 'Martin has a bit too much of a reputation for this already.'

'See you after lunch,' Ben said.

44

'MISS DOYCE, BEFORE lunch you told the jury that the shadow – the man – who came into the sleeping quarters of the *Rosemary D* hit Frank twice on the head with whatever he was holding in his hand, and that the second time, he pulled Frank up and off you, is that right?'

'Yes.'

'Let me just ask you this. It may be obvious. Had you or Frank invited anyone else on board the *Rosemary D*? Were you expecting anyone?'

'No, of course not.'

'When you went on board, were you aware of anyone else in the vicinity of the boat?'

'No.'

'Did you meet or see anyone in the meadow as you were making your way from St Ives?'

She shook her head slowly, looking into the distance, as if searching her memory.

'I'm sure the meadow was deserted at that time of night,' she said. 'I'm sure I would have remembered if we had seen anyone.'

'Yes. What happened to Frank after the man had hit him the second time?'

'He fell off the bed, to my left, on to the floor, and I didn't see him again.'

'Did he say anything, or do anything?'

'No. He was completely silent.'

'Had the man spoken at all? Did he say anything?'

'No. I don't think so. Not that I remember.'

The handkerchief went up to the eyes again. Pilkington paused. 'What happened next?'

'The man was climbing on to the bed, on top of me. I remember screaming and telling him "no, get off me" – but he was very strong. I…'

'Miss Doyce, can you describe this man at all? Do you remember anything about his appearance, or his clothing?'

She shook her head.

'No. It was very dark. I seem to remember that one of our flashlights was on, and I have this strange memory of it being on the floor, facing away from the bed towards the river. So it wasn't really any use. Where the other flashlight was, I don't know. It was totally dark on the bed. I couldn't see him at all.'

'What did he do?'

'He was holding my arms down by my sides. I was… well, I had no way to defend myself. My knickers were down around my ankles. I remember him lifting my skirt up. And that was when I felt his penis. That's how I know it was a man. He had his erect penis against my leg, and he was trying to penetrate me.'

'What did you do?'

'I'm not sure. I was screaming and begging him to stop. I think at some point I spat in his face, since I couldn't move my arms.'

'And what did he do?'

She sobbed violently again. Without turning to Dr Walker, Andrew began to ask the judge for a break. But Jennifer held up her hand.

'No. I want to get this over with.'

'All right,' Andrew said. 'Take your time.'

'I was waiting for him to penetrate me. But instead, he hit me over the head. Twice, I think.'

'Can you say what he hit you with?'

'I didn't see it. It was a heavy object of some kind. It wasn't just his hand. It felt like it was made of metal.'

'You said, you thought he hit you twice?'

Her eyes lost themselves somewhere above the jury box again.

'I can't be sure. The first one knocked me into the middle of next week. Everything after that is a blur. I couldn't see properly. I couldn't speak. I couldn't have been fully conscious. Then there was a second blow, and it was like I went out like a light then, after some time, God knows how long, I drifted back into consciousness a little, then out again, then in again, then out again. I had no control over my body. At one point I am pretty sure I felt something, which I assumed to be his penis, inside me, but then I blacked out again.'

'And did you…?'

'But even when I was partly conscious, it felt as though I was a spectator, watching something happening to someone else.'

'Miss Doyce, during this time – and I appreciate that you have said you were not always fully conscious – were you aware of any sound?'

'Yes.'

'Please tell my Lord and the jury what it was.'

'I heard the man singing in a soft voice.'

'Indeed. Were you able to recognise what it was he was singing?'

'Yes. It was the *Lincolnshire Poacher*.'

'Is that a song you were familiar with before?'

'Yes. My family sings songs around the piano every New Year's Eve. It's a long tradition. I have sung that song often. It's in the book of English folk songs we have at home.'

'And what was going on while he was singing? What was he doing?'

'It was while I was drifting in and out, and he was raping me. And whether he was singing the whole time, or for periods of time, and for how long, I have no idea at all. I just remember the silence, and then instead of the silence there was this singing of the *Lincolnshire Poacher*, then perhaps there was another silence and then more singing. I don't know for sure.'

'Yes, I see,' Andrew said. 'And what is the last memory you have of that night?'

She was absent again for some time.

'Watching this woman on the bed being raped. Listening to the singing. At some point it all went black and stayed black. That is the last thing I remember.'

'What is your next memory?'

'Waking up in hospital. My mother. Everyone being so excited that I was awake. I had no idea where I was. I had no idea even who I was for quite some time. It was as if a new life was beginning and I couldn't account for or explain anything that had happened before.'

Andrew nodded. 'Finally, Miss Doyce, you told my Lord and the jury that you were wearing your gold cross and chain, Exhibit Five, when you left your house on the evening of the 25 January. Did you take it off, or did it leave your body, at any time before the man attacked you?'

'No. I'm sure I did not take it off. There would have been no reason for me to take it off.'

'When did you first realise that it was missing?'

'Not until a day or two after I woke up at Addenbrookes and the memory of the night began to come back to me. I asked about it and my mother said the police had not been able to find it among my things or on the boat.'

'The doctors found a mark on your neck where the chain might have been resting. Do you have any recollection of anyone removing the chain?'

'No.'

'Did you give any person permission to take your gold cross and chain from your body, or to take it away?'

'No. I did not.'

'Miss Doyce, thank you very much. Please wait there. There will be some more questions.'

* * *

As he rose to his feet, Ben felt every eye in the courtroom on him. He had barely spoken a word in the trial before now. Most of those present would not know who he was or why he was there. If they noticed anything amiss at all, it would have been that Martin Hardcastle was not present, rather than that Ben was. He was sure that even the judge must be reaching for his copy of the daily list to remind himself of Ben's name.

The eyes upon him were not friendly. Jennifer Doyce had clearly suffered during her evidence, even her evidence in chief, answering questions from the prosecution. Ben knew that many of the spectators would be assuming that he would unleash a brutal cross-examination – and that the press might actually be hoping for it. In Ben's imagination, every one of them seemed poised to leap to Jennifer's defence, to jump on him and bring him down if he caused her any further suffering. But the only eyes he could allow himself to care about were those in the jury box, those which, he could only hope, were concerned with the evidence and nothing else.

'Yes, Mr Schroeder,' the judge was saying.

'May it please your Lordship. Miss Doyce, I do not intend to take long, and I certainly do not intend to cause you any further distress. If you would like me to ask his Lordship for a short break, please do so, and I invite Dr Walker to do the same.'

She nodded slightly. 'Thank you.'

'You told my Lord and the jury that you and Frank did not notice anyone in the meadows as you made your way to Holywell Fen, is that right?

'Yes.'

'Or anyone hanging around near the *Rosemary D*?'

'No. No one.'

'What about when you left the Oliver Cromwell? Were you aware of anyone following you when you left the pub?'

'No.'

'Or when you left the corner shop after you had bought the cigarettes?'

'No.'

Ben looked down and scanned his notes. The next piece of his short cross-examination was the one he knew he could not control. He asked himself again whether he had to put the questions to her, and concluded that he did.

'You also told the jury that you were wearing your gold cross and chain when you left your house?'

'Yes.'

'And that you had no occasion to take it off while you were on board the *Rosemary D*?'

'No reason at all.'

'Am I right in thinking this? If whoever attacked you stole the cross and chain, he must have done so after he had attacked Frank, and when Frank was lying on the floor, unconscious?'

She thought for a moment.

'Yes. That is correct.'

Ben hesitated.

'Do you generally take off the cross and chain before going to bed?'

'Yes, I take it off then. It's too heavy to sleep with it on.'

'That is what I was wondering. It would be uncomfortable, wouldn't it?'

'I am sure it would.'

'You were about to go to bed with Frank on the *Rosemary D*, weren't you? I wondered whether…'

The suggestion seemed to irritate, rather than distress her. She replied almost defiantly.

'That's not the same thing at all. I told you, we couldn't take our clothes off. It was too cold. I had a blouse and a jumper on. It was not uncomfortable at all.'

'I mean no offence, Miss Doyce. But you were about to exchange virginities,' Ben reminded her. 'Isn't it possible that you would have preferred not to wear your grandmother's cross and chain while…?'

Jennifer straightened up in her wheelchair and spoke, not loudly or angrily, though she was by now clearly very angry, but quietly, and with a devastating dignity.

'My grandmother eloped with her thirty-year-old lover when she was sixteen,' she replied. 'She would have been cheering me on. I wouldn't have been embarrassed for her, any more than I was for myself.'

'*Once in a while,*' Gareth had told him, early in his pupillage over a pint in the Devereux, '*a witness will knee you right in the balls, and there is nothing you can do about it. Just make sure they don't see your eyes watering. Carry on as confidently as you can, as if nothing had gone wrong.*'

Ben nodded and searched his notes, trying to forget that out of the corner of his eye he had seen several members of the jury nodding towards Jennifer with sympathetic smiles. It had been a gamble and he had lost. But he had had to risk it. And he had been right to deal with the theft of the cross and chain in the middle of the cross-examination, and save a better point to close on. He held on to that thought as firmly as he could.

'There is just one more thing, Miss Doyce. You described hearing your assailant singing the *Lincolnshire Poacher*, and you said you recognised that song from many New Year parties at your home, is that right?'

'That's right.'

'But that was at a time when you had already been seriously

injured by two savage blows to the head, which we now know had caused at least one fracture to your skull?'

'Yes.'

'And while you were, in your own words, drifting in and out of consciousness?'

'That is quite true.'

'When did you first remember that you had heard the man singing the *Lincolnshire Poacher*?'

'When did I first remember?'

'Yes. You told the jury that when you first woke up in Addenbrookes, you could not remember who you were, much less what had happened. Isn't that right? If I am being unfair, please tell me.'

She nodded. 'No, that is correct.' She lowered her head and considered for some time. 'Everything came back to me in patches, like pieces of a jigsaw puzzle. I remembered the attack on me first, but not all of it. I remembered the shadow, then the shadow hitting me, then I remembered about him hitting Frank.'

She looked up suddenly.

'That was when I asked my mother about Frank, you know, how he was, whether he was in hospital as well. She didn't want to tell me anything, but she didn't have to. I knew straight away.'

The tears returned. Ben paused, found Andrew Pilkington and then Dr Walker with his eyes. Neither gave any signal, and Ben allowed her to regain her composure.

'Then, gradually, it all came back, almost in reverse order,' she said. 'And at some point, the *Lincolnshire Poacher* came back as well, probably when I was remembering the rape.'

She looked up again and added another answer, almost randomly.

'And of course, the police were doing their best to help me remember.'

Ben felt a rush. He heard Barratt Davis sit up in his seat behind him.

'Really? How did the police help you to remember, exactly?'

'Obviously, they told me what they had found on the boat; they told me when they recovered the cross and chain…'

'They told you when they found the winch handle they believed had been used to assault you and Frank?'

'Yes.'

'They told you when they arrested Mr Cottage?'

'Yes.'

'Which officers would come to see you at the hospital?'

'It was mostly PC Willis, but Superintendent Arnold and Inspector Phillips came once or twice as well. They were all very kind.'

'Yes, I'm sure.'

Ben paused. He felt a tug on his gown. He turned slightly. Barratt was shaking his head almost imperceptibly. He was right. Ben was reaching the same conclusion. He had no evidence that the police had planted the *Lincolnshire Poacher* in her head, and a negative answer would take the point away without hope of recovery. The door was open for the jury to walk through if they chose to do so, but he could not guide them any further.

'It would be fair to say then, that they brought you up to date with the investigation as, and when, there were any developments?'

'Yes.'

Ben nodded. 'Thank you, Miss Doyce. My Lord, I have nothing further.'

Mr Justice Lancaster nodded, looking Ben directly in the eye. The look said, '*thank you for keeping it short and not hurting her again*'. He knew who Ben was, now. A note landed on the table in front of him. '*Nicely done,*' it read, in Barratt's handwriting. Andrew Pilkington was on his feet. He was about to take a calculated risk, Ben knew. From the point of view of good advocacy, the best course might be to let the point pass. Ben had not suggested, could not suggest, that any of the police officers had acted improperly, and the judge would have been hard on the defence if he had. But an officer might have let something drop quite innocently, perhaps to the mother, or in front of the medical staff, and if it had got back to Jennifer, in the state she was in, who knew what effect it might have had? Andrew was a principled prosecutor. Ben had made a decent point, and there was a question of fairness.

'Miss Doyce, can I just take you back to the *Lincolnshire Poacher*? If you cannot answer this question, please just say so. But as far as you can tell us, is the singing of the *Lincolnshire Poacher* something you remember, or is it possible that it is something that was suggested to you by someone else?'

The question seemed to take her by surprise.

'There was no one else there to hear it,' she pointed out.

'No, I understand that,' Andrew replied. 'But you said that the police were doing their best to help you to remember what had happened. Is it at all possible that the police – or someone else, for that matter – suggested to you that the attacker had sung the *Lincolnshire Poacher*, or asked you whether that had happened?'

'Why would they do that?' she asked.

'I'm not suggesting they did,' Andrew replied. 'I am just asking whether you can rule that possibility out in your mind?'

She thought for a very long time.

'I do believe I heard it,' she replied eventually. 'I don't recall anyone talking to me about it. But it has been a difficult time, you know. I have been confused. I've done my best. For Frank. I've done my best for him.'

'Yes, I know,' Andrew said. 'Miss Doyce, thank you very much. Unless your Lordship has any questions?'

'No,' Mr Justice Lancaster replied. 'Thank you. Miss Doyce, I know this has not been easy for you. Thank you for coming to court and giving evidence. You are now free to go, and I wish you well in your recovery.'

'Thank you, my Lord,' she said, as Dr Walker stepped forward, smiling, to wheel her out of the courtroom.

'My Lord, may I have five minutes before I call Detective Superintendent Arnold?' Andrew asked.

'Yes, of course,' the judge replied.

* * *

'A Silk couldn't have done it better,' Barratt said, as they gratefully breathed the fresh air of the Square, 'even if we had one.'

'She killed me on the cross and chain,' Ben replied ruefully.

'Of course she did,' Barratt said. 'We don't have a good answer to that. You tried. It was all you could have done. You could hardly have left it alone, could you?'

'No,' Ben replied firmly. 'I couldn't. Any word from the George?'

'Yes,' Jess replied. 'Our Silk has graciously agreed to meet us to take a lemonade at the conclusion of today's proceedings. Apparently he finds lemonade good for food poisoning. I may be ready for something stronger myself.'

Ben smiled. 'Yes, me too. Well, there won't be anything else to do today. Arnold is going to be some time in the box. He has to deal with the arrest and the interviews and the investigation generally, so we won't get anywhere near cross this afternoon. Martin can have him tomorrow morning.'

'Do we have much for him?' Barratt asked.

'No, I don't think so. Cottage hasn't denied the content of the interviews at all. Martin may want to clear up one or two points about the investigation. Pilkington may want to ask him about the *Lincolnshire Poacher*, but there's not much we can do about that.' He paused. 'So we should finish the prosecution case tomorrow. And then...'

* * *

'Do I have to give evidence?' Billy Cottage asked sullenly. 'I don't want to. And I don't want Eve giving evidence.'

The voice in his head had intensified during Jennifer Doyce's evidence. He had not dared to look at her. He was doing his best to tune out her evidence, but that had proved impossible. He was quite sure that she, like the judge, like the jury, like that prosecuting counsel, was just daring him, egging him on. *'Come on, Billy. Give us a verse or two of the Lincolnshire Poacher.'* It had been welling up in him throughout the day. When the temptation was particularly strong he had to bend forward and hold his head in his hands for a while, hoping that would make it go away. It did not. He was aware of people looking at him, the jury looking at him, but there was nothing he could do. If he gave evidence and they asked him about the *Lincolnshire Poacher*, what would he do? What would Eve do, if they asked her? She knew the song as well as he did. And she could tell them some things... His barrister was saying something. But it was not his main barrister, his real barrister. Where was he? Ill, they said. How could he get ill now? Didn't he know Billy could be hanged...? The walls of the cell were closing in on him again.

'We understand how you feel. But you've got to tell the jury your side of the story,' Ben was saying. 'We've been over this before. The jury is bound to want to hear from you. They want to hear you say you didn't do it. They want to hear you say you are not guilty.'

Billy shook his head. 'You told me it was up to me,' he said.

'It *is* up to you,' Ben confirmed. 'But our job is to advise you. And our advice is that both you and Eve must give evidence. Your life is at stake here, Mr Cottage. Surely you understand that?'

'I know that,' Cottage insisted. 'I'm just saying I don't like the idea. What if I say something I shouldn't?'

Ben paused.

'Why do you think you will say something you shouldn't?' he asked. 'Look, we have told you before. As long as you tell the jury the truth you have nothing to worry about.'

Ben looked at Barratt, who was standing alongside him in front of the cell.

'Billy, if you have anything you want to tell us, now is the time. Don't wait till you are in the witness box. By then there will be nothing we can do.'

'You must listen to counsel, Billy,' Barratt agreed. 'No one likes giving evidence. It's not pleasant. But if there is anything you need to say to us…'

Billy folded his arms across his chest without replying. Ben and Barratt exchanged a glance of frustration.

'I don't want to talk any more,' Billy said.

Ben allowed a few moments to pass.

'Will you give evidence?' he asked quietly. 'Will you at least discuss this with Mr Hardcastle tomorrow morning? Will you at least listen to what he has to say?'

'I'll give evidence, I suppose,' he replied grudgingly. 'If I have to.'

'And you will talk to Mr Hardcastle tomorrow?'

Billy stared at Ben before nodding. Well, it couldn't do any harm to talk to his real barrister. But the voice was still telling him otherwise. He wasn't going to give evidence, and neither was Eve, if he had anything to do with it. He turned and walked to his seat at the back of the cell.

45

WHEN THEY ARRIVED back at the George, Martin Hardcastle was sitting, looking slightly sheepish, in an armchair in the bar, a glass of lemonade, barely touched, on the table at his side. He was dressed in a casual brown sweater and brown trousers. He was pale and unshaven. Ben excused himself to go to his room to change, asking Jess to order him a pint of bitter. When he came downstairs a few minutes later, she and Barratt had joined Martin at the table and the drinks had been served. Martin was still nursing the same lemonade. As Ben took his seat, Martin looked at him and smiled.

'Barratt was telling me about today's proceedings, Ben,' he said. 'You did well, really well. Thank you.'

The use of his first name took Ben so much by surprise that, for some seconds, he was not sure what to say.

'Thank you... Martin...' he replied as soon as he was able, conscious that Barratt, beside him, was grinning broadly. 'She killed us on the cross and chain.'

'Of course she did,' Martin replied immediately. 'We don't have any coherent case on that, and that's the biggest problem we face.'

'The second biggest problem, perhaps,' Barratt said. 'He still doesn't want to give evidence, and he doesn't want his sister to give evidence. He is very serious about it.'

'Aha.' Martin turned away and stared out of the window towards All Saints Church for some time. He turned back. 'Well, he may be right.'

Ben and Barratt stared at each other.

'What?' Ben asked quietly.

Martin brought his hands together in front of his face and lowered them slowly.

'Think about it for a moment. Ben, you are Andrew Pilkington. What is the first question you would ask him in cross-examination?'

'"How do you explain your fingerprint on the window ledge in the sleeping quarters?"' Ben replied.

'Exactly.'

Martin picked up his cigarettes and lit one. He pointed it at Ben.

'First of the day,' he smiled. 'Bloody food poisoning. I'll be right as rain tomorrow. This is what you get for staying in these provincial hotels. But my man John is sorting me out a fresh salad for this evening. They can't do any harm with that, surely?'

After the silence, he continued.

'So, think about it for a moment. Do you really want to put him up there to answer that? He's got no answer to it, except that nonsense about boarding the *Rosemary D* because she's a hazard to navigation. Well, apparently the River Board doesn't agree with him about that, because she's still moored up at Holywell Fen. And even if he was concerned about her as a hazard, why does that mean he had to leave a fingerprint in the sleeping quarters? It would be better if he said he took a girl there himself. Actually, that would be really good news, any way you look at it. But he doesn't say that, and he didn't take a girl there.'

'But we don't have enough to create a doubt in the jury's minds without some explanation,' Ben replied. 'They want to hear him say that he wasn't there on the 25 of January. If they want to have lurid thoughts about why he might have been there before – as a peeping Tom, perhaps – fair enough. They know he has form for that, and it's a far cry from rape and murder. But if he tells the jury that, at least we are alive. And we have made real progress with the *Lincolnshire Poacher*. When we started this trial, you would have put money on that being enough to hang him in itself. Now, I don't see how the jury can rely on that evidence.'

Barratt shook his head. 'We have done better with that than we had any right to expect,' he admitted. 'Especially today, with her answers about the police talking to her, and "doing it for Frank" and so on – again, well done, Ben – but we have to face facts. It hasn't gone away, and it won't go away.'

'Be that as it may,' Martin replied, 'I fear that we are failing to face up to an unpleasant reality.'

'Namely…?' Barratt asked after a pause, putting his glass down on the table.

'Namely, that there is a strong probability that Billy Cottage murdered Frank Gilliam. Regardless of the progress we have made – and we have made some – that is the picture which is emerging from this trial, isn't it? We don't know whether he did or not. His instructions are that he did not, and we have to act accordingly. But the evidence strongly suggests that he did. We have a responsibility to ensure, if we can, that a strong probability does not evolve into proof beyond reasonable doubt.'

He looked around the table.

'The question is, how best to do that? It is, I fear, a matter of playing the odds. Whatever we do, it will be a gamble. That is what it has come down to now. But consider what is likely to happen if we call the evidence of the alibi. Cottage doesn't want to give evidence – never a good sign. His account of his movements is vague, to put it mildly. Andrew Pilkington will take the alibi apart and scatter it to the four winds. And then, the sister. She can't even support the alibi, really, can she? All she says is that her brother was there when she woke up the next morning. Even if you believe every word she says, it doesn't rule Cottage out as the murderer. But Pilkington will have a field day with her.'

He paused.

'Look, let's be honest. Neither of them is too bright. If they have concocted the alibi – even with the purest of motives, if he really didn't do it – the alibi will go down in flames and it will take with it any hope of saving Cottage from conviction.'

He lit another cigarette, turning to Ben.

'You are right, Ben, of course, in saying that the jury want to hear him say he didn't do it. Of course they do. But I don't think we can afford the price he would pay for giving them what they want. At the end of the day, the case against Cottage is circumstantial. That gives us some hope that it doesn't pass the reasonable doubt test. We can admit that it looks suspicious, even extremely suspicious. But the judge is going to tell the jury that's not enough. And if we don't call evidence, Pilkington may not make a closing speech. Even if he does – after all, it is a murder case – it will be a short one, and he will have nothing new to say. So, at the end of the day, they may well end up hanging Billy Cottage, but at least he won't hang himself.'

Ben breathed out slowly.

'I see what you're saying, Martin, but...'

He paused as John approached from the bar.

'Excuse me,' he said. 'Is it Mr Schroeder?'

Ben looked up in surprise. 'Yes?'

He handed Ben a written message.

'Sorry to interrupt you, sir, but there was a call for you a bit earlier. Your mother. She left her number, sir, though I am sure you know it. She said it was about your grandfather. He's been taken ill. She said you should call as soon as you can, sir. I am sorry. If there is anything I can do, please let me know.'

'Is there a phone I can use?'

'Of course, sir. You can use the manager's office. Come this way, please.'

Ben scrambled to his feet. As he left the table, Jess caught his hand and squeezed it gently.

The manager's office was a very small, claustrophobic space behind the reception area. It was a cluttered morass of files and stacks of paper – invoice forms, typing paper, carbon paper. On the wall was a calendar with pictures of sheep-dog trials. There was barely room on the desk for anything except the phone and a small typewriter. He picked up the receiver and dialled the number without reference to the message John had handed him.

Jess stood as Ben returned to the table.

'My grandfather has had a heart attack – at least, that's what they think,' he said. Jess saw at once that he was pale and a bit unsteady on his feet. 'They have taken him to the London Hospital. They are not sure about his condition yet.'

'You need to go,' she said at once.

Ben looked at his watch.

'I'll have to wait for a train, then get myself across town. I'm not sure how long it will all take, how soon I can get back.'

Jess looked at Barratt. 'Can I take the car?'

Barratt nodded. 'Of course.'

'I'll drive you. It's the quickest way,' she said to Ben. 'I'm sure you wouldn't have any trouble getting there by train, but coming back may be a different story. If he is well enough for you to leave, you can be back for tomorrow morning if we drive. We can work on our own timetable. I just need to go to my room for a couple of minutes to get some things. I will be straight back.'

Ben turned to Martin and Barratt.

'Would that be all right?'

'Of course it is,' Barratt replied. 'I hope it's not too serious.'

'We will hold the fort,' Martin said. 'Nothing too onerous to do tomorrow.'

Jess was back within five minutes.

'Come on,' she said. 'Let's get started.'

As he was walking towards the door, Ben turned back.

'Barratt,' he said. 'Why don't you call Merlin at Chambers? Gareth was keen for his new pupil, Clive Overton, to see something of this trial. Gareth said he might send him if he didn't have anything too pressing on. If he has nothing better to do, Clive might be able to come up tomorrow morning, take a note, and generally make himself useful to you and Martin.'

Barratt raised a hand.

'Good idea,' he replied. 'I will.'

46

BARRATT'S DARK BLUE Rover 2000 was parked in the car park at the rear of the George. As soon as they had climbed in, Jess reached into a large brown bag she had brought from her room.

'Road map,' she said, reaching across and putting the map in Ben's lap. 'Flashlight.' She threw the bag behind her on to the rear seat and started the engine. 'I'm pretty sure of my way until we get into London. We will take the A14 towards Cambridge, at Cambridge we will pick up the A10 to London, continue into London and turn left when we hit the North Circular. But you will have to direct me from there. The East End is a bit off my radar.'

He nodded. 'Thanks for this,' he said.

She smiled. 'Don't mention it. I'm glad to help and, besides, I'm sure we can both do without listening to Martin Hardcastle grumbling about his food poisoning for the rest of the evening. We will have to stop for petrol once we are on the A10, but hopefully we will miss the worst of the traffic.'

As they pulled out of a Shell station with a full petrol tank, Jess looked at Ben. The A10 was quiet, and she gave the Rover's powerful engine its head as they made swift progress south towards London. She kept a relaxed watch on the road, alert for oncoming traffic, but took time for occasional sideways glances, studying the outline of his face. He had said barely a word since they had left the George.

'I know how much your grandfather means to you,' she said, after some time. 'You talked about him that time we had dinner after you took me to see West Ham.'

'He has always been the one who believed in me most, the one who was most on my side,' he replied, after some time. 'It's not that I'm not close to my parents. I am. We are a close family – probably too much so, in some ways – and I love them all. But, I don't know, sometimes it seems easier to talk to grandparents than it is to your parents. It's always been that way for me.'

'They don't have the main responsibility for bringing you up,' Jess said. 'It gives them a little space to stand back and see who you really are.'

'Yes,' Ben agreed. 'They don't have to worry about you quite as much, so perhaps they are free to start treating you as an adult before your parents can. I wouldn't be at the Bar but for his support.'

He sat back in his seat and was silent for some time.

'I don't know what I will do if he dies, Jess,' he said. 'And with everything that is going on...'

She shook her head.

'You can't think about that,' she insisted. 'Nobody has said he is going to die. We just know that he is not well and you are going to visit him in hospital. Let's just concentrate on one thing at a time.'

It was almost an hour before they spoke again, as they were driving through the northern suburbs of London.

'I've never learned to drive,' Ben said suddenly. 'I never saw the point, living in London. It's so easy to get around on public transport. Do you think I should?'

'If you're going to practise in places like Huntingdonshire, it might be a useful skill to have,' she smiled. 'Why don't you find where we are on the map? It's not much farther to the North Circular, and then you are going to have to navigate for me.'

Despite everything that was weighing on his mind, Ben's navigation was flawless. Jess brought the Rover to rest outside the Schroeder family home in Brady Street at just after 8.30. He knocked at the door. His mother, Ruth, answered. She was dressed to go out, in a blouse and skirt, but she had obviously been keeping herself busy – she wore an apron over them and there were spots of water on it. She had been crying and, as she hugged Ben, the tears returned.

'There's no more news,' she said. 'Your father and your Uncle Eli are at the hospital. I was there earlier, and I said I would go back later, so that there is always someone there. They are still assessing him. The doctor said they don't want to operate if they can avoid it. At his age, that could be very dangerous, they said. So they are treating him with something, and keeping him under observation. We haven't been able to see him yet...'

She stopped suddenly as she noticed Jess and the car.

'Mother, this is Jess Farrar,' Ben said. 'We are working together on the murder case up in Huntingdon. Jess offered to drive me when they gave me your message at the hotel.'

Ruth dried her eyes.

'That's very kind of you,' she said. 'Please come in. I am sure you could do with a cup of tea after your journey.'

She closed the door behind them as they entered.

'The hospital is just around the corner, as Ben knows. They will call if anything happens, so there is no need to rush round there, is there?'

She ushered them into the living room.

'Have a seat, please, and I will make some tea.'

She disappeared into the kitchen.

Jess sat next to Ben on the large sofa and took in the homely clutter, the books and the family pictures, the pieces of kitsch everywhere, crammed into the smallest spaces; a home, she thought, never to be moved from – there would be far too much to undo, far too much to sort out, too much of too many lives ever to transplant anywhere else. She heard a soft sob from the kitchen. She touched Ben's hand, stood, and made her way towards the sound.

'Can I do anything to help?' she asked.

'No, thank you, my dear,' Ruth replied with a sniffle. 'It's all under control. The kettle will boil in a minute... well, you could get the biscuits for me, if you don't mind. They are in the pantry in the corner, and there are plates in that cupboard on the left.'

'Of course,' Jess said.

As she placed the biscuits and plates on the kitchen table, Ruth filled the tea pot from the boiling kettle. She turned towards Jess.

'I was here when it happened,' she said quietly. 'He was sitting there at the kitchen table, having his coffee, as he always does after lunch. And he just dropped his cup. I heard it break on the floor. I had my back to him, so I was asking him what he was doing, and that's when I saw he had slumped to the floor, and there was coffee and bits of china everywhere. It happened just like that. I didn't have anyone else at home. David and Eli were at the shop and, of course, Ben's brother and sister were at school. So I had to call for the ambulance and go with him...'

Her voice trailed away. Impulsively, Jess walked over to Ruth and pulled her into a hug.

'It's all right, Mrs Schroeder,' she said. 'I'm sure it is going to be all right. He is in the best place and they are looking after him.'

Suddenly, Ruth pulled away slightly, but only enough to allow her to look directly into Jess's face.

'Thank you, my dear,' she said. She paused, pulling herself together.

'So, you work with Ben, do you?' she asked, after a few moments. 'Are you a barrister?'

Unaccountably, Jess felt herself blush as her eyes met Ruth's.

'No. No. I work for Bourne & Davis. We are the solicitors instructing Ben in this case.'

'Oh, I see.'

'So, of course, we worked together before the trial, and we have to attend the trial as well,' she heard herself add, quite unnecessarily.

Ruth smiled as she moved gently away and picked up the tea tray.

'Well. That must be very interesting... Do you mind bringing the biscuits?'

47

THE LONDON HOSPITAL was quiet when they arrived. Parts of it seemed deserted as they made their way, following the instructions provided by the nurse at the reception desk, to the intensive care ward in which Joshua Schroeder lay. Ruth had accompanied Ben and Jess in the car. Her husband had been keeping vigil ever since the ambulance had brought his father to the hospital. Ruth intended to persuade him to return home to sleep for a while, to let her take over the waiting if there was no immediate crisis, though she did not really expect him to agree.

There was no admittance to intensive care without the permission of the attending physician, so relatives and friends waited in a grey waiting room with fluorescent lighting, which the hospital had tried to brighten up with vivid red chairs and tables; and a few works by local artists featuring cheerful subjects – vases full of flowers, a bowl of fruit next to a dark green wine bottle, a pastoral scene with a shepherd in a field. Ben's father David and his uncle Eli were sitting gazing silently at the closed doors of the ward. Ben approached his father and tapped him gently on the shoulder. David turned his head and, without a word, stood to embrace Ben. Uncle Eli was next. Ruth in turn hugged her husband.

'There is no news yet,' David said. 'The doctor came to see us about half an hour ago. There has been no change in his condition.'

'Not that we are sure what his condition is,' Eli added. 'But if it hasn't changed, that means it hasn't changed for the worse, so...' He spread his arms out wide by his side.

'What did they tell you when they brought him in?' Ben asked.

David hesitated.

'They said he had had a heart attack,' Eli replied. 'They said that, at his age, it was serious, but they wouldn't know how serious for some time. They were going to keep him under observation. They didn't want to take any further action for now. The doctor comes and talks to us once an hour but, so far, there has been nothing new. So, who knows?'

Then Eli spotted Jess. She had been standing quietly to one side, anxious not to intrude, wondering whether she should take herself off in search of a café.

'And who is this young lady?' he asked.

The question set her thinking of the most unobtrusive way to make her apologies and leave. But Ben came over to put an arm around her and brought her into the circle.

'This is Jess Farrar. She drove me here from Huntingdon when we got the news. She works for the solicitors in the case I'm doing. Jess, this is my father, David, and my Uncle Eli.'

David shook Jess's hand politely before resuming his seat and his gaze towards the ward. Ruth sat down beside David and held his hand. But Eli remained standing and took Jess's hand in his.

'Don't mind David,' he said quietly. 'He's very upset, and he doesn't say much when he's upset.'

'Oh, please don't worry,' she replied. 'I'm just concerned that I don't get in the way. Ben, why don't I...?'

'You are not in the way,' Eli replied. 'And thank you for bringing Ben to us.'

He released her hand with a slight squeeze, and turned to Ben.

'So, Ben, this is some case you have in Huntingdon.'

Ben smiled. 'Yes.'

'From what the papers are saying, it doesn't look too good for your man. What does he have to say about it all?'

'He will be giving evidence tomorrow or the next day,' Ben replied. 'He has an alibi. He says he was never at the scene of the crime and he didn't do it.'

Eli considered this for a few moments.

'But what about the fingerprint? What about the gold cross and chain?'

Jess could not help laughing. 'You have been following the case, Mr Schroeder, haven't you?'

Eli smiled. 'It's Eli. None of that "Mr Schroeder" stuff. Not if you're a friend of Ben.' He put an arm around both their shoulders.

'Yes, I have been keeping up with the case every day. I read every word they write about it. Well, I'm proud of the boy, my father is too, getting himself in a big case like this.'

'You should be,' she said, returning the smile.

'Of course. We all are. He is the first one in the family. We are expecting big things of him.'

'Viceroy of India, so I hear,' she said.

Eli laughed. 'Ben told you about that? Good.' He turned to Ben. 'But I think we agreed to settle for less, given the political situation in India, Ben. What was it?'

'Lord Chief Justice,' Ben reminded him.

'Lord Chief Justice, that's it. He's going to be Lord Chief Justice.'

'I wouldn't be at all surprised,' Jess said.

Eli smiled again, looking at her a little more closely. She was momentarily embarrassed and looked away.

'Well,' Eli said. 'Why don't the three of us make ourselves useful? There is a tea and coffee bar on the next floor down. I think they should still be open. Let's go and get some drinks for everyone. We should be able to carry them between us if we all go.'

* * *

It was almost midnight before the attending physician came again. The tea and coffee bar had closed and they had nothing to do but sit in the brightly coloured chairs and wait. As the doctor entered, they all rose to their feet in a single movement. The doctor looked tired, but he was smiling.

'Well, we have had Mr Schroeder under observation for several hours now,' he said. 'We have been monitoring his vital signs. He has had a heart attack and it wasn't just a mild one, but at present there is no sign that it has done any long-term damage. We won't know for sure for some time, but his signs are good for now. He's going to have to stay in hospital for observation for a few days. I am going to start him on some medication to control his blood pressure, which is a bit high. But the most important thing is for him to rest, and it's better that he should do that here at first, so that we can monitor him and get an early warning if anything goes wrong. He is awake and he is talking to the nurse, so if you want to go in and see him for a minute or two, I have no objection. But don't all go in at once, and don't stay more than a minute or two. You can do the same tomorrow. The nurse will tell you all about visiting hours.'

'Thank you, doctor, thank you,' Eli said. 'David, why don't you and Ruth go in first?'

'You come, too, Eli,' Ruth insisted.

They followed the doctor into the ward, leaving Ben and Jess together. He held his head in his hands and took several deep breaths. She hugged him.

'I'm so glad, Ben,' she said.

The doctor had meant what he said about limiting any visit to a minute or two. Ben's parents and uncle returned very quickly.

'Your turn, Ben,' Ruth said.

Joshua was sitting up now, leaning against two pillows. He looked pale, but Ben saw at once that the twinkle in his eyes had survived the heart attack.

'Viceroy,' he said, holding out his hands. The voice was weak and croaky but his breathing seemed strong. 'I am very glad to see you. I didn't expect this. How is the big case going?'

They embraced.

'We are still fighting,' Ben replied. 'We won't know for a few days.'

'I missed the report in today's paper,' Joshua said, 'what with all the excitement. But this is even better, to get a first-hand report from one of the barristers. You can't beat that, can you?'

'I came as soon as I heard,' Ben said.

'I know. Your mother told me you have a very pretty girlfriend who brought you.'

'She's not my girlfriend,' Ben protested quietly. 'She works for my instructing solicitors.'

'Whatever you say, Viceroy,' Joshua replied. 'The important thing is that you are here. But you could at least bring her in so that I can see her and say thank you.'

Ben hesitated. 'Are you sure? I don't want to tire you. The doctor said…'

Joshua waved a hand dismissively.

'I'm not going to die because I spend a minute or two talking,' he said. 'And I am sure I will fall asleep as soon as you go.'

Ben smiled. He walked to the door of the ward, opened it, and beckoned Jess. She looked at him questioningly, but he repeated the gesture.

'He just wants to thank you for bringing me to see him,' he whispered.

'This is Jess Farrar,' he said as they approached the bed. 'This is my grandfather, Joshua.'

Joshua took both her hands in his.

'I am very pleased to meet you,' he said. 'Thank you for bringing the Viceroy to see me. It means a lot for me to see him.' He smiled. 'You might say it does my heart good.'

'I'm sure it does' she replied. 'I'm very pleased that I could do it. And I am very pleased to meet you, and that you are feeling a little better.'

The nurse was giving them a look.

'We should probably go,' Ben said, leaning over to embrace his grandfather. 'I'll come again as soon as I can.'

Joshua smiled. 'Billy Cottage needs you more than I do at the moment,' he said. 'Come when you can.'

He shook hands again with Jess.

'If it goes the wrong way with the case,' he said quietly, 'make sure you tell him that's the way it goes sometimes and he has to move on to the next one. He can be too hard on himself, sometimes.'

'I will,' she replied.

* * *

It was almost 1.30 when they all arrived back at the family home in Brady Street.

Jess looked at Ben. 'If you want to head back…' she began.

Ruth was shaking her head.

'Not at this time of night,' she insisted. 'Not with the kind of day you've had. I'm sure you are far too tired. Stay here. I will get you up in the morning and make you some breakfast. When you are rested you can go more safely.'

Jess looked at Ben.

'I don't see why Martin Hardcastle can't do a morning on his own,' he said. 'After all, I did.'

She smiled. 'Good,' she replied. 'I have to admit, I would prefer not to drive back. I can curl up on the sofa here.'

'There's no need for that, Jess,' Ruth said. 'We have more than enough room. We have the whole house. You can have a bedroom to yourself upstairs. And I always keep Ben's room ready in case he needs it.'

'The family started out with just the top floor in my grandfather's day,' Eli said, with a wink at Ben. 'The lower floors were occupied by several other families. Over time, we terrorised the others until they moved out, and we bought up the house bit by bit.'

Jess laughed.

'It's true,' Ben said, 'apart from the bit about terrorising people. I'm sure they moved out voluntarily.'

Eli held up his hands.

'Voluntarily, yes,' he said. 'Of course, they did.'

When Ruth came into their rooms to wake them with a cup of tea, it was 9 o'clock. When they arrived downstairs, a cooked breakfast awaited them. They set out for Huntingdon before 11.

As they left, Ruth embraced them in turn.

'Come back soon,' she said. 'Both of you.'

48

AFTER SO MANY years of experience, there was not much that bothered Detective Superintendent Stanley Arnold when he went into the witness box. He had long since become accustomed to having his evidence challenged; his competence questioned; and to being called a liar to his face by some fresh-faced young man wearing a bright white wig. It was never a pleasant experience, but over the years Arnold had learned to suppress his indignation before his blood pressure began to rise, and to respond in a calm professional manner. If he had anything to do with it, his evidence, and that of his colleague Detective Inspector Ted Phillips, would be the final nail in Billy Cottage's coffin. Despite the strain of being the officer in charge of a capital murder case, Arnold felt no anxiety about his evidence. The course of the investigation had been meticulously recorded. DI Phillips had written a verbatim note of the interviews with Cottage as they occurred. Andrew Pilkington had told him that Martin Hardcastle did not challenge his evidence, and had only a few questions about the investigation generally. As he waited outside court to be called, Arnold felt relaxed. That changed abruptly when he entered the witness box and saw Clive Overton dressed as a barrister and seated behind Martin Hardcastle.

Barratt Davis had taken Ben's advice, and had asked Merlin to send Clive to Huntingdon to take a note of the evidence in Ben's absence. Gareth Morgan-Davies had been only too pleased to part with his pupil for the day to expose him to the experience of a trial of this kind. Arnold had already taken the oath when his eyes settled on Overton, and Andrew Pilkington's first question, asking him to identify himself, bypassed him completely. He simply stared at Clive in disbelief.

Clive gave no sign of recognition, even though, when he had arrived at court and spoken to Barratt Davis, Arnold's name was immediately familiar. For a moment he experienced a sense of rising panic. He had a sudden flashback to the time of his arrest. He had been lying, in a drunken sleep, on his bed in his room at college when Arnold and Phillips came for him. It had been after 3 o'clock in the morning. He had been taken to the police station and thrown, hung over and dishevelled, into a cell until the time came for his first appearance before the Cambridge magistrates. It had been just over three years ago, but it felt like another life. He had moved on. He had fallen in love in America and Bonnie had come to England with him as his wife. He had completed his degree and been called to the Bar. He was a new man. But he had always known that there would be reminders. He had to learn to deal with them when they came. He had to concentrate. His head was bent over his blue notebook, ready to record every word Arnold said.

'Your name and rank, please,' Andrew Pilkington was saying for the second time.

Arnold suddenly became aware that Clive Overton was the only person in court not looking at him. He turned towards Andrew.

'I'm sorry, sir. Stanley Arnold, Detective Superintendent, attached to Cambridge Police Station, my Lord.'

'Are you the officer in overall charge of the case?'

'I am, sir.'

'And did you make notes of your activities during the investigation?'

'For the most part, sir, I did, yes. There were occasions when my colleague DI Phillips made notes of certain things and I verified them at or near the time, while the events were fresh in my memory.'

'I see. Thank you, Superintendent. Then, if you would produce your notebook, please.'

Arnold glanced across once more at Clive, which caused him to fumble more than usual while extracting his notebook from his inside pocket. Then he wrenched his eyes away and began to focus on his evidence.

More than an hour later, Arnold's evidence in chief having been completed, Mr Justice Lancaster decided on a short break, and Arnold gratefully left the court and walked out of the building into the fresh air of Market Square. Turning to his left he almost bumped into Clive Overton, who had felt the need of the same relief. Arnold's first reaction was to turn and walk the other way. But this time, Clive was looking at him.

'Superintendent,' he said, with a courteous nod.

'Mr Overton.'

'I'm sure you are surprised to run into me here,' Clive said.

'To be honest, sir, there's not a lot that surprises me these days.' He paused. 'I had heard that you had come back from America.'

'Yes. Some time ago.'

'And you have qualified as a barrister. Congratulations.'

'Thank you.'

'Are you in your father's Chambers, with Mr Hardcastle?'

'No. No, I am with Bernard Wesley QC, with Mr Schroeder.'

'I see.' Arnold smiled thinly. 'Your father cross-examined me once,' he said, 'at the Cambridge Assize. It was not a pleasant experience.'

Clive smiled.

'I'm sure it wasn't. I know all about that. I grew up with it, believe me.'

There was an awkward silence.

'Superintendent,' Clive began, 'I know you must have been angry about what happened, with the charges being dropped...'

Arnold shook his head.

'Nothing to do with me, sir,' he replied. 'All the decisions were taken by the Director of Public Prosecutions. I am sure he had good reasons for whatever he decided.'

He allowed a moment to pass before turning back towards the entrance to the Town Hall. He began to walk away, then suddenly turned back to face Clive.

'I heard that you went to visit William Bosworth's family in Yorkshire?'

'Yes, I did,' Clive replied.

Arnold nodded.

'That must have taken a great deal of courage,' he said.

He pulled the door open and entered the Town Hall without waiting for a reply.

49

WHEN BEN AND Jess arrived back at the George, it was after 1 o'clock. Ben was about to go upstairs to his room to change for court when he noticed Barratt Davis and Martin Hardcastle sitting at a table in the lounge, each with a pint of beer in front of him. Glancing at Jess with surprise, he walked over to join them. Jess followed and took the fourth seat.

'Early day?' Ben asked.

Barratt nodded. 'Adjourned until tomorrow morning,' he confirmed.

'Oh? Have we finished the prosecution's case?'

'Yes,' Barratt replied. 'Nothing very interesting in the police evidence. The interviews hurt us, of course, but we knew that was coming, and Cottage didn't challenge the evidence.'

'And we are not starting Cottage's evidence today?'

Barratt looked down at the table and then up again.

'There will be no evidence from Billy Cottage,' he replied. 'The judge adjourned to allow us to prepare our speeches for tomorrow morning.'

Ben stared at him for some time. He found himself struggling for words.

'What? We told the judge that Cottage would not give evidence?'

'I gave the judge that information, yes,' Martin Hardcastle said. 'Do you have something you want to say about it?'

Ben fought to keep his composure.

'Yes,' he replied. 'I do. We were still discussing the question of whether to call him when I left. No decision had been taken.'

'I took the decision while you were away, Ben,' Hardcastle replied, 'to advise Cottage not to give evidence. I took your views into account, but as leading counsel, it was a matter for me. In fact, regardless of any advice you or I might give him, Cottage does not want to give evidence, and he does not want his sister called to give evidence. It is his decision, after all.'

Ben shook his head in frustration. His voice was animated.

'I'm perfectly aware that it is his decision,' he replied. 'But you know as well as I do that he has been shaky about it all the way through. Of course he's not keen on giving evidence. How could he be? But we have been working with him, and he had come to see that he has no choice. He would have given evidence if we told him to.'

'I don't think that would be the right thing to do at all,' Hardcastle said.

'Well, I do.'

Hardcastle shook his head.

'Ben, listen to me. If he gives evidence he won't last five minutes. I'm not even sure he could get through evidence in chief, let alone cross-examination.'

'Why not? Don't you think he would be telling the truth?'

'If I thought that, I couldn't call him to give evidence,' Hardcastle pointed out. 'I can't put evidence I believe to be false before the court.'

'Not if you *know* it's false,' Ben replied. 'But that's not what we are talking about here. We have no basis for saying he is not telling the truth. In fact, he could perfectly well be telling the truth. And his sister supports him.'

'His sister says he was at home when she woke up on Sunday morning,' Hardcastle said, 'which no doubt he was. Her evidence doesn't help us in the slightest, and Andrew Pilkington will be asking questions about whether she saw him during the night.'

'I agree there is a risk that we will be hurt by the cross-examination,' Ben said. 'But that's a chance we have to take. We cannot justify advising this man not to give evidence of a plausible alibi which is not contradicted by the prosecution's evidence. It may be his only hope.'

There was a silence.

'Ben,' Hardcastle said, 'the time has come for us to face up to reality. Cottage's best hope is that the jury will not buy the prosecution's argument that the killing was in the course or furtherance of theft.

In that case, he will be convicted of murder, but the sentence will be life imprisonment rather than death. At this point, I think that result would represent a success.'

'We can't concede that he is guilty of murder.'

'We are not going to concede anything,' Hardcastle replied. 'We can argue that the prosecution's evidence is insufficient for a conviction. But our back-up is that, if he is guilty, he is guilty of non-capital murder only. It offers the jury a compromise if they are undecided, and it still keeps us in the game for a not guilty.'

He paused.

'If we let him give evidence and Andrew tears him limb from limb, which I believe to be the most likely outcome – because, let's be honest, if we put his intelligence and his sister's together, it hardly registers on the scale – we may have lost the theft point beyond any hope of recovery. The jury will still have the interviews ringing in their ears. Let's not forget – he couldn't even give the police a consistent account of something as simple as where he found the cross and chain. Andrew is bound to ask him about that, and he's got ammunition to contradict him, whatever he says. It would be a disaster. Andrew may well prove course and furtherance of theft once and for all, and then we have no straws left to grasp at.'

Ben took a deep breath, waving away a waiter who was asking whether he wanted anything.

'Barratt, what do you think about this?'

'Barratt agrees with you in principle,' Hardcastle said. 'But I think he has begun to see that I am right about what might happen. I'm sorry, Barratt, I shouldn't presume to speak for you.'

Barratt thought for some time.

'Speaking as a solicitor,' he said, 'it is my view that whatever we do is a gamble. The prosecution has built a pretty strong case against Cottage and, whatever we do, we can't guarantee that it won't go horribly wrong. That being said, Cottage has maintained from the beginning that he has an alibi and, in my mind, I can't justify not calling him to give evidence about it. If he is exposed as a liar, then so be it. But Martin, just think for a minute about him being hanged without telling his story. I think that he ought at least to hear what Ben has to say tomorrow morning.'

Hardcastle shrugged.

'All right,' he replied. 'Let him hear what Ben has to say. But he's going to hear from me again at the same time.'

There was another silence. Hardcastle drank the remains of his pint, and stood.

'I'm going to my room now, to think about my speech,' he said. 'But before I do, Ben, let me make one last point which you may not have thought of. If Cottage is convicted after not giving evidence on my advice, it gives you something extra to complain about to the Court of Criminal Appeal, doesn't it? Just in case they get bored with the course and furtherance of theft.'

He began to turn away.

'How is your grandfather, by the way?'

'He is going be all right,' Ben replied. 'Thank you.'

50

'Mr Hardcastle is my main barrister,' Billy Cottage said. 'I'm going to do what he advises. So is Eve.'

It was just after 10 o'clock, less than half an hour before closing speeches were due to be made, and Court 1 was filling up for what the public expected to be a dramatic session. Ben and Martin had once more made their way along the narrow corridor and were standing outside Billy Cottage's cell with Barratt and Jess.

'You are entitled to do that,' Ben replied. 'But I have a responsibility to tell you what I think. So does Mr Davis. We have talked about this before, haven't we? I know you don't want to give evidence and be asked lots of questions. Of course, you don't. No one would. But there is no other way for the jury to know that you weren't there on the *Rosemary D* that night. I thought you understood that.'

'Mr Hardcastle can tell them,' Cottage replied.

'No, I can't,' Hardcastle intervened at once. 'I told you that yesterday. I can't give evidence. All I can do is argue to the jury based on the evidence.'

'But you said...'

'I said that my advice was not to give evidence. I have listened to what Mr Schroeder has said, and that remains my advice. But I can't tell them what happened for you. That is up to you.'

Cottage turned his back and walked slowly around his cell once or twice.

'But you still think I should not give evidence?' he asked Hardcastle.

'That is my advice,' Hardcastle replied.

'Mr Hardcastle is my main barrister,' Cottage said. 'I'm going to take his advice.'

He folded his arms across his chest defiantly.

* * *

The trial ended just before 3 o'clock. Mr Justice Lancaster had the gift of summing a case up clearly and succinctly, and he had chosen to sit through the usual lunch hour to make sure of getting the jury out that afternoon.

'So, in conclusion, members of the jury' he said, as he ended the summing-up, 'remember what counsel has told you. Mr Pilkington says that the evidence in this case, although circumstantial, is overwhelming. Mr Hardcastle says that the evidence is not sufficient for proof beyond reasonable doubt – that the prosecution has simply failed to prove its case. He adds that even if you were to convict of murder, there is no evidence that the murder was in the course or furtherance of theft.'

'As I said before, ask yourselves first whether the prosecution has proved beyond reasonable doubt that the accused, William Cottage, and no one else, murdered Frank Gilliam. If that is not proved beyond reasonable doubt, Cottage is not guilty of anything. If you do find it proved beyond reasonable doubt that Cottage murdered Frank Gilliam, then you must also consider whether it is proved, to the same standard, that the murder was in the course or furtherance of theft. If it is, then your verdict will be one of capital murder. If not, your verdict will be one of non-capital murder.'

After a few more words, the judge sent the jury to their room to begin their deliberations.

51

PAUL, THE USHER, suggested that they return to the George to await the verdict. He would summon them to court by phone when the time came. There was no way of telling when that might be. The members of the jury were not permitted to separate now until they reached a unanimous verdict, and if they found it difficult to agree, it might mean a very late night. The press and the public appeared to have no intention of leaving the Town Hall either, and there was nowhere quiet or comfortable to wait there. They gratefully took Paul's advice.

They spent about an hour together in the lounge, drinking coffee and toying with sandwiches. The conversation was spasmodic and strained. Eventually they abandoned the effort altogether and went to their respective rooms to pass the time as comfortably as they could. There was never an easy way to wait for a jury. Even in a less serious case it could be a nerve-wracking time. In this case, it was almost unbearable. Dinner time came, but the thought of food was not appealing. It was 9.30 when Paul phoned through and asked them to return to court.

* * *

The judge entered court with his chaplain and his clerk, who both sat to his right. There was total silence as the judge took his seat. Philip Eaves picked up the indictment from his bench, turned to the judge, bowed, then turned to the jury.

'Members of the jury,' he called out 'who shall speak as your foreman?'

The foreman of the jury was a tall, distinguished-looking man who had taught mathematics locally before his recent retirement.

'I am the foreman, sir,' he replied.

'Members of the jury,' Eaves continued, 'has the jury reached a verdict on which all twelve of you are agreed?'

'We have, sir.'

'Members of the jury, on this indictment, charging the accused William Cottage with capital murder, how say you? Do you find William Cottage guilty or not guilty?'

The foreman turned briefly towards the dock and then back to Philip Eaves.

'We find the accused, William Cottage, guilty of capital murder,' he replied.

'You find the accused guilty of capital murder, and that is the verdict of you all?'

'It is, sir.'

Eaves turned and bowed to Mr Justice Lancaster, handing him the indictment, on which a verdict had now been returned, to symbolise the end of the trial.

As a matter of courtesy, the judge looked briefly down at Martin Hardcastle, who shook his head. There was nothing to say, no question of mitigation. The penalty was fixed by law. The judge's clerk approached with the black cap, which he placed on top of the judge's wig.

'William Cottage,' the judge said, 'the jury has convicted you of capital murder. Have you anything to say before sentence is passed upon you?'

Billy stared straight ahead. His main barrister had said... what was it? Didn't he say he would be found not guilty? He could not understand what had happened. Something had gone wrong. But his main barrister was not saying anything to the judge, so Billy did not say anything either.

'William Cottage, the judgment of the Court is that you suffer death in the manner authorised by law. The sentence will be carried out at Her Majesty's Prison at Bedford, and you are committed to the custody of the Sheriff of Bedfordshire, who is to be responsible for executing the judgment of the Court.'

Moments later, the prison officers led Billy Cottage out of court to his cell.

* * *

Most of those present in the courtroom had left before Ben slowly picked up his papers and notebook and rose to his feet. Ben could not conceive what impact the sentence had had on Billy Cottage, but he knew the effect it had had on him. He felt as if someone had punched him hard in the stomach. His breath had been taken away. Briefly, he thought he might faint, but he managed to recover by gripping the side of the bench in front of him until his fingers hurt.

When he eventually made his way out of the courtroom, he looked around him, thinking he was the last person to leave. He was wrong. Eve Cottage was curled up, unnoticed, on a corner seat in the upstairs public gallery. She remained in court for almost an hour, until she was found by the building's janitor who was preparing to lock up for the night. He shepherded her gently out of court and out of the Town Hall into Market Square, where she stood alone, wondering what to do next.

By the time Ben got as far as the cells, Martin and Barratt were about to leave. They had commiserated with Cottage and promised to pursue an appeal against conviction. Ben approached, fully intending to add his own sorrow at the verdict. But Billy Cottage was sitting on his seat at the rear of the cell, rocking backwards and forwards, his hands folded in front of him. As he stood in front of the cell, Ben could hear him singing, faintly, to himself. The tune was recognisable, in fact unmistakable. Ben turned abruptly and walked away.

* * *

They said little when they returned to the George.

Martin found John, slipped him some money, then retired to his room to await the relief that John would soon bring him.

Ben placed a call home on the hotel's phone to learn that Joshua continued to improve and that the doctor's opinion remained the same. The family had found Joshua in good spirits and still pleased that the Viceroy had found time to visit him.

Barratt took over the hotel phone after Ben and called Suzie at home, reversing the charges. 'Talk to me,' he said.

'About what?'

'About what you did at the boutique today, about what you saw from the bus, on the streets. Talk to me about life, about people being alive.'

Suzie had been through this before. She talked to him gently about her day for more than an hour.

Jess sat in her room, staring out of the window into the courtyard, for some time. Well after midnight she made her way to Ben's room. He was lying on his bed, wide awake, but got up when she knocked. Without a word, she entered, took his hand, and led him back to the bed. They both lay down. She switched off the light, turned him on to his side facing her, and held his head against her breast. Within a few minutes they were both fast asleep.

52

Flashback

'WELL, COME ON then, how does it work?' Terry demanded, after a silence.

How did it work? Not in any way Arthur could have imagined before he made his way to Pentonville Prison. The letter had instructed him to report to the prison engineer by 10 o'clock, which meant travelling to London the previous afternoon and spending the night with a cousin of his mother who lived in Mill Hill. He told the cousin only that he was exploring opportunities in the capital. His mother, who was mortified by what she saw as this morbid interest on the part of her son, had strictly forbidden him to reveal his true purpose, and in any case he would have preferred to keep it from his hostess. He was not yet ready to answer too many questions, and those his mother had asked had been enough.

To the extent that he had imagined an execution before, Arthur had never focused on the place where it would happen. He dimly pictured it as a grubby shed of some kind somewhere in the prison grounds. When Bill, the prison engineer, unlocked the door to a room on the ground floor of the wing, Arthur gasped with astonishment. Looking up, he saw an almost empty space, three storeys high and two cells wide, cut from the middle of the wing, as if a roaring river had simply swept the cells on three floors away, creating a concrete and steel canyon. The whole space was spotlessly clean.

'On the top floor,' Bill said, 'you have some beams in the ceiling, and you can see some chains hanging down from the beams. That's where you fasten your rope. You've got to calculate the drop first, of course. Once you've done that, you know what length to mark off on the rope, and you can work out where to attach it to the chain. On the floor immediately above us is the condemned cell and the drop. That's our next port of call. This level is where you lower the body down into the coffin after the execution and, once the doctor has pronounced him dead, they take it away for burial.'

'How do you calculate the drop?' Arthur asked nervously.

'Very carefully,' Bill replied, without smiling. 'Come on, let's go upstairs and I'll show you.'

'This is the condemned cell,' Bill said, unlocking a door on the floor above. 'Currently unoccupied, fortunately, for our purposes. There is another one next door. There is a double drop too, so we are set up for a double execution, but executioners don't like doubles. They require two assistants and they are a bit more complicated.' He ushered Arthur inside. 'Perfectly possible, of course, but you don't see them often. I think the last time was before the War, so they may have gone out of fashion.'

He turned and touched the door of a wardrobe to their right.

'What the condemned doesn't know – at least until 8 o'clock in the morning – is that the exit to the drop is just behind this wardrobe. He thinks he has to go through the cell door and take a long walk somewhere. He probably doesn't have a clear picture of where and how long, but he tries to imagine it. So he is completely taken by surprise when the officers move the wardrobe aside and he finds he has only a few feet to walk. Before he has a chance to recover from the shock of that, the executioner has him on the drop, the hood is over his head, the noose is in position, and Bob's your uncle. The whole thing shouldn't take more than ten seconds.'

'Ten seconds?' Arthur gasped.

Bill smiled. 'Actually,' he said, 'the current standard, originally set by Tom Pierrepoint, is eight seconds. Uncle Tom, as we called him, could enter the condemned cell on the first stroke of 8 o'clock by the church clock and have the condemned dangling on the end of the rope before the last stroke. He usually left his little cigar burning in an ashtray just outside, and he was taking a puff, with the job well done, before it had a chance to go out. So we aim for eight seconds, but don't fret about that. If you are doing it in fifteen before you leave tomorrow, I will be happy. After that, it's just practice and repetition. The more you do it, the faster you get. Of course, it ran in the family with Uncle Tom. His brother Henry was also an executioner, as was

Henry's son Albert until he retired a couple of years ago. First rate, all three of them.'

He waved Arthur into a small chair with a small table in front of it.

'This is where the condemned writes his last letter home,' he said, nodding towards the table. 'Now, you asked about calculating the drop, so let's talk about that before we start on the practical work. This is the bible – the official Home Office approved table of drops, 1913 edition.'

He handed Arthur a slim dog-eared grey booklet, the pages stapled together untidily.

'And if you think that's going to solve all your problems, you can forget about it. It consists of approximations based on assumptions. It's useful as a starting point, but these days, all executioners agree that there are certain corrections that have to be made. The only way to guarantee the result is by observation and experience.'

He opened the book for Arthur, standing behind him and looking over his right shoulder.

'Now, what do I mean by "guarantee the result"? What is the result? The result is instantaneous death, and it is your job to provide it. Instantaneous death is caused by a drop which severs the spinal cord near the second or third cervical vertebra. The first thing to remember is that this only happens if you adjust the noose correctly. It has to be firm and tight under the left jawbone. Never under the right. Never. Why? Because the drop causes the noose to turn a quarter-circle clockwise, so the tug of the rope finishes under the chin and throws the head back. Result: fracture of the spinal cord. If you adjust to the right, the rope ends up on the back of the neck, pushing the head forward and resulting in slow strangulation. That may be acceptable in other countries, but not here. That happens once, you're off the list, and once you're off, you don't get back on. There is no room for mistakes, and there are no excuses.'

Bill pointed to the table of drops.

'Assuming you have adjusted the noose correctly, the next thing is the length of the drop. The Home Office table is based on the weight of the condemned. The table tells you that drops of less than five feet or more than eight feet six are not allowed. Why? It can't be too short because you don't want the head visible above the drop –

upsets the official witnesses. But on the other hand, it can't be too long – you don't want him bouncing up off the floor below. But the table is only a guide. You have to observe. You get the chance to watch him taking exercise. You are here the day before, to make sure the equipment is in order and set everything up. You have to stretch the ropes overnight with sandbags. So while you are here, you watch him. The prison will give you his weight. But you need more than that. You need to see his build, how solid, or otherwise, he is, the condition of his muscles.'

Arthur looked up over his shoulder.

'It sounds as though you would need a lot of experience to judge all that,' he commented.

'Good,' Bill replied. 'I'm glad you said that. I am nervous when I get someone who thinks it's easy. That's why you will assist at so many executions before you work as number one. You get experience by watching your number one work, by watching the condemned together. You can talk to your number one, ask him why he is using a particular drop. Talk to him, ask as many questions as you like, as long as it's not at 8 o'clock on the day.'

Bill walked around the table to face Arthur.

'You see, Arthur, you've got to get it right. If the drop is too short, you won't sever the spinal cord and, if he dies at all, it will be through strangulation. No good. Like I said, that happens once, you're off the list. There is no room for mistakes, and there are no excuses. If the drop is too long, you'll pull his head off. No good. That happens once, you're off the list. There is no room for mistakes, and there are no excuses. No use saying, "that's what it said in the Home Office table". There are no excuses.'

Bill pulled a pipe from his top pocket and tamped down the tobacco with a finger.

'Look inside the back cover. There's a sheet with some weights in pounds. They are exercises, just to get you used to applying the formula in the table. I hope your arithmetic is all right. Got a pen? Good. Let's see if you get the drop about right. But, Arthur, listen. Once you get to a prison as number one, you'll get advice from everyone, whether you ask for it or not – the governor, the prison doctor, your assistant, even the prison officers. My advice? Listen to everyone, look at the table, but make your own decision. Because the governor, the prison doctor, they have never hanged a human being. Never have, never will. Same with me. You can ask me whatever you want. I know the table inside out, and I can show you exactly how to conduct an execution. But I've never done it, and I never will, thank you very much. It's your responsibility, Arthur. You've got to get it right.'

* * *

Bill looked at Arthur's results with approval. He had been smoking his pipe as Arthur worked and the aroma of Players Navy Flake hung in the air. He put the pipe in a tin ashtray, walked to the far corner of the cell, and picked up a wooden box, which he placed on the table. Returning to the corner, he retrieved a floppy life-sized dummy.

'This is Bert,' he said, smiling. 'You and I are going to hang him a lot today. Don't worry about him. He is used to it. It won't do him any harm. So if you're going to make a mistake, this is the time to do it. It won't count against you now. Stand up, please.'

Arthur stood. Bill sat Bert in the chair, leaning slightly forward.

'Right, this box has all the tools of the trade. Straps for pinioning the arms and legs, ropes, white cap. Now, what drop did you decide on for Prisoner 1?'

'Six feet four', Arthur replied.

'Good', Bill nodded. 'That's correct in terms of the table, plus the necessary correction. And, by a happy coincidence, that's the length of the rope I set up for you to practice with. I'll show you how to do that when we go upstairs later. So, let's make a start. Give me a hand with the wardrobe, there's a good lad.'

Arthur gasped yet again. The wardrobe was very light, and moving it almost effortless. Once it was pushed aside, a door behind it led directly to the drop, a walk of only three or four feet. Arthur was astonished. No wonder the condemned was taken by surprise. No wonder Uncle Tom could do it in eight seconds.

'Right. Now, come over to the door of the cell. It's 8 o'clock on the day. You are standing outside, you and your assistant. The governor is with you. The chaplain may be inside the condemned cell, ministering to the condemned. You enter as the clock begins to strike eight. Prison officers move the wardrobe away, opening the door for you to get through to the drop. You pinion the condemned's arms, and walk him briskly to the drop. Once he is on the drop, your assistant pinions the legs. In the meanwhile, you put the white cap – it's a hood really, but we always call it the cap – over the head and position the noose. As soon as the assistant is off the drop you pull the lever. The drop is just two trap doors secured with a bolt. When you push the lever, you release the bolt. The condemned falls through the drop and Bob's your uncle. The first time, I'll be number one, and you will be my assistant. Your only job is to pinion the legs and get off that drop as if you are starting the hundred yards. Ready?'

Arthur nodded.

'Right,' Bill said. 'Grab your strap. It's eight o'clock. Go.'

At a brisk pace, Bill helped Bert up from the chair and, in a flash, turned him, pinioned his arms behind him and walked through the door towards the drop. In a matter of one or two seconds Bert was on the drop with the white cap on his head, and Bill was adjusting the noose. Arthur had almost frozen, bewildered by the sheer speed of it all.

'Move! Get on with it!' Bill shouted. 'He's going to die of old age before I can hang him, for God's sake.'

Arthur forced himself into action. He jumped on to the drop, fell to his knees, and at the second attempt, pinioned Bert's legs near the ankles. He jumped backwards off the drop. A split second later, there was a deafening bang and Bert disappeared from sight, only a length of rope visible, swaying almost imperceptibly from side to side. Arthur put his fingers in his ears, which were ringing.

Bill was grinning. 'It is a bit loud, isn't it?' he said. 'Don't worry. You'll get used to it. Now, the pinion wasn't great, a bit too low, wants to be a bit higher. But the main thing was, you were too bloody slow. I was ready to push the lever a good two seconds before you started to move off the trap. You've got to have him pinioned as I am adjusting the noose. You can't leave number one standing there biding his time. You've got to be off that drop as though your life depends on it.'

Bill began to haul Bert back up. 'There was a famous accident once,' he said. 'This was at the old Newgate prison in 1896. The assistant was a bit slow getting off the drop and number one pushed the lever before he was clear. It ended up with the assistant grabbing the condemned's legs to save himself as he dropped. He ended up swinging there. Fortunately, the condemned was dead and the assistant suffered nothing worse than a nasty shock. And in fairness to the number one, that was a triple execution, and he probably couldn't see everyone. We don't do triples today, and that's one reason why. Too complicated. Too much can go wrong. But it can still go wrong with just one condemned. That's why you have to be careful.'

'Whose fault was it?' Arthur asked. 'The accident?'

'Number one,' Bill replied, without hesitation. 'He took his eye off the ball. He's got to wait for his assistant to clear the drop. But don't make him wait, that's the rule. Not if you want to stay on the list. Right, come on. We'll try that again.'

After Bert had been hanged six more times, Bill pronounced himself satisfied.

'Now, you can be number one,' he said, hauling Bert up yet again. 'We are not going to worry about time for now. Just go through the motions. So, put Bert back in his chair and let's stand by the door.'

'Would he be sitting down?' Arthur asked.

'Good question,' Bill replied. 'The answer is, be prepared for anything. He may be standing with the chaplain if the chaplain is present. You have to size the room up immediately on entering. You have to notice if you've got two dozy officers who are taking too long moving the wardrobe. If so, take a second more with the pinioning of the arms. Make the whole sequence as smooth as you can. You don't want to stop and start. Make sure your path to the drop is clear before you start walking. Now, a tip. Wear the white cap in your top pocket, like a fluted handkerchief. That way, the condemned has no idea what it is. Uncle Tom came up with that, I think. Uncle Tom's brother Henry, our Albert's dad, had a peculiarity too, by the way. He used to adjust the noose first and put the cap over it. But I would not recommend that. It may have worked for Henry, but it's not standard procedure.'

Arthur fluted the cap in the top pocket of his jacket. Bill handed him the arm strap.

'It's eight o'clock. Go!'

Arthur strode forward, lifted Bert up, and tried to hold his arms behind his body while fiddling with the strap. He dropped the strap once, and needed two attempts before fitting it. But he then lost no time in standing the dummy on the drop. Bill had the legs pinioned and was off the drop before Arthur had got the cap fully on. But Arthur took his time and adjusted the noose over the cap. He pushed the lever. The deafening noise rang through the empty chamber again and Bert dropped.

Bill nodded.

'Not bad for a first try, Arthur. We will have to work on the arm strap. But it's just technique. The position of the noose looked very good. We are not worrying about time at this stage, as I said, so that wasn't bad at all.'

'You were right fast off the trap,' Arthur said.

Bill smiled. 'I'm taking no chances with a beginner like you,' he replied. 'I don't want you pushing the lever too soon, do I?'

They practised for the remainder of that day and a good deal of the next. Arthur's last hanging of Bert as number one was accomplished in twelve seconds, and with no mistakes.

'I'm not supposed to say this,' Bill remarked as they shook hands at the door of the wing, 'but I think you will do very well. They will send you a letter eventually. It may take a while, so be patient. Then you will just have to assist at one execution before your position on the list is confirmed. Good luck.'

* * *

Arthur's test execution took place three months later. The execution took place at Pentonville, so Arthur had the confidence of knowing his way around the prison and having seen the condemned cell and the drop before. The condemned man had killed his wife for no apparent reason, and said that he was sorry for what he had done. He had not resisted at all. It all happened so quickly that Arthur could later remember almost nothing except for the man's last words of remorse. He was supposed to be studying his number one's technique but, apart from the sheer speed of the action, it was all a bit of a blur. His leg pinion had gone perfectly and he had raced off the drop. The deafening noise seemed to come at the very moment when his rear foot was leaving the trap. In the ensuing silence he walked silently back through the condemned cell with his number one, the assistant governor, and the prison doctor. There was a required wait of one hour before the body could be hauled down for the doctor to pronounce the cause of death, though there was no doubt about the cause of death. Death had been instantaneous.

The prison doctor approached Arthur unexpectedly.

'Give me your wrist, please,' he said.

Taken aback, Arthur hesitated before extending his left wrist. The doctor held the wrist with a finger on his pulse, and consulted a silver pocket watch he had taken from the pocket of his waistcoat. He held his finger in position for a full minute. Eventually he released the wrist with a nod to the assistant governor.

'Calm as you like,' he observed. 'He will do.'

Number one patted him on the back.

'Well done, Arthur,' he said. 'Come on, time for breakfast. Let's try the prison bacon and eggs. They are not bad here, usually.'

The other thing Arthur learned in connection with that execution was that Thwaites would extend him a day's unpaid leave whenever he was called away to an execution. He had made the request to his manager rather sheepishly but, to his surprise, the firm seemed only too pleased to have someone performing an important public service. Naturally enough, in return, they wanted to hear all about it when he reported for work the following day, and Arthur had to quickly learn the discretion required of an executioner in not talking about the detail of his work with the curious and the pruriently minded.

Within three years he had conducted his first execution as number one. The condemned was an East London villain who had used too much force on a guard in what was supposed to be a routine lorry hijacking. When Arthur entered the condemned cell he seemed paralysed with fear, and Arthur conducted the execution in a respectable eleven seconds. The result was the fracture of the spinal cord between the second and third cervical vertebrae – and instantaneous death. The assistant governor was delighted and congratulated Arthur warmly before inviting him to breakfast.

53

1964
14 July

COURT 4, THE LORD Chief Justice's court, is the showpiece of the Royal Courts of Justice, a large, richly appointed courtroom full of dark wood and brass fittings, the Royal Coat of Arms above the judicial bench hand-carved, the sheer dimensions of the place calculated to strike terror into any young barrister, without even considering the ordeal of an appearance before the Court of Criminal Appeal. The room was big enough to make any advocate worry about whether his voice would even carry to the judges' bench, and Ben had many times heard a familiar joke at the Bar that you could only see the judges from counsel's row after any morning fog had lifted.

The Court had been created by Parliament in 1907 as a contemporary appellate court, to appease public concern about the fairness of jury trials, in the wake of several notorious miscarriages of justice. Unlike its predecessor, the Court for Crown Cases Reserved, the Court of Criminal Appeal was empowered to consider the facts of a case, as well as the law, and so was designed to provide an added layer of protection for defendants convicted by juries. But, even to experienced advocates, Court 4 did not feel reassuring. The Court, which consisted of the Lord Chief Justice and two High Court judges, had a reputation for having little tolerance for weak arguments or weak advocates. Anything less than a compelling argument, attractively presented, tended to get short shrift. The three members of the Court sat on high on their bench, far above the Bar, intimidating in their austere black robes, offset only slightly by the subdued pale grey of their wigs.

As a pupil Ben had watched proceedings in Court 4 with

Gareth Morgan-Davies, and had witnessed the judges' propensity to dissect without mercy and reduce to nothing what at first had seemed promising grounds of appeal. Despite Gareth's reassurance about how much the Court had mellowed under Lord Chief Justice Parker, the aura of the place hit him as he walked into court at 10.20, ten minutes before the Court was due to sit. As a capital murder conviction, Ben's case had priority over other cases, and was first in the list. The list was substantial and other members of the Bar were already milling around, talking jovially to each other and to the usher. Ben sat quietly in junior counsel's row, doing his best to tune them out. They were not carrying the burden he carried. Perhaps they were representing a burglar, or a fence who had been given a year or two for some act of routine, mediocre dishonesty. Perhaps some wayward lad who had gone a bit too far with a beer glass in a pub brawl. You could afford to be jovial when you had a case like that. The defendant probably had a long record and doubtless deserved every day of his sentence, so when the inevitable happened you could hardly feel too bad about it. You had another war story to share with your colleagues, the story of how abrasive they were to you in the Court of Criminal Appeal, and of how you had bravely stood your ground and gone down with all guns blazing. Certainly, no one was going to blame you if the appeal was dismissed. It was only to be expected. But you had an outside chance of persuading the Court that the trial judge had erred in law, leaving the Court with no alternative, albeit with the great regret which always accompanied the triumph of form and technicality over substance and merit, but to allow the appeal. Some appeals had to be won, and if yours was one of them, it was a triumph, another feather in your cap, evidence that your advocacy was respected in high places.

But these were not Ben's concerns. Ben had an altogether different case. His client had not committed an act of routine, mediocre dishonesty, or gone too far in a pub brawl. He would not do a year or two and then be released. Ben's first appeal in this court was a case of life and death. If his appeal was dismissed, the court's judgment would be a second death sentence, and this time it would be final. His stomach still churned from the recent experience of the verdict of guilty and the death sentence passed at the Assize Court in Huntingdon. Now, with little time to recover emotionally, here he was in the Court of Criminal Appeal, facing the only chance left to any lawyer to save the life of Billy Cottage. Even worse, his leader, Martin Hardcastle, had abandoned ship under cover of embarrassment that his professional conduct was being questioned. As it should be, Ben reflected, but surely Billy Cottage ought to be represented by someone more senior, someone the court was more likely to heed. He should not have been left alone in this place. The only relief was that Billy Cottage would not be produced for the hearing. He would be notified of the outcome by the prison governor in due course. Ben thought that he could not have coped with his client, in addition to the court. His head was throbbing and his starched collar stuck stubbornly to his neck as if determined to hold his head in a fixed position. He looked up at the clock on the side wall of the courtroom. Two minutes to go. Around him barristers were slipping quietly into their places and untying the lengths of ribbon that held their briefs. The jovial banter had stopped now. Barratt Davis tugged gently on his gown from the row behind and whispered 'good luck'. Andrew Pilkington nodded in a friendly way from his place on the other side of counsel's row.

At exactly 10.30, an usher knocked loudly from outside court on the door leading to the judges' corridor, as another loudly ordered all in court to rise. The three members of the Court entered briskly. The Lord Chief Justice, Lord Parker, took his seat quickly in the middle, with Mr Justice Carver to his right and Mr Justice Melrose to his left. The robed associate stood.

'My Lords, the first case in your Lordships' list is the appeal of William Cottage against conviction.'

Ben stood. Lord Parker was searching the bench for the list of counsel appearing before him, as judges often did when counsel had not yet become a familiar face.

'Yes, Mr... Schroeder,' the Lord Chief Justice said. Ben caught the briefest of glances that passed between the three judges, and knew exactly what it meant. What was junior counsel doing arguing an appeal in a capital murder case? If they gave him a chance, they would find out. His obviously junior status offered a slim hope of some sympathy. But not if he failed to make an impression. He felt, rather than saw, every eye in the courtroom on him as the Bar asked the same silent question as the judges. 'Who are you, and why are you here in this case?' He had to subdue his churning stomach and aching head, and answer their question.

'May it please your Lordships,' he began, 'I appear for the appellant, William Cottage. My learned friend Mr Pilkington appears for the Crown.'

He thought his voice sounded confident enough. None of the judges seemed to be straining to hear. He felt a slight surge in confidence.

'My Lords, the appellant was convicted of capital murder at the Huntingdon Assize before Mr Justice Lancaster and a jury, on the 26 June of this year, and was sentenced to death. There are three grounds of appeal. The first relates to the learned judge's decision to allow the Crown to adduce evidence that Jennifer Doyce was raped.'

Ben studied the court's reaction. He saw a faint smile cross the face of the Lord Chief Justice.

'A point which your learned leader abandoned in front of the trial judge,' Mr Justice Carver observed.

So, has Mr Justice Carver been designated to take the lead?, Ben wondered. One judge took the lead and had responsibility for delivering the judgment of the Court in each case, so that there was a fair division of work between them. It seemed that the Lord Chief Justice might have called on Mr Justice Carver for Cottage's case. '*He likes to think of himself as tough but fair, a no nonsense kind of judge,*' Gareth had said, when Ben told him who the members of the Court were. But Ben was not ready to appeal to fairness directly – at least not yet. That would come later, after they had disposed of the points of law.

'Yes, my Lord , but...'

'And he was right to do so, was he not? As the learned judge himself pointed out, if the jury focused on the rape, that would provide the best opportunity for them to reject the allegation of the course or furtherance of theft.'

'My Lord, yes. But it increased the appellant's chances of being convicted of murder, and did so in a highly prejudicial way.'

'Why do you say that?' the Lord Chief Justice asked. 'The issue was really the identity of the killer, wasn't it? Whoever it was committed an act of rape, but that in itself did not incriminate Cottage at all.'

'In addition,' Mr Justice Melrose chimed in, 'why should the Crown not be entitled to lead the evidence of rape? It was part and parcel of the whole transaction, wasn't it?'

Ben reeled under the force of the combined onslaught. He was now experiencing at first hand the horror stories he had heard about the summary demolition job of which this court was capable. He felt himself bathed in sweat, and his field of vision seemed to have shrunk to a narrow tunnel connecting him to the Lord Chief Justice. He struggled desperately for a reply.

'Why don't you move on to the second ground of appeal?' Mr Justice Carver suggested. 'That involves a point of law, does it not?'

Ben took the hint.

'Your Lordship is quite right,' Ben agreed. 'There is a question of law. As the case was presented by the Crown, on any view, this was not a case of killing in the course or furtherance of theft and, therefore, was not a case of capital murder. My learned friend very fairly opened and presented the case on the basis that the defendant killed Frank Gilliam primarily in order to further his intent to rape Jennifer Doyce. That was the Crown's case throughout. They portrayed Mr Cottage as a sexual predator, even adducing his previous conviction for indecent exposure, and the jury must have convicted on that basis.'

Ben saw that the Lord Chief Justice had been about to speak, but that he then deferred to Mr Justice Carver. Now, Ben was sure who he was dealing with.

'But, Mr Schroeder, there was evidence, was there not, from which the jury was entitled to infer that Cottage stole Miss Doyce's cross and chain at some time during the events that occurred on board the house boat, the *Rosemary D*, on that evening?'

'My Lord, I must accept that there was.'

'Well, in that case…'

'But, my Lord, there was no evidence that the killing of Frank Gilliam was in any way directed to that end. The evidence was equally consistent with any theft having been no more than an afterthought at the conclusion of the rape of Miss Doyce, by which time a substantial time had elapsed since the killing of Mr Gilliam.'

The judge nodded.

'Is there the law on that point?'

Suddenly, Ben felt on stronger ground. He had the feeling that he was warming to the courtroom.

'My Lords, the Homicide Act 1957 provides that killing in the course or furtherance of theft is one of the categories of capital murder. The term "in the course or furtherance of theft" is not defined, except that by virtue of section 5 (5) (e) : *"theft includes any offence which involves stealing or is done with intent to steal"*. It is straining the meaning of "in the course or furtherance" to suggest that it covers a case in which the killing may have been committed before any intention was formed to steal, and in which all the direct evidence pointed to an intention to rape.'

'But that is not a point of pure law, is it?' Mr Justice Melrose was asking. 'Surely everything depends on the view the jury took of the evidence?'

'My Lord, not if there was no proper basis on which the jury could be invited to draw that conclusion. It was so improbable in the light of the evidence as a whole that it cannot have been safe to invite them to draw it. There was no evidence that the murderer knew of the existence of the cross and chain, much less formed any intent to steal it, until Frank Gilliam was already dead.'

They were not shooting him down summarily on this ground, Ben noted with satisfaction.

'I believe your Lordships have been provided with a copy of the case of *Jones*, reported in the first volume of the Queens' Bench Division Reports for 1959, in which Lord Parker gave the judgment of the Court.'

'Yes, I remember the case, Mr Schroeder,' the Lord Chief Justice said, smiling. 'But that was a case where the accused committed a murder in order to facilitate his escape after the theft had been completed.'

'My Lord, it was. And I cite it in the hope of persuading your Lordships that there is a clear point of distinction. Where the theft has been completed, it does follow, as your Lordship held, that killing to make good one's escape should be regarded as being in the course or furtherance of theft. But where the killing occurs, not only before the theft occurs, but before there is any intent to steal, the same logic cannot apply. Indeed, it would seem that the only conclusion the jury could properly reach is that the killing was wholly unrelated to the theft.'

'But I am not sure why the jury could not properly conclude that there was an intent to steal before Gilliam was killed,' Mr Justice Melrose persisted. 'If that is the case, surely the learned judge was right in leaving that issue to them. He directed the jury that they must first consider whether Cottage murdered Frank Gilliam. If they were not sure of that, then the verdict would be one of not guilty. If they were sure of that, they must go on to consider whether the murder was in the course or furtherance of theft. If it was, they would convict of capital murder; if not, they would convict of non-capital murder. Surely, the learned judge took exactly the right approach?'

'Yes,' Lord Parker intervened, to Ben's surprise, 'but the point Mr Schroeder is making is that, while that may be the proper course generally speaking, it was not the proper course here because the evidence to support a finding of course or furtherance was too tenuous to be left safely to the jury. Isn't that right, Mr Schroeder?'

Ben inclined his head slightly in gratitude.

'Yes, my Lord. It seems remarkable, as the Crown invites the Court to do, to impute to Parliament an intention that a conviction for capital murder would be proper in these circumstances, in the absence of a clear provision to that effect. It seems to be a case which Parliament never considered. If they had, I submit that they might well have regarded such a conclusion as unjust, and unnecessary for the public policy purposes which underlie the Act.'

Lord Parker looked at Mr Justice Carver.

'I would like to hear from the prosecution on that point,' he said quietly. 'I confess that I find it far from easy. Perhaps we could move on to the final ground?'

Carver nodded.

'We have your argument on the second ground, Mr Schroeder.'

Ben took a deep breath.

'Yes, my Lord. The third ground concerns the fact that Cottage did not give evidence in his defence, and did not call a witness who was available to him. He was prepared to give evidence of an alibi, namely that he made his way home after leaving work at the Oliver Cromwell public house, and remained at home throughout the night until the following morning. His sister, Eve Cottage, would have said that, although she did not know what time her brother returned home on the night of the twenty fifth, because she has the habit of retiring early, nonetheless, he was in the house when she woke up the next morning at 7 o'clock.'

'And why was that evidence not called?' Mr Carver asked.

Ben hesitated.

'My Lord…'

The Lord Chief Justice intervened.

'You need have no concerns about seeming to giving evidence, Mr Schroeder. Our practice is to accept the facts from Counsel. We need to understand what happened.'

'Yes, my Lord. My Lord, I concede that Cottage was initially reluctant to give evidence, or to ask his sister to give evidence on his behalf, simply because of apprehension. He is a person of limited education, as is his sister, and he was afraid that he would not be understood or that he might not be able to explain himself adequately. But both I, and my instructing solicitor, Mr Davis, who sits behind me, had spent considerable time with him, and we believe that we had convinced him that he had to put aside any nervousness and tell the jury about what happened on the night in question. It was our clear understanding that he accepted that position.'

'You believed that there was a case to answer?' Mr Justice Melrose asked.

'Yes, my Lord,' Ben replied immediately. 'We were clear about that.'

'But…?' Mr Justice Carver asked.

'My Lord, there came a day on which Mr Hardcastle was indisposed, because of… apparent food poisoning. This was the day on which Jennifer Doyce was called to give evidence and…'

'And the day on which you cross-examined her,' the Lord Chief Justice observed, with a smile.

'Yes, my Lord. Mr Hardcastle had not raised the question of defence evidence until then. But after the court had risen on that day, he had recovered sufficiently to meet Mr Davis and myself. He advanced the idea that it was unnecessary for Cottage to give evidence, or call evidence, because we had weakened the prosecution case to such an extent that the best course was to leave it to the jury on the prosecution case, and argue that the case had not been proved beyond reasonable doubt.'

'What view did you and Mr Davis take about that?' Mr Justice Carver asked.

'My Lord, I think it is fair to say that we were sceptical. We believed that Mr Hardcastle had misjudged and underestimated the strength of the prosecution case,' Ben replied. He looked up and saw all three members of the Court nod, as if in agreement.

'But before the question could be resolved,' Ben continued, 'I was called away for the night because of the serious illness of a close relative. When I returned the next morning, I found that Mr Hardcastle had seen Cottage and had advised him that on no account should he give evidence, or call his sister to give evidence. I went to see Cottage myself with Mr Davis, but we were unable to persuade him otherwise. It was in those circumstances that no evidence was called for the defence.'

There was a lengthy silence. Ben bit his lip.

'With considerable regret,' he said, 'I believe it to be my duty to submit to your Lordships that Mr Hardcastle was guilty of a serious error of judgment, which deprived the jury of vital evidence – evidence, which, if believed, might very well have resulted in an acquittal.'

The Lord Chief Justice sat up in his chair.

'Mr Schroeder, it was for the appellant to decide whether or not to give evidence, was it not?'

'Yes, my Lord.'

'Of course, he would listen to the advice of leading counsel but, at the end of the day, it was his decision. He listened to all points of view put to him and made his decision. Isn't that right?'

Ben drew himself up to his full height.

'My Lord, as a matter of legal theory, your Lordship is quite right. But this appellant is a man of limited education, a lock keeper by trade, charged with a capital offence. I am sure your Lordships can imagine only too well the strain of his situation. A man in his position is unlikely to go against the advice of leading counsel. And if leading counsel makes an error of judgment as egregious as that made by Mr Hardcastle in this case, I submit that the interests of justice demand that your Lordships should intervene. It is a matter of basic fairness.'

Ben stood back to try to assess the effect his words might have had. But the judges gave little away.

'Unless I can assist your Lordships further?'

'No,' the Lord Chief Justice said. 'Thank you very much, Mr Schroeder. We are much obliged to you. Mr Pilkington?'

* * *

Andrew Pilkington stood, but did not begin immediately. He saw that the three judges were conferring quietly. At length Mr Justice Carver looked down from the bench.

'Mr Pilkington, we require your assistance only in relation to the second ground of appeal. It does seem strange, does it not, that a man can be convicted of capital murder in the course or furtherance of theft when there is no evidence of theft, or an intent to steal, before the killing takes place?'

Andrew nodded.

'My Lord, if that were the case, it would be somewhat strange. But that was not the state of the evidence. My learned friend Mr Schroeder has argued, with his customary eloquence, and as his leader did at trial, that the prosecution's case was based solely on the motive to rape Jennifer Doyce. That was not the case. The prosecution's case was that the appellant intended to commit whatever offences he could find to commit for his own gratification. The rape was, of course, one such offence. But, by the same token, so was the theft. If the jury found that the appellant stole Miss Doyce's gold cross and chain, as they were entitled to find, it was also open to them to find that the appellant had formed the intent to steal anything he found worth stealing once he had boarded the *Rosemary D*, and once he had overcome resistance by killing Frank Gilliam. The jury's verdict shows that that was the conclusion they reached, after a careful summing-up by the learned judge, of which no complaint is made. My Lords, that verdict is consistent with the intent of Parliament, as expressed in section 5 of the Homicide Act 1957, that murder in the course or furtherance of theft should be prosecuted as capital murder. With respect, it is not for your Lordships' Court to seek to overturn that parliamentary intent, which is what my learned friend, in effect, seeks to persuade your Lordships to do. On the contrary, your Lordships are bound to give effect to the plain wording of the Act. No real question of law was involved here. It was a question of fact. It was a matter for the jury.'

After a respectful pause to await any questions from the bench, Andrew resumed his seat. The judges conferred again.

'We will retire to consider our decision in this case,' Lord Parker announced. In a second or two, the judges were gone.

54

A MEMBER OF THE Bar whom Ben did not know smiled at him from his left.

'Well done,' he said. 'It's not often you get this lot to retire. It's usually a quick mutter to each other, appeal dismissed, and on to the next one. Someone said this was your first time, is that right?'

'Yes,' Ben replied quietly.

'Well, bloody well done. The first time is the worst. Once you've lost your virginity it's not quite as bad. But I must say, I've been doing it for a few years now, and it still gives me the willies before I'm even on my feet.'

Ben smiled.

It was ten minutes before the judges returned. The same member of the Bar leaned over towards Ben as they rose to their feet. 'It's especially unusual to get them to rise for ten minutes,' he said.

Lord Parker looked up.

'Mr Justice Carver will give the judgment of the Court in this case.'

Carver picked up his reading glasses from the bench and put them on. He pulled together a number of sheets of paper from the bench in front of him and arranged them in order. He glanced down at counsel before returning his gaze to his papers.

'On the 26 June of this year,' he began, 'the Appellant William Cottage was convicted of capital murder before Mr Justice Lancaster and a jury at the Assize at Huntingdon, and was sentenced to death. The facts of the case can be stated quite shortly…

'*Whenever a judge says that the facts of the case can be stated quite shortly,*' Gareth had said one day after they had listened to a judgment in a civil case, '*you can resign yourself to a long wait before you know which way they are going to go. They love to make you wait for the result while they show off how well they have mastered the facts of the case. It gives them a feeling of power.'*

Gareth's words came back to Ben as he listened to Mr Justice Carver recite the history of the conviction of Billy Cottage. There was nothing to do but wait. Ben tried hard to look more confident than he felt as he made a pretence of writing a note, or studying the hand-carved coat of arms above the bench. But the wait seemed like an eternity. At last, Mr Justice Carver seemed to be getting to the point.

'In the judgment of this Court,' the judge was saying, 'the evidence to which I have referred fully justified the verdict of guilty of murder returned by the jury. They were aided by an impeccable summing-up by the learned trial judge, of which no criticism has been made, or could be made, before this Court. But the appellant has taken three points which we must consider. They have been very ably put to us by Mr Schroeder who, for reasons which will become clear in the course of this judgment, did not have the assistance of leading counsel who appeared at trial, Mr Hardcastle QC. In our judgment, the appeal did not suffer because of that. The grounds of appeal could not have been more clearly presented and we are grateful to Mr Schroeder.

'The first ground is that the learned judge erred in permitting evidence to be given that Jennifer Doyce was raped. The Crown alleged that this was a case of capital murder because the murder was committed in the course or furtherance of theft. The defence say that, on that basis, evidence of the act of rape was irrelevant and inadmissible, and caused the defence such prejudice that the verdict of the jury was not safe and satisfactory. We deal with this point very shortly. In our judgment, the learned judge was entirely correct in admitting the evidence. It was a part of the assault committed against Jennifer Doyce, which in turn formed part of the background, not only of the killing of Frank Gilliam, but also of the act of theft. Moreover, we note that Mr Hardcastle did not press his application to exclude the evidence before the trial judge – in our view, quite rightly. There is no merit in that ground of appeal.

'The second ground is that the learned judge erred in law by holding that the appellant could be convicted of capital murder on the facts of the case. At most, it is said, this was a non-capital murder. The Crown alleged that the murder of Frank Gilliam was committed in the course or furtherance of theft. This would make the murder a capital crime under section 5(1)(a) of the Homicide Act 1957. This allegation depended on the jury being satisfied that the appellant stole Miss Doyce's gold cross and chain. Mr Hardcastle took the point before the accused was arraigned, and again at the conclusion of the evidence, and invited the learned judge to order that the indictment should allege non-capital murder only, and to direct the jury that non-capital murder was the only charge for them to consider. The judge declined to do so. As I have indicated, the evidence tendered to support the allegation of theft was circumstantial, and depended on the appellant's possession of the cross and chain and his unsatisfactory attempts to explain how he had come by it. In the view of this Court, the jury was perfectly entitled to reach the conclusion that the appellant stole it. But Mr Schroeder argues that, even if the jury were to reach that conclusion, they could not properly convict of capital murder because the killing of Frank Gilliam was not "in the course or furtherance of theft". He argues that the evidence showed that the main motive for the killing of Mr Gilliam was not theft, but the rape of Miss Doyce; and that, even if the appellant took the cross and chain from her person, Mr Gilliam must already have been dead some time before that. The first of those arguments is, if we may say so, rather ironic, given that in the first ground of appeal argued before us today it was suggested that evidence of the rape should not have been admitted, but we understand that counsel has a duty to advance every arguable ground on his client's behalf.

'Mr Schroeder referred us to the decision of this Court in the case of *Jones* in 1959, in which the appellant stole property from a cooperative store, and was about to leave the premises when he saw the manager enter. Fearing detection, he struck the manager on the head, causing several fractures of the skull, from which the manager died. He argued on appeal that, even if he were guilty of murder, it could not be capital murder because the theft was already complete when the blow was struck. My Lord, Lord Parker, gave the judgment of the Court, rejecting the argument. He said:

"This was a case where the appellant was caught, if one may use the expression, red-handed, and in order to avoid detection, and while still on the scene of his

theft, he committed murder. It is difficult to see why that should not be within the words 'in the course of theft'."

'Although the present case is not identical to *Jones* on the facts, we see no reason to depart from the clear decision reached in that case, merely because the killing in this case preceded the theft, rather than following the theft as it did in *Jones*. The appellant, as My Lord put it, was "still on the scene". We take the view that the jury was entitled to find that the killing was "in the course of theft". But in any case, we have concluded that, even if it was not in the course of theft, the jury was clearly entitled to find that it was "in furtherance of theft". Under the Act, either is enough to found a charge of capital murder. Mr Schroeder rightly pointed out that the Court in *Jones* left open the meaning of the phrase "furtherance of theft". In this case, unlike *Jones*, it was open to the jury to infer that the appellant intended to steal anything of value he might find, and that the killing of Frank Gilliam facilitated, and was intended to facilitate, the appellant's act of theft of the cross and chain from Miss Doyce. In those circumstances, the killing of Frank Gilliam was in furtherance of the theft as well as in the course of theft. The fact that the killing also facilitated the rape of Miss Doyce makes no difference to that conclusion at all. For these reasons, the second ground of appeal is dismissed.

'The third and final ground is that the appellant was deprived of a fair trial because his leading counsel made a strategic decision not to call the appellant, or his sister Eve Cottage, to give evidence in support of an alibi. Mr Schroeder has told us that the appellant maintains that he went straight home on the night in question after completing his shift as a barman at the Oliver Cromwell public house in St Ives, and remained at home until the next day. Eve Cottage, it is said, would have given evidence in support of that contention. If that account of events were to be accepted, then of course it would follow that the appellant could not be convicted of the murder of Frank Gilliam, or indeed of any offence committed aboard the *Rosemary D*. That the appellant was working at the Oliver Cromwell earlier that evening was not in doubt. Indeed, it was a part of the Crown's case that he was working, because it was said that the appellant saw Frank Gilliam and Jennifer Doyce drinking in that public house immediately before walking along the river bank to the *Rosemary D*.

The landlord of the house, Charles Edwards, was called to prove that the appellant had been working on that evening, though he also said that the appellant had left somewhat early, and shortly after Mr Gilliam and Miss Doyce had left the premises.

'We begin with two general observations. Firstly, the decision whether to give evidence was the appellant's decision, and not that of his counsel. Of course, it is part of counsel's duty to give appropriate advice on that question, and sometimes that advice will and must be robust. But at the end of the day, the appellant must make his own decision. Secondly, we regard it as unsatisfactory that leading counsel should not appear before us to give some account of the sequence of events which led to the appellant deciding not to give evidence. We were told that Mr Hardcastle considered it more prudent to allow Mr Schroeder to make the argument, so that he could be free to criticise the conduct of leading counsel. Having heard Mr Schroeder, we do not consider it to be in the least likely that he would have been inhibited from making such a criticism, and it would have been of some assistance to us to hear about what happened directly from Mr Hardcastle.

'In the event, we have concluded that it can make no difference to the outcome of the appeal. It appears that Mr Hardcastle considered that it was unlikely that the jury would believe the evidence of alibi once it had been submitted to cross-examination on behalf of the prosecution. He considered that he had done not inconsiderable damage to the prosecution's case, and that the appellant's best hope lay in seeking to persuade the jury that the case against him had not been proved beyond reasonable doubt. Mr Schroeder and the appellant's instructing solicitor took the opposite view, and both views were presented forcefully to the appellant, who then made his decision. It is the duty of leading counsel to advise the course of action he believes to be in the best interests of his client. It is part of the skill and judgment required of counsel engaged in such important and difficult cases to assess the chances of conviction and acquittal, and to conduct the defence accordingly. Counsel who has heard the evidence, seen the witnesses, and spoken with the client at length is in a far better position to do this than anyone else. We consider that we might have taken a different view in Mr Hardcastle's position, but we cannot say that we would have been correct to do so, because there may have been important considerations which he took into account, of which we know nothing. At the end of the day, our system of criminal justice relies on the experience and skill of counsel to take such difficult decisions. It is not for this Court to substitute its own view for that of counsel engaged in the case. It is the common experience of the members of this Court that, however much damage is done to the prosecution case by cross-examination, the pendulum swings back very quickly if the accused's evidence is not to be believed, and we have no doubt that Mr Hardcastle had that reality very much in mind.

'The appellant was represented by experienced leading counsel, and there is no basis for finding that he was denied a fair trial. The prosecution case was left to the jury, it was summed up to them properly, and they made a decision. The appellant's guilt or innocence was for them to decide. It was, as Mr Pilkington said on behalf of the Crown, a matter for the jury. For these reasons, the third ground also fails and the appeal must be dismissed.'

Ben rose slowly.

'My Lords, the second ground of appeal, in my submission, involves a point of law of general public importance. I seek leave to appeal to the House of Lords on that ground.'

The three members of the Court conferred briefly.

'We are against you, Mr Schroeder,' Lord Parker replied. 'In our view this is a question of mixed law and fact, and we do not think it is one of general public importance.'

Ben bowed and collapsed back into his seat.

'That doesn't prevent you from seeking leave from the House, of course,' Lord Parker added.

'Yes, I'm much obliged to your Lordship,' Ben replied.

* * *

'Come on,' Barratt said, putting his hand on Ben's shoulder. 'Let's go down to the crypt and have a coffee.'

They had left court as the next appeal was getting underway, and as the reality of what had just occurred was becoming clear. Ben nodded wearily. He took off his wig and followed Barratt as he led the way through the labyrinthine corridors of the Royal Courts of

Justice to the basement café. They sat in silence, sipping their coffee, for some time.

'That was probably his last chance,' Ben said. 'And I feel as though I've just been mauled by a pride of lions.'

'That's the Court of Criminal Appeal for you,' Barratt replied sympathetically. 'You did all you could have done, Ben. As the Court said, the case was put as clearly as it could have been put.'

Ben nodded. 'Yes.'

They fell silent again.

'Will you ask the House of Lords for leave to appeal?' Barratt asked eventually.

'Yes,' Ben replied. 'But I don't hold out much hope. The Court we had today seemed to think it was a pretty clear case. That's why they refused leave to appeal. The test is whether the case raises a point of law of general public importance. Our problem is that it's essentially factual. It's simply a question of what is meant by "in the course or furtherance", which is generally a jury question. We will be asking the House of Lords to interpret an Act of Parliament which is not obviously ambiguous on its face. I doubt they will want to do that. Still, we can but try.'

Barratt nodded. 'I think the Court today got it wrong, but I agree with you about the House of Lords. So, now I have to put together my package for the Home Secretary on the subject of a reprieve. Your job is done, Ben, but I would value your thoughts when we have got the materials together.'

'Yes, of course. What avenues are you exploring?'

'I've set wheels in motion on two fronts,' Barratt replied. 'First, I have asked John Singer to comb through any school or medical records he can find in St Ives that might tend to suggest any mental slowness in Cottage – anything, really. I'm clutching at straws. I'm not very hopeful. Second, I have been in touch with Sydney Silverman MP. He is a bit of a maverick, but he is the acknowledged leader of the abolitionist movement, and he is widely respected for that.'

Ben sat up in his chair. 'And Silverman is prepared to help?' he asked.

'I think so,' Barratt replied. 'But there is a limit to what he can do. Most reprieves are granted in cases where the defendant is sympathetic in some way, or the case has exceptional features which would make it wrong to apply the death penalty. None of that applies to Cottage. It was a brutal attack for which there is no mitigation at all.'

'So, what would he…?'

'Silverman's view is that everyone knows abolition is coming. Legislation is on the way, and there is probably enough support in both Houses of Parliament, or there will be soon. So Silverman's argument is that it must be wrong to execute anyone so late in the day, when capital punishment will end in a year or two anyway.'

'That's not a bad argument,' Ben observed.

'No, it's not. Silverman will write to the Home Secretary, Henry Brooke, and he will try to arrange a meeting with him at the House of Commons. Our job will be to provide him with any materials which may help but, to be honest, I'm not sure what those would be in this case. Our problem is that, once Cottage is convicted, this is a bad case – a really bad case.'

'What is Brooke's record on capital punishment?'

'Little known, but not all that promising. He is on record as having no objection in principle to the death penalty, though he is said to be a stickler for the law, and he has said that each case has to be judged on its merits.'

Ben reflected for a moment.

'I think the law may help us with Brooke,' he said, 'despite what happened today.'

'Oh?'

'Yes. All right, the Court of Criminal Appeal decided that we fall within the "course or furtherance" provision. Let's concede that for the sake of argument. Let's assume they have interpreted the Act correctly. Even so, there must be a question of whether Parliament really intended it to be capital murder when the murder was complete before any intention to steal was formed. It seems that Parliament failed to consider that point when they enacted section 5.'

'They told us what "course or furtherance" means.'

'Well, not really, because they ignored the question of when the intent to steal is formed – they didn't really address the timing point.'

Barratt was nodding.

'And if they had considered it…?'

'They might have provided a more precise definition of "course or furtherance". It's a point Silverman may be able to make with the Home Secretary. We don't even have to say that the Court of Criminal Appeal got it wrong today. We can simply say that the law is in an unsatisfactory state because Parliament has not defined its terms, and that it must be wrong to execute a man when we don't know what the boundaries of this kind of capital murder are.'

Barratt clapped his hands together.

'Can you write me an opinion, saying that?'

'I will have it with you tomorrow.'

'Good,' Barratt said. 'I'm afraid we may not have much time. A date for execution is usually fixed quite quickly once the appeal is out of the way – usually within two or three weeks. The House of Lords may buy us a few days, but not long.'

'I'll make a start as soon as I get back to Chambers,' Ben promised. 'Keep me up to date, so that I can look at the full package before you send it off.'

'I will,' Barratt replied.

* * *

The three judges of the Court of Criminal Appeal had just risen for lunch, and were standing in the corridor outside their court. Lord Parker turned to Mr Justice Carver.

'Young Schroeder did very well, didn't he?'

'He did indeed,' Carver replied. 'We didn't give him an easy ride, but he didn't seem intimidated, did he?'

The Lord Chief Justice thought for a moment.

'What do you think we should do about Hardcastle?'

Carver shook his head.

'It's a problem,' he replied. 'On his day, the man is as good as anyone at the Bar, capable of brilliance at times. But we have been hearing rather disturbing rumours for quite some time now, haven't we?'

'I've certainly heard rumours of drinking, and not turning up at court from time to time,' Lord Parker said. 'And what's worse is that the rumours come from a number of sources. If you hear such things from one man – well, you know what the Bar is like, it's the world's biggest rumour mill – you might be disposed to disregard it.

But when you are hearing it from everyone, it's a different matter. You saw the letter Steven Lancaster wrote to me about the Cottage case once the grounds of appeal had been filed.'

'Yes.'

'I didn't think it would make any difference to the way we looked at the case, and it didn't. But Lancaster said that Hardcastle failed to appear on a rather crucial day during the trial, claiming to be suffering from food poisoning, and left Schroeder to cross-examine Jennifer Doyce.'

'What do you think?' Carver asked.

'Well,' Lord Parker replied, 'the problem as I see it is that, like all Silks, he may be carrying on in the happy expectation of a tap on the shoulder for the High Court bench one of these days. I think we need to bring that expectation to an end.'

'So you will…?'

'Unless either of you disagrees, I will have a quiet word with the Lord Chancellor's people and suggest that they offer him something at the County Court level. Hopefully, he can't do too much damage there, and even if he does, the Lord Chancellor can dismiss him for misconduct.'

'I don't disagree at all,' Carver replied.

'Neither do I,' said Mr Justice Melrose.

55

BEN PUT HIS head around the door of the clerks' room for the briefest of moments and exchanged a wave of the hand with Merlin to signal his return to Chambers. The senior clerk did not press him to come in. His experience had long ago taught him that there were times to talk to his barristers, and there were times to leave them alone with their thoughts.

Ben was grateful for Merlin's consideration. He walked quickly across the narrow landing which ran between flights of stairs and led to his room on the opposite side of Chambers. Closing the door behind him, he threw the bag containing his robes on to the floor in the corner of the room behind his desk and flopped into his chair. He hurriedly opened a notebook and wrote a heading: *'Application for Leave to Appeal to the House of Lords'*. It sounded hopeless even before he had completed the title. He sat and stared at it blankly, incapable of making a start.

As he gazed through the large windows of his room out into space and began to come to terms with his feelings, they seemed unexpectedly familiar to him and, to his surprise, memories quickly came flooding back. He had been here before. At the Old Bailey, during his first jury trial, he had found himself having to stand up to the fearsome Judge Milton Janner who was interfering with his vital cross-examination of the prosecution's main witness. Ben had bluntly defied the judge at 1 o'clock, just before lunch, and had been rewarded at 2 o'clock when the judge, recognising his error, apologised. But during that lunch hour, the same demons had come. Seated in a dark corner of the bar mess with a cup of coffee, fully expecting to be disciplined and expelled from Chambers, he had asked himself why he was there. During that one hour, he tortured himself with every imaginable doubt about his ability to succeed as a barrister. Now the demons returned with a vengeance. He had spoken with Billy Cottage. He had shaken his hand. Cottage had placed his trust in him. But Billy Cottage had been sentenced to death, and today Ben had lost him his last real hope of avoiding the gallows. His rational side told him that he must keep his role in perspective. He was junior counsel, and he lacked the power to restrain a forceful but wayward Silk like Martin Hardcastle. But his feelings did not end there, with the rational view. They never did.

Darkest of all was the thought that he did not belong to the barristers' club – the white Anglo-Saxon public school and Oxbridge clique which seemed to surround him everywhere he looked – and that he did not belong to it, not because of any lack of ability, but because of who he was. He was a Jewish kid from the East End. He came from the wrong family. He had been to the wrong school, the wrong university. Who did he think he was? During that lunch hour at the Old Bailey, he had almost talked himself into taking the next bus to Whitechapel and announcing that he was, after all, ready to devote his life to a career at Schroeder's Furs and Fine Apparel.

The memory of his trial at the Old Bailey led him to remember his grief for his mentor, Arthur Creighton. Ben had only just returned from Arthur's funeral in Scotland when Merlin presented him with the Old Bailey brief, and it was Arthur Creighton who had, as if by premonition, reminded him of the duty to stand up to unfair judges, the last time they had met. He wondered what Arthur would have had to say about his first foray into the Court of Criminal Appeal. He smiled despite himself, remembering what Arthur had said on another occasion when all seemed hopeless. *'Remember, Ben, we don't make the facts. The clients do that all on their own and, having made them, they sometimes have to live with them.'* Perhaps that was what had happened to Billy Cottage. He had made the facts and now he was living with them – and dying with them.

He started as the door opened. Harriet Fisk came in and stopped awkwardly in her tracks as she saw him.

'I'm sorry, Ben. I didn't know you were back.' She paused. 'I hear it didn't go too well over the road this morning.'

'Bad news travels fast,' Ben replied. 'Merlin had heard all about it by the time I got back, I'm sure. He didn't say anything, but I could tell.'

'Merlin would have heard before anyone, with his network,' she smiled. 'I really am sorry, Ben. But I heard they were nice to you…?'

He looked up at her as if considering the question carefully.

'Yes, in their own way, I suppose they were,' he replied. 'They didn't have me thrown in the Tower, or disbar me, or order me to pay all the costs.' He laughed. 'It's strange what passes for niceness when you're over there in front of that lot. Anything other than outright abuse, I think.'

'I heard they were a lot nicer to you than that,' she said. 'And… well, you had grounds that could have… well… could have gone either way, couldn't they?'

'Hopeless, you mean?'

'No… I…'

'No, I'm sure you're right,' he said. 'You have to believe in your own grounds of appeal, don't you? If you don't believe in them, why should the judges? But that doesn't mean you are going to win the appeal. I'm sure I will see it all in a more objective light at some point. Just not today.'

She walked across to her desk and threw down the heavy brief she had hauled back from her hearing in the Queen's Bench Division's applications court, in a recess of the Royal Courts of Justice affectionately known as the Bear Garden.

'Come on,' she said decisively. 'On your feet.'

'Why? Where are we going?'

'The Edgar Wallace, for lunch,' she replied. 'On me. There's no point in sitting here getting ever more depressed. Let's try a pint and some bangers and mash. If it doesn't work, you're no worse off. And let's not pretend you're going to get any work done today.'

He shook his head.

'I have to start a petition for leave…'

'Anything you write today, you will tear up tomorrow,' she said. 'Aubrey taught me that. Never try to draft grounds of appeal on the same day you lose a case. You have to give yourself a day to get over it – sometimes more than a day. *"You can't take a case to the next level until you have come to terms with the last level."* – A Smith-Gurney, circa 1963.'

Ben reluctantly pushed his chair back.

Oh, Harriet,' he said wearily. 'The trouble with you is that you are always so bloody logical.'

'Thank you,' she replied, smiling.

* * *

The Edgar Wallace, which stands on Essex Street, just outside Middle Temple and a stone's throw from the offices of Bourne & Davis, has a pleasant, airy dining room upstairs and, as they arrived just before the 1 o'clock rush, they were able to secure a corner table for two.

'The truth is, Ben,' she said, once the drinks and bangers and mash had been ordered, 'that I can't imagine what you are feeling. Aubrey would never touch crime, so I've never seen a client go to prison, much less sentenced to death. You are fully entitled to be as miserable as you like. I will listen until you can't stand the sight of me any more, then I'll go.'

He smiled, and they allowed some time to pass in silence.

'I suppose, when it comes right down to it, it's not about the Court of Criminal Appeal. As you put it so nicely, the grounds could have gone either way – even though I still think we were right.'

'Of course,' she said.

'It's really about me. Wondering what I should have done differently, how I could have dealt with Martin Hardcastle differently. Perhaps if I'd made more of a scene at the time, perhaps even told the judge that I wasn't happy with what was happening.'

She was shaking her head.

'I know, I know,' he said. 'I couldn't do that, and it probably wouldn't have made any difference anyway. Even if Cottage had given evidence… perhaps Martin was right.'

'And perhaps at some point, Ben,' she said, 'you should try to contemplate the possibility that Billy Cottage is the monster the prosecution say he is, and that he attacked those two young people as savagely as they say he did, and that he deserves everything that's coming to him. Perhaps it wouldn't have made any difference what you did, or what Martin Hardcastle did. Have you thought of that?'

'Yes, he replied. 'I have thought of that, and I know that it may well be the truth. But he is my client, and…' He allowed his voice to trail away.

She looked at him closely. He turned his eyes away from her. She gave him some time.

'Ben, we know each other too well. This is not really about Billy

Cottage, is it?' she asked gently. 'It's about you. You're still beating yourself up, questioning whether you have the right to be at the Bar, aren't you?'

He nodded.

'Well, I'm going to give you the same answer I've given you before. You *are* at the Bar, and you are a member of our Chambers because you are good at what you do, and you have every talent you need to succeed. You just need to believe it. You did everything you could have done for Billy Cottage, including going into the Court of Criminal Appeal without a leader. And they complimented you on your argument.'

The drinks arrived. Ben gratefully raised his glass in a toast.

'Thank you,' he said, simply.

He took a deep draught of beer.

'To better days,' she replied, raising her own glass.

There was a pause while they both savoured their drinks, then Ben suddenly sat up straight as if he had just remembered something.

'Harriet, I have to know what happened when I was taken on in Chambers,' he said suddenly.

There was real urgency in his voice. The change of tone took her aback.

'I thought we had been through that,' she said, after a pause. 'When you talked to Gareth, didn't he...?'

'I got part of the story from Gareth,' he replied, 'but there's something missing. Gareth told me that there was a problem in Chambers because of Anne Gaskell's divorce case. Well, we all knew that. Bernard Wesley had to do something to make it all right, and that involved only taking one of us on. That one was going to be you. But somehow, we were both voted in.'

Harriet had been nodding.

'Yes,' she replied. 'Did it ever occur to you that Chambers realised what a huge mistake they would be making if they let you go?'

He shook his head.

'There's more to it,' he said. 'There must be. Anthony Norris...'

'Anthony Norris is an anti-semitic bigot,' she replied with fervour. 'We both know that. You can't let a man like that rule your life. And Ben, even Norris was impressed with the work you did. Aubrey told me he was ready to vote for you. I really think he had changed his mind. I know it doesn't make it any easier that we have a man like that in our Chambers. But let's not give him power over us. He took much the same approach towards women, you know.'

She looked at him again for some time. He did not respond.

'All right,' she said. 'I will tell you everything I know. You do know almost the whole story. But there is one piece of the puzzle you don't have, and the reason you don't have it is that only Bernard Wesley and I know what happened. It's not something Gareth could have told you about.'

Ben was leaning forward, his arms crossed in front of him on the table. Harriet looked around the room. She saw no one she recognised.

'And you have to promise that this will stay between us.'

'I promise,' he replied.

She nodded and leaned in towards him.

'Kenneth Gaskell had an affair with Anne while he was acting as her counsel in the divorce case,' she began. 'They were old flames and it all flared up again. Why they couldn't have waited until… anyway, there it was. Bernard was leading Kenneth. They had a very strong case. The husband drank and was violent – well, you know all this through talking to Simon, probably. Miles Overton was on the other side, leading Ginny Castle. Their instructing solicitor had the idea of having Anne followed by a private detective. They struck gold, including photographs.'

'How do you know that?' Ben asked.

'Through my father.'

'Your father?'

'All will become clear. Give me time.'

She sipped her gin and tonic.

'Armed with this, Miles had lunch with Bernard at the Club and essentially blackmailed him. He gave Bernard seven days to allow the husband incredibly generous terms, or Miles would serve a cross-petition naming Kenneth as a Party Cited and asking for damages for adultery.'

'Which would have been the end…'

'It would have been the end – for Chambers, not just for Kenneth,' she agreed. 'Remember, Ben, Anne was a client of Herbert Harper. You know how much work Harper Sutton & Harper send to

Chambers. So Bernard had seven days to save Chambers.'

'How did he do it?' Ben asked.

Harriet took another sip and smiled.

'Partly by good fortune, and partly by sheer animal cunning,' she replied. 'The good fortune was that Miles Overton's son, Clive, now Gareth's pupil of course, asked Chambers for help. He was a friend of Donald Weston, Kenneth's pupil. You know the background to that story, of course. Everyone does now. When Clive was up at Cambridge, he was ringleader in a drunken escapade after the college rugby club dinner. They threw another student into the river and he drowned. Miles disowned Clive and sent him abroad, to America, where he remained, until he happened to call Donald during the aforesaid period of seven days. He told Donald he wanted to come back to England and that he wanted to come to the Bar. Donald offered to help, and he went to Bernard. Bernard saw a glimmer of light.'

'I don't follow.'

'Clive was at my father's college,' she replied. 'That is where the rugby club incident happened. Miles and Bernard are also college men. Bernard put two and two together and made four. He realised that someone must have covered up what Clive and the other hearties had done – after all, no charges were pursued against any of them – and it wasn't too much of a stretch to conclude that Miles was probably behind it. The problem was, Bernard couldn't prove that.'

'But your father could?'

She nodded.

'Of course. As Master he knew everything that went on,' she replied. 'And I'm pretty sure he helped Miles to do it, though he would never admit that to me. Bernard went up to college to confront him about it. Of course, that meant that Bernard had to tell my father everything that was going on in Chambers. The idea was to sell Miles a way to bring Clive back. Miles couldn't do that himself, of course. He had sworn never to speak to Clive again. My father agreed to help Bernard – on certain conditions, needless to say.'

Ben smiled.

'You would be offered a place in Chambers.'

'Yes. I had no knowledge of that, Ben, I swear.'

He nodded.

'I remember you told me that Bernard was going to Cambridge to see your father, but you didn't know why. It was that day we were both at the Willesden County Court and we had a drink at the pub at lunch time.'

'Yes. Well, after that, Aubrey told me that I was going to be elected. What I didn't know until later was that Gareth had had to abandon you because Chambers only wanted one new member.'

'I had worked most of that out,' Ben said, 'from what Gareth told me. But I'm still mystified…'

She took a deep breath.

'I went to see Bernard, about five minutes before the Chambers meeting,' she said. 'It was a conversation that was just between the two of us.'

Ben had his pint glass in his hand, but suddenly replaced it on the table.

'I told him to his face that they could not treat you like that, and that I would not accept a place in Chambers unless they took you too.'

Ben suddenly felt himself go hot and cold. A lump formed in his throat, and he was not sure he could speak.

'Harriet…' he began weakly.

She laughed and shook her head.

'No, no. Ben, before you prostrate yourself at my feet in gratitude, I must be honest. I knew Bernard could not allow me to turn my place down. The whole deal would have crumbled. Bernard, of course, used the information my father gave him to blackmail Miles back, and make him agree to a reasonable settlement – one which let Kenneth and Chambers off the hook and allowed Clive to come to the Bar with a pupillage all arranged. But without the proof my father gave him – whatever that was – he could not have brought any of that off. Of course, as we all know, that's exactly what he did. And in any case…'

'In any case…?'

'I told Bernard the truth, Ben. I didn't want to be in a set of Chambers that turned a good man down because he was Jewish. I would have left if you had been voted down. I have my own work, as you know. I could have gone elsewhere, and Bernard knew that. But fortunately, Bernard did the right thing. Aubrey told me he actually threatened to leave Chambers if they didn't vote you in.'

She sipped again.

'So we all lived happily ever after.'

She smiled. He reached across for her hand, and she saw that there were tears in his eyes. She smiled, but said nothing more.

At that moment their waitress appeared with their bangers and mash, saying that she was sorry it had taken so long.

56

'MARTIN,' JEREMY SAWYER said, getting up briskly to greet his visitor. 'Thank you for coming. I'm glad you could spare the time.'

'Not at all,' Martin Hardcastle replied, shaking Sawyer's proffered hand. The phrase 'spare the time' was a bit ironic, Hardcastle reflected. The invitation to attend Sawyer's office in the House of Lords had come suddenly, without warning, and without any suggestion that the date or time could be postponed if it should be inconvenient. It was, in truth, more of a summons than an invitation. He had had to scramble to make arrangements to comply.

'Would you like some coffee?'

'No. Thank you.'

'Well, come and have a seat, please.'

Sawyer's office was spacious, sparingly but elegantly furnished with reproduction Regency chairs and tables, and overlooked the river. It was the office of a man used to wielding considerable authority. Once Hardcastle was seated in front of his desk, Sawyer took his own seat and spread his hands in front of him. He eyed Hardcastle carefully. He had chosen the appointment time of 9 o'clock in the morning deliberately. He detected nothing untoward in Hardcastle's manner, but it had been worth checking.

'Martin, you may or may not know this already. I'm the Lord Chancellor's right-hand man on judicial appointments.'

'Yes, indeed,' Hardcastle replied. Everyone in Silk knew who Jeremy Sawyer was, and what he did. Under certain circumstances, an invitation to Sawyer's office was the harbinger of good news. The Lord Chancellor had concluded that the time had come to launch a man into his new career on the High Court bench. Hardcastle would have loved to believe that his turn had come. But he did not believe it. He had probably not been in Silk long enough. He was still a bit young. But, more significantly, the Lord Chancellor never made such a move without taking soundings from a number of senior judges before whom a Silk had appeared recently. Hardcastle was no longer sure of his standing with the senior judges. The Cottage case gave him particular cause for alarm. He had read the judgment of the Court of Criminal Appeal. It did not augur well.

'I'm sure you have a busy day ahead, so I'll come straight to the point,' Sawyer said. 'The Lord Chancellor has asked me to inform you of his intention to appoint you to the County Court bench. He would like you to sit in London, but the opportunity may well arise for a chairmanship of Quarter Sessions, or perhaps a recordership in due course, so that you can do some crime as well. Usually, this kind of appointment takes a fair amount of time to arrange, but it so happens that we are in rather urgent need of a judge to sit at West London. So the Lord Chancellor sees no need to delay. May I be the first to congratulate you?'

Hardcastle suddenly felt short of breath. He found it difficult to focus on what Sawyer had said. To a member of the public, it might have seemed that Sawyer was paying him a compliment, that he was offering him a professional honour. But in the world which Hardcastle and Sawyer both inhabited, his words had an altogether different meaning. Hardcastle's career had just been holed below the water line. Sawyer's cultured voice and carefully chosen words conveyed to him as clearly as could be that he would be denied access to the highest echelons of the profession to which Queen's Counsel aspired. The County Court bench was not just an offer; it was the end. Sawyer seemed to sense the effect his words had produced, and he did not try to hurry Hardcastle into a reply. He seemed content to shift his gaze and look out over the river.

'This comes as something of a surprise, Jeremy,' Hardcastle replied. 'I had understood that it was the Lord Chancellor's practice to sound people out about whether they would wish for this kind of appointment, to allow them some time to think about it, to consider their options.'

'That is the usual practice,' Sawyer agreed, without diverting his gaze from the river. 'But in this case, the Lord Chancellor feels unusually strongly about the matter and, as I say, we have a vacancy to fill almost at once. I'm not saying you can't have time to think about it. Of course you can. Take all the time you wish. And, of course, we will work with you on the timing of your appointment, so that you can deal with any cases you may feel professionally obliged to see through to the end.'

Hardcastle looked down at the floor.

'And if I should decide that, grateful as I am to the Lord Chancellor for the confidence he is placing in me, I would prefer to remain in practice as Queen's Counsel?'

Sawyer turned back to face him.

'You're perfectly entitled to respond in that way, Martin. The Lord Chancellor has no power, and indeed would not wish to force anyone to take an appointment. But I have been asked to make it clear to you that the Lord Chancellor does not envisage offering you an appointment at a higher level.'

Hardcastle sat back in his chair.

'I see,' he said quietly.

'And while you are free to continue in practice as Queen's Counsel as long as you wish, the Lord Chancellor has asked me to remind you of the professional standards which he expects of Queen's Counsel.'

Hardcastle felt his blood pressure start to rise.

'Now, look here, Sawyer. You can't bring me here and try to intimidate me like this. I am...'

Sawyer shook his head dismissively.

'People are talking, Martin,' he said. 'More importantly, judges are talking. You are living on borrowed time – professionally speaking, that is. It has not escaped the Lord Chancellor's attention. And please don't make it awkward for both of us by asking me what I mean. You know perfectly well what I mean. Don't make me spell it out.'

Hardcastle sat back in his chair, deflated.

'Martin, we feel we owe you something,' Sawyer continued. 'You are in Silk, after all. That is why the Lord Chancellor invited you here this morning. But please understand, there is only so far we can go.'

He stood and proffered his hand.

'Take the appointment, Martin. That is my strong advice to you.'

He walked around his desk and placed his hand on Hardcastle's forearm.

'Don't look so downcast, my dear fellow. I think you will rather enjoy the bench once you get used to it. Let me know when you have made a decision. I'm sure you can find your own way out, can't you?'

57

AT EXTREMELY SHORT notice, Virginia Castle had been put in charge
of organising Martin Hardcastle's congratulatory – and farewell –
party. Miles Overton was anxious to hold it as soon as possible. If
the truth were told, most members of Overton's Chambers were
not entirely unhappy to see Martin go. He was a successful and
ambitious Silk, and over the years he had done more than his fair
share of keeping Chambers' solicitors happy and introducing new
solicitors to Chambers. For some years that contribution was an
asset which outweighed the liability of the rumours. But, as time
went by and the successes grew less frequent, the balance began to
shift, and there had been mutterings in the ranks to the effect that
it was time for him either to make changes or move on. The Lord
Chancellor's decision to appoint Martin a county court judge not
only confirmed the suspicions, but also came as a welcome relief
to most members of Chambers. They would never say so except in
whispered conversations, of course, but in private they felt a burden
being lifted.

Virginia was a rising star in court, but was also known for her
deft touch in social and diplomatic situations. She had no trace of
the pomposity of the Bar, and had an engaging and irreverent sense
of humour. Even those who were too stuffy to approve fully found
themselves drawn irresistibly to her. Miles Overton had asked her
for something tasteful, but not too elaborate – or too long-lasting.
Virginia immediately ruled out a formal Chambers dinner, and very
quickly ruled out a venue outside Chambers. She opted for a Friday
evening reception in Chambers with champagne and *hors d'oeuvres*,
an event which would run from six until eight and which allowed

people to come and go as they wished. Using Chambers instead of an outside venue also reduced the risk of embarrassment and gave her more to spend on food and drink. When her plans were complete, and had been approved by Miles Overton, she announced them to Martin as a *fait accompli*, and with such enthusiasm that it did not occur to him that there could ever have been an alternative.

Nervous as she was as the organiser, Virginia began to relax after the first hour. It seemed to be a happy occasion after all. She had taken care to invite numerous barristers from other Chambers, which discouraged any back-biting or outbreak of Chambers politics. Everyone was honour-bound to be civil to each other, and almost all of them were doing so with a good grace. After tonight, any problems Martin had caused would melt away and, as he was leaving to take up judicial office rather than because of any overt scandal, his instructing solicitors would have no reason not to allow their work to filter down to others in Chambers. Moreover, the door would be open for at least one other member to consider applying for Silk. Most importantly, Martin himself seemed to be in the best of moods.

After he had left Jeremy Sawyer's office in the House of Lords ten days earlier, he had wandered, feeling lost and helpless, around Westminster. He was feeling too angry to trust himself to go to Chambers, and cancelled his appointments for the day with a curt call to his clerk. Eventually, he found a pub opposite St James's Park underground station and drank whisky until he felt on a sufficiently even keel to make his way home. At home he systematically threw half a dozen water glasses at the wall until they shattered, imagining Jeremy Sawyer's supercilious face grinning at him from the cream paint as they collided with it, and felt somewhat better. But any serious thinking about his predicament had to wait until after a bout of drinking, which ended three days later when he remembered that he had a trial beginning at the Old Bailey at the start of the following week. The trial was likely to last for five or six weeks, and would be his last before he took up his appointment. It was also, by Martin's standards, a leisurely affair. His client was the last of six on an indictment for fraud, and counsel ahead of him on the indictment would do most of the heavy work. He could lurk in obscurity and snipe at witnesses, or not, as he chose.

This gave him a chance to come to terms with his coerced future. In some ways, he reflected, it might be a godsend. On his worst day as a judge in the county court, the pressure would be far less than the unrelenting stress he endured on his best days as a Silk at the Assize or in the High Court. The legal issues would pose little challenge – especially with counsel or solicitors to assist him – and the facts would hardly tax his brain after the complex and tangled webs he dealt with every day now. Most importantly, he would no longer have to deal with clients. At 4 o'clock, or shortly after, he would wend his happy way home with no client to appease and reassure, with no solicitor to flatter – without a care in the world. His weekends would be his own, and he could not even remember when that had last happened.

Of course, he would have to be careful. They would be watching him. There could be no question of failing to show up for court any more. For one thing, there would be no judge to ask or apologise to; he would *be* the judge, and if he failed to attend, a whole court full of litigants and their legal advisers would want to know why. And that bastard Sawyer would be watching him like a hawk. If he gave him even half a chance Sawyer would not hesitate to talk to the Lord Chancellor about dismissal. Martin was sure it would not be a problem. He just needed to be careful. He would set up a new regime. Perhaps he would look up one or two of his old girlfriends; even seek out a new one. After all, he would have some free time now.

By the time of the reception Martin had, for the most part, convinced himself that his appointment was just what he wanted, just what he needed. There was still some anger, but it would fade with time. He enjoyed himself hugely, making the rounds and greeting every guest. As he left, he hugged Virginia and thanked her profusely.

* * *

It was 6.30 in the morning when the phone rang in Virginia's flat. She was half awake, and trying to decide whether to try to get back to sleep for a while, or whether to surrender to the inevitable and make herself get up. It was a Saturday and the weekend lay ahead, though some papers in a civil case which needed an urgent opinion were competing for her time. Her lover, Michael Smart, had been up for some time, and was in the bathroom. They spent nights in each other's homes regularly, but had not yet moved in together. The Bar Council took a dim view of barristers fraternising with solicitors, especially those who instructed the barrister in question, and any permanent liaison would require some political work. Miles Overton had offered to intercede, but it would take some time.

'I am sorry to disturb you, Miss Castle,' Vernon, her clerk, said. 'I know it's a Saturday morning, but I need you to go to Clerkenwell Magistrates' Court for 10.30.'

Virginia began to protest, but Vernon cut her off, and spoke quietly but intensely to her for some two minutes.

Virginia hurriedly made two cups of instant coffee and rushed into the bathroom as soon as Michael emerged.

'You look remarkably awake,' he smiled, kissing her as they passed in the doorway.

'I am either completely awake or I'm in a real nightmare,' she replied, returning the kiss.

Michael laughed and settled down happily with his coffee and *The Times* until it was time to think about breakfast.

Virginia had no brief for her appearance at Clerkenwell Magistrates' Court, but Edwin McCullough, a solicitor intensely loyal to Miles Overton, had agreed to be at court personally by 9 o'clock with a backsheet marked with a modest fee, which technically amounted to a brief, and was just about enough to ensure that she had the instructions without which no barrister could appear in court.

Virginia knew McCullough. He had begun to send her some work in the last year, and as soon as she found him in the lobby of the court, she took him discreetly aside.

'How bad is it?' she asked.

'I'm not really sure, Miss Castle,' the solicitor replied. 'All the warrant officer knows is that he was arrested in the early hours for being drunk and disorderly and obstructing an officer in the execution of his duty. We won't know any more until the arresting officer gets here.' He paused. 'Whatever it is, it can't be good, can it?'

'No,' Virginia agreed quietly.

PC Nathan Smith was unshaven and looked tired and dishevelled. He had snatched no more than an hour or two of sleep at the police station before he made his way to court, fortified by some strong coffee, to complete his shift by dealing with the one miscreant he had had occasion to arrest while on duty the previous night. Smith was a brawny, muscular man who filled his uniform almost to bursting point. He had a shock of thick red hair. He seemed bemused to find both counsel and solicitor present and taking an interest in the most mundane of arrests.

'What can I tell you?' he replied, in answer to Virginia's question. He produced a crumpled notebook from the breast pocket of his uniform and opened it, running his fingers along the lines of the paper as he narrated the events.

'Let me see. This was at about 2.10 this morning. I was on duty in full uniform on foot patrol in Gray's Inn Road, near the junction with Theobald's Road, when I observed a white male who appeared to be urinating against the wall of a building. The man was about six feet in height, slightly built, wearing a smart, formal grey suit and a tie, hanging loose around his neck. I approached the male and asked him what he was doing. He replied: "What does it bloody look like? I'm taking a piss." I noticed that his speech was slurred and, as I approached, I was able to smell alcohol on his breath. He stopped urinating and, with some difficulty, adjusted his trousers. He appeared to have poor coordination and was unsteady on his feet. He was very drunk. I asked the male to identify himself. He said: "Fuck off. Don't you know who I am?" I said: "No, I don't know who you are, that's why I am asking you to identify yourself." He then became violent and aggressive, and repeatedly tried to push me away. He continued to swear and be abusive, and continued to refuse to identify himself. I called for assistance. I then told the male he was under arrest for being drunk and disorderly and for obstructing me in the execution of my duty. I cautioned him, and he said: "I know all about that, you moron. I'm a bloody judge. You can't do anything to me." When my colleague PC James arrived with a car, he resisted our efforts to detain him, but we were eventually able to handcuff him and take him to the police station where he was detained overnight.'

PC Smith concluded his recitation and smiled. 'That was a good one, Miss, about him being a judge. I haven't come across that one before.'

'No,' Virginia replied. 'I don't imagine you have.' She paused. 'Look, would you be heartbroken if I talked the inspector into dropping the obstruction and proceeding on the drunk and disorderly?'

PC Smith smiled broadly.

'Miss, if I can get home and take a nice bath, have a bite to eat, see the missus, and grab a bit of kip, my heart will not be troubled in any way.'

Virginia smiled.

'Thank you,' she said.

* * *

The duty sergeant showed no inclination to lock her in the cell.

'Now that we know who he is, we are satisfied he's not a flight risk,' he grinned. 'You can go inside or stay in the corridor, Miss, as you wish.'

The sergeant opened the door of the cell with a large key and disappeared along the corridor. Martin Hardcastle was sitting on the hard wooden bench, without his jacket, shoes and tie, looking very sick. On seeing Virginia he nodded.

'Is McCullough here?' he asked quietly.

'Yes,' Virginia replied. 'I left him upstairs to check for any sign of the press taking an interest. We haven't seen any indication yet. I'm going to pull some strings to get us on first, and with any luck we will be away before anyone knows.'

'The police know,' Martin said miserably. 'After all the abuse I've heaped on police officers during my career, I'm sure they will be only too glad to spread the word. The press are bound to pick it up.'

'We shall see,' Virginia replied. 'In any case, first things first. They have agreed to drop the obstruction charge if you plead to drunk and disorderly. I assume you have no problem with that?'

Martin shook his head.

'In which case,' she continued, 'the magistrates will deal with it by way of a fine. I'll ask for seven days to pay to clear a cheque.'

'Thank you,' he replied.

There was an awkward silence.

'If I didn't say so last night,' he said, 'it was a great party. Thank you.'

She nodded.

'I'll see you upstairs,' she said.

She walked away, leaving the door of the cell open to the empty corridor.

58

3 August

'YOU WANTED TO dictate a letter, Mr Sawyer?' Annette asked brightly as she entered his office.

'Yes, thank you,' Jeremy Sawyer replied, waving her into her chair.

She took her seat, opened her notebook, crossed her right leg over the left, and was immediately poised for action, pen in hand.

As was his custom, Sawyer walked around his office while dictating, passing a small green rubber ball from hand to hand, and occasionally throwing it up into the air to catch it again.

'It's to Martin Hardcastle QC, at his Chambers,' he said. 'You will find the address in his file.'

He looked out over the river, playing with the ball.

Dear Martin,

The Lord Chancellor was saddened to hear of your plea of guilty, over the weekend, before the Clerkenwell Magistrates' Court, to an offence of being drunk and disorderly. As you know, as Head of the Judiciary, it is the Lord Chancellor's responsibility to uphold the standards of conduct which are expected of those who hold judicial office. I am directed by the Lord Chancellor to inform you that, as a result of your conviction of this offence, he is obliged to withdraw the offer previously made to you of an appointment to the county court bench. I am sure you will understand that, in the circumstances, he has no choice in the matter. If you have any questions, please do not hesitate to let me know.

Yours ever,

Jeremy Sawyer

He stopped.

'That's it, Annette. Can it go out this afternoon?'

She smiled.

'Yes, of course, Mr Sawyer.'

59

WHEN HIS ASSISTANT approached him with quiet, respectful steps, Arthur Ludlow was observing Billy Cottage at exercise in the yard. A window was cut into the wall of the execution suite, adjacent to the small exercise yard reserved for condemned prisoners. Its purpose was to allow the executioner to see the prisoner and make an assessment of his physical condition for the purpose of calculating the drop. Arthur moved slightly to his left to allow the younger man to stand alongside and share the view. The number two was a reliable fellow named Ken Aitcheson who hailed from Southend-on-Sea. It was the day before Billy Cottage's scheduled execution, and it was time to make their final preparations.

'How does it look up there?' Arthur asked.

'It looks good, Arthur,' Ken replied. 'I've been up to the top and looked at all the tackle. It is in order. Everything is working. I've hung two ropes up with sandbags to stretch overnight, so you'll have your choice of the two in the morning. I checked the lever and the trap doors on the drop and there's no problem there. They are working.'

'Good lad,' Arthur replied approvingly. 'Now, take a look at Billy, and tell me what you see.'

'He's well-built, isn't he?' Ken asked. 'He looks strong. Good muscles.'

'Aye,' Arthur replied. 'He looks right strong. He's a lock keeper, apparently, lots of hard physical work. So you'd expect him to be in good shape. And his neck is right thick, an' all.'

Ken nodded. 'Yes, I see that.'

'Good. So, what would you give him for the drop?' Arthur asked.

Ken produced a small notebook from the breast pocket of his jacket.

'Well, yesterday he weighed in at 180 pounds.'

'Right,' Arthur confirmed.

'So according to the Home Office table, we would need a drop of 5 feet 7 inches.'

Arthur nodded. 'But today...'

'But today, we would add 9 inches to that so that gives us...' He paused to check a calculation he had made in pencil. 'If we add 9 inches, that gives us a drop of 6 feet 4 inches.'

Arthur nodded again.

'That's right enough, and I don't think you would have any problem with it. But looking at his build, I think we would be safe with 6 feet 1 inch or thereabouts. Remember to always err on the side of shorter, as long as you don't go too far. I'm going to say 6 feet 1½ inches. Any problem with that?'

'No problem at all, Arthur,' Ken replied.

'Good,' Arthur said. 'That's all till tomorrow morning, then. And now it's tea time. Let's go and see if they've got any of that fruit cake left.'

* * *

After his period of exercise, the prison officers took Billy Cottage back to the condemned cell. He was to have a visitor. Eve had made an appointment to see her brother for the last time. For one last time, she had made her way to Bedford Gaol by train and bus, and had patiently submitted to every security check at the prison, including a demeaning personal body search. At long last an officer admitted her to the condemned cell. She looked around sadly. The cell seemed drab, hopeless, and an officer was standing just a few feet away from where Billy sat at the small table. There was to be no privacy as they said their goodbyes.

She seated herself across from him at the table.

'It doesn't look very nice in here, Billy,' she observed, without rancour. 'How are they treating you?'

'It's not very nice,' he replied. 'The worst thing is, they leave the lights on all day and all night, so it's not easy to get to sleep at night. I get tired.'

'Well, that's not right,' Eve said, eyeing the officer critically. 'There's no reason to leave the lights on all the time, is there? Quite apart from the money it must cost.'

He did not reply.

'Are you eating properly?' she asked.

'Yes. The same as usual.'

A silence.

'How about you? All right?'

She looked down at the table and held both hands in her lap.

'Well, the money is still very short,' she said. 'It's not the same as when you were working. I'm worried about the bills. I don't know how long I can make ends meet. There are some things that need doing around the house, and I can't afford anyone to do them. You know, the roof at the back needs some new slates. And there are some pipes that need lagging, and I don't know what all.'

She looked up.

'And they are still saying that I won't be able to stay on in the house after… if you can't come back to work. They will need it for a new lock keeper, you see.'

She suddenly put her hands on the table and became animated for the first time.

'Have you spoken to Mr Davis, Billy? What did he say?'

Billy looked down uncomfortably.

'Mr Davis said it's up to Mr Henry Brooke now,' he replied. 'He can stop them from hanging me. Mr Davis has given him some papers, and my second barrister Mr Schroeder has looked at them as well. And Mr Sydney Silverman, the MP, said he would help. He is going to talk to Mr Henry Brooke.'

'He hasn't got much time left, has he?' she said, without thinking. 'What I mean is, Billy, I hope he's getting on with it quickly. Is he?'

'Yes, of course he is,' Billy replied hurriedly. 'I'm expecting to hear from him this evening.'

She nodded.

'That's good, Billy,' she said. 'Even so, you will be here in prison for a long time, won't you?'

'Yes. It looks like it,' he replied.

'So you won't be back to work. Not unless they can prove you didn't do it after all.'

'No. Not unless they can prove that.'

'I'm sorry I didn't give evidence for you, Billy,' she said suddenly. He saw tears in her eyes.

'No. You mustn't worry about that,' he replied. 'My main barrister, Mr Hardcastle, told me we didn't have to. He said it was our best chance not to say anything.'

'He was wrong though, wasn't he?' she replied. 'I could have said you were at home all night.'

He leaned forward in the hope that the officer would not hear. If the officer was listening, he gave no sign of it. He was staring away from them across the room, as if he was unaware they were even there.

'They would have asked you about us,' he said.

'I would have told them,' she replied. The tears were in full flow now. 'I wouldn't have cared. What difference would it have made? What would it have mattered?'

He shook his head.

'It wouldn't have done any good,' he said. 'He was my main barrister. We had to trust him.'

He waited for her to dry her eyes. It took a long time for her to compose herself.

'Is the River Board still making sure to cut back the rushes?'

'Yes. They do it every week,' she replied. 'A man comes. He's very nice. Fred, he's called.'

'Because if you don't do it at least once a week, it gets out of hand, and it's the devil's own job to get it clear again once it gets away from you.'

'Yes, I know,' she said.

She suddenly stood.

'I'm going now,' she said. She stood, walked around the table and kissed him once on the cheek.

'Billy,' she said. 'Tell me the truth. That cross and chain you gave me. Where did it come from?'

'I told you,' he replied. 'I found it.'

She was looking straight into his eyes.

'Did you?' she asked. 'Did you, Billy?'

He looked down at the table and said nothing. She walked slowly to the door, turned, and faced him.

'You were always good to me, Billy,' she said, as she left the condemned cell. 'Thank you for that.'

'Goodbye, Eve,' he said, long after she had closed the door behind her.

60

BARRATT DAVIS HAD asked Ben to come to his office in Essex Street for what he called 'the wake' by 6.30 that evening. The application for leave to appeal to the House of Lords had been dismissed two days earlier. When he had found out Ben had called Barratt, who sounded distracted, but not particularly surprised. Ben had always known that that result was inevitable, but the receipt of the formal notice from the Appeals Committee had still felt like a hammer blow. He had been sitting in his room, fretting helplessly, for most of the afternoon, despite Harriet's best efforts to distract and calm him. At 6.25 he gratefully set out for the short walk up Middle Temple Lane. He arrived exactly on time.

Barratt's office, when Ben entered, bore no resemblance whatsoever to the scene of a wake. Papers and books were scattered over his desk and, on the two small side tables, even more were piled on chairs. Barratt was in his shirt-sleeves, the sleeves rolled up. Jess also looked as though the day had been a frantic one. Her hair was coming down and her blouse was uncharacteristically crumpled. John Singer alone seemed calm and somehow removed from the fray. He was sitting quietly, wearing his suit jacket and with his tie firmly in place, on Barratt's sofa.

'Welcome, Ben,' Barratt said. 'Excuse the mess. We have been going over the paperwork, just to see if we have missed anything. I don't think we have. If we find anything now, it would have to be sent over to the House of Commons without delay, but we can arrange that. John was kind enough to take everything over there for Sydney Silverman this afternoon. Just as you saw it. We haven't changed anything.'

'This afternoon?' Ben asked. 'Isn't that a bit...?'

Barratt nodded.

'Yes. It is a bit late by normal standards. Usually the Home Secretary's people want it all several days in advance. But in this case Brooke could not meet Sydney Silverman until this afternoon. Sydney asked us to leave the paperwork with him so that he could take the Home Secretary through it personally. We have to rely on him as our guide, of course. It's not exactly voluminous, so it won't take him all that long to go through it. Sydney believes Brooke to be conscientious. He will read every word before he makes a decision. It may be late this evening, but better late than never.'

Ben turned to John Singer.

'Did Silverman make any comment on the papers?'

'No. Not really,' Singer replied. 'Not surprisingly.' He paused. 'I mean, let's be honest, we've done our best. But we are not dealing with Derek Bentley or Ruth Ellis, are we? Today, if we had one of those cases, in the context of what's happening now, we might...'

'Yes, point taken,' Barratt agreed.

'I had hoped to come up with something useful in St Ives,' Singer continued. 'I spoke to everyone I could find – teachers, people who knew him on the river, his sister Eve, of course. They all seem to agree that he's not the brightest candle on the altar, but there's nothing about his mental state which cries out for a reprieve.'

'I'm sure Sydney is pinning most of his hopes on the abolition argument,' Barratt said.

'Well, we have given him plenty of ammunition for that,' Ben said. 'He's got the whole parliamentary history, current legislative plans, and a lot of evidence of how many MPs would support abolition if it came up before the House of Commons tomorrow.'

'It's the House of Lords you have to worry about when it comes to abolition, more than the Commons,' Singer observed.

Barratt nodded.

'Well, in any case we have done what we can,' he said. 'At a certain point you have to stop or you risk weakening your case by diluting good arguments with bad ones. Essentially, I think Sydney is going to plant in Henry Brooke's mind the thought that he does not want to wake up two years from now with a guilty conscience, after the country has repudiated the death penalty and he could have spared one of its last victims. That's not an easy task, of course, given the uncertainty. But if anyone can do it, I fancy Sydney can.'

'That's what we have to hope for,' Ben replied. He lowered himself into an empty armchair. 'How do we find out?' he asked. 'Does John have to go back to the House of Commons?'

'No,' Singer replied. 'Silverman said the usual protocol is that the Home Secretary communicates with the condemned and his solicitor – Barratt, that is – in writing. But in this case, because we are getting down to the wire, Brooke has agreed to have his Permanent Under-Secretary call Barratt here when they have a decision.'

'At which point,' Barratt said, 'we will hold a celebration or a wake, whichever is appropriate. Meanwhile, all we can do is wait and be prepared to spring into action if Brooke needs more information.'

John Singer stood.

'Well, Barratt, I've made the only contribution I can and, to be honest, I don't have the stomach for waiting around under these circumstances.'

'No, of course,' Barratt replied. 'You've done all you could, John, and I really appreciate it. Take yourself off home. We will be in contact, of course, once we know.'

Singer picked up his briefcase and began to walk to the door. Then he hesitated.

'Actually,' he said, 'there is one other thing I have to tell you. I wish I could avoid it, but I'm afraid it's going to be in all the papers tomorrow, and I would rather you heard it from me, unpleasant as it is.'

The room suddenly grew silent.

'Nothing to do with this case. You remember the Reverend Ignatius Little, I'm sure.'

Ben and Barratt exchanged smiles.

'Who could forget?' Barratt asked.

'I got a call while I was at Silverman's office this afternoon,' John continued. 'The Diocese of Ely transferred him after the trial. I don't know whether you knew that?'

'No, I don't think so,' Barratt replied.

'Yes, well, it was with his full agreement. We all felt it would be best for him to make a fresh start somewhere else. The Diocese of Chester agreed to take him, and they gave him a curacy there, with a living in sight after a year or two if everyone was happy.'

'But I take it not everybody is happy?' Ben asked.

'The Queen versus Ignatius Little, number two?' Barratt asked. 'Isn't Chester off circuit for you, Ben? Could you venture into the frozen north? Do you need permission from the powers that be?'

John Singer took a deep breath.

'He was arrested last night in Liverpool for importuning a 12-year-old boy in a public lavatory. What Little failed to appreciate was that the boy's father was waiting outside and, as it turns out, he is a police officer – off duty at the time, but that didn't stop him making an arrest.'

'God Almighty,' Ben muttered.

Barratt shook his head, smiling grimly.

'But there won't be a trial in Chester – or anywhere else,' Singer added. 'He was held in custody overnight before being brought before the magistrates this morning. But he never got that far. An officer found him when he took his breakfast into the cell. He had hanged himself with a couple of sheets they gave him for his cot.'

The room fell silent again. Jess collapsed on to the sofa.

'Has anyone told Joan Heppenstall?' she asked quietly.

'I don't imagine so,' Singer replied. 'The Liverpool police would have no reason to know about her. I'm not sure what information his Bishop has. I suppose that is one more unpleasant job for yours truly.'

'I would like to tell her myself, if you don't mind,' Jess said. 'I should try to speak to her before the press gets hold of it.'

'I would be very grateful to you,' Singer said. 'I'm going to be fending off the Diocese of Chester for a few days, and it would be a blessing not to have to deal with her too.'

He left. Ben and Barratt looked at her.

'I was the one who talked her into giving evidence for him,' she said simply. 'I owe it to her.'

Quietly, she left the room.

'Surely to God,' Ben asked, after some time, 'it is not possible to have two clients hang in the same week?'

'That would have to be something of a record, wouldn't it?' Barratt replied. He walked over to Ben's chair and put both hands on his shoulders.

'Ben,' he said. 'Listen to me. Not even you can blame yourself for the hanging of Ignatius Little.'

* * *

The call from Henry Brooke's Permanent Under-Secretary came at 11.15.

'I see. Thank you,' Barratt said, replacing the receiver.

He turned to Ben and Jess, who were sitting, their nerves long since torn to shreds, on the edge of their seats.

'The Home Secretary regrets that the law must take its course,' he said.

He walked behind his desk, opened a drawer, and took out a bottle of a fine whisky. In one fluent, violent movement he swept every last sheet of paper off his desk on to the floor.

'I hereby declare the wake to be formally open,' he said, unscrewing the top of the bottle. 'Glasses, Jess, if you please.'

The wake passed with little conversation. Ben would later remember a fragment, during the early hours, as he drifted somewhere between sleep and wakefulness.

'Barratt, why are we having this wake?' he had asked.

Barratt had taken some time to reply.

'Where do you stand on capital punishment, Ben?' he asked.

'I never thought about it much before this case,' Ben admitted. 'Now, after this case, if I was ever in favour of it, I have turned against it.'

'Good,' Barratt said.

He stood and re-filled all the glasses, though Jess was asleep.

'I know this is your first time – and hopefully it will be your last. But we have the wake in the interests of our reformation, our welfare.'

'Reformation?'

'Yes. We are a bit like Scrooge, Ben. During this night we will be visited by three spirits. For me, the Spirit of Executions Past and the Spirit of Executions Present. For you, mercifully, just the Present.'

He took a long drink.

'The only good news in this miserable bloody drama,' he said, 'is that, very soon, they may have some trouble casting the part of the Spirit of Executions Yet to Come.'

He raised his glass.

'Let's drink to that thought, anyway.'

'I can't do another of these, Barratt,' Ben said.

'That's what I always say,' Barratt replied.

61

6 August

AT PRECISELY THREE minutes to eight, Arthur Ludlow had stopped outside the door of the condemned cell. He was formally dressed in a dark grey suit and a blue tie, and he had the white hood which would shortly be fitted over Billy Cottage's head tucked away neatly like a fluted handkerchief in the top pocket of his jacket – the refinement introduced to the trade by the legendary Tom Pierrepoint. He held the strap with which he would pinion Billy's arms in one hand behind his back. His number two stood at his side, wearing a suit of a lighter shade and holding his leg strap behind him. Ken was a good lad, Arthur reflected. It was a pity, with all this talk of abolition, that Ken might never get the chance to act as number one. He was well trained and had good nerves; number one material, no doubt in Arthur's mind. But he was running out of time. That was the way of things now. Change; always change; the end of a way of life. Executions would be consigned to history if that man Silverman and the like had their way. Behind the executioners was the assistant governor holding the small cup of brandy that would be offered to the condemned in case of need – a modern concession, perhaps, to the historic practice in the days of public executions of allowing the condemned's friends and relatives to supply him with enough drink to induce a state of intoxication during the long last journey by cart from Newgate Prison to Tyburn. Time to focus. Arthur knew exactly what he would find when he entered the condemned cell.

As he heard the church clock sound the first stroke of the hour, signalling 8 o'clock, Arthur entered the cell briskly. As he expected, two prison officers stood poised by the large wardrobe.

The chaplain, book in hand and fully robed, stood at Billy Cottage's side. Arthur's only concern about chaplains was that they had a habit of getting in the way. It was not deliberate – not these days, although the Pierrepoints had told some stories about chaplains in Ireland who clung to the condemned as he walked to the drop, in the days when they conducted executions there. Now, in England, it was just because they did not always react quickly enough when the executioner entered the cell. You couldn't blame them. It was Arthur's job to deal with the problem if it arose. But this man evidently had every intention of keeping well out of the way. As Arthur entered he moved sharply away to the side of the cell. Arthur approached Billy, bringing the hand which held the strap round in front of him. At the same time, the prison officers were moving the wardrobe aside, and opening the door.

Billy stared at Arthur, wondering who he was. Then it came to him. Of course.

When I was bound apprentice in famous Lincolnshire

'Mr Brooke?' Billy Cottage asked. 'I was wondering when you would come.'

Arthur thought he detected something of a smile on Billy's face. He wondered briefly why this man thought his name was Brooke. But he dismissed the thought, as he had trained himself to dismiss all extraneous thoughts when he was working. You had to. You had to stay focused. You had to tune out whatever the condemned had to say. You never knew what it would be. Some said nothing at all. Some confessed to their crimes at the last moment. Some said things that did not make sense. Usually it wasn't hard to let it pass by. Only when the condemned protested his innocence did Arthur need a moment to readjust. That would not be the case today.

Full well I served my master for nigh on seven years

'Turn around please,' Arthur said, although he was already turning Billy, holding him by his right shoulder. He brought Billy's hands around behind his back and pinioned them in a flash. He looked up. The wardrobe was gone and the path to the drop was clear.

Arthur turned Billy again and positioned himself in front, as Ken fell in behind Billy with the assistant governor bringing up the rear. The two officers who had moved the wardrobe were now stationed on either side of the drop, just in case of trouble. Their presence was reassuring, but Arthur sensed that there would be no trouble today. Not with this one.

'Follow me, please.'

Till I took up to poaching as you shall quickly hear

The walk to the drop was a matter of a few feet. As Ken moved swiftly to his position behind the huge metal trap doors, Arthur walked Billy on to the drop, where Billy saw the rope, ending in a noose, at his side, at head height. What was that for? They wouldn't need that unless they were going to... Something had gone wrong. Perhaps this man was not Mr Brooke. Perhaps none of these people was Mr Brooke. He had to tell these people that something had gone wrong. But the words would not come. Where was Mr Davis? Where was his main barrister? Where was his other barrister?

Oh, 'tis my delight on a shiny night in the season of the year

He felt pressure against his legs as Ken pinioned them.

Success to every gentleman that lives in Lincolnshire,

Then it went dark. Arthur had taken the white hood from his pocket and placed it over Billy's head. What had happened? Had someone turned the lights out? Was he still alive, or had it happened already?

Success to every poacher that wants to sell a hare

More pressure, this time up by his neck. Arthur was adjusting the noose, tight under the left jaw for the quarter-circle rotation.

Bad luck to every gamekeeper that will not sell his deer

Arthur checked that Ken was well clear of the drop. He reached for the lever. The clock sounded the final stroke for the hour.

Oh, 'tis my delight

62

THE ALARM WOKE all three with a shocking clarity. Barratt switched on the small radio he had placed on his desk the previous evening.

This is the BBC Home Service. It is 9 o'clock on Thursday the 6 of August 1964. Here is the news.

The crisis in the Congo took a decisive turn yesterday as Simba rebel forces led by Christopher Gbenye and Pierre Mulela entered the outskirts of the capital, Stanleyville, amid fierce fighting. Sources in the country say that the city will fall today, giving the rebels a decisive advantage in the civil war. Many thousands of people have fled their homes, and the United Nations has called on both sides to give safe passage to all refugees. It seems unlikely that there will be any lull in the fighting for some time.

And in the Far East, the United States has launched a bombing campaign against military targets in North Vietnam. The move follows a confrontation yesterday in the Gulf of Tonkin, in which North Vietnamese gunboats attacked the United States destroyers USS Maddox and USS Turner Joy. A spokesman for the Department of State told reporters that the attack had been repulsed with the aid of air support, with the loss of one Vietnamese gunboat. North Vietnam has made no comment on the incident.

In Rome, Pope Paul VI has issued the encyclical 'Ecclesiam Suam', in which he likens the Church to the body of Christ. The encyclical, which has taken several years to compile, is expected to be controversial among non-Catholics because of the privileged position it suggests for the Roman Catholic Church to the exclusion of other denominations.

At the Great Basin National Park near Baker, Nevada, Prometheus, which had been claimed to be the world's oldest tree, has been felled. The tree, a Great Basin Bristlecone Pine, was believed by many scientists to be at least 4862, and possibly more than 5000, years old. The cutting down of Prometheus has sparked outrage among scientists and conservationists, but the team which felled the tree claims that there is no compelling evidence of such an advanced age, that they were unaware of the true age of the tree, and that the tree will yield important information for future research into diseases affecting trees.

William Cottage, a 28-year-old lock keeper from Fenstanton, Huntingdonshire, was hanged this morning at Bedford Gaol for the murder of Frank Gilliam. Cottage was convicted of capital murder at the Huntingdonshire Assize in June. The prosecution alleged that Cottage launched a frenzied attack on Frank Gilliam and his girl friend, Jennifer Doyce, on a houseboat on the Great Ouse river near St Ives in January. Jennifer Doyce, although critically injured, survived the attack, but Frank Gilliam died instantly.

And finally, they say New York is full of surprises, but no one could have been more surprised than a man who found himself walking past City Hall in Manhattan yesterday, when he was asked to step inside and act as a witness for the wedding ceremony of a couple who wanted to get married straight away. The surprise? The couple turned out to be comedian and script writer Mel Brooks and actress Anne Bancroft. As they say over there, 'that's show business!'.

And that's the news at 9 o'clock. The weather report and shipping forecast will follow in one minute.

Barratt reached out a hand and switched the radio off. He stood by his desk and stretched out his arms towards Ben and Jess as if giving a final benediction.

'*Ite, missa est*,' he said. 'It's over. It's time to carry on with our lives. It's time for the next case.'

Jess took Ben's hand and led him to the door of Barratt's office without a word, pausing only to kiss Barratt on the cheek. He in turn placed a hand on both their shoulders as they left.

* * *

In the kitchen of the lock keeper's house at Fenstanton, Eve Cottage also switched her radio off as the news ended. She sat in her chair for some time in the silence of the house. Then she put on her hat and got ready to walk into town to do her shopping for the day.

63

BEN AND JESS EMERGED from Barratt's office into the already bright sunlight, which promised another hot day. Standing in Essex Street, watching Londoners hurrying to work, listening to the noise of the traffic on the Strand, Ben had a strange sense of detachment, even of alienation, as though he were observing the scene as a visitor from some other universe. The hubbub around him was one he saw every day as part of his working life, but today he was not a part of it. He felt utterly disorientated. A few yards from the Temple, around which his life revolved, he felt lost; he was not sure he could find the way back to Chambers. After some time, he became aware of Jess standing close by his side.

'Come on,' she said. 'Barratt says we can take the car.'

He followed without a word. He settled into the front seat of the Rover, wound down his window, and stretched out his legs. As Jess expertly weaved her way into the morning rush-hour traffic, he allowed the cooling breeze to play on his face and through his hair. In a matter of minutes, he sank into a deep, dreamless sleep.

When he awoke, they were pulling into a long driveway. The noise of traffic had vanished, and the air felt different; it was fresh and relaxing, despite the increasing heat of the day. Around him he saw nothing but trees and grass, and some bright flower beds around the perimeter of the house resplendent with reds, yellows and mauves. She switched off the engine, and turned towards him. As their eyes met, she saw his lost-boy look and touched his hand.

'You're in a magic place, in Sussex,' she explained. 'This is my Uncle Jim and Aunt Ellen's house. They spend their summers at their place in France. I've had a key for the last couple of years. They like someone staying once in a while and keeping an eye on the house for them. We will stay for a few days, till you're ready to go back. Uncle Jim's shirts should fit you pretty well. Mrs Digby, their housekeeper, will have laid in some basic supplies – bread, milk, that kind of thing. We will walk down to the village shop tomorrow, or later this afternoon, if you feel like it.'

It took him some time to digest the information. He turned to her. 'Jess, what am I doing here? What about Chambers?'

She turned and held him by both arms.

'Ben, you remember what Barratt said. He will have talked to Merlin by now. Barratt has the number here, if anything should come up, but it won't. Come on.'

She climbed out of the car, walked around, and opened his door for him. He took her hand and she led him through the elegantly furnished house and into the back garden, which looked out over acre upon acre of green rolling countryside. Two benches and a table, made of dark, heavy rust-red wood, stood under a portico on the stone patio.

'Sit there and relax for a while,' she said. 'I will go and make some coffee before we do anything else.'

She brought the coffee and set it before him, then sat on the edge of the bench and pulled off her shoes and stockings. Next she knelt and took his off also. She threw them all into the far corner of the patio.

'We won't need those for a while,' she said, as she sat down beside him.

He was taken aback for a moment, but the country air had begun to ease him into relaxation. He smiled his thanks. They savoured the coffee and the view together for a long time as the sun traced its afternoon arc towards the West. They listened to the breeze and the birdsong and the distant humming of bees on the flower beds.

'Thank you for bringing me here, Jess,' he said. 'But why did you? What made you think of it?'

She eased herself off the bench and came to kneel in front of him. She took his hands in hers.

'They had a saying in the Middle Ages,' she said. '*In media vita in morte sumus*. In the midst of life we are in death. It seems appropriate to your profession, Ben, especially today. So I was thinking that perhaps we could stand it on its head. In the midst of death, perhaps we can find life.'

She kissed him full on the lips.

'You told me that the world ended for you a few years ago,' she said. 'I thought it was high time we made a new world, and set it spinning around its axis.'

Postscript

The Times, February 1991

Tests Confirm Old Murder Conviction, say Scientists

By Our Legal Correspondent

A TEAM OF SCIENTISTS working at University College, London, announced yesterday that tests involving the use of DNA profiling have confirmed the guilt of a man hanged for murder following one of the last capital murder trials to be held in England before the death penalty was abolished in 1965. William Cottage, a lock keeper from Fenstanton in Huntingdonshire, was convicted in June 1964 of the murder of Frank Gilliam. The prosecution alleged that on the night of 25 January 1964 Cottage repeatedly beat Gilliam over the head with a heavy winch handle in a frenzied attack on board a houseboat, the *Rosemary D*, on the Great Ouse river, near St Ives. Gilliam's girlfriend, Jennifer Doyce, was also savagely attacked and raped. Her injuries were very serious and she lay unconscious on the boat for more than thirty hours before being discovered, but she was able to give evidence at the trial and subsequently made a complete recovery.

The case against Cottage at trial was circumstantial. His fingerprint was found on a window ledge in the sleeping quarters of the *Rosemary D*, where the crime was committed, but the prosecution was unable to prove that the print had been left on the same occasion. A few days after the murder, Cottage was found to be in possession of a gold cross and chain which Jennifer Doyce had worn on the night of the attack. Miss Doyce gave evidence that her attacker sang verses of a folk-song, the *Lincolnshire Poacher*, to himself while raping her, and there was evidence that Cottage had sung the same song earlier the same evening, and on an earlier occasion when he was arrested for indecent exposure in 1961, an offence to which he pleaded guilty. But there was no direct evidence against him, and he declined to give evidence or call witnesses in his defence. Cottage was convicted, and after an unsuccessful appeal to the Court of Criminal Appeal and a plea for a reprieve to the then Home Secretary, Henry Brooke, he was hanged at Bedford Gaol on 6 August 1964.

The case has been a controversial one ever since. Cottage had no relatives to take up the cause. His only known close relative, his sister Eve, died in 1965, in her gas-filled kitchen, in an apparent suicide, though no note was found and an open verdict was recorded by the Coroner. But a number of legal scholars have questioned the conviction and several calls were made to successive Home Secretaries, without success, for a public inquiry into the case. One matter for concern is that, under the law at the time, the Homicide Act 1957, Cottage could not have been convicted of capital murder unless he killed Gilliam in the course and furtherance of theft. Not only did Cottage steal from Jennifer Doyce, and not from Frank Gilliam, the scholars say, but the evidence suggested that Gilliam was already dead before the theft was committed. But the Court of Criminal Appeal held that this did not affect the correctness of Cottage's conviction for capital murder. Another recurring complaint has been the absence of direct evidence to prove that Cottage was the murderer.

But the scientist who oversaw the testing, Dr Paul Burgess, says that this second point can now be laid to rest. The scientific evidence available to the prosecution in 1964 was inconclusive. But, Dr Burgess says, new DNA profiling identifies Cottage as the murderer. Profiling by means of DNA – deoxyribonucleic acid – was first announced as a technique in 1984 by a team at Leicester University led by Professor Alec Jeffreys. DNA is a molecule which contains the genetic instructions for all known organisms, and its use for profiling involves the use of encrypted sets of numbers to identify the unique genetic profile of the subject. This can then be compared to other profiles. For some years the profile was regarded as too expensive and complex for commercial purposes, but since 1987 it has become increasingly available. Dr Burgess and his team, who have employed DNA profiling to look into a number of instances of alleged miscarriages of justice, compared a DNA sample taken from a specimen of Cottage's blood to the DNA found in two vaginal swabs taken from Jennifer Doyce. The result was a match. Dr Burgess told *The Times* that the probability of anyone other than William Cottage being the source of the DNA found on the vaginal swabs was many millions to one against.

Five years after Cottage's execution, Jennifer Doyce married Edgar McHugh, an Edinburgh banker. They have two children. They live quietly in Scotland. Jennifer McHugh has never commented on the case publicly. But yesterday, the family released a statement through their family solicitor, thanking Dr Burgess and his team for their work, and expressing satisfaction that the question of Cottage's guilt had finally been resolved.

'It is as close to scientific proof as you could wish,' Dr Burgess said of the test results. He added that DNA profiling has heralded a new era of certainty in criminal trials, and that it can be expected to become routine within the next few years, considerably reducing the risk of miscarriages of justice. It seems that William Cottage was indeed guilty of the murder of Frank Gilliam. Whether he should have been hanged for it is a controversy which may never be resolved.

Acknowledgments

While this book is not based on the case of James Hanratty, I have made use of some of the details, and of the evidential problems which arose in that case. I acknowledge my debt to Bob Woffinden's *Hanratty: the Final Verdict* (Macmillan, London, 1997) and to Louis Blom-Cooper's *The A6 murder: Regina v. James Hanratty, the Semblance of Truth* (Penguin Books, Harmondsworth, 1963). I have drawn liberally on Albert Pierrepoint's autobiography, *Executioner: Pierrepoint* (Harrap & Co Ltd, London, 1974), for detail of the preparation for and conduct of executions, and the training of executioners in this country. Last but not least, *Archbold: Criminal Pleading, Evidence and Practice*, 1962 edition (Eds. Butler and Garsia, Sweet & Maxwell, London 1962) was an invaluable source for the law and practice in capital murder cases.

Also by Peter Murphy

A HIGHER DUTY

Ben Schroeder, a talented young man from an East End Jewish family, has been accepted as a pupil into the Chambers of Bernard Wesley QC. But Schroeder is an outsider, not part of this privileged society, where wealth and an Oxbridge education are essentials. He encounters prejudice, intrigue and scandal.

Kenneth Gaskell, a rising star of Wesley's Chambers has become involved in an affair with a high-profile client and the relationship, if known, could ruin his career, and the careers of all those around him. But Bernard Wesley has some information – he knows about a student prank that went terribly wrong – can he use this knowledge in a desperate gamble to save his Chambers and turn the tables on his old rival, Miles Overton QC?

Ben Schroeder has proved his ability, but he is no more than a pawn in this game. Can he survive in this world where nothing, not even justice, is sacred?

ISBN: 9781842436684
Price: £7.99

REMOVAL

A compromised President, his murdered mistress, enemies foreign and domestic, and a rogue Marine Commander lusting for power: the impeachment is the least of America's problems…

President Steve Wade believes his latest affair with a beautiful Lebanese woman, Lucia Benoni, is a secret. When Lucia is murdered in mysterious circumstances, FBI Agent Kelly Smith is called in to investigate and uncovers links between Lucia, a hostile foreign power, a group of vicious white supremacists and a shadowy high-placed Washington figure known only as 'Fox'. As Wade continues to deny the affair, the press gets on the trail. Because of the national security implications, there are demands in Congress for Wade's impeachment but if this were to happen, the law provides that Vice President Ellen Trevathan should become President.

'Fox' and his associates have other plans, which do not include allowing the lawful succession to take place. As time runs out Kelly may hold the key to preventing a coup d'état and a possible civil war.

ISBN: 9781842435984
Price: £7.99

TEST OF RESOLVE

A denounced President, her kidnapped daughter, a Hindu extremist group and the threat of nuclear war: America is once again thrown into turmoil in Peter Murphy's sequel to *Removal*.

As Ellen Trevathan settles int   ent to
come out as a lesbian to the   ashes
a storm of criticism against h   omes
increasingly unstable when he   ed by
a Hindu extremist group, Sva   f the
FBI, Kelly Smith, is called in t   d in a
situation with far wider implic

Under pressure to comply w   as to
tackle the threat of nuclear   and
ensure the safety of her daugh   duty
and personal concerns are thr   the
situation demands that one ha   can
choose...

ISBN: 9781843441885
Price: £7.99